A NOVEL

SIXERS

A NOVEL

SIXERS

John Patrick
KAVANAGH

TM
LYNX
BOOKS

Library of Congress Cataloging-in-Publication Data

Kavanagh, John Patrick, 1950–
  Sixers.

  I. Title.
PS3561.A8694S59   1989   813'.54   88-27346
ISBN 1-55802-366-6

First Edition

This book is published by Lynx Books, a division of Lynx Communications, Inc., 41 Madison Avenue, New York, New York, 10010. The name "Lynx" and the logo consisting of a stylized head of a lynx are trademarks of Lynx Communications, Inc.

Printed in the United States of America

0 9 8 7 6 5 4 3 2 1

For my mother
and
in memory of
Lt. Col. James M. Kavanagh
03AUG42-07MAR84

ACKNOWLEDGMENTS

—to United Airlines for providing the Red Carpet Clubs and DC-10s in which most of this manuscript was written.

—to Marriott for providing the rooms where the rest of it was composed.

—to Lori Perkins, my literary agent, for finding me and guiding me, and for her relentless insistence on improvement.

—to Judy Stern, my editor, for picking me and polishing me.

—to Mike Fine and Lou Wolfe, my publishers, for their confidence and encouragement.

—to Dave Lersch, for a wrapping about which manuscripts dream.

—to all my friends who have tolerated all my tangents for all these years.

Finally, if I may, two words of advice to all the readers who have thought on occasion that they have a novel inside of them: Write it.

A NOVEL

SIXERS

PROLOGUE

THE ENVELOPE SAT ON A DESK IN RURAL GEORGIA, UNOPENED AND half hidden under a pile of magazines and circulars. Camden had tossed it there weeks before and absently buried it deeper each day. A visitor asked when he planned to catch up on his mail. "When somebody sends me something worthwhile," he replied.

The envelope contained another certified check. The envelope contained another pamphlet. The envelope contained another registered letter.

Dear Dr. Camden:

Enclosed is Southern United Enterprises check number J203609 in the amount of fourteen million, five hundred ninety-one thousand, five hundred sixteen dollars ($14,591,516), representing the final payment due you under your separation agreement with the Company. As per that agreement, our accountants will make available to you or your representatives the calculations employed in arriving at this final figure.

Along these lines, the Company requests that you respond to our recent inquiries concerning your plans regarding checks J197442 ($7,198,733) and J192677 ($8,901,500). The difficulties inherent in carrying this additional sixteen million dollars on our books for ninety and one hundred eighty days respectively are quite involved. We would appreciate your cooperation in presenting them, along with the enclosed check, for payment.

Miss Lane requested that I forward to you the latest installment of our CYD information brochure.

Please feel free to contact me if I may be of further assistance in this matter.

Sincerely,

Julie Marx
Assistant to the Group Vice President

The pamphlet was vintage Lane—part information, part misinformation, and part propaganda, with the usual doses of criticism and pessimism mixed in for flavor.

CYD Update

The following information is provided to our Southern United Enterprises customers concerning the latest developments in the global war against the devastation of Camden-Young's Disease.

For our new or younger readers, a brief explanation of what is currently known about the cause and spread of this affliction should prove helpful. Some of the following information is borrowed from the recently published *Sixth Report of the CYD Task Force*. (The CYD Task Force presently has two hundred and thirty subscribing organizations. The board of directors executive committee consists of representatives from the World Health Organization, the Centers for Disease Control, the National Institutes of Health, the Pasteur Institute of Paris, SUE, and four other international health care leaders.)

There is now no real debate concerning the genesis of this epidemic. Virtually all recognized authorities on the subject agree that the envirus known as CYD was accidentally created during experiments at the Perkins Genetic Engineering Laboratories near San Diego, California. The explosion and destruction of that facility undoubtedly marked the entrance of the envirus into the general population. Once this Pandora's box was opened, it could not be closed.

Theories on how the envirus spread throughout the Northern Hemisphere continue to be debated, but three interrelated possibilities are most often proposed:

1) The CYD envirus was carried across the continental United States by prevailing weather patterns. Wind or rain was the most probable initial vehicle of delivery. This theory would account for the spread of CYD throughout the rest of the planet.

2) The CYD envirus first infected cattle in the Southwest and Midwest, and then spread to the general population through beef products. While the sudden death of seventy-one percent of the cattle population of the United States in the second- and third-generation herds after the PGE explosion has been clearly linked to the CYD envirus, the transmission of the envirus via this medium has not been definitively demonstrated.

3) The CYD envirus linked with beef-related feed products such as Soyaplus IV, and was spread through the general population via consumption of contaminated meat.

Unfortunately progress in vaccinating against or curing CYD has been hampered by the fact that science is just beginning to understand the fundamentals of the broad subject of envirus technology. It is difficult to fight an enemy that has never been wounded and apparently requires neither food nor shelter nor sleep. (Perhaps the time has come to drop the name Camden-Young's Disease and rename this affliction Nemesis, as has been suggested by many authorities.)

The recent spectacular breakthroughs in the treatment and cure of other blood-related disorders have not transferred well to CYD research. While Acquired Immune Deficiency Syndrome has all but been eradicated, and leukemia is becoming a memory, CYD continues to evade its trackers. Those organizations attempting to develop vaccines and cures have thus far, unfortunately, failed in their efforts. A few other organizations, including Southern United Enterprises, have nonetheless made significant progress in treatment. The SUE Febrifuge Blue series continues to be the standard against which all other medications are measured.

The Tourraix-Camden Blood Composite, developed by Southern United Enterprises, remains the definitive diagnostic tool for predictive analysis of CYD infection. This test has been administered to almost three quarters of the United States population between the ages of eighteen and thirty-two, the only persons apparently vulnerable to the CYD envirus. An explanation for these mysteries continues to elude us.

With tens of millions of sets of data available from Tourcam tests and follow-up reports, SUE has created the definitive profile of the pandemic proportions of the current crisis. While we may not know what CYD is, we do know what it does. And it can be treated, as all users of Febrifuge Blue know.

Nineteen percent of all individuals tested and continuously monitored have been identified as Class A carriers. All Class A carriers show the blood clue that evidences the envirus. All Class A carriers develop the same set of primary symptoms.

The first outward sign of active CYD is a deep, persistent reddening of the eyes and a marked sensitivity to light. (Anyone who develops these symptoms and maintains them for more than forty-eight hours should consult his or her physician.)

Within three weeks of the onset of CYD, Class A carriers typically develop a low-grade fever of a half to a full degree above normal. Within a few days of this elevation in temperature, increasing thirst becomes apparent, and the individual may experience tremors in the extremities. Lung congestion, especially in older members of the target population, is common.

The only other primary symptom of a Class A progression is the frequent loss of all hair approximately four months after onset.

Following hair loss, Class A carriers will follow one of five prognosis profiles, four of which respond favorably to Febrifuge Blue tablets or injections.

Class A-1 carriers (32%) experience only episodic bouts of eye redness, thirst, and an occasional low-grade fever which lasts from two to five days.

Class A-2 carriers (29%) develop a mild set of secondary

symptoms, including a chronic fever between one and one-and-a-half degrees above normal, a general malaise, and an increased intake of liquids equal to approximately four percent of body weight per day.

Class A-3 carriers (27%) develop a more marked set of symptoms, including a chronic fever of between one-and-a-half and two degrees above normal, episodic muscle weakness, transitory confusion, mild aural hallucinations, and an increased intake of liquids equal to approximately eight percent of body weight per day. Death from these symptoms is rare.

Class A-4 carriers (10%) experience transitory bouts of severe symptoms, including fevers in the 103–104° range, persistent muscle cramps, moderate aural and visual hallucinations, chronic dehydration, nausea, and damage to various organs caused by the high level of stress placed on the body by these secondary symptoms. Death within three months of the first episode is sometimes reported.

Class A-5 carriers (2%) experience fevers approaching 107 degrees as soon as the hair-loss phase ends. Blindness, severe hallucinations, and coma are common. Death usually follows within seventy-two hours, although some individuals, especially those who have embarked on a program of supervised care, do survive.

Unfortunately recent studies confirm that any individual diagnosed as being a Class A carrier runs the risk of developing Class A-5 symptoms at any time. Use of the Febrifuge Blue line of products may, we believe, diminish this risk.

Twenty-one percent of all individuals tested and monitored have been identified as Class B carriers. All Class B carriers evidence the same blood clue as Class A carriers and report the same primary symptoms. Hair loss, however, is sporadic, partial, and temporary and is followed by a dormant period of between ten and thirty-six months. Then the individual may manifest one of the five Class A prognosis profiles.

Thirty-three percent of all individuals tested and monitored have been identified as Class C carriers. These individuals carry an alternate blood clue and experience a very mild set of primary symptoms. Typically the Class C carrier suffers a less severe reddening of the eyes and transitory headache. After two weeks these symptoms fade and return only for brief periods at increasingly longer intervals.

Approximately one in four Class C carriers, however, experiences one of the five Class A prognosis profiles within six to twenty-five months of onset.

Twenty-six percent of all individuals tested and monitored have been identified as Class D carriers. The Class D designation is a misnomer, however. Class D carriers evidence neither blood clues nor symptoms. Class D carriers are apparently immune to Camden-Young's Disease, although the nature of this immunity has yet to be explained. Recent reports concerning an antibody blood clue in Class D carriers are clearly premature in their conclusions. Likewise, reports indicating that Class D carriers possess a genetic predisposition not held by other carriers are equally premature in their conclusions.

The Febrifuge Blue line of products is extremely effective in the treatment of general CYD symptoms, especially fever and thirst, and serve no other purpose. Febrifuge Blue should be used only under the direction of a doctor or a registered CYD treatment center. Febrifuge Blue is not a cure or vaccine. Those afflicted with CYD should take only recommended doses. *Those not afflicted with CYD should not use Febrifuge Blue products.* The improper consumption of any drug can result in serious harm to the user.

If you are eighteen to thirty-two years of age, we recommend a basic Tourcam or the recently introduced Tourcam Three. Diagnosis is the first step in a successful program of CYD treatment. If you have reached age thirty-three and have experienced no CYD symptoms and have previously tested negative, consider having a follow-up test to verify your good fortune. This will also assist in the ongoing collection of data on which thousands of lives may depend.

Before concluding, two myths should be dispelled:

First, CYD is not contagious and is not passed from individual to individual. It is present in our environment, and every American in every one of the fifty states has no doubt been exposed. Alaskans and Hawaiians are no exception.

Secondly, the twenty-six percent of the population not afflicted with CYD are not necessarily healthier than the other seventy-four percent. They are, possibly, simply different in their blood chemistry. That difference may someday be exploited to the benefit of all, but currently it holds only a hope, not a promise. Along these lines, the practice of transfusing the blood of a Class D carrier for purposes of establishing immunity should be avoided. We expect it will soon be outlawed.

Some of the competitors of Southern United Enterprises make excellent products. Some do not. Some of our competitors have only the best interests of the consumer in mind. Some do not. We at SUE believe in excellent products and the best interests of the consumer. And we believe in truth.

Some irresponsible journalists and irresponsible competitors continue to promote the worn-out story that the Febrifuge Blue line of products has somehow entered its twilight. Nothing could be further from the truth.

Under the direction of Dr. Randolph Hickey, the Febrifuge Blue line of products has experienced a spectacular evolution during the past two years, and we expect even greater success in the upcoming months. Our research team is the best it has ever been, and so is our product.

Remember-Rainbows come in colors, but only Febrifuge comes in blue. When your doctor asks if you have a preference, tell him you don't want a best seller, you want *the* best seller.

As we are certain you have heard Wexford, the rock music phenomenon, say: "There are a lot of twos and threes and sixes in the world, but only a single one. Febrifuge." Febrifuge. It only comes in blue.

(Copies of this brochure are provided as a public service and are available through pharmacies, treatment centers, and physicians selling or distributing the Febrifuge Blue line of products.)

Febrifuge and Febrifuge Blue are trademarks of Southern United Enterprises.

CHAPTER 1

IT WAS GOOD TO BE HOME, STONETREE THOUGHT. SOMETIMES vacations are more trouble than they're worth.

From his position beneath the comforter, he could not tell if it was early or late, sunny or cloudy. The rattling of the windows was a remnant of the previous evening's thunderstorm. The slightest smell of coffee told him that Sharon was already up. It was not enough of a clue, however, to tell him if she was still in the house. Probably, he supposed, she was sitting at the kitchen table, fiddling with her fingers as she always did when she was nervous. Probably, he guessed, she was waiting for him to come downstairs to continue the conversation they should have finished the night before.

When the flight from London touched down at nine P.M., five hours late, they were both too exhausted to do much more than gather up the baggage and stagger through Customs. Then a cab back to his town house in the suburbs. Once there, they flopped onto the two oversize love seats in the living room and did nothing but stare out the half-open blinds for what must have been a good half hour. No lights, no stereo, no unpacking, no talk. Only exquisite, drained silence, broken occasionally by a random car passing on the street, or the distant growl of thunder.

He finally mustered enough strength to get himself a scotch, her a glass of wine. As he held it out before sitting down across from his guest, he could see a tear had been wiped away from her cheek.

He asked what was wrong. All she gave in response was a slow shake of her head. He ventured she was just tired and maybe a bit shaken from the violent landing, but she gave no reply. He chuckled and said he had been scared too. He offered it was appropriate that the voyage had ended with a bang, hoping she would remember they almost missed the outbound flight a week before by making love quickly and passionately when they should have been finishing their packing leisurely and carefully. He forgot his robe and shaving cream while Sharon overlooked a hair dryer, a favorite pair of sneakers, and their entire supply of maps and pamphlets.

He considered crawling over to her and tugging at her leg like a puppy seeking attention. She was curled tightly into a corner of the love seat, distancing herself from the vacation, from him, from everything but her own troubled thoughts. He sensed if he held her she'd cry, so they sat again in silence until he eventually fell asleep. He couldn't remember getting up later, or undressing, or making his way to bed, or if she'd kissed him good night. The weariness he felt before dozing off was now replaced by apprehension. Being home might bring more to an end than only a trip.

As he tossed the comforter to one side, he noticed the television glowing silently against the far wall. The hosts and the weatherman of "The Today Show" chatted and laughed, so it must be earlier than nine. He couldn't recall turning the TV on the night before.

After showering and tossing on the abandoned robe, he trudged downstairs, quietly enough not to startle Sharon if she was there, but loud enough to let her know he was coming. His suitcase was still in the front hallway, but hers had been moved and was now wedged against the door. He walked through the dining room and peeked into the kitchen. She was sitting on the family room coffee table, idly paging through a magazine. She looked up after a moment and smiled weakly, as one smiles when the bad news has not been as bad as expected.

"So, it looks like you have continued your unbroken ten-month string of getting up before I do," he began. "The milk in the refrigerator must be awful by this time. What did you put in your coffee?"

"It is," she replied. "Just sugar."

"I really slept like a rock. How about you?"

Sharon shrugged. Stonetree fumbled through a cabinet looking for his favorite cup, trying to stretch his neck to relieve the tightness rising from his shoulders.

"I'm surprised I slept that well," he continued. "The last time I got back from Europe I couldn't get two hours of solid sleep for a couple of days. I didn't know if I was supposed to be asleep or awake or eating or working. It was crazy. And after that landing last night. Jesus! I'm amazed I could even close my eyes. Do you want some more?"

She stood and shuffled to the kitchen table. She sat down in what she called the "visitor's chair," nudging her mug a few inches toward him. After leaning across the table to fill it, he sat down and toyed with the sugar bowl, wondering how long she had been up and how long he could delay asking her the obvious question. He was fairly certain why she was behaving this way but did not want to confront her. He did not like disruption and he did not like pain.

He wanted everything to be like it was in those first heady months they knew each other. He did not want to resign himself to the fact that those times were now farther away than Buckingham Palace or Speaker's Corner. Vacation was over. The time for everyday reality had arrived. He would have sifted through the bowl for an hour, but she placed her hand on his and whispered, "Come on, David. Let's talk."

He raised his head and stared into a face that seemed to sport a genuine smile. Sharon wasn't wearing any makeup, scrubbed and fresh, just like the morning they met. Her chestnut-bordering-on-red hair, long and tousled, gave her the look of a college student, not a twenty-nine-year-old woman. An uncountable number of freckles and her small, childlike nose added to an impression that more often than not called for the production of proof of her age.

If only her eyes could be as brilliantly green as they had once been. If only they could be as crystalline as they were the day he ambled into the bookstore in search of some forgotten magazine. If only today could bring a replay of their first conversation, their first phone call, their first date, their first kiss. Now her eyes were glassy and flat, filled with tiny red lines. The source of those lines could not be mistaken by anyone who had seen the same lines in other sad eyes.

"They don't look too good, do they?" Sharon sighed. Her hand rose to hide them from the light or from Stonetree, or both. Reaching up, he gently pulled her hand back to the table and held it under his own.

"What?" he inquired with a dose of curiosity that sounded contrived even to him.

"My eyes, David. Look at my eyes."

"What about them? They look a little bloodshot. You're tired. How did you sleep last night?"

"Not for a month," she moaned. "I haven't been tired for a *month*. Would being tired cause tremors, David? Do your hands shake when you don't get enough sleep?"

She thrust her hands forward, and Stonetree recoiled slightly. The trembling was not obvious, but it was there. She froze for a moment and then gradually pulled them back, finally locking her fingers behind her neck and letting out a long, resigned sigh.

"Not jet lag?" he asked.

"Not jet lag," she replied.

The first time he speculated that Sharon might have Camden-Young's Disease was one Sunday a few weeks before they went to London. They had spent the previous day visiting friends and the previous night watching television and reading. They went to bed reasonably early and slept late. He noticed the next morning over breakfast that she looked as though she had a serious hangover. She said she felt fine, but as the day wore on, it was apparent she was ill.

When he saw her the following weekend, he again noticed her ragged look, although this time it was not quite as pronounced. She said she thought it was an allergic reaction to something and was taking antihistamines. Just before the trip she seemed to improve, so he put his anxieties on a mental shelf. During their entire stay in England, however, he would glance at her each time he saw a cruiser on the streets or in a pub. She might be using Ocu-Clear, but the insidious red lines were still noticeable, at least to him.

"So what do you think?" he finally asked.

"What do you think?" Sharon shot back. "You're the expert, I'm not."

"I've got a CPA," he retorted. "Not an M.D. I didn't go to medical school. I don't work in a doctor's office. The company only makes . . ."

He stopped. He'd gone too far. His suspicion was no longer a secret, and he could never, ever retract the accusatory tone that permeated his voice.

"They only make what?" she said, the venom in her words apparent. "They only make what, David?"

"Sharon," he said calmly, "let's not argue. Let's bring this conversation down to a little more rational level, okay?"

She nodded. "I'm sorry. I'm just upset. I don't know what to think. I'm scared."

"And you're tired and traveled out," he reassured her. "So am I. But we had a good time. Right?"

"Uh-huh."

"And we promised each other that we'd go back again, didn't we?"

"Uh-huh."

This time her response was a little weaker than the first, and he could feel the beginnings of a crack in her voice. He stood up and moved behind her, delicately massaging her shoulders. Why did this have to happen to him, he wondered. Why couldn't she just be like she was when they met? Why couldn't they just have a couple more days off to do nothing but recover from all the rushing around? Why did the fantasy that was London have to come to such a disappointing end? Why couldn't it be like it was before? He could feel her start to tremble.

He moved his hands to the tops of her arms and squeezed them, pulling her back. She stood up and wrapped her arms around him, holding him tightly. She began to sob, then to cry, and then to gasp, all in such quick succession that Stonetree was certain she would faint.

He guided her to the couch in the family room and held her until she caught her breath and relaxed with her head against his chest. For a moment he tried to imagine what it would be like if their positions were reversed but quickly shook the thought from his mind. She looked up and touched a finger to his cheek.

"What am I going to do?" she pleaded.

Stonetree propped her up and looked her directly in the eye, hoping his expression would not show the pain and fear evident in hers.

"Okay," he began. "There is no point in the two of us panicking. First of all, we don't know that there is anything to panic about. Secondly, if there is . . ." He hesitated. What if there *was* something to panic about? Then what? "If there is something to panic about," he concluded, "well, I guess we'll have to panic about it together, right?"

The nonsensical nature of his remark seemed to stun her at first, but then she began to laugh uncontrollably, shaking harder than before. He decided if they had to talk about it, maybe keeping it light would help. He waited until her laughter subsided, but before he could speak again, she excused herself to use the bathroom. She muttered, "This is insane," before closing the door. It was just then that the telephone began to chirp.

He looked around the room for the cordless. He reached for it on the coffee table, and after flipping up the antenna, said hello.

"David? David, how was the trip?" It was his secretary, Elaine.

"Oh, it was great. Lots of fun. I'm really beat, though. I could use another."

"Well," she replied, "according to my screen you took only a couple of days in January, no days in February, it's the end of this month, and you have used up a total of eight—"

"Make that nine," he interrupted. "I'm not coming in today. That was the deal. Remember? Remember when I was walking out last Wednesday and you told me to have a good trip and I said 'Thank you' and you said 'I'll see you next Friday' and I said 'No you won't' . . ."

"And that's why I'm calling you, David. I'm only a messenger."

Stonetree could feel his face tingle. They were going to do it to him. They couldn't leave him alone on his first day back from vacation. They didn't understand that he just didn't care whether they needed him for something or not. SUE just wasn't that important.

"Listen, Elaine," he said with a sigh. "Do you still have my stats up? Do you see how—better yet, tell me how many more vacation days I'm entitled to this year."

"Counting today or not?"

"This isn't funny, Elaine. Let me off, all right?"

"Well, I'm sure glad you came back with such a wonderful attitude. Wouldn't the King have you over for tea?"

Stonetree chuckled. If there was one person in the world who could be counted on to match him attitude for attitude, it was Elaine. Still, he was not in the mood to visit Southern United Enterprises, despite the fact that he had almost planned on being down near the Home Office anyway. He loved the city on Fridays. The beginning of spring only made it better.

"So how many days?" he asked.

"Uh, if you don't take off today, it looks like you have another twelve coming, and that doesn't count the wonderful fourteen paid holidays sweet SUE gives us all—even the peons."

"Let's do this the easy way." He smiled, though she couldn't see his expression, of course. "Make it an even eleven, and I'll see you on Monday. Thanks for calling. I know you miss me. Good luck and good-bye."

He switched off the phone and began to count the seconds backward from fifteen. The phone chirped at seven.

"No, Elaine," he said as he walked to the sink with his cold cup of coffee. "I told you, vacation. Spell it with a capital V. Tell whoever wants me I can't be reached. Tell them I'm having mental problems."

"You *do* have mental problems," she replied.

"Well, tell them they've gotten worse. Okay, who wants me? Is it a problem with the quarterlies? Once they're out of Division, it's not our problem anymore."

"I don't know."

"Does Wallace want to see me?"

"I think Mr. Walker is out of the office until Monday."

"Well, Wallace is the boss, and if he doesn't need to see me, then it can wait—"

He caught himself. He realized he was starting to act as if it *was* important, whatever it was Elaine had called about. And it simply wasn't. So why get excited?

"Time out," he continued. "I'll take a breather. Who needs what?"

"Trisha Lane called down here a couple of minutes ago and said that if it was at all possible, she wanted to see you before the end of the day."

"And you said?"

"And I said that you were out of town and wouldn't be back until Monday."

"And she said?"

"She asked if I'd be talking to you."

"And you said?"

"I didn't know."

"And . . ."

"And she said it was important, that I should get in touch with you and give you the message. Click."

"Is Mr. Riley around? Let me talk to him. Maybe he can see what she wants."

"I thought of that, David," she continued, "but he's out. I think he's sick again."

"Great. Uh, let me think for a minute."

Without being able to talk to either Riley, the vice president of the Technology Division, or Wallace Walker, the group vice president over the Technology, Communications, and Transportation divisions, Stonetree was in a difficult position. Trisha Lane was arguably the most powerful of SUE's three group vice presidents, controlling both Pharmaceuticals and Entertainment, and was not known to take well to real or perceived insubordination. So why aggravate someone in an influential position? Still, it was only SUE.

"I don't know," he said. "I've got a lot of things to take care of today. . . ."

Sharon walked back into the room, looking refreshed. She'd put on a bit of makeup and pinned her hair up as she typically did when she had something she wanted to get out of the way. Stonetree thought it was a good sign. He held up his index finger to indicate he'd soon be done with the phone call and then motioned for her to get some fresh coffee.

"So what do you want me to do?" Elaine asked.

"Are you in the mood to lie for me?" Stonetree asked.

"Anything for you, David."

"If Lane calls back, tell her you couldn't get in touch with me." He hesitated. "Did she call or did her secretary call?"

"She did."

"And what did she want, exactly?"

"To see you today."

"Yeah, well, if she calls back, just say you couldn't reach me. Riley and Walker are both out, huh?"

"Yes."

"Maybe I'll check back later. Did the guy ever call back about the Mustang?"

"Is his name Hendricks?"

"That's him."

"He called on Monday and said to tell you it hadn't been sold and, if you wanted to see it, you should contact him before Saturday. He said that was as long as he would hold it."

"Did he leave his number?"

"No. I asked, but he said you had it."

"I do? Oh, it's . . . no, it's somewhere in my office. Okay, maybe I'll be in—I don't know." He looked over at Sharon as she sat down at the table. "I'll call back later. If Lane calls again, tell her you couldn't reach me."

"As ordered."

"Bye."

Stonetree turned the phone off and walked to the table, sitting down across from Sharon again. She rubbed the side of her nose methodically, as if she were giving Stonetree a signal. He did the same, and they both laughed. He felt better, and she seemed to be herself for the first time since they boarded the jet at London's Heathrow Airport.

"You think you've got it, don't you?" he began. "Is that it?"

Sharon looked at him blankly and then toyed with her watches. Maybe he was mistaken. Was it possible there was something *else* wrong? She frowned slightly and looked out the window.

"What do you think?" she replied.

"Like I said before—"

"I know, David," she interrupted him as she looked back at him and propped her chin on her hand. "You're not a doctor, and the company only makes treatments for the symptoms, not cures for the damn disease. Is that about right?"

Stonetree nodded. It was the most he could offer or, at that point, anyone could offer.

Despite the fact that CYD was a global obsession that one could not read a newspaper or watch a news broadcast without hearing about, Stonetree rarely thought about the affliction. He used to worry about it a great deal and thought about it every day. The last time he could remember giving it any serious consideration was fourteen months before, on his thirty-third birthday.

His Tourcam was clean. He didn't have a hint of primary symptoms. Nevertheless, he avoided the typically outrageous behavior a sixer was supposed to engage in when the milestone was reached. He spent the day alone, not even mentioning it to his friends. As he studied Sharon's face, he remembered how he had scratched his head, wondering how he had lucked out.

He could imagine what was going through her mind. She had entered what the psychiatrists called the realization phase without harming herself, which meant she was at least on the right track. The neutral phase would follow and would last, he guessed, a good two months. And then she would shift into crisis phase.

Crisis phase was more dangerous than CYD itself, especially for women. The devastating effect of the hair loss, combined with the already existent sense of doom, pushed hundreds of thousands of victims "out on the wire" each year. Many made at least one suicide attempt, usually employing whatever method was in vogue at the time. Those who failed were often maimed or scarred for life.

Sometimes self-destruction wasn't enough. Paranoia was a common secondary symptom during crisis phase, and oftentimes cruisers would take a sixer or two with them as they exited life. If suicide was not in the plan, they would frequently go after someone else for practice just to unload some anger. The bodyguard business was booming. Stonetree did a quick calculation. No, he couldn't afford one.

He glanced at Sharon and wondered if she possessed the capacity to kill either herself or someone else. If exposure to negative behavior was a factor, she certainly wasn't lacking. Both her younger sisters, the twins, torched themselves on the lawn at their parents' house. Her best friend, Becky, was raped and murdered by two cruisers before they piped themselves down the block. Three months before, a young customer at the bookstore discovered she didn't have enough money to purchase the latest book on hair restoration. So she returned it to the display and pulled a wine bottle from her shopping bag. After smashing it against the book rack, she calmly slashed first her wrists then her throat.

Sharon stood and picked up her coffee cup. She took a sip, set it down, and went to the refrigerator. She returned with a bottle of orange juice and positioned it at the center of the table. She asked Stonetree if he wanted some. He declined.

"I'll drink yours if you don't," she offered.

"It's been about a month, hasn't it?" he asked.

"I figured you suspected." She nodded. "And I love you for not making it an issue before vacation. I really appreciate that. Ocu-Clear can do just so much, and then I'm on my own." She laughed and shook her head.

"It's not an issue now."

She went to the cabinet and brought back a large glass, which she filled to the top. She gulped half of it, then propped her chin again and gazed at Stonetree, her eyes filled with question marks. After waiting a few moments, she said, "Talk to me."

"What do you want me to say?" he asked.

"I don't know. Anything."

"I guess the first thing to do is get you in for a Tourcam."

"Already did."

Stonetree winced. "When?"

"A couple days before we left."

"So you didn't get results?"

"They told me about a week. I told them I wasn't in a hurry."

"Which one did you have?"

"The whole shot. A T-three. I figured it was worth it."

"I guess they're doing quite a job with the residual reads," Stonetree said enthusiastically. "It might be real good."

"Or it might not."

He leaned forward. "But it might. It hasn't been more than a month. You might be—"

"A B-girl?" she snapped. "Lucky me! But I guess it beats the alternatives. I doubt you'd want your friends to catch you with a skinhead!"

Stonetree recoiled at the term. Although an entire language had grown out of the CYD crisis and was part of everyday communications, some of the slang still made him cringe. Carrier designations were the most popular subjects, and certainly the most graphic.

Class D carriers were most often and most acceptably referred to as sixers, from the twenty-six percent of the target population they represented. Deezers was the first popular term for sixers, but was now usually used only by older people and foreigners. Corkers was rarely heard anymore. Bluebloods was regaining its former status.

As the phrase went, however, "a sixer is a sixer to a sixer." Or to the press or to the commentators or to the Hawaiians. A sixer was not a sixer to cruisers. To them, a sixer was a highlander or a winker or a figleaf. Sometimes a sixer was white-eyes or fishface or oyster. Sometimes, to a cruiser, a sixer was a lukifuk or blueball, and Stonetree would not even think some of the terms used exclusively for females.

Class C carriers did not generate nearly as much interest as sixers. Ceezers was coined at the same time as deezers, and never seemed to disappear. Occasionally terms like flats and five-speeds and clams came into popularity, but ceezers remained at the top of the list. One term that presented the only serious competition was woks. Woks derived, it was thought, from the fact that Tourcam test results from Japan recently confirmed what most observers had known for years. More than half the native target population of the island was Class C. When coupled with the disproportionate thirty-nine percent Class D population, CYD was no more a threat to the Japanese than a particularly virulent strain of flu.

Class B carriers were still popularly known as beezers, a term that retained an almost warm acceptance with most people. Being a beezer gave those carriers both the yin and yang of Camden-Young's Disease. On the one hand, the specter of imminent death or impairment was avoided. On the other, beezers knew to a one that eventually they would be faced with Class A roulette. While their hair loss might be partial, they often looked worse for CYD's incomplete assault.

Some hair, however, was better than no hair. They kept what they had and waited for nature to take its course. Rather than the melancholy and despair of Class A carriers, beezers usually appreciated the reprieve and often tried to cram a lifetime into a year.

Beezers. Crew cuts. Kangaroos. Shorts. Climbers. They all described a life marked by equal parts of reckless abandon, hedonism, and unbelievable social climbing. Beezers knew what they wanted and were not afraid to ask. If asking was not enough, they'd demand it. After sixers, beezers were the focus of most advertising, especially for consumables and luxury items. They were the darlings of the arts and, one on one, the worst nightmare of a cruiser bent on destruction. Beezers did not want the party to end. The search for gratification, however, often did bring the party to a very abrupt end. They were addicts. Alcohol, drugs, sex, thrills, skinhead-cracking. Most of them were into at least one, or attracted to some other pastime that eventually took its toll. It was not uncommon for an otherwise middle class B-girl to turn a few tricks in the neighborhood occasionally. It was not uncommon for an otherwise middle class B-boy to do a number on someone in the neighborhood. They all had habits, but usually the habits were overlooked. Everyone loved a beezer.

Class A carriers took the brunt of the CYD epidemic, and the slang category was no exception. The term a-zer never caught on with the public. They were cruisers from the start. The term remained the kindest, if not the most popular. Skinhead was the rage and had been for the past six months.

Bad spokes. Cyclers. Reddies. Boneheads. Pluckers. Bugeyes. Jumpers. Chokers. Beef eaters. San Diego chickens. Cactus brains. Shakers. Pukers. Cashouts. Wishing wells. Water eaters. And the one that summed them all up—wigs.

"Sharon, don't."

"What do you mean, 'don't'?" she cried. "I've got to get used to it."

"No, you don't," he argued. "Never. Don't get yourself involved in that crap."

"Easy for you to say," she retorted with a bit of a sneer. "You've got your position. You're one of the chosen. Don't tell me what to say, David. You've got no room to criticize."

"I'm not being critical." He sighed. "I just don't like hearing you talk about . . . yourself that way."

"Why not?" she continued. "I've heard you with your pals. When they say 'Did you catch the wig that just walked by— wouldn't touch her with a ten-foot pole,' or 'That climber will be fine as long as she keeps taking her pills' . . ."

"Sharon, please, not now."

"Or," she snapped, "the ultimate compliment—'A true blueblood, a true sixer if I ever saw one.' A true blueblood, David. A true sixer. Yeah, I thought I was one too. I guess we can say good-bye to those days, huh?"

She began to shake. He wanted to hold her and comfort her but was repelled by her temper and her accusations. He would not be drawn into her petulance or her anger. They were, he believed, wasted emotions. Instead, he raised his hand, spreading his fingers in front of her, silently requesting her to relax. In a moment, she did.

"You might only be Class B," he began. "That's no big deal. You take the drugs for a while, they find a cure, and it's over."

"And if I'm Class A?"

"And if you're Class A, you take the drugs for a while, they find a cure, and it's over."

"That simple, huh?"

"Sharon, we could argue about this—Jesus, this isn't an argument! We could talk about this until hell freezes over, but it isn't going to change anything. And it won't change us."

"Promise?" she asked.

"I promise. Come on."

Stonetree stepped away from the table, motioning for her to follow. She took his hand and they walked to the living room where they sunk into one of the love seats, not speaking for a long while.

When they finally continued their conversation, it concerned other topics. Sharon wanted to check on things at the shop, see if her apartment was still in one piece, pick up the mail, and go to the grocery store. Stonetree told her about the call from Elaine, wondered aloud about the Mustang, and said he might go into the city in the afternoon. Everything was as normal as could be, until Sharon got up to leave.

"I don't want to call them, David. I don't want to know—not yet. Can we wait until Monday?"

"Anything can wait till Monday." He smiled as he pulled her close. "How do you feel? Aside from pissed off."

"You're so sweet," she responded. "Pretty good. A little tired. I might have a temperature."

Stonetree raised his palm to her forehead.

"You feel okay to me."

"No, I've got a temperature. I've been taking it. About ninety-nine, ninety-nine and a half. It wasn't too bad this morning. Almost normal."

"That's a good sign. We'll wait till Monday. Stop at the drugstore and get some seven hundred. Better yet, I've got some nine hundred upstairs. Want some?"

"I guess, if you've got it."

"I've got a couple of Bradshaw-4 Injectors too."

"Those are pretty expensive. Where'd you get them?"

"It was after one of the promotions last year. They had cases of them sitting around up in Marketing. A guy I know, Boonie, I'd done a favor for him, he gave me a half dozen. I showed them to you, remember?"

"When?"

"You remember," he said with a smile. "It was just after you and Jim and Tracey took over the store. Mike and Midge came over, and we had our first annual world championship PRISMPLEX tournament."

If CYD was one of the darkest points of the past few years, PRISMPLEX was one of the brightest. The board game was timed perfectly. Its appearance was compared to The Beatles surfacing a few months after the Kennedy assassination, like Japan's Project Pearl Harbor after the Hawaiian earthquake. It was the bright ray of hope, the ebullient diversion that distracted the American public's attention from the seemingly inescapable tragedy around it. Unlike its ancestors from Liverpool and Tokyo, however, PRISMPLEX was home-grown, the creation of a cantankerous attorney from Manitowoc, Wisconsin, who also happened to be a close friend of another of America's favorite diversions, its first Mrs. President.

"Oh, yeah!" she said, returning his smile. "Midge was incredible! She really should have entered the Nationals."

"And we had the champagne . . ."

"While they were here, and then after . . ."

"Now you're catching my drift." He laughed. "Your memory's still there."

"Can we do that again?" she asked. "Maybe leaving out Mike and Midge and PRISMPLEX!"

"Anytime you want."

"Tonight?"

"No, not tonight," he said. "You've got your errands to run. Maybe over the weekend. How about tomorrow?"

"Promise?"

"Look," he said with a bit of excitement, "you come over tomorrow afternoon, and we'll drive upstate to see this guy Hendricks about the car and come back here and have a nice quiet evening."

"How quiet?"

"Quiet enough that you'll sleep well."

Stonetree ran upstairs and returned with the device and the capsules. He carried the suitcase out to her car and, after agreeing to return to London in the autumn, kissed her good-bye. As he stood on the edge of the street, watching her drive away, he tried to organize his thoughts. There were a number of things he could do with the rest of the day, but only a few held any interest.

After unpacking and throwing a load of clothes into the washer, he drained what was left in the coffeepot and perched himself on one of the kitchen counters, watching the second hand of the clock above the pantry tick around its face. It was close to eleven A.M. He wandered around the house for fifteen minutes, examining the plants, writing his initials in the light film of dust on the dining room table, and wondering how much Hendricks wanted for the Mustang.

Sitting on the stairway was the box of Bradshaw Injectors. He reached into it and removed one of the three remaining devices. It was smaller and lighter than the Bradshaw-2's, maybe three quarters the size of a pack of cigarettes, despite its doubled capacity. Peeling off the cellophane wrapper, he pressed the injection button, and the ready light indicated it was fully charged. The two high-pitched beeps confirmed it.

He flicked open the front cover and peered into the four small chambers. Instead of being the dark brown they turned after thirty or forty uses, the barrels were enamel white. Maybe, he thought, getting cool would put the day into better perspective. He pushed the injection button a few more times, watching the tiny green light flicker on and off, listening to the unit's invitation.

He went upstairs to the den and opened the earthenware jar on top of the desk. It contained perhaps eighty capsules, roughly divided between Febrifuge Blue 800 and 900. There were also ten stray Febrifuge Blue 700 capsules he guessed must be over a year old. He poured the contents onto the desk, picked out the 700's, and tossed them into the wastebasket. He then swept the remaining capsules back into the jar, leaving four each of 800's and 900's. While some people enjoyed the effect of blending, Stonetree always felt a bit queasy after combining different series. He thought for a moment.

He pushed the four 800's aside and loaded one of the remaining capsules into the Brad. Closing the cover, he held the injector to the underside of his left wrist. Perhaps, he mused, maybe two would be better. Reopening the unit, he popped an additional 900 in and squeezed the cover closed again. Repositioning the device, he took a deep breath and pressed the injection button.

A bright crackle sounded from the unit, and he felt the familiar slight pinch on his wrist. In a few seconds he smelled the exhaust, which until now he had never been able to categorize. Febrifuge Blue 900 was manufactured with an additive to mask the antiseptic, sour medicine odor of all the earlier compounds. Curry, he thought. It smells like burnt curry.

He closed his eyes for a moment to savor the cool wave that washed through his body. He felt a light pressure in his scalp, as if someone were gently pushing down on the top of his head. The wave receded almost as quickly as it had rushed across him, replaced by a sensation he always associated with lying in the sun on a brisk, breezy day. The room seemed to darken a bit, as if the sky had suddenly clouded over, but soon regained its normal appearance. He chuckled and lifted up the blind on the window in front of his desk. Tricked again. Not a cloud to be seen.

Another wave washed through his body, colder than the first. The shiver, however, lasted only a few seconds. Again he felt the relaxed, dreamlike sensation he loved, and he closed his eyes. Sometime, somewhere in his past, he had felt this way all the time. Exactly where and when he could not recall. It was so peaceful.

Not that he cared much about the technicalities. He felt it now, and feeling it now was what mattered. Artificial peace beat organic anxiety any day of the week. He did not need an excuse to use Febrifuge Blue 900. The drug was an excuse in itself.

When he finally opened his eyes, nothing was different. Except the minute hands on his watches, which had moved from the ones to the fours. Tricked again. It seemed like no more than a minute or two.

Leaning back in his chair, he slowly opened the unit's cover and emptied the residue into an ashtray. He took a deep breath and closed his eyes again. He pictured three telephones in his mind. On one was a card with the name Carl Zigeras, on the second Trisha Lane, and on the third Dr. Fitzgerald. Stonetree rested there awhile, exploring the different combinations and examining the important question of whom he should call first.

CHAPTER 2

Stonetree guessed he and his buddy Carl might get into some mischief that night, so he took the Bullet into the city. The forty-minute ride allowed him to read through *Newsglance*, his glossy, eight-page daily source of news, information, and opinion. Its succinct, bite-size features and columns were well tailored to his short attention span.

International led with a report from the Vatican stating the massive wave of conversions to Catholicism, especially in the Mid- and Far East, over the past three years had established it as the foremost religion in the world.

The French government reported that contributions for rebuilding the recently destroyed Eiffel Tower, the victim of a terrorist, were so generous during the first twenty-four hours of fund-raising that no additional gifts would be necessary.

Moscow was again calling for the United States to remove its armed forces from Europe. Australia and Japan agreed in principle to tighten the immigration restrictions of the PICO treaty, and Brazil acknowledged it would be bankrupt within weeks unless its creditors and lenders could work out an acceptable debt repayment schedule.

National led with the Supreme Court decision upholding a Texas law making parents responsible for property damage caused by their children (of any age) during the commission of an act designed to take a human life. In a related story, the

FDA refused to consider the application of Upjohn for approval of a cyanide-based "resignation" capsule.

House Speaker Daniel Hersch was calling for an FBI investigation into the recent deaths of five members of Congress, despite the fact that all were ruled isolated events.

The NASA funding bill was defeated for the second year in a row. Alaska, Hawaii, and Washington continued to increase their populations at an unprecedented rate, and under pressure from the Cabinet, the President would soon announce her support for an experimental federal middle-school system.

City trumpeted the plea bargain, after the third day of trial, of sportscaster Kari Katz. The state agreed to drop soliciting and public indecency charges for a guilty plea to the lesser crime of disorderly conduct. The defendant also announced she would resign her position even if she did not receive a jail sentence.

The mayor charged the council's majority bloc with conflict of interest in their refusal to fund the city's second Body Retrieval Team (BRITE Squad). The first team, he claimed, was overworked and underequipped.

An explosion on a bus two nights before had claimed its twelfth victim. Members of the PTA were picketing City Hall to protest the refusal of the Board of Education to fund any additional lunch program milk purchases, and the Streets and Parks Department expected to hire up to three thousand part-time workers for the summer.

In Money, the lead story concerned yet another investigation of the insider/short-selling practices that may have contributed to the devastation of the fast-food industry. In a related story, McDonald's announced that all its remaining outlets would close within two weeks in anticipation of the complete restructuring of its product line and marketing.

The stock market was up 29.31 points, closing at a new high for the year of 4887.75. Analysts, however, did not believe this to be more than a small step toward reaching the Dow's apogee of 6991.81, set two years earlier.

Hair America Ltd. reported yet another stock split, its third in seven months. The Continental Commodities Exchange said it would consider the recommendation that there was a sophisticated enough structure in place to allow a trial program for European Antique futures, and the most popular investment vehicles in the first quarter, and the most profitable, were Alaskan real estate and real estate trusts.

Sports led with a story on Stephanie Van Til's win at the Australian World Invitational Tennis Tournament in Sydney. The record three-million-dollar first prize, Van Til announced, would be donated to CYD research. In a related story, it was revealed that tennis star Ian Winters committed suicide two days before the tournament began.

Roosevelt Wilkins, undisputed bare-knuckles boxing champion, announced he was retiring from the ring next week, on his twenty-first birthday. This followed a grand jury's refusal to indict him on second-degree murder charges involving the death of one of his opponents the previous month.

A golfer in Toledo shot a typical ninety-four over the weekend despite sinking three holes-in-one. The University of California Board of Regents announced a phaseout of most sports programs in the system, and Major League Baseball Commissioner Will Bainisi announced all bat and ball boys and girls could not reach or exceed their sixteenth birthday while employed.

Stonetree skipped the Living page, skipped the Fashion page, and finished with his favorite, Entertainment.

The summer movie season was expected to be a blockbuster, with Hollywood offering new installments of James Bond, Indiana Jones, and Chin-Chin Davis. Entertainment stocks were hot, and a story on them would be in Money tomorrow.

Artist Jean Lionne-Demilunes failed in his lawsuit to reclaim four examples of his COMBAT ART executed prior to its trademark registration. The four three-by-three canvases, drab gray and stenciled with that phrase and one other word each (Obsession, Nightmare, Risk, and Sixers) had been purchased by his broker from Lionne-Demilunes's former lover for eighty thousand dollars each. A post-trademark version of Sixers, Sixers II, recently sold at auction for 6.8 million dollars.

Domination of the popular music charts by the Pacific Wave groups continued, with five of the top twenty going to Australians and three to Hawaiian natives or residents; however, a re-release of the 1986 recording by The B-52's titled "Wig" remained in the number-one position for the fifth consecutive week.

The fall television schedules for the six major networks were announced, and once again they could be summed up in two words: nostalgia and fluff. Westerns, Victorian dramas, and sixties fare occupied close to a third of the schedule, with sitcoms and sports taking another half.

Of special interest to Stonetree was an article stating Wexford, his manager, Doug Smite, and a number of his associates had been cleared by a grand jury investigating the bombing of a police station in suburban Pittsburgh the previous September. The night before the incident, the pop star was the target of the fourth assassination attempt on him or members of his band in less than a year. This time a delirious teenager approached the stage and threw two hand grenades, both of which fell short of their mark. They landed in the crowd, killing fourteen fans and injuring another thirty.

The youth was taken into custody, charged with murder, and held pending his arraignment the next day. At seven o'clock the following morning, the holding cells were literally leveled by a massive blast thought to have emanated from a suitcase filled with explosives.

Following the previous assassination attempt, Wexford's manager was quoted as saying that the next person who threatened Wexford's life would be dealt with "the way butchers handle pigs" and offered $500,000 to anyone who brought "the next crackpot to justice."

After the decision of the grand jury was announced, Smite held a brief meeting with reporters. He told them that until further notice Wexford would no longer make concert appearances, would no longer sit for interviews, would not comment on the possibility of a third Search for Survival blood drive, and would answer everyone's questions about his recent divorce, the attack, and his plans in his next album.

When he emerged from the Bullet station, Stonetree looked up at the Citicorp clock. It was 1:15. He had told Lane he would be at her office at 1:30. Noting that SUE Plaza was only two blocks away, he decided to stop at a magazine shop to page through a copy of *Car Collector*. He wanted to see what he could expect to pay for the Mustang he hoped to purchase. He couldn't find one that rivaled the credentials of the one he planned to look at, but those that came close were selling in the twelve- to fifteen-thousand-dollar range.

As he walked to the Plaza, he played with figures in his mind. At the very most, Hendricks could ask $20,000 for the car, which was extremely generous. Now, what exactly was $20,000? It was about a sixth of his annual salary. It was an awful lot to spend on a toy. It was about three fifths of what he paid for his "real" car, the recently introduced Toyota Turbostar. Loaded. It was about twelve percent of the remaining balance of the mortgage on his town house. It was more than half of what the typical family of four was supposed to survive on each year and probably a small fraction of what Wexford made each morning by waking up.

Instead of the Mustang, Stonetree could buy five new stereo systems, thirty new suits, or a dozen cases of great wine. He could go on four vacations in Europe or take a two-month unpaid leave of absence from work. He could spend a year going to Sirius every night, or visit Dr. Fitzgerald for two hundred fifteen-minute sessions, or take Sharon to one hundred nice restaurants. He could buy her a couple of leather coats. He could buy her an engagement ring. He could buy her a nice funeral.

He didn't have his employee badge when he reached Security, so he filled out the Lack of Badge form. This was despite the fact that he and the guard on duty had been on a first-name basis for at least three years. Stonetree asked how many demerits he could expect for not having his badge, and Eddie replied, wide-eyed, that he didn't think demerit records were kept on management-level employees.

Picking up a visitor's ID, Stonetree ambled to the executive access elevator. He shook his head and wondered why he worked for a company that more often than not treated its staff the way an annoyed teacher dealt with errant students.

After signing in and flirting with Security Sheila on eighteen, he hurried to the men's room to straighten his tie and comb his hair. That done, he made his way to eighteen-north to say hello to Wallace Walker. As he neared the corner office, he noticed it was dark and recalled Elaine telling him Walker was out. He walked back to eighteen-south, stopping again to flirt with Security Sheila.

He finally arrived at his destination. It was 1:40. Lane's secretary wasn't there, but he could hear her boss talking on the phone, so he busied himself with trying to read the papers on the secretary's desk. He'd never been good at reading upside down and still wasn't. He almost figured out what the executive bonus structure would be for the following year when he heard a voice from Lane's office call, "Mary? Bring in your book, please."

Stonetree peeked into her office, waved, and deadpanned, "Sorry. Only me."

Lane smiled pleasantly and motioned for him to come in and sit down. She pointed to the two couches at the near end of the office. She closed an appointment book and set it to one side of her large, deep mahogany desk. She stood up and walked to the other coach to join him.

She was, he thought to himself, probably the most striking woman he had ever met. Although he had talked to her only three times in the past, he certainly knew her better than she knew him. Lane was the stuff of which corporate legends were made.

Her rise through the ranks of SUE management was nothing short of spectacular, but there were still a few chapters left to be written. Her history was well documented in newspaper and magazine articles, the rest being filled in by conventional company wisdom and cafeteria gossip.

Although she majored in mass media in college, she could not find a position in the electronic media upon graduation. So she took the first job that was offered to her, a sales position with Baxter.

According to one account, she volunteered to take the toughest territory with the lowest sales and worst physicians. Impressed with her spunk but put off by her arrogance, the man who hired her granted her wish.

Sales remained flat for nine months but then slowly began to turn around. After her first year, the territory had moved from an adjusted twenty-fifth in her zone to an adjusted twenty-first. The second year saw it move up to fourteenth, the third year to an adjusted fifth. The end of her fourth year brought her up to number three. The sales manager died, she took his job, promptly had the number-one and -two reps transferred out of the zone, fired all but her remaining top five producers, and in two years built a staff that was easily the best in the industry. Then she quit.

She spent the next six months of her life at a ranch outside Tucson, horseback riding two or three hours a day, doing some nontechnical climbing, and reading. Stonetree had seen a reprint of a picture of her taken back then. She sat majestically atop a stallion, her black jeans blending into the horse's body, her red sleeveless T-shirt in sharp contrast to the desolate background. Although probably not planned to be, it was one of the most sensual photographs he could ever remember seeing.

When she returned to the city, there were a dozen job offers or inquiries waiting for her, a few promising terms that most people would murder to get. Instead of accepting any of them, she wrote polite refusals to all of her suitors and filed a job application with Southern United Enterprises, which had just surfaced out of the merger. Hundreds of workers were being terminated, retired, or laid off, but Lane refused to take no for an answer, and with her track record, she was difficult to turn away. She was eventually given a mid-level marketing position in Pharmaceuticals, but was transferred six months later to the then-struggling Entertainment division. Her starting pay was a third of the highest offer she had refused.

Entertainment was picked up whole when Southern Technology acquired and then merged with United Science and Communications. At that time, Entertainment consisted of two small record labels, a music publishing company, a fleet of six Gulfstream V executive jets, three radio stations, and a beer distributorship. Lane, on her own initiative, drafted a plan that argued against the proposed sale of the entire unit. She boldly approached SUE's chairman, Pierre Ruth, with her scheme.

Her outline called for the termination of most of the contracts with Entertainment's existing roster of performers, the sale of four of the jets, the disposal of the three radio stations and the beer distributorship, and the sacking of her vice president. She proposed the acquisition or construction of state-of-the-art audio and video recording studios and the use of the remaining two jets to taxi performers who used the facilities.

A recent increase in the sale of albums, cassettes, compact discs, DATs, and sonics, along with a similarly expanding market in videos, told her profits were to be made. She concluded that strengthening Entertainment's publishing operation would also help.

The masterstroke of her scheme was her perception of a faintly emerging breed of folk singers and pop performers who presented material containing three recurring, interrelated themes. The first was the specter of young, violent death and its ramifications. The second was the new and disturbing class structure surfacing in the United States, based on financial standing, the ability to face or inflict violence, and Tourcam results. The third theme dealt with hope for a better day, no matter what fate might deal out.

Pierre Ruth had molded Southern Technology from a minor collection of specialty manufacturing companies into a major industrial concern. He bet his future and that of ST on the development, manufacture, and sale of Febrifuge Blue 100 seven years before. His bet paid off beyond his greatest expectations, and SUE now held a forty-percent share of the entire world market for CYD treatment. This ever-expanding money machine had created billions of dollars in profits for SUE shareholders and made Ruth one of the wealthiest men in the country.

The story went that upon being shown the plan by Lane, Ruth was struck with its insight and daring. He immediately summoned her superior, the now-immortalized corporate martyr, Henry Schuster. Schuster studied the five-page outline and summed up his opinion of it with the statement, "Pierre, it just doesn't work here at SUE." To which Ruth supposedly responded, "And, Henry, neither do you."

With checkbook in hand and the new title of Vice President, Entertainment, on her SUE business card, Lane plunged into the work of putting her plan into action. Within a couple of months she had signed a number of new performers, including Peggy Quinlan, The Razors, and Impostor Michael. She also chanced one night in Philadelphia upon a plain, unremarkable, shy twenty-four-year-old folk singer who was the opener for a popular East Coast act.

She'd gone to see the headliners but immediately saw the potential of the young man whose name was not even announced when he took the stage. According to popular accounts, after his set she stepped backstage to meet him. She introduced herself as "Trisha Lane, a recording executive" and he introduced himself as "Wexford, an unemployed sandwich maker." The fuse on the Entertainment division's skyrocket was ignited, and the rest is history.

Tenacious was a popular adjective used in describing Lane both then and now. Her propensity to pick a fight with anyone who stood in the path of her singular vision was known both inside and outside the company. When some of the other adjectives were added to the equation—precise, distant, intense, driven—it wasn't hard to appreciate that her rivals had all but become extinct.

The former vice president of Pharmaceuticals objected to the second Search for Survival blood drive as a crass, ridiculous, and unseemly gimmick to sell records and pander to disturbed adolescents. He found himself out of a job in less than two months. When the former group vice president over both divisions was faced with a direct challenge for position from Lane, he wisely accepted a generous early-retirement package. He also joined the ranks of what had become known as the Lane Alumni Association.

And, of course, there was the showdown with Dr. Camden a few years before.

It seemed, however, that beyond her professional life, the profiles and whispers offered very little more than speculation. She was notorious for not attending SUE parties and apparently had no social life outside the company. He had never heard anybody referred to as a friend of hers, and could not recall anyone ever having seen her anyplace except at the office or at the airport.

Her office yielded no clues to her private life and very little about her status. It was slightly smaller than he expected, although certainly four times the size of anywhere he would ever park his desk. It was decorated in subtle rust and cream and beige, the walls empty except for a large painting that dominated the inside wall. It looked to be early Jasper Johns, but he could find no signature.

There were no plaques, no awards, no certificates, no photographs. There were no plants, no magazines, no bric-a-brac, no clutter. In fact, except for her appointment book and a legal pad on the desk, there was no paper in sight. Aside from her telephone, there were no electronics to be seen. The view, however, was impressive.

But Stonetree was more impressed with the way she carried herself. She was close to five foot eight, he guessed, and moved her slender frame with the grace of a gymnast. Her long, thin hands sported perfect nails but no jewelry. She had a thick, almost black, mane of wavy hair that always looked perfect —this in striking counterpoint to her flawless porcelain skin and her pale blue eyes set over a perfect set of cheekbones. Not her only perfect set, he mused as she approached him.

"Do you like the necklace?" she asked as she sat down across from him, casually pulling the chain away from her white silk blouse.

"I do," he said, and smiled. "It must have been expensive."

"Very," she replied. "But fortunately, not for me. Wexford's manager gave it to me when 'The Shortened Life' passed forty million units. A little extravagant for my tastes, but I try to wear it once in a while when I'm going to see him. I wouldn't want to appear ungrateful. We've got a new contract coming up next year."

"I read today that the grand jury wrapped up the bombing inquiry."

"That was idiotic from the start," she said. "You would think the authorities have better things to do with their time than to harass people they ought to be expending energy on to protect. One of the prosecutors involved in that witch hunt had the gall to ask Wexford for an autograph after he testified. Here is one of our overpaid public servants trying to put a man in prison for life and then wanting to kiss and make up so he can tell his wife that he and our boy are old buddies. That's really aggravating."

Stonetree nodded.

"People should invest themselves in their jobs," she continued. "Do them well and accept success and failure with equal dignity." She paused for a moment. "Which is why I wanted to speak to you this afternoon. Thank you for stopping by. You were in London?"

Stonetree felt his stomach muscles tighten and a lump rise in his throat. He never, his thoughts racing, really invested himself in his job. He certainly worked diligently when there and received what he judged to be adequate raises and promotions. Neither SUE nor his previous employer, Tribe Electronics, however, was ever a consuming fire.

He wasn't even that keen on being an accountant, but he figured it was preferable to working on a punchpress. He rarely stayed at SUE past five o'clock and had no interest in showing up on weekends. Steven Riley respected his work and tolerated his occasional oversights, and that was enough for him as long as he was left alone to do his work. He would not pledge allegiance to the corporation to the exclusion of his personal life. He was reasonably happy. Maybe Lane heard from Personnel that he was always forgetting his badge. Maybe he was about to join the "alumni association."

"Yes, I was in London," he offered.

"Enjoy yourself?"

"Yes, I did." He wanted to add it was good to get away from SUE for a week, but decided that was better left unsaid.

"I haven't had a vacation in two years," she replied, glancing over to her desk. "And probably won't for another two."

This was it, he thought. Carl would have a field day. He always said Stonetree's days were numbered.

She crossed her legs, locked both hands around one knee, and leaned forward a bit, looking at him intently.

"I had a conversation with Steve Riley last week, and we spoke about you," she began. "Did you know he was back in the hospital?"

"No, I didn't. When?"

"I believe he was admitted on Friday, possibly Saturday."

"That's terrible," he said.

"Evidently they didn't take care of all his difficulties in November," she continued. "I understand his prognosis is not very encouraging. In any event, in speaking with Mr. Ruth, he indicated Steve would not be returning for at least six weeks and might possibly resign his position with the corporation."

"That's awful."

"It's unfortunate," she agreed. "He's an asset to the company. He brought you over from Tribe when he came to Technology, didn't he?"

"Yes, he did," Stonetree replied. "Not actually with him. I think it was more like six months after he left."

"And you'd worked with him how long at Tribe?"

"About three years."

"As I said, it's a loss to the company."

Lane looked at him as if to wait for a response. He said nothing.

"I would imagine," she continued, leaning back a bit, "that Mr. Walker will continue his program of promoting from without and will bring in someone from the outside to take over Technology."

"I don't know."

"And, as is the case with those of us who acquire new responsibilities, it's probable the new person might make some alterations in the staff."

"I guess."

"Which is not to say that your position would be altered, David," she said earnestly. "Steve speaks very highly of you. I think Mr. Walker likes your work, too, although he is much more inclined to the technical aspects of his divisions than the financial ones."

"Mr. Riley has been good to me, as has Mr. Walker. I don't have any complaints, at least none that are important."

Maybe. Maybe not. These guys are good administrators and all that, but they don't, Stonetree thought, really appreciate what they've got. There is some dead wood that they tolerate, encourage, or just ignore. There are drunks and jerks who simply linger, like lumber waiting for the fire. That's the way the corporation works.

"That's refreshing to hear," she countered. "Some employees are not as pleased with their positions as others are. You know Julie Marx, my staff assistant?"

"Sure. We've worked together on the annuals and a few other projects."

"Julie's last day here at SUE is today. Actually, she's already gone. She is going to pursue some other career possibilities."

Stonetree's eyes widened a bit, but he said nothing. Julie was always enthusiastic about her job and bragged about being groomed to be a unit vice president, possibly of Studios or even of Publishing.

"In examining replacement possibilities, I decided I was interested in someone with a financial background rather than someone with an industry background. I don't have the time to educate someone on the ins and outs of the corporation and would prefer a person who already understands the basics. I want someone who can jump in and get involved immediately."

Stonetree nodded his head slowly, not knowing why he was nodding.

"You know Jim Ling over in World Trade?"

"Sure," he replied. "He's a good man."

"And Susan Kanzia in Corporate Planning?"

"I've heard the name. I don't think I've ever worked with her."

"Well," she continued, leaning forward again, "in asking around internally, those three names came up."

"Which three?"

"Yours, Ling's, and Kanzia's."

"Really?"

"And as I said, time is at a premiun right now. If it sounds like something you might be interested in, I'd like to discuss it now."

"Sure."

"If not, I'll understand."

"No," Stonetree said, "I'd like to discuss it."

He couldn't believe what he was hearing. Trisha Lane had been discussing him. His name had been uttered from her lips. She had said the words "David Stonetree," probably like she said, when asked about her painting, "Jasper Johns."

"Mary?" she said firmly, looking up to the door.

"Yes, Miss Lane," her secretary called back.

"Please bring in that set of material I asked you to get from Archives, along with the memos I had you copy."

"Yes, Miss Lane."

She stared toward her desk and appeared to be running through a list, almost as if she were in a trance. She tilted her head slightly, then returned her gaze to Stonetree.

"Julie had a rather amorphous set of responsibilities when she worked for me, but this time I would like the position to be more clearly defined. Of course, your primary duty would be to help me keep things moving and to handle certain tasks that I delegate to you. As a major project, I have been thinking for the past few weeks that we need to get a better grasp on why we were able to cut our adjusted net expenses last quarter by only five percent. I would think seven percent is much more like it. I want to find out who is wasting what and put a stop to it. That would be an ongoing project, but you would have to get it started. Of course, you'd have the cooperation of all the units. . . ."

Mary struggled into the office, laboring under a stack of papers and reports that looked to Stonetree to be two feet high.

"Mary, be sensible," Lane said. "Put them over on the table," she continued, motioning with her hand.

"So I'd essentially be running an audit on all the units?"

"No," she said, shaking her head. "I just want to key in on expenses. Each of the units has its own audit process. I want you to interpret what they give us and determine where the leaks are."

"Oh." He nodded.

"Of course, I'd want you to get involved with some other projects that would be of special interest to you. I think it helps to have one's own territory. Julie was interested in intellecual properties, so I got her involved in the publishing unit. Top to bottom. If she'd stayed another six months, she might have picked up the whole thing."

She shrugged her shoulders, and a look of disbelief crossed her face. Mary struggled into the office again with a stack as large as the first. She set it on the table and walked out of the office, breathing an exaggerated sigh of relief.

"If I recall correctly," Lane said with a smile, brushing her hair back with both of her hands and snapping her head once, "you expressed to me an interest in . . . was it The Bahamas?"

Stonetee was flattered and couldn't help but smile. The last time he had talked to Lane was when they shared a company limo to the airport last year. She asked him what he thought of Wexford's recent album and how it compared to his previous efforts. He wisely praised it, which was not difficult to do because he genuinely enjoyed it. Then he contrasted it with that of a relatively unknown group that had just released its first album on a different label. A song Stonetree particularly stressed, "Everybody's Green," eventually made the Top Ten. A month later Lane stopped him in the hallway and thanked him for alerting her to the act.

"Right. I remember that."

"It was a good album, but they could do much better. Columbia, you might be interested to know, will probably not release a second album. I think they are a bit too conservative to deal with that act's philosophy, much less their childish demands. I've spoken to Columbia and I'd say, oh, within a few months, we might bring them over here. A number of details need to be worked out. Perhaps we could involve you in the transition."

"Really. I'd like that. Quite a bit different from doing quarterlies."

Lane laughed. "Yes, David, quite a bit different. My Group is not the same as Mr. Walker's or Mr. Paneligan's. We have more intensity here. You might like it."

"What do you mean by the transition with The Bahamas?" he asked.

"Everything. The contracts. The recording. Maybe marketing."

"But I really don't know much about those things," he responded a bit too sincerely.

"You'll learn," she said, standing up and offering her hand. "We all do."

He also stood, and shook her hand. Her grasp was strong and somewhat warmer than he expected.

"So, do we have an agreement?" she asked.

"When do you need to know?"

She looked at him with a mixture of surprise and disbelief. "I need to know by Monday," she said curtly, turning and walking to her desk. "I'd like to know today."

"Well," he said, following her to the other end of the office, "it does sound good. . . ."

He waited until she looked up from her appointment book before he continued. "But it's a big move. I'd like to talk to Mr. Riley too."

She weighed his reply, setting her elbows on the desktop and folding her hands. "I suppose that's reasonable," she stated matter-of-factly. "As I told you, he recommended you for consideration and, in all honesty, David, I doubt he'll be back."

"Probably not," he agreed.

She reached to her left and pulled a pen from its holder, then took a sheet of note paper from a drawer to her right.

"I'm going to Mexico City Monday morning to visit our

pharmaceutical manufacturing plant. Then I have to go to Seattle, then Honolulu. I won't be back till Friday. Here's my home phone number. I'll be there or here all weekend except tomorrow night. Let me know one way or the other by, let's say, nine Sunday night. Is that enough time for you?"

She handed him the slip. "Yes," he said. "That's fine. Thank you. I do want to talk to Mr. Riley, though."

"If you accept this position, and Mr. Riley returns to work, and you choose to go back to Technology—"

"Yes?" Stonetree interrupted her, excited that he was going to get to have it both ways.

"You will be in big trouble," she said with an affected snarl.

They both laughed. "I figured," he replied, nodding his head again.

"By the way, David," she continued, "are you acquainted with Robin McReynolds?"

"Robin?" he blurted out, dumbstruck. "Sure! We go way back. He's really something. Do you know him?"

"No, I don't," she replied. "Just *of* him at present. He has a little something to do with our conversation this afternoon."

"No kidding. How?"

"First your decision," she said tauntingly, raising one eyebrow. "First your decision. Then we'll discuss Mr. McReynolds."

"Robin," he said to himself.

"And if you decide to accept this position, I'd appreciate your reading through those materials Mary brought in. It should get you up to speed on what's going on in both Entertainment and Pharmaceuticals."

"By when?" he asked, turning toward the two stacks of papers.

"Next Friday. With quarterlies out of the way, I'm sure you'll be able to disengage with a minimum of difficulty."

"Friday?" he asked.

"I'll look forward to hearing from you over the weekend," she said as she stood and again offered her hand. "Give it serious consideration."

"I will," he replied, and then turned and confidently walked out of the office, glancing one last time at the two stacks of papers, wondering if he could absorb them all by next Friday if he started that minute. Probably not, he concluded.

CHAPTER 3

As HE RODE IN A CAB TO DR. FITZGERALD'S OFFICE, STONETREE mulled over his conversation with Lane. On the positive side, there was the fact that Lane probably held the inside track on assuming the presidency of SUE. He could attach himself to something better than counting beans all day. He might be able to work with some of his favorite recording artists, actually be part of their careers, and he someday might even meet and work with Wexford. He could picture it in his mind—"Wexford's Greatest Hits"—and in the credits, under special thanks, "And, of course, my good friend and confidant, David Stonetree." And the devil he knew was better than the devil he didn't.

The devil he knew, however, would probably expect fifty or sixty hours of work from him each week. That was half again more than he currently logged at SUE. He would really have to *work* rather than move along at the more reasonable pace he developed over the past few years in Technology. Inappropriate assessments would not be as readily forgiven as they were by Steve Riley. A serious mistake could cost him his job rather than merit him a five-minute lecture on precision. Was it really worth the money?

The money! God, what an idiot, he thought. "I didn't talk to her about the money," he mumbled. The cab driver turned and asked him to repeat himself.

"Nothing," Stonetree sighed.

He didn't know how much Julie Marx was paid and didn't know enough about the pure management function to even hazard a guess. It must be more than he earned, he reasoned, or why would Lane think he'd be interested at all? For the challenge? To fill in some of his free time? Of course, it would be more—but how much? Five thousand? Ten thousand? He tried to remember Julie's title. He sent memos to her in the past but could not recall how they were addressed. She wasn't an officer, he knew, so she must be a director. The pay ranges for both were wide and overlapping, so her title might not be very helpful. Maybe when he talked to Riley, he concluded, he'd find out the answer.

Before leaving the Home Office, Stonetree stopped down to his office to use the telephone. He called Hendricks to arrange to see the Mustang, and the voice on the other end told him anytime the next day would be fine. He took the directions, and they discussed the car briefly, but Hendricks refused to quote him a price, saying only that it needed to be seen to be appreciated. A second call to Robin McReynolds got him a recording saying the number was not working. He called Sharon, but she did not answer.

When he arrived at Fitzgerald's office, the reception room was empty and the receptionist was gone. After waiting a few minutes, the doctor himself walked into the front room through his private office door and greeted Stonetree with a nod. Fitzgerald was large and round, and his thin blond hair barely covered his head. He wasn't yet fifty, Stonetree knew, but could easily pass for fifty-five or sixty. After dropping a chart on top of a file cabinet, he motioned for his patient to follow him down the corridor. They stopped at the second examination room, and the doctor ushered him in.

Stonetree immediately sat down in the deep leather recliner, and Fitzgerald sat down next to him after raising the lights.

"So," the doctor began, "how was the trip?"

"Enjoyable," he responded. "I had a nice time."

"You don't sound too sincere."

"Maybe we can look into that today." Stonetree shrugged.

Fitzgerald was one of only two psychologists in the city who practiced their trade in conjunction with Selfscan, a piece of technology new enough and controversial enough to be widely decried by the medical journals as being nothing more than sideshow quackery and nothing less than dangerously Orwellian. Stonetree first came to see Fitzgerald on a lark but was so impressed with his first results he returned several more times when he found himself struggling with indecision. At one hundred dollars a visit, not covered by his medical insurance, he still believed it was worth it.

"I think I'm ready to give it a try alone today," he said, motioning toward the wall opposite him.

"How many times before?" the doctor asked.

"I think it's been four," he replied.

"Maybe," Fitzgerald nodded. "You relax for a moment, and I'll get your file."

Stonetree toyed with the control box attached to the recliner until the doctor returned.

"Let's see," Fitzgerald said as he came back into the room. "Yes, it has been four visits. When did you get back?"

"Yesterday."

"I see. And how did you sleep last night?"

"Fine."

"I see. And how many cups of coffee this morning?"

"Two, maybe three."

"I see. Any alcohol in the past two hours?"

"No."

"Cigarettes?"

"No."

"Medicine?"

Stonetree hesitated. "No."

"And your general health?"

"Good."

"All right, David," the doctor said, closing the file. "Let's check the pulse." It was sixty-eight. "So you think you're ready to try it alone, eh?"

"Sure. Why not?"

"Well, you've progressed rapidly. I figure your last visit you hit a steady eighty-five rating, which is very good. I think maybe you can get along without me."

"So what do I do?" Stonetree inquired.

"Essentially what we've done in the past, except I won't be in the room with you. I'll just set you up, and you'll be on your own. You'll have to keep track of your questions and any statements you make that don't involve a direct inquiry. That way I'll be able to check the reading if you have any problems with interpretation, which I imagine might cause you some difficulty on some issues."

"Like what?"

"Not so much particular concepts." The doctor patted Stonetree's shoulder. "Just what you see up on the screen. Tell me what you expect."

"Truth."

"I know that," Fitzgerald said with a chuckle. "That's why you're here. I mean, tell me what goes on on the screen. How do you interpret it?"

"Oh, I get it," Stonetree responded. "Well, I stare at the black circle in the center, wait until I'm ready, then press the clear button. I ask the question . . ."

"Try to make statements."

"Okay. I make the statement and then clear my mind and watch the . . . what's it called?"

"The color flow."

"I watch the color flow as it expands to the edges of the screen, ignoring the changes until the screen is full."

"Covered."

"Right. The color I end up with is the reading. The green-blue-purple side of the spectrum is truth . . ."

"Or what you believe is truth . . ."

"And the yellow-orange-red side is false, or at least what I believe is false. The purpler the better, the redder the worse."

"That's about it. We can get a little subtler as time goes on, but that will get you through for now."

"So let's do it."

Fitzgerald nodded. He instructed Stonetree to insert the little and ring fingers of his left hand into the sensors on the arm of the chair and then busied himself with setting the controls. He mentioned that a new model of Selfscan was coming out with an audio function and asked Stonetree what he thought of the idea.

"I suppose it would be interesting," he responded. "That reminds me—I've been meaning to ask you about something. A friend of mine told me I should get a mood ring, that I could save some money. What do you think?"

"David," he moaned. "Not today. You're my last patient. Be a good boy, and we'll get started. Mood rings."

Stonetree laughed.

"All right. Look at the focal point, please."

Stonetree gazed at the middle of the six-foot disc on the wall in front of him as the luminescence increased. Clouds of color floated across the shimmering, electronic silver fuzz on the screen. Fitzgerald tuned out the color patches and reduced the static to a soothing glow.

"At the focal, please," the doctor ordered.

Stonetree relaxed against the headrest and stared at the six-inch black circle in the center of the disc.

"Now the clear button."

He pressed it, and the screen brightened a bit.

"Give me a positive."

"I want a mood ring."

Fitzgerald reached across him and pressed the clear button. "I told you," he said in mock sternness.

"I'm sorry, Doctor." Stonetree giggled. "I couldn't resist."

"Let's try it again. A positive, please."

"My name is David Stonetree."

He watched as green, blue, and purple spokes began to radiate from the focal. They thickened and slowly began to rotate clockwise around the black circle, expanding toward the edges of the screen, blending into each other. In about thirty seconds the screen was dark blue.

"You're not sure today?" the doctor inquired. "Clear it and try again."

Stonetree repeated the process, and again the result was another dark blue reading.

"How many cups of coffee?" Fitzgerald asked, a puzzled expression on his face.

"Maybe two or three."

"Hmmm. Any medications at all today?"

"Some Febrifuge Blue 900. One at about eleven-thirty," he fibbed.

"I see. That's probably it." He adjusted the controls. "Again, please."

This time the screen turned a deep purple.

"That should do it." Fitzgerald smiled. "How dark do you want it?"

"About medium," Stonetree replied.

"Just come out when you're done," the doctor said as he

walked to the door and dimmed the lights. "And remember, David—always seek the truth, no matter how painful it might be."

Stonetree, now alone in the cool, darkened room, stared absently at the focal and tried to organize his thoughts. He felt apprehensive and a bit warm, probably a result of the dissipation of the temperature-lowering characteristic of the Febrifuge. He sat there for a moment, waiting, as if something was about to happen. The only distraction was the glow of the disc and its muted electronic hum. He pressed the clear button and gazed at the black circle.

"Well, it's great to be back here at Selfscan," he said in an announcer's voice.

Two yellow spokes and one green splashed from the focal, followed by a second green spoke which began to swirl with them. By the time they blended and reached the edges, the screen had turned a pale yellowish-green. This, he knew, was essentially neutral territory. It indicated, at least according to his subconscious, conscious, and emotional responses as interpreted by the voice analyzer and body sensors, that he had no strong feelings about what he said. Or, if he did, he wasn't actually thinking about the concept his words represented. He smiled. "And this at a hundred bucks a crack. Oops!"

He watched as two blue, one green, and a thick orange spoke pushed away from the focal and began to swirl. He hadn't pressed the clear button before he spoke, so he was now getting an overlay on the screen which still remained yellowish-green in the areas that had not turned a gooey brown.

He smiled and pressed the clear button, returning the screen to silver. He hesitated a moment and then spoke.

"I really enjoyed myself in London."

Two green spokes, one thick and one thin, and a stunted blue spoke appeared on the screen. At the end of the swirl, the disc had settled into a turquoise shade. He stared at the shimmering circle of color and felt disappointed, almost as if he'd betrayed himself. He thought maybe his inflection was off or he was not concentrating enough. He pressed the clear button and repeated the sentence.

This time five spokes emerged, three green, one thin blue, and an even thinner purple one. As they snaked around the focal, he was encouraged by the bluer tint he was getting. Still,

48   · JOHN PATRICK KAVANAGH ·

by the time the process was finished, he was again left with an essentially turquoise reading. *I'll be damned*, he thought.

He cleared the disc and stared at the focal. "I didn't enjoy myself because of Sharon," he said.

Almost perfectly symmetrical pairs of blue and purple spokes broke quickly from the focal and, spiraling together as if they were fitted parts, rapidly covered the screen with a deep blue tint. He sighed, looking toward the door, wondering if he'd had enough. He pressed the clear button.

"If Sharon has Class A CYD, will I—" He stopped and reset the device.

"I will not care about Sharon—" He tapped the clear button with the side of his clenched fist and stared again at the black circle. He was getting agitated.

"If Sharon is a cruiser, things between us will be different," he said in a slightly questioning tone.

Three thick purple spokes oozed from the focal, followed by two thinner, lighter blue shafts. He didn't feel he needed to see the actual blend but waited for it anyway. In a moment the disc was a deep purplish-blue. He pressed the clear button.

You asshole, he thought. *She's the best thing that ever happened to you, and you know it. When are you going to get it through your head that life is not perfect? Remember the blind guy selling newspapers in the tube station at Sloane Square? How you thought his eyes would be raised toward the sky forever but he wouldn't see a damn thing? Wake up! No one has a guarantee. On anything.*

You asshole, he thought again. *You pitiful crybaby. Pay attention. Wake up. When are you going to shake this grating, boring self-absorption, this continual fascination with yourself? Pay attention. Wake up. No guarantees.*

He took a deep breath and stared at the screen.

"I'll pay up to twenty thousand dollars for the Mustang," he said.

A yellow spoke emerged, followed by an orange, then a green, then a blue. The blend on the screen indicated neutrality leaning toward false. He thought for a moment and said, "Let me elaborate on that," and pressed the clear button.

"What I meant to say," he continued, striking the button again, "is that I will not pay more than twenty thousand for the Mustang."

This time the results were more in line with his expectations. The red and orange rays circling the screen told him that his ride the next day might turn into a fairly expensive proposition.

"But that's all I can afford," he added.

A new set of yellow and orange spokes darted from the focal.

"Maybe two or three thousand more, but I just can't spend everything."

Two stubby blue spokes and a green one appeared. He cleared the screen.

"The most I will pay is twenty-two thousand five hundred."

Four purple rays shot from the black disc along with three blue ones. *All right*, he thought and smiled. That was it. Twenty-two five, and not a nickel more. He punched the clear button.

"Finally," Stonetree said, "let's check out this thing with Lane." He watched a single plump purple spoke move idly out of the focal. He'd never seen a single spoke response and watched as it lazily spun across the silver background, forming an ever-widening spiral. The silver in between was imperceptively being replaced by the purple hue, but he grew bored with the display and cleared it once again.

"I'd like to work for Lane."

He was a bit surprised by the initial appearance of a yellow and a green ray, but these were soon overcome by two blue rays and finally a small orange one. The overall composite indicated that he was more attuned to working for her than he was happy about his trip to London. He pressed the clear button one last time and said, "I should really get a mood ring."

Without looking at the screen, he pulled his fingers from the sensors and walked out of the office. He found Fitzgerald at the receptionist's desk.

"So how did you do?" Fitzgerald asked.

"Not bad," he replied. "I've got just one question. On my third to last statement I presented a thought that was essentially neutral, like saying, 'Let's talk about the weather,' and all I got was one huge purple spoke. What's that about?"

"David," the doctor blurted out, slapping his forehead and laughing. "What kind of a place do you think this is?"

"I don't get it," he responded, a bit perturbed at Fitzgerald's mocking tone.

"I'm sorry," the therapist continued. "It's sort of a joke, a slang expression in Selfscan terminology. They don't know why it happens, but they have a good idea what causes it. Does that make sense? It's called the purple pleasure pattern."

"Which is?"

"Your libido, David. Whatever you said to the machine, it determined you might want to know it better. Did it involve a female?"

Stonetree hesitated. "Yes," he responded sheepishly. "It did."

"Well, you'll have to talk to her about it, not me." He chuckled, leading Stonetree back toward the "truth zone." "Any other checks you want, any other help with interpretation?"

"No, Doctor. I think I got what I came for. Toss it into the file. And, by the way," he said, grinning, "my last question was whether I should get one of those mood rings. Why don't we take a look at the answer."

They walked into the examination room and peeked at the screen. It was deep purple.

CHAPTER 4

AFTER COMPLETING A FEW ERRANDS, INCLUDING A STOP AT A bookstore to pick up a paperback he'd ordered on vintage automobiles, Stonetree arrived at Sirius just a few minutes after seven. The doorman nodded a friendly "good evening" as he opened one of the two massive metal gates that kept out the uninvited. When Stonetree reached the second barrier, about forty feet from the first, another doorman said hello but only partially opened the gate.

"I know you're one of our members," the burly young man said apologetically, "but could I just see that card again?"

"Sure," Stonetree responded, reaching into his wallet and handing over his membership with a five-dollar bill. "Try to remember a little better next time, okay?"

The doorman returned the card, nodding slightly. "Yes, sir, I will. Thank you." The gate was opened.

Stonetree walked to the glass entrance door and was admitted without question. Just before reaching the coat-check room, he was stopped by a slight woman with a broad smile and excited face.

"There's a twenty-dollar cover charge for gentlemen tonight," she said.

"Twenty bucks!" he cried. "That's after seven, isn't it?"

"That's right. And it's after seven."

He looked at his watches. He was about eight minutes late.

"Come on, Marianne," he said, looking at her nameplate. "You know me. I always get here a little late. It's only five after."

"I'm sorry, but the rules are the rules."

"Wait a minute. Do you know Carl? Carl Zigeras?"

"I don't believe so."

"Sure you do. You waitress here, too, don't you?"

"No. I only collect cover charges."

"Oh. Well, then how about giving me a break tonight? What's the cover before seven?"

"Five dollars."

"Five. Of course. That's what I always pay." He reached into his wallet and then thought for a minute.

"Wait!" he continued. "That's what I gave the guy at the gate outside. I gave him five. I thought it was the cover."

She looked at him suspiciously.

"Go ask him," Stonetree urged. "He's right out there. Check with him. It's true." He thought a moment. "And here's five for you," he said, handing her a bill. "Get yourself a drink later."

"This looks like a bribe to me." She smiled.

"It is!" he agreed, shaking his head rapidly. Just then Carl walked up.

"Marianne," he said, getting her attention and pointing at Stonetree. "Is this guy giving you a hard time? Call Kennard over here, and we'll straighten this joker out."

"Oh, he's no trouble. He's just being cute. Is he a friend of yours?"

"With a face like that?" Carl laughed, squeezing Stonetree's chin. "Not on your life. Hey, how you doin', Stoney?"

"Thanks for coming to the rescue."

Carl reached into his pocket and pulled out a rumpled ten-dollar bill.

"Is he trying to get around the cover, Marianne?" Carl howled. "The big corporate executive must be hurting this week!" He handed her the money and sent her on her way with the advice that she shouldn't worry about it.

"So," Carl began as he led Stonetree away. "London Davey returns to the big city. I suppose everyone's been asking you how the trip was, huh?"

"You got it."

"Well, then I'll dispense with my prepared questions. In fact, I don't care how it was. I just want to know if you got to meet the Queen and get your hands on the royal melons."

Carl roared with laughter and slapped his thigh with his hand.

"Can you imagine being breast-fed by her?" he continued. "That would make me absolutely crazy. Come to think of it, those sons of hers have a kind of crazy look about them. I mean, what do they have to look forward to now?"

He laughed again, Stonetree along with him.

The two had met at a company function. Carl was recently divorced, Stonetree was single, and they were both in pursuit of a trainee called Dutch who recently started at SUE. When the makings of a triangle were mentioned to Carl by a mutual friend, he immediately sought out Stonetree, offering to have a drink with him and talk it over.

She looked to be in her mid-twenties, Stonetree guessed. Medium-length hair. Great eyes. Great figure. A little taller than usual. But it was the way she walked that caught the eye. Chin raised a bit higher than others. Posture a bit better than others. Demeanor a bit cooler than others. Everyone knew her as The Dutchess within a month of her arrival.

Stonetree was struck with Carl's open manner and comic bearing, and Dutch was forgotten as they spent the rest of the party discussing their mutual interests in cars, music, and travel. In fact, it was Carl who first gave Stonetree some Febrifuge Blue 600, then a prescription drug, for his recreational use. Since that time they'd become fairly good friends, but now saw each other only at Sirius.

Carl had worked in SUE's World Trade Division, handling speculation in foreign currencies, currencies that paid for a sizable portion of SUE's gross pharmaceutical sales. A question arose with a broker who disputed an order which Carl transmitted to buy Swiss francs, and SUE management took the broker's side of the argument. After Carl presented his side of the story, management shifted to his point of view. He demanded an apology from his vice president but received none. So he resigned.

After taking a long vacation, he returned to the city and studied the gold market for a few months. He contacted a broker and entered a tenuous partnership based on Carl's money and research and the broker's license. Within three weeks all that remained was Carl's knowledge.

Carl was a cruiser, probably an A-2 or an A-3, Stonetree guessed. This particular night he looked a bit worse than usual. His eyes were red and droopy, and a thin damp coating covered his forehead. They had not reached the upstairs landing where they usually enjoyed their first drink when Carl pulled out a well-used Bradshaw-2.

"Did you bring the equipment with you tonight?" Carl asked. "It's just about refrigeration time."

Stonetree nodded. "You may recall, Mr. Zigeras," he said in a solemn tone, "that you agreed to provide me a new membership card to this fine establishment upon my triumphant return from Europe—"

"Go ahead," Carl interrupted.

"—in exchange for a new or only slightly used Bradshaw-4 Injector. Is my understanding correct?"

"Yes, your lordship," Carl replied, bowing deeply with a sweep of his hand. "It shall be yours just as soon as you tender said device."

"How about the card first?"

"Stoney, be my man. Give me the Brad, and I'll get you a card."

"When?"

"Tonight. Now, quit stalling. Those memberships are going up to four or five hundred next month. They are getting serious here at Sirius."

Both of them laughed.

"Five hundred?" Stonetree asked. "That's pretty steep. What are they now? Two-fifty?"

"Two-fifty," Carl replied. "But for you, one injector."

"These things are going for two seventy-five or three hundred in the pharmacies right now," Stonetree said as he removed the Bradshaw-4 from his pocket and handed it to Carl. "Will this do?"

Carl popped open the lid and peered into the chambers. He pressed the injection button. He smiled.

"Nice. Very nice," he answered. "Compliments of our favorite company, sweet, sweet SUE?"

"Now, would I do that?" Stonetree retorted. "Of course I would!"

They laughed again, and then Carl began to cough.

"You okay?" Stonetree asked.

"How do I look?" Carl responded.

"Like shit. The hairpiece looks pretty sharp, though. When did you get it?"

"A couple of weeks ago," Carl replied, patting the top of his head gently. "Not human hair. Can't afford one of those. But it's pretty good for plastic."

"How much?"

"Too much. But what are you going to do? I can't go walking around on the streets looking like a department-store dummy."

"You've got the brains of one!" Stonetree howled. "So why not look like one?"

"Easy for you to say, you fucking deezer. Just wait until all of your hair falls out. You'll be singing a different tune."

"Come on," Stonetree chided his friend. "What's the big deal. It's only hair." He thought for a moment about how Sharon might look.

"Only hair to you, but not to me. You know the policy here—no hair, no chair!"

They both roared, then Carl broke into a fit of coughing that lasted close to thirty seconds.

"So what are we going to do?" he continued after taking a few uninterrupted breaths. "Are we going to get a drink, are you going to give me the Brad—what's going on?"

"So how does the membership-card deal work?" Stonetree asked.

"Let me go talk to the guy." He hesitated a moment, then moved closer to Stonetree and addressed him in a conspiratorial tone. "Here's what I'm gonna do. There's this kid who cleans up the place, buses glasses and stuff, who got hold of a couple cards, signatures and everything. So I was talking to him and I said, 'What do you want for them,' and he said, 'You can have them both for an injector,' and I ask him, 'Which model,' and he says, 'Anything.'"

Stonetree shook his head. He knew his friend well enough to be able to predict the outcome.

"So what I'm gonna do," Carl continued, looking innocent, "is go downstairs and give this little guy my Bradshaw-2, which I cleaned today, and he'll give me the cards and I'll give you one. He gets his 2, you get your card, and I get a new

Brad-4, plus an extra card to use at my discretion, hopefully"—he smiled as two young women passed them—"to help convince one of those two little climbers I am a man of integrity and wealth, if not bubbling health." He coughed again.

"Are the symptoms coming on or going away?" Stonetree asked.

"Coming on," Carl responded. "I've been fine for the last six weeks or so. God, even longer than that. I started feeling sick again last night."

He reached into his pocket and pulled out a dozen capsules.

"I—was—on—fire," he continued. "Feel better today, though. Let's see—what shall we use to baptize the new unit? How about an eight hundred and a thousand?"

"You've got thousands?" Stonetree asked. "I thought those were still in the testing stage. Are you in a program?"

"Nah," Carl said. "I've got a guy who can get anything. They've been on the streets for a couple weeks, if you know where to look. And they are something. Much better than the nine hundreds. A lot smoother. Longer lasting." He loaded the two capsules into Stonetree's injector and placed it against his wrist. "You're next," he said with a smile as he pushed the button.

"No, not now," Stonetree replied. "Maybe later. I think I'm more in the mood for some Chivas."

Carl stared at him blankly.

"And then maybe we can run down the street, catch some rats, and eat them raw," Stonetree added, realizing that Carl probably was oblivious to what he was saying. "And then we could invite those two climbers over there to join us for a discussion concerning the pros and cons of life here at Sirius."

"You want to what?" Carl finally replied after blinking his eyes a few times.

"I want you to go get my membership card, you drughead."

"Oh, yeah." Carl smiled. "I must have iced over a little. You gotta check it out, Stoney. Try it later, okay? Probably lots of fun for a sixer."

"Maybe."

Carl left via the right-side stairs, and Stonetree made his way to the small upstairs bar to order a scotch. Drink in hand, he returned to the balcony railing and gazed down into the club. It was, as they always billed it, a piece of heaven and a piece of hell on earth.

The Sirius Club had been opened a year earlier by Kennard and Raynard Brown, two of the sleazier worms inhabiting the Western world. Collectively they'd been arrested for every known vice crime, plus a few others, but always seemed to land on both feet when the charges against them were eventually tossed out of court.

Kennard was married to a large, cross-looking Japanese woman who now ran the place when neither brother was in town. Raynard could more often than not be found slumped in a corner unconscious each night, long before the two A.M. closing time.

Sirius was the top club in the city. It permitted very limited access to nonmembers and was surely the most spectacular facility, outdoing its private rival, The Roulette. The Brown brothers named the club after the brightest star in the sky on the advice of a strung-out fortune-teller they'd met in the holding pen one night.

They incorporated their philosophy of life into the place— we're all going to burn in hell eventually, so let's enjoy life while we can. They were the perfect Pied Pipers for a generation of people with short fuses and often shorter life spans. It was not the dying they sought for clients, however; it was the ones they thought were survivors.

The Brown brothers were both in their early forties and did not have much compassion for people afflicted with CYD. They made no bones about the fact that they were not fond of admitting persons with red eyes into their establishment. In fact, the club was at one time planned around a U.S. Cavalry motif and was to be called White-Eyes, a phrase the Browns liked to use affectionately toward their customers.

White-Eyes. How ironic. Stonetree remembered seeing a video of an ancient television show, Amos and somebody. Blacks with huge white eyes, a comic creation of some white producers. It wouldn't surprise him in the least if pretty soon there would be a renegade television show called "Amos and Somebody," whites with huge red eyes, a comic creation of some black producers. Because now, he knew, they were taking over the game.

No one had divined the answer to the riddle, but everyone

knew the result. If CYD was nothing more than a case of the flu to the Japanese, it was nothing more than a sniffle to blacks. The more grade A, as in African, blood a person possessed, the more the CYD attacker was held at bay. They were the survivors. They were the ones getting into the top schools, the top training programs, the top jobs. It started out as economics, but now was becoming a part of the culture. All things considered, your Average Black Dude would outlive your Average White Dude any day of the week. And survival of the fittest was no longer an exercise limited to the fans of Chuck Darwin. It was becoming a driving force propelling much of everyday life.

Stonetree had his chance a few months before. Her name was Denae. He met her at Sirius one night, somehow getting her attention after she brushed off a half-dozen other Average White Dudes over the space of an hour. She liked his tie.

After an hour or so, a few drinks, a few dances, she agreed to go out for dinner with him the following night. Convenient enough because Sharon was busy with inventory.

The date turned out to be half a date. They met back at Sirius, and Denae got his life story out of him during the course of a thirty-minute interview. He cleared as a sixer but came up short on some other points. Wrong job, wrong place to live, what did she call him? "Not quite up in front." She suggested he ought to save his money and go back to the suburbs. In a very nice way. He persisted and was brushed off just like all the pretenders the night before.

White-Eyes. Those Brown brothers were funny guys. And black as a barrel of Saudi primo crude.

It took the owners a few months to get their in-house policies in place, but once they did they rarely made exceptions.

Initially, almost anyone could get into the club with a ten-dollar cover charge, and a fairly regular clientele was established. Membership passes were distributed to the most attractive females, with a tacit understanding that those passes were subject to revocation if the women brought around too many friends with no hair or bloodshot eyes. Males needed a fifty-dollar temporary membership. They were still required to pay the varying cover charges, but because of the "white-eyes only" policy, there was no lack of takers.

Sirius quickly obtained a reputation as a "special" club, and

· JOHN PATRICK KAVANAGH ·

after a while it became a hangout for upper-income males and healthy-looking females. The Browns soon raised the male memberships to one hundred dollars every six months, then two hundred dollars. New applicants were told quite bluntly that they shouldn't waste their money if they were sensitive to bright lights, and the owners were not beyond throwing out customers they reckoned to be liars. They found the ten-dollar cover was keeping out some otherwise qualified females, so unescorted women were eventually admitted free. Escorted females were charged ten dollars. Carl would always have a home there because he was friendly with the owners, but he still avoided Kennard when his CYD was acting up.

Stonetree noticed the crowd had changed in the past few months. Although there were always a few celebrity types around, their numbers seemed to be on the rise. Show people, athletes, politicians. There were always a few higher-paid call girls frequenting Sirius, but their numbers were waning. The most striking change was in the women who now called Sirius home. They were getting younger. Not younger as in early twenties—younger as in eighteen or even sixteen.

The after-work crowd of professional women and their imitators was being pushed out by a growing group of regulars who literally had no other interests except "the show." The show was part of Sirius the day it opened but was becoming more bizarre with each passing week.

What used to be high fashion was now outrageous fashion. What used to be trendy hairstyling gave way to incredibly elaborate wigs. Opaque contact lenses in luminescent colors that covered the entire eye were the rage. The place, Stonetree mused, was getting spooky.

The other attractions Sirius offered were many. Below the small upper landing encountered when entering the club, there stretched a massive lower level where most of the action took place. Directly below the balcony were two octagonal bars with seating for fifty at each. To the sides were groups of tables, couches, and lounge chairs used by those who were not up on the generous, cleverly illuminated dance floor that occupied the center of the room. The sound system was an engineering marvel, structured in such a way that those dancing were treated to high-energy sound, while those not gyrating to the music heard it only as background, easily spoken over with normal conversation. Ringing the far side of the dance floor was a long, narrow ledge on which patrons could set their drinks and stand and watch.

About thirty feet beyond the ledge, against the far wall, was the furnace. The twelve-foot-high, fifty-foot-long inferno immediately caught the eye of anyone entering the club and often stopped first-timers in their tracks. From the base of the furnace rose hundreds of jets of pure, hot glowing fire spaced closely together in three staggered lines, presenting one massive, foreboding wall of flame. The color was occasionally brought to pure white, but the disc jockey who controlled it usually kept it shimmering in blues and greens and reds.

The only sound the furnace made was a deep rumble that could be heard if one was beyond the rail, and the heat it emitted was more sensed than actually felt, at least from farther away than the final ten feet. Although the practice was frowned upon, customers who purchased bottles of champagne or expensive cognacs were allowed to toss their empty glasses into the flames and watch them instantly vaporize.

On New Year's Eve, a despondent couple had elected to avoid paying their tab by diving into the furnace, a gesture that brought the club to a close early and some thought permanently. But a few days later Sirius was open for business as usual, the furnace lit, with the addition of a large reproduction of the headline describing the event hung above the steel-gray mantel.

Sharon didn't enjoy Sirius the first time Stonetree took her there. After two more visits she told him he was welcome to go whenever he wanted, but not with her. So Friday was now their "free" night. Stonetree sometimes went to the club while Sharon went out with her friends, worked, or simply stayed at home. She said she hated the "crowd," which Stonetree interpreted to mean the women. That was her choice, and he respected it. In some ways he even liked it. She was too good for the place.

In a few moments Carl returned, looking refreshed and relaxed, and handed Stonetree the membership card.

"Pretty good group tonight," he offered.

Stonetree nodded. "So what's new in the workplace these days, Ziggy? When are you getting off the unemployment rolls?"

"Uh, let's see. I talked to Smitty a couple of days ago, and he says that he ought to have his license back in another month. Then we're gonna put together a group, you know, maybe twenty grand from fifty people—"

"Twenty grand each?"

"Yeah, twenty grand each. A million. Then we're going to dig in, recoup some losses, and build up some profits. Interested?"

"Who, me?" Stonetree recoiled. "Let me off on this one. I don't have twenty thousand dollars to give to anyone, let alone to finance one of your harebrained schemes."

"No, no, wait a minute, Stoney. This is the real thing. We're going to do it right. We just made some bad moves last time."

"Let me think about it. So what else is new?"

"How about hair?" Carl asked excitedly. "I know a guy whose got about ten pounds of primo, grade A, number-one European hair. Probably hot. He's in a hurry to unload it. We could turn it around in a couple days and pick up five thousand each, easy. What do you say?"

"No." Stonetree frowned. "Too risky. So what else is new?"

"I know this other character, he's got blasting caps. Things keep going the way they are out on the streets, if we hold them, in a couple of months we could clean up. He's got two cases. All he wants is three grand."

"No," Stonetree replied. "Too dangerous. So what else is new?"

"Well . . . oh, I know. I was in here Wednesday night and this guy I'd never seen before, I think he's with one of the ball clubs or something, decides that he has to be a big act. So he walks downstairs and sets a bowling ball down on the bar and has a couple drinks. Then he pulls out the old injector, loads it up twice with four capsules, probably nine hundreds, refrigerates his brain, and then his pal starts buying him shooters. I go over to Kennard and I tell him, 'Kennard, this guy over here is looking for trouble.' He tells me thanks and just ignores this jerk. About fifteen minutes later the guy picks up the bowling ball—"

"Don't tell me. I can guess."

"He picks up this huge black bowling ball and walks across the dance floor over to the ledge, sets the ball down, and orders another drink with his pal."

"I know what's coming," Stonetree said, shaking his head.

"You bet your ass you do, Davey. So, sure enough, a couple minutes later the guy picks it up and tosses the ball from where he's standing right into the furnace. It was like a fucking bomb went off. You should have seen the looks on people's faces. It was great!"

"That's incredible. Did anyone get hurt?"

"No, not except for the guy and his pal. Kennard walks over with a couple of the boys and proceeds to kick the shit out of them. Bad. But the crowd loved it. Everyone applauded."

"This place *is* getting bad. You want a drink?"

"Yeah, I could use one," Carl agreed. "I feel like I put away a bathtub full of water today. Let's get down to the good stuff." He motioned to a waitress. "Kristin, would you bring me a rum and Coke and a scotch for Mr. Stonetree? Thanks."

"So what's new with you?" Carl continued. "How's the girl?"

"Sharon? Oh, she's getting along. She thinks she's got A symptoms. She'll find out more on Monday."

"No kidding. How's she taking it?"

"Not bad, not bad at all," Stonetree replied earnestly. "She's a good trooper. She activated before we went on the trip, but she never said a word."

"Oh, man, that's too bad. I know she's not crazy about me, but it's still a shame. You ought to get her into one of the one thousand programs. I hear the stuff is pretty good when the old CYD is just coming on. You could probably do that through somebody at work."

"Yeah," Stonetree responded. "That *is* a good idea. Who should I see?"

"I'd try someone in Pharms. They essentially control it, don't they? That's what I'd do."

Stonetree thought back to his conversation with Lane. She could probably arrange it. Arrange it? Demand it!

"So what's the hot gossip over at sweet SUE these days, those bastards."

"Oh, you'll love this one." Stonetree waited until the waitress delivered their drinks. "I had a chat today with one of your old flames, at least a flame of your dreams."

"Really? Who?"

"Guess."

"Well, one of my all-time favorites was that lady who worked up in Leasing, you know, with the curly hair and contorted mouth."

"Nope."

"How about Randi from my old operation?"

"Nope."

"Don't tell me Sheila?"

Stonetree's eyes brightened. "As a matter of fact, I did talk to her today. Your name didn't come up, though."

"Man, I'd like to play guns with her sometime. Okay, who?"

"Two more guesses."

"Not Dutch," he replied, his eyes brightening as best they could. "Not Dutch. Don't tell me Dutch. I still dream about her. She's dressed in a French maid's outfit. I discover her in my bedroom, walking back and forth in front of a full-length mirror. She's practicing." He paused. "Not Dutch."

"Better."

"Doesn't exist."

"The best."

"Not Trisha Lane?"

"You win a free round of drinks."

"*You* were talking with the goddess we mortals only fantasize about? And you didn't invite me? Hey! Share and share alike. This is your buddy Carl you're talking to."

"I thought you'd like that."

"Like it!" Carl moaned. "I love it. Every inch of it." He wrapped his arm around Stonetree's neck. "Oh, please bring me with you the next time, Mr. Stonetree. I'll do anything. I'll even wait till you're done!"

They laughed so hard, most of the drinks spilled. Carl motioned for another round while Stonetree wiped off his sleeve with a handkerchief.

"This conversation is getting me hot," Carl said, pulling out the Bradshaw. "Time for more medicine. You want some this round? At the rate we're going, you're not going to get much of a buzz from the cheap booze they sell here."

"Maybe," he responded. "It has been a long day. But you ought to go easy on it. You just cooled a few minutes ago."

"Listen, Mr. Sixer," he replied in a mock snarl. "Mr. I-went-to-Europe Sixer. I have a temperature and I don't want it. If you want it, you can have it. And then," he continued, "you bring up Dutch, which doesn't help at all. Cut me some huss, White-Eyes."

Carl dropped two more capsules into the cylinders and quickly injected them, handing Stonetree the still-smoking unit.

"Try just one of the thousands," Carl urged. "They're a lot better than the eight or nine hundreds. That eight hundred and thousand mix would probably knock you over. You have to go easy on this stuff, though. Hell, I just take them to feel normal. I can imagine what it does to you."

"No mixes, thanks," Stonetree replied, opening the device and shaking it. "But maybe I'll try a thousand. Only one."

"Here you go." Carl smiled, handing him a capsule. "But I'm telling you, try the eight hundred and thousand combo. You'll love it. I think *I* even get a little shiver from it."

"Okay, okay. Give me the eight hundred too."

"You want to go downstairs first? Get comfortable?"

"Maybe. Catch some tunes. Let's do it."

"Screw the tunes. Let's socialize with some of the local talent. What, are you getting married or something?"

Stonetree gave him a disappointed look and motioned toward the stairs.

After sitting down in a lounge chair, Stonetree glanced around at the faces near him. It wasn't that he was afraid of getting caught using a drug that, at least for him, was illegal. Everybody seemed to use Febrifuge or one of its competitors, and no one raised an eyebrow. People took Febrifuge like they took aspirin. Nobody asked to see Tourcams or looked into eyes. They used the drug on street corners, in offices, on trains, in cars, in Sirius.

It was like the way some people smoked cigarettes. It was like the way some people chewed gum or sported wigs. It was like the way some people wore two wristwatches instead of one. It was like coffee in the morning. It was like ignoring trouble out in the street. It was a part of life. It was ordinary.

Febrifuge Blue. The most popular legal drug in the country. For seventy-four percent of young adults, it was a godsend, a state-of-the-art shock absorber that softened the rough road that CYD had paved over the world, over their lives.

Febrifuge Blue. The most popular illicit drug in the country. For twenty-six percent of young adults, it was a godsend, a state-of-the-art shock absorber which softened life's hard corners into smooth contours.

Sixers used it with impunity. Sixers used it with an almost imperceptible smugness. Febrifuge Blue used by sixers was reaching epidemic proportions, but there was no way it would stop until somebody, somewhere, came up with a plausible reason to dissuade its disciples—perhaps something like the "Surgeon General's Report on the Relationship between Cocaine and Thoracic Cancer," a document that in one swipe virtually terminated cocaine use in America. Oh, there were still pockets of people here and there who didn't get the message. Most, however, took the position that life without the powder was preferable to their throats rotting away from the inside out.

The Addiction Research Center in Baltimore, though, had recently reported after an exhaustive study that Febrifuge Blue and its chemical cousins had no lasting addictive qualities and caused minimal harm to its typical user. The comfort it provided to three quarters of its customers was simply more consequential than the immoral high it provided to the other quarter. Febrifuge Blue was like a prize bull roaming the streets of Calcutta, going where it wanted, revered by most who came in contact with it.

On busy nights the crackles came from everywhere. By midnight the entire place would smell of exhaust. He felt a little uneasy about using a drug that made him feel wonderful when others needed it to maintain their health, but so much for philosophy. He pushed away his watches to make room for the unit, and pressed the button.

He stared into the wall of flames, not paying attention to the shapes of those standing at the ledge. The first wave coursed through him, its effect lasting longer than he was accustomed to—a smoother, deeper flow. The furnace grew dim, but just to him. He chuckled. Tricked again.

He thought he heard Carl say something but ignored it, focusing instead on a woman in a white minidress with a black stripe down the front. It was bare on one shoulder, a tight sleeve down her other arm. The thick waves of her sequined red wig dropped down past her waist. The opaque green contacts hid the direction she was looking. The six-inch heels of her shoes contributed to her insectlike appearance.

She was sensually sweeping her outstretched arms back and forth in time with the music. Now playing was "Everybody's Green," the song he had mentioned to Lane. He wondered what it would be like to dance with her, if in fact she danced at all. He pictured the two of them sitting in her office, just as they had that afternoon. He'd look at the skyline and say, "Well, that's enough for the day. Let's go dancing." And she'd respond, "I'd love to."

The second wave washed over him, leaving a bit of dizziness in its wake. The peaceful, contented sensation seemed—how could he describe it?—closer than usual. It was larger than usual. The idea of a feeling being large or small made him smile.

Carl nudged him. "Not bad stuff, huh?"

"No, not bad at all. I like it. It sure cools you down, though."

"That's the idea, isn't it?" Carl snickered. "Come on, we'll warm you up. I'll take you over and toss you into the furnace. Kennard would probably thank me and give me a lifetime membership. SUE might even hire me back."

Stonetree looked back at the dancer and thought about Lane. Then he thought about Sharon. In some respects they were alike but in many ways so different. They both had something to offer him, but both came at a price. What was the price? How could it be paid? He felt a third wave.

"So tell me what Trisha had to say today. Did she ask about me?"

"Nope," Stonetree responded. "Just business. She's looking for a new assistant."

"And she wants you?"

"We're talking about it. I'm thinking it over."

"I wouldn't think about it!" Carl squealed. "I'd be over there right now on my hands and knees begging her for more work! I'd take a cut in pay. I'd be happy just to follow her around all day. Christ!" he exclaimed, slapping his head. "She wants you to work for her, and you're sitting in this dive with me? What, have you lost your mind, Davey?"

"There's a little more to it than that, Zigs. I mean, large amounts of work. You should have seen the pile of stuff she wants me to read. Not tomorrow. Now! I could end up living there."

"I guess," Carl responded knowingly. "That woman does have one tough reputation. She grinds them up and spits them out like a Yamaha blender. She's gonna be running that whole operation someday, you wait and see. I wouldn't be surprised if she dumped old Pierre himself. If she can get rid of Camden, she can probably wipe out anybody. Could be a good career move, though."

"I know," Stonetree agreed. "And I'd be getting into some really interesting things."

"Like her pants?"

Stonetree sighed. Carl had a way of moving from cleverness to tedium, and Stonetree had things on his mind of greater concern than his friend's adolescent sex drive.

"Look," he finally said, staring around the room. "There's a woman over there, the one in the black dress and earrings. Go give her the other membership, and I'm sure she'll take care of you."

Carl frowned. "She doesn't need a membership card. That's why they call her a she. If she wasn't a she, she'd be a he, and I wouldn't give a shit!"

They both laughed. Maybe tonight wasn't the time for concerns. Stonetree had his fill for the day. It was time to loosen up, at least for a little while.

Carl popped for another round, and they moved over to one side of the room, where a crowd had gathered to watch a high-stakes game of PRISMPLEX Doubles going on. A hundred bucks a point. Lots of action on the side. Zigeras recognized one of the teams, two art dealers from Yokohama who showed up in the city once a month to skim the best off the top of the galleries and ship it back to the Land of the Rising Sun. He'd seen them in action before and recommended that some easy money was to be made if they gave odds against the locals.

Stonetree put up two fifties, his friend adding four hundred and booking three-to-two on the art dealers in the next game. By the time contract eight arrived, Mr. Ichiro and Mr. Yoshida had mathematically eliminated the locals from any hope of winning. At the end of contract ten, Carl's dupes handed over the five hundred and skulked away.

"You gotta loosen up that wallet of yours, Stoney," Carl said.

He handed his friend the four fifties. "You gotta trust your buddy's intuition!"

After another round and a brief conversation with a few women Carl had his eye on, Stonetree said good-bye. He walked into the cool, quiet night and leisurely made his way to the Bullet, wide awake and filled with anticipation about the next few days. On the ride home he questioned whether he should accept Lane's offer. If things didn't work out to her satisfaction or his, he still had a standing offer from Tribe to go back and maybe even get Riley's old spot when it became available. Maybe it was time to get a fresh start.

But it was disturbing to him to have to conceptualize the changes such a decision might bring. All the work, all the trouble, all the hassle. His life was finally settling into an even pace, like a creek two weeks after the last rain. Meandering along, no problem, no sweat. Plenty of time to do nothing but, well, nothing. For hours on end. Sleeping late. Missing work once every few months just because he needed an entire day to do nothing.

Opportunity, though, is seductive. Like Dutch, he thought, smiling. The decision was made.

CHAPTER 5

THE FOLLOWING MORNING THE FIRST TELEPHONE CALL STONE-tree made was to Riley's home. One of his children answered and gave him the number of the hospital where Riley was a patient. Calling there, he spoke with Riley's wife. She told him Steve was having tests completed and would probably not be back in the room until later in the afternoon. She told him he was very sick and, if at all possible, she would appreciate his being left alone. Lung cancer can get pretty ugly. Stonetree asked when she thought he'd be up to having a conversation involving work-related matters, and she hung up the phone.

His next call was to Sharon's apartment, but there was no answer. He then tried the bookstore. She was there but could talk for only a few minutes. One of her part-time employees had just quit, another worker was sick, and the shop had been in an uproar since the previous Monday. She told him she had been there until eleven P.M. the previous night and re-turned at seven this morning. She said she was running a slight fever and felt tired and achy, like she had the flu, but was otherwise holding her own. There was no way she could take the rest of the day off and would probably have to stay late again that evening.

Stonetree asked if he could come over to help out. She dismissed the offer, saying she wouldn't be of much help to him if he was behind in accounting work at SUE. He was taken aback by her curtness but did not pursue the issue. The pressure she was under was tremendous, he thought, certainly more than he had ever experienced. The threat of Class A CYD would be enough to put anyone on the edge.

He asked if she wanted to go out for dinner later or come over to his place. The best she could say was that she'd have to see how she felt as the day wore on, see how much she could get accomplished at the store. He told her he was set on going to see the Mustang but didn't want to make the long drive alone. She suggested he drop by Sirius to see if he could latch on to "one of those strays." He didn't feel it would be very productive to continue the conversation, so he told her he'd give her another call when he returned.

After hanging up, he considered phoning back to tell her about Riley and about Trisha Lane's proposal. He decided it might only put her in a worse mood.

He checked his home listing for Robin McReynolds and called him again. He got the same recording saying the number was not in service. He then dialed Lane's work number but hung up before making the connection.

He thought about calling Carl, or his friend Mike, or another friend, Lynn, to see if any of them might want to go for a long ride. On second thought, he decided that he'd be better off going alone because, after all, this was serious business. He was getting ready to pay his entire cash savings for a second car he didn't need.

Somewhere, sometime in a past he couldn't remember, he had seen one—a red 1967 Ford Mustang. It might have been in a movie or a book or part of a real event. Probably, he guessed, when he was very young. In his twenties he could have saved and borrowed and purchased one in good running order, but his real dream was a fully restored beauty. A classic. And it had to be for cash. Only for cash.

He had reached a state in life, at least financially, where he felt he could afford this luxury. For the past year or so he had been looking into prices and conditions and rust and oil leaks. He'd actually gone to see four different cars, but none of them seemed to match the model he pictured in his mind. The one Hendricks was selling sounded like the best possibility yet; if worse came to worst, he'd spend a spring day on a ride in the country.

The Turbostar was a great car, no question about that. It

was red with a black leather interior, just like his previous one. Terrific handling. The stereo system his friend Sy installed was marvelous. He didn't drive more than eight or nine thousand miles a year, so it would last him a good five. But that wasn't the issue. The critical question was "Is this a red 1967 Mustang?" The answer was no.

A few hours later, when he pulled up to the address written in his organizer, he was surprised by what he saw. Somehow he expected a run-down green cottage with four or five abandoned car frames strewn about the yard. He pictured a pile of tires here, a leaking battery there, a pregnant woman holding a child's hand and standing on the broken-down stairs. Instead, he found himself in front of a good-size modern house with an immaculate front yard in a relatively new neighborhood. There was a school down the street, sitting quietly in the sun, and a large park full of mature trees just beyond it.

He walked to the front door and rang the bell. He waited for a moment and rang it again. He started to look up at the address when he heard the lock being unbolted. The door opened, and a man, a little older-looking than himself, smiled and asked, "Mr. Stonetree?" After a nod of acknowledgment, he was ushered into the hallway.

The interior was open and bright, with paintings and rugs and lithographs covering most of the walls. Soft jazz played in the background. Hendricks asked if he would like a beer, and Stonetree agreed a cold one would be fine. He sat down on a couch in the living room and amused himself for a few moments by reading the titles from a pile of books stacked neatly in a corner and by looking at a collection of bric-a-brac scattered about the coffee table. Hendricks returned shortly with two cans and an ashtray. He pulled up a chair next to the table and lit a cigarette.

He looked tan and relaxed, as if he had just returned from vacation. Although not emaciated, he appeared to Stonetree to be capable of carrying another ten pounds on his frame without any trouble. He wore a pair of gray denims and a fashionably tailored shirt, his thick brown hair parted down the middle, a little long and a little messed.

"So, Mr. Stonetree," he began, "what can I do for you today? You've come a long way."

"Well, Mr. Hendricks—"

"Call me Jay. Please."

"Well, Jay," he continued, "I believe you have an automobile I might be interested in purchasing."

"That's a new Turbostar you've got out there, isn't it?" the man asked. "What would a person with a car like that want with a 'sixty-seven Mustang? Do you have a kid who just got a license?"

"No, nothing like that," Stonetree replied. "I've just always wanted one, I guess. Where is it?"

"In the garage. Are you sure you aren't a dealer?"

"No, really," he protested. "I just want a car. A Mustang. You did tell me it was red, didn't you?"

"Yeah, it's red. Black leather interior."

"No kidding! I don't think I've ever seen one with a leather interior."

"Custom black leather. It gets pretty hot in the summer."

"Oh, that's okay. I've had leather interiors before. I've got one now," he replied, a slight nonchalance in his voice.

Hendricks took a drag on his cigarette, then a sip of beer, eyeing Stonetree with an apparent mixture of suspicion and amusement. "You sure you're not a dealer?" he asked again.

"Really. Uh, if I can ask, Mr. Hendricks—Jay—why do you care whether I'm a dealer or not?"

"Oh, I don't know. I suppose I'd like to see the car go to a good home rather than put it out on the streets with just anybody. Did you ever have a dog?"

"No."

"I had a dog once. When I left for law school, my mother was going to move to a smaller place, somewhere the dog wouldn't have room to run."

Stonetree didn't respond.

"So we gave it a shot," he continued. "Seemed to be the right thing to do at the time. You follow me?"

Stonetree nodded. "I think so." He didn't.

"Anyway, I just want to make sure it's not stripped down for parts or left up at somebody's summer house to rust." He hesitated for a moment. "I'm sorry. Am I making any sense to you?"

"Sure. I think I understand. You must have had it for a long time."

"No. Just a couple of years. That's it."

Stonetree leaned back on the couch and absently scratched his elbow.

"Now *I'm* sorry. I guess I am a little confused."

Hendricks reached for another cigarette and left the room for a moment, apparently to change the record that had just ended. "Anything you'd like to hear?" he called.

"No, thanks."

Stonetree soon heard a more pop-sounding tune coming from the speakers but couldn't place the artist. A female with a rich, resonant voice sang about being away from the city beat, safe from crime. Hendricks returned, a small basset hound trailing after him. "Rick," he said, addressing the animal. "I want you to keep your mouth shut and listen to this conversation. You might learn something." He turned to Stonetree.

"So what's the top end on that car of yours?" he asked, sitting down again.

"The Turbostar? I really don't know. I've had it up to seventy-five a couple of times. I suppose it could do ninety, maybe a hundred. I think the speedometer only goes up to eighty-five."

Hendricks chuckled. "You might be in for a treat, then. The Mustang has a three ninety V-8 in it with a four-barrel carburetor. I took it out in the country last November and buried the damn needle before I got pulled over. Cop said I was doing a hundred and twenty-eight—"

Stonetree winced.

"—but he only wrote eighty on the ticket. Nice guy. Never showed up in court, either. That car can fly when you want it to."

"I don't know," Stonetree replied. "I've never driven a car that fast."

"Neither had I," Hendricks replied. "I was just in an aggressive mood. Wanted to blow off a little steam." He paused. "Not as good as a weight bag, but better than a massage."

They sat not speaking for a moment. Hendricks stared vacantly at one of the paintings on the wall, and Stonetree tried to make sense out of the snippets of information about the car and about Hendricks but couldn't find a pattern. The vocalist on the stereo was now singing a song about someone named Davey.

"Did you put this on for my benefit?" he inquired.

"What?" Hendricks replied, broken from his reverie. "Put what on?"

"This album. The song—about Davey."

"Oh." He smiled. "No, I hadn't thought about it. What do you do for a living?"

"Right now I'm an accountant."

"You like it?"

"Yeah, it's all right. Why?"

"Just curious."

"And you're an attorney?" Stonetree inquired.

"Used to be," Hendricks said. "I wised up, though. I think I did, anyway. Maybe not."

"So what do you do now?"

"I do public relations work. Travel. Paint. Invent things. Hang out."

"I don't mean to be rude," Stonetree said with a hint of apology in his voice, "but I would like to see the car now, if you don't mind."

"Grab your beer and wait on the driveway," Hendricks said as he pointed to the door. "I'll bring it right out."

Stonetree walked outside and leaned against a small tree. He could hear sounds coming from the garage, like cloth being pulled and folded. Probably a tarp, he guessed. A good omen, he thought. At least this guy cared about appearance.

In a moment he heard a car door open, followed by an engine turning over.

The garage door opened, and Hendricks backed the car slowly onto the driveway, pausing a moment more before shutting the engine off and gingerly sliding out of the front seat. Stonetree could not believe his eyes. He was seeing a vision.

The car sparkling before him could easily have been plucked from a showroom in Detroit in 1967, then magically transported to the spot on which it now stood—that was how good it looked. The body and paint were immaculate, not a dent or scratch to be seen. He slowly circled it, trying to find an imperfection, but could see none. The finish gleamed in the mid-day sun. There was not a hint of corrosion or even dirt. The bumpers were perfect. The tires seemed to have most of their tread. The hubcaps twinkled. It was too good to be true.

Hendricks unlocked the trunk, and Stonetree moved eagerly

to join him. He wanted to see what treasures the compartment contained. It was spotless. It held only a spare tire, a jack assembly, a cardboard box, and a black briefcase which the owner removed. Hendricks motioned for Stonetree to follow him back into the house, which he did, transfixed. He gazed at the car for as long as he could, tripping over the front stoop in the process.

"I'd like a fresh one," Hendricks said, picking up his beer can and shaking it. "Could I interest you?"

"Please."

"Do any of your friends think you're a little, uh, strange?" Stonetree inquired when Hendricks returned, a bit surprised he would ask such a question of a relative stranger, especially one who possessed something he wanted.

Hendricks rubbed his chin a few times, finally grasping it between his thumb and forefinger. "How do you mean?"

"I don't know," Stonetree continued, frantically trying to find a way out. "Just an impression. The paintings. Your dog."

"I never connected the two of them," his host replied. "What do you think it means?"

"I'm not sure," Stonetree mumbled. "It's nothing. Honestly. Just an impression. I didn't mean to . . ."

"Do *you* know, Rick?" Hendricks asked, looking at the dog. "Surely you must know. You're an intelligent animal."

The dog did not respond. Hendricks turned to Stonetree and shrugged his shoulders. "He really is an intelligent creature," he said.

"You seem, I don't know, detached," Stonetree finally said.

"I get paid to be detached. That's what my life is all about." He thought for a moment. "And in response to your question—yes, some of them do think I'm a little squirrelly at times. But they like me anyway." He thought another moment. "I'm sure your friends like you too. That's why they're friends."

Stonetree took a sip of his beer. "I take it the briefcase has something to do with the car?" he asked, eyeing it cautiously.

"What makes you think that?" Hendricks responded blankly.

"It was in the trunk."

"Do you have a briefcase?"

"Sure."

"Do you ever put it in the trunk of your car?"

"Sure."

Hendricks shrugged his shoulders again and reached for his can. Stonetree motioned with his hand to get him to elaborate, but Hendricks only grinned and shrugged a third time.

He took another sip of his beer and asked Hendricks if he could have a cigarette. Hendricks tossed him the pack and pointed to a large ornate lighter at Stonetree's end of the table. After lighting it and inhaling deeply, he looked at Hendricks and asked how long he'd lived in the house.

"About four years now. It needs a good cleaning but, aside from that, not a bad crib."

"Do you live here alone?"

"Right now I do. Used to be married—actually I guess I still am. My wife took her kids back to England a year ago. Said she needed to think. I haven't heard from her. I guess she's still thinking." He stood up and stretched. "Have you ever been married, Dave?"

"No. Not yet."

"It's got its good points. It's got its bad points. If the good outweigh the bad, you've got no problems."

"Did your wife own the Mustang?" he asked.

Hendricks laughed. "No, no. I'm sorry. We're really getting off the track." He looked at Stonetree intently. "I'm just building up the suspense, setting you up for the kill." They both laughed now, and Hendricks sat down, plopping the briefcase onto his lap and patting the top of it with his hand. "The story of the Mustang is all in here," he said quietly.

Hendricks pointed to the pack sitting on the coffee table. Stonetree removed another cigarette for himself and set it on the couch. He then tossed the pack back. He was eager to see the contents. Hendricks lit another cigarette and sank into his chair, crossing his legs and blowing a stream of smoke toward the ceiling. "Let me give you a little background on that car out there," he began.

"My brother was in college in the early sixties, and for some reason got tossed out. Busy playing baseball or something. Anyway, he came back home and got a job in a bank. A few months later he received a draft notice and, seeing he'd taken some ROTC, he enlisted in the army, hoping he'd be able to get into Officers' Candidate School.

"They accepted him into OCS, and after he graduated they

shipped him over to Southeast Asia to command a company or platoon, whatever it is the second lieutenants were given. He was about three months away from the end of his hitch when he and his boys got sent out to a fire camp. I'm not sure what that is, either, but it was out in the middle of nowhere. So each morning they had to go out and walk around this camp to see if any bombs or booby traps had been set the night before. Let me know if this gets too boring for you."

Stonetree shook his head.

"So they're walking through the bush, about five yards apart from each other, talking about what they were going to do when they get home. One guy wanted to go to Florida, one guy wanted to go back to school, one guy wanted to open a store. The guy walking next to my brother, his radio operator, said all he wanted to do was buy a new car. A red 1967 Mustang.

"So they get about fifty feet away from the camp and somebody trips a wire rigged to a detonator. This land mine goes off and his radio guy, his medic, and seven other of his men are killed. A couple more lose an arm or a leg. My brother gets blown back about thirty feet and gets up, not a scratch on him."

Stonetree drew on his cigarette and took another, larger sip of beer. Hendricks picked up his can, but then set it back on the table.

"Anyway," he continued, "when my brother got back from Vietnam, one of the first things he did was to go out and buy this car, right off the lot, with almost every option available. Air-conditioning, power steering, power brakes, AM-FM radio, custom leather interior, big engine. Everything. But he didn't buy it to drive it. He bought it to remember life can be fragile, that you should stop once in a while and be thankful for things you might otherwise take for granted."

"I don't get that last part," Stonetree said. "I mean, what's the difference?"

"The difference," Hendricks continued, "is that the car became a symbol of sorts, I don't know, his own way of thanking whoever or whatever controls all of this."

He looked at Stonetree, who stared back as blankly as Rick.

"The day he bought the Mustang, he bought another car. A Buick or something. The Mustang got put away in storage, under a tarp up on blocks. He would drive it only two days a year. On his birthday and on Thanksgiving. That was it. He never saw combat again, but he stayed in the service for twenty years.

"Got out a full bird, a colonel, and started a security-consulting business. He had that damn thing shipped all over the world and had it put up on blocks every winter. It went anywhere he went. Cost him a fortune. But he took it out only twice a year. One day each in August and November. It was in Illinois, Germany twice, Colorado twice, Japan, Hawaii. You name it. It was there."

Stonetree was stunned. He had to have it. He'd never wanted anything more in his life.

"Pretty good story, huh?" Hendricks asked.

"I'm speechless," he volunteered. "Only two days a year?"

"Well," Hendricks said with a sigh, "maybe two days a year is a bit of hyperbole. My brother didn't count 'maintenance runs,' as he called them. Driving it to a dock, taking it home, putting it in storage. You can judge yourself from the log."

"The log?"

"Yeah," Hendricks replied, picking up the briefcase and opening it. "He kept a kind of journal, if you will, about where the car went, how many miles, when he drove it. This case has got some great stuff in it. What the weather was like, who was with him, what he was thinking about."

Stonetree got up to look as Hendricks set it down on the coffee table.

"Let's see." He sorted through the contents. "He's got the owner's manual. Here's the original price sticker from the window. Four thousand one hundred dollars. Can you believe that? Here's the warranty—that's not worth too much any-more. He's got all of the shipping documents, all of the maintenance work, all the receipts for gas."

Stonetree wanted to touch the papers but instead sat down on the edge of the couch.

"I've got the original plates from the car. There's a 1967 Maywood, Illinois, vehicle sticker that's still on the windshield. It's all here. Even the stuff I've added." He stopped and thought for a second. "And I've driven it only twice a year. On Thanksgiving and on his birthday."

Stonetree leaned back into the thick cushions. He felt exhausted, as if he had just spent an entire night watching the vigil at a shrine. This wasn't a car, he thought. It wasn't an antique. It was a relic.

"All of the equipment is original," Hendricks said. "The brakes, the tires, the shocks, the transmission, the engine. Even the lights. The battery was replaced, I think, in 1984, and, of course, all the filters have long since been changed. The oil's been drained every winter, along with the gas tank. It's been waxed every spring. And tuned. I forgot to look when I pulled it out, but I think the mileage is eight thousand three hundred and forty-three."

Stonetree took a deep breath. "Eight thousand three hundred and forty-three miles? That's it?"

"That is it. The only addition is a new stereo system in the dash and a couple of triaxials I installed under the package carrier in the back. Those go with it. You could have them removed, and no one would ever know they'd been there. I've still got the original radio, if you want to switch. It's in the box in the trunk, with the factory speakers."

"There must not be another car like this in the world," Stonetree said, amazed by it all. "How can you . . ."

"How can I what?"

"How can you sell it?"

"Oh, I'm sure there are cars like this in the world. Maybe not as well cared for or documented, but I'm sure there are others."

"But I mean," Stonetree continued, "how can you give it up?"

"My brother gave it up. I can give it up."

"What happened? Is he still around?"

"No," Hendricks said, a whimsical grin creeping onto his face. "He died a few years ago. Heart attack—in his sleep. He left it to me in his will. Said I ought to do something creative with it."

"And?"

"And I'm going to do something creative with it. Not with the car, with the money." He picked up his beer and rolled the can in his hands. "I've made copies of all the things in the briefcase. Up there," he continued, pointing to a large photograph on the wall of the upstairs landing, "I've got a picture of him I took with the car in Hawaii. The best view is from the edge of the cliff." He paused. "Material things all disappear eventually, but good memories live on forever."

"What are you going to do with the money?"

"That's my concern, not yours."

"Oh."

Stonetree thought for a moment. Should he make an offer or should he wait for a price to counter? Hendricks seemed reasonable enough. Maybe if he put all his cards on the table at once, he could clinch the deal.

"Well," Stonetree began, "I've been doing a lot of reading on Mustangs during the past year, and I've got a pretty good idea what they're worth." He spoke with an affected air of authority.

"Go on."

" 'Sixty-seven models like yours, in superior condition, are selling in the range of between ten and fifteen thousand dollars."

Hendricks motioned him to continue.

"Of course, this car has things to offer that they probably don't, so I would be willing to talk about something a little higher."

Hendricks nodded.

"Would you consider, say, eighteen thousand?"

"Yes." Hendricks laughed. "As an insult."

Stonetree sank back into the couch.

"Look, Dave," Hendricks began, "I don't know how much the books say they're worth. I haven't read them. I do know that a friend of mine mentioned the car to a broker she met in Dallas, and the broker called me and wanted to buy it. I'll guess this broker takes about ten or fifteen percent of the price, so I think I've got a vague idea about what it's worth. My only problem is being satisfied with who gets it."

"Are you satisfied with me?" Stonetree asked self-consciously.

"We could talk a bit more. I've been watching you. I imagine you'd qualify."

"Uh, how about a trade? The Turbostar is probably worth now, I don't know, twenty-five maybe. Twenty-two."

"I've got a year-old Chrysler out on the street. I don't need a new car. And I don't know how much you drive or where you drive, but I wouldn't advise running that Mustang up and down freeways every day. It's not cut out for it, not anymore. You'd destroy it in a year. What do you want it for, anyway?"

"I'm not sure," Stonetree replied. "I just want it. To have it."

"Well," Hendricks said as he repacked the briefcase, "why don't you think about it and give me a call when you get your thoughts together?"

"We can talk now," Stonetree protested. "This is my money we're talking about."

"Are we talking about fifty thousand dollars' worth of your money?" Hendricks queried. "If not, then we ain't talking."

And they didn't. But Stonetree promised he would be in touch soon.

CHAPTER 6

As he drove into the city the following Friday morning, Stonetree tried as best he could to place the events of the preceding week into perspective. Despite the massive amount of time he'd spent poring over the background material on Pharmaceuticals and Entertainment, sometimes reading until two in the morning, he felt mentally alert. He did not feel assured he could take on more if asked to do so, however. He was not completely confident he was making the right judgments and properly managing the things within his control. And the things he couldn't master had begun to gnaw at him.

His conversation with Lane before she left for Mexico City filled him with a sense of purpose he had not experienced before in his professional life. She was enthusiastic, almost delighted, he thought, when he told her he would take the job. They spent a good forty minutes on the phone discussing the immediate actions Stonetree would take and speculated about what the future might hold for him. When she told him about her conversation with Robin McReynolds, it was almost as if she were conversing with an old friend rather than with a new assistant.

McReynolds had been commissioned by *Fortune* magazine to do an in-depth article on Southern United Enterprises and was now finishing it by conducting background interviews with key SUE executives. Pierre Ruth, as usual, refused to talk with *Fortune*, but instead delegated the task to the three group vice presidents.

Walker and Paneligan were pleased with the opportunity, but Lane, between her own previous difficulties with the press and her imminent travel schedule, declined. She was obligated to provide her divisions' input, though, and during a telephone conference McReynolds mentioned offhandedly that he knew a few employees of SUE. Of course, Stonetree's name came up.

Seeing he was already on her list of prospective assistants, she sensed the serendipity of the situation and decided on the spot that Stonetree would be the first to be offered the position. One of his first actions as the new director/corporate projects was to contact McReynolds and arrange the meeting.

The remuneration accompanying the new title was not as great as he had hoped, but the long-term possibilities were more enticing. Although his salary would increase by only eight thousand dollars, his new bonus structure was much better than that in Technology. There, he usually received between eight and twelve percent of his salary each year. He never thought it bore much relation to his performance.

Lane was very adamant about the fact that she thought bonuses should be earned and not granted. While a lackluster execution of his responsibilities might merit nothing, Lane was prepared to award him up to thirty percent of his salary for a sterling performance—taking into account, of course, the bottom line of her two divisions and the general corporate profit picture.

Despite the fact that she was maintaining a hectic schedule on the road, Lane saw to it that the transition for Stonetree was as smooth as possible. It was Walker who contacted him, not vice versa, and congratulated him on his promotion. Personnel gave him priority status and took care of virtually all the details of the switch in a single day. Operations came in on Monday morning and gutted Marx's old office, fifty feet away from Lane's and half again as big as his last one.

He was allowed to choose his own furniture from the warehouse rather than be assigned the standard company groupings he was used to. He also was given the option of keeping Marx's old secretary or bringing Elaine over with him, a courtesy that SUE's red tape typically did not allow. Elaine was thrilled with the prospect of moving over to the Entertainment side and made her choice before Stonetree finished explaining her options.

At the end of his conversation with Lane, Stonetree mentioned that a close friend of his had recently come down with phase one CYD and inquired about the Febrifuge Blue 1000 program. Lane replied she would be happy to front for an addition to the testing and told Stonetree to put his friend in touch with the Pharmaceutical Marketing VP. It would be arranged.

He thought Sharon would be tickled with the news, but she took it with little enthusiasm. She reacted in similar fashion to the accounts of his promotion and his visit with Hendricks.

Her Tourcam results tested about where they expected. The analysis confirmed she was indeed a carrier of Camden-Young's Disease. The residual readings indicated she might, as was said on the streets, escape with a warning rather than a heavy fine. The breakout on the scan pointed to an encouraging sixty-two percent on the extended Class B threshold. This meant she had better than an even chance of weathering her current symptoms and going on her way as if nothing had happened.

On the Class A threshold she showed an equally favorable fifty-two as to A-1, twenty-six as to A-2, nine as to A-3, seven as to A-4, and only six as to A-5. Although there was an outside chance that she might be experiencing extended Class C, the alternative blood clue did not test positive. All told, her doctor was very encouraging and prescribed an average-strength dosage of Febrifine Green 800. She found the recommendation amusing, as Green 800 was the most popular competitor of SUE's Febrifuge Blue products.

Stonetree was troubled by the condescending tone she used when addressing his decision to work for Lane. On at least one occasion he could remember, he'd characterized Lane as being the embodiment of many of the things he disliked about SUE. Admittedly it seemed he was now making a departure from his earlier assessment. Sharon seemed intent on turning this fact into a bigger issue than he thought it was. She took him to task for what she considered an abandonment of his principles just so he could get ahead. When she referred to Lane as an "overrated, ambitious bitch," Stonetree dismissed her entire harangue as nothing more than depression over her illness, her struggles at work, and her continuing difficulty with a decidedly jealous disposition.

Sometimes her possessiveness amused him, sometimes it all but choked him. If she could only give him a little room, they might by now be living together, if not married. But she had this black guardian angel of suspicion that seemed glued to her shoulder. "What did you do last night?" was never enough. "What time? With who? Why with them? What did you talk about?" If he answered, it just encouraged further interrogation. If he didn't, he acknowledged a massive conspiracy.

Then there was the phone call to Hendricks. Stonetree called to double-check the fact that he really said $50,000. Having confirmed it, he went on to tell Jay the price was so far out of line with reality that it bordered on science fiction. Hendricks replied he had no particular interest in reality and wished Stonetree luck in finding the same car at any price.

Stonetree pleaded and cajoled, trying to get five or ten thousand taken off, but Hendricks would have none of it. As soon as he got his price, the car would be gone—end of conversation. He told Stonetree he sympathized with him and didn't himself believe the car was worth that much. Seeing he was under no compulsion to sell, however, his mind was made up.

As he rode the elevator up to McReynolds's apartment in the new luxurious Wilson Towers, Stonetree wondered how Robin had been faring of late. McReynolds had married a college friend of theirs, and Stonetree had met him at an annual get-together about a dozen former classmates held each summer.

The match of Sasha and Robin seemed perfect. They were both intelligent, artistically bent, attractive, and, if the truth be known, cute and cuddly, Robin towering over her exact five feet by about eight inches. But two years earlier she had thrown her lot in with the Equus Society, a fringe environmental/religious movement, and departed for destinations unknown with most of the money and both of the kids.

Stonetree and he did not see each other as much as they had just after her disappearance. Still, they now and again got together for lunch or cocktails and always enjoyed their wide-ranging, albeit cynical conversations about life.

McReynolds greeted him with an enthusiastic handshake and ushered him into his small but stylish one-bedroom condominium. Robin, as usual, did not appear to have aged a day since Stonetree last saw him, or, for that matter, since the day they met. His short brown hair and classically boyish, well-scrubbed looks, which always seemed to attract maternally instinctive waitresses or socialites, were all intact.

He was one of those charmingly arrogant men who could run a 10K race, work on a couple of writing projects while enjoying a few martinis and half a pack of cigarettes, and then think about dinner. He'd go to the grocery store to pick up a steak or some apples and end up explaining his projects in the ten-items-or-less checkout line to a recently divorced stewardess who happened to be a gourmet cook, former model, and literature teacher.

Inevitably he'd be invited back to her place and inevitably he'd explain to her how no one understood him. Three hours later she'd be hopelessly in love, and Robin would be dragged into the bedroom so he could discover that, yes, someone did understand. Then he'd leave the next morning, off to Tanzania to do research. Robin was the only person Stonetree knew who always referred to the city library as Tanzania.

If only he could be more like Robin, Stonetree thought. If only he could move through life with the ease and detachment and confidence his friend so simply commanded. He'd watched him on many occasions, drawing people into conversations, casting his spell over anyone within earshot. He could speak with authority about almost anything, ask questions to which only he seemed to know the answers. Pick a subject, McReynolds was the source. And if he didn't know the answer, he would bluff his way through his analysis so convincingly that the lie became the truth.

A lot of people were put off by his directness, his cleverness, but Stonetree loved it. If only there were a way to master it. If only there were a way never to have a doubt. If only there were a way to create truth the way McReynolds did.

The first thing McReynolds did was show Stonetree some new toys he purchased with the money he received from *Fortune*. There was a new Minolta camera and three different telephoto lenses. There was a new Mont Blanc fountain pen.

Finally he pulled out a small blue box and gingerly opened it. Inside was a Beretta .25 automatic.

"Isn't she a beauty?" McReynolds asked gleefully. "You've got to have one these days. I keep it loaded just in case."

He pressed a button, and the barrel popped open. He pulled a small shell from it, then pressed another button to release the clip, which held six more. He handed the weapon to Stonetree, who closed the barrel and raised the gun toward a vase. He stared over the sight and thumbed at the hammer.

"This *is* a beauty," he agreed. "How much?"

"Three hundred. Plus the guy threw in a free box of ammo. I've been getting some weird phone calls since I moved in here. Had to change the number a couple times. You know, 'We're going to get you,' and they hang up. It rattles me every once in a while. An article like this other one I'm working on can bring out the weird ones."

"Oh, yeah?" Stonetree responded. "What are you doing now? A lobotomy on Burger King? They're about ready to give up the ghost."

"Sorry," McReynolds said. "Top, top secret. Here," he commanded, pointing to the chair. "Sit down at the desk like you were writing and swivel in the chair toward me and look bright. They said I'd get an additional five hundred if they used a picture I took. It might be the size of a postage stamp, but your puss might show up in the article. Let's give it a try, anyway." Stonetree complied.

"I was under the impression I was just background," he said as McReynolds fooled with the camera. "Isn't that right?"

"Yeah," McReynolds replied as he fired off ten frames. "That's true. But I could mention to my editor that you're a rising star. He might bite."

"Okay." Stonetree smiled into the lens. "But no leg shots."

"No leg shots," McReynolds agreed. "And put that gun down. It just adds to the perception that SUE is robbing everybody."

After a brief tour of the apartment, which was dominated by unpacked cartons of books from Robin's large collection, the two sat down at the newspaper-strewn kitchen table to catch up on the events of the past months. McReynolds finally abandoned the house he and Sasha had shared north of the city. He also recently gave up his job at an advertising firm to concentrate on journalism.

McReynolds had become fairly well known at a young age for his ability to craft devastating articles on large corporations but had set aside his freelance work for the stability of a regular paycheck. Since Sasha ran off, he'd thought more and more about returning to his earlier profession, and finally made the break when he was offered the chance to do a hatchet job on American Airlines. The piece was never published, but his editors at *Fortune* liked it enough to assign him the present project.

"Well, the better this little story comes out, the more likely you'll be out on the streets," he told Stonetree as he poured the coffee. "I suppose you're aware of that fact."

"I'm just here to preach the corporate gospel," Stonetree lobbed back.

"Okay, I'll go easy on you. You're not the one I wanted, anyway. Although I know you're a diamond in the rough, Dave, I really wanted your boss."

"You and everybody else."

"No, seriously," McReynolds continued. "What's the problem with Trisha? I didn't have problems with those other two characters. They were very cooperative, in fact. But, Jesus! The day I talked to her, I got two minutes and I was sent packing."

"So you met her, huh?"

"No. She was going somewhere. Said she'd be in touch. And here you are."

"A martyr for the cause. She lives here, too, doesn't she?"

"Does she?" McReynolds replied. "That's news to me. I've never seen her here, and you can bet I'd remember if I had. She's got good taste, though, if she does. I think I've actually slept here a total of ten nights since I got the place, so the Pope and the entire Vatican Guard could be holed up in one of the penthouses and I wouldn't know about it. I think the building is only half occupied. I don't see many people coming and going."

"Ten nights? In three months?"

"You know how it is," he said with a wink. "No rest for the wicked! I've been traveling a lot, too, digging up dirt about your company and working on the other piece I latched on to."

"You're enjoying the single life, then?"

"Ah, it's all right. But it tends to get old after a while. If Sash could shake herself from that group of horse worshipers she fell in with, I suppose I'd take her back."

"Honestly?"

"Maybe. I don't know." He paused. "So, anyway, what's old Trisha's problem? Is it that piece in *Money* a few years ago?"

"It could be," Stonetree said. "I doubt she'll ever live that one down."

The article was the feature story of the monthly, cashing in on the tremendous growth of SUE after the merger. It highlighted the various executives who contributed to the expansion. The article was glowing in its praise of the conglomerate, and Lane was singled out as one of the brightest stars. But the cover picture turned out to be a big surprise to everyone.

Pierre Ruth and his management team were invited to sit for a photo session, and the usual group and subgroup pictures were shot for the accompanying text. Photos of Ruth and his lieutenants were taken against a plain background, with some of them standing and others on high stools. These head-and-shoulder shots were common, and no one gave them a second thought.

The final cover photo, though, was edited slightly. It turned out to be a full-length shot of only Lane with the others blocked out. She was perched on a stool with her skirt riding a little too high up her crossed legs. To compound the problem, she sported what could only be called a saucy look on her face. The caption, in huge yellow letters, read SUE HEATS UP.

"I think that issue must have sold out the morning it hit the newsstands," Stonetree said with a laugh. "It was everywhere! You couldn't go ten feet and not see it on another person's desk. I don't think we got in an hour of work that day."

"And what was the applause thing?"

"Oh, yeah," he continued. "I guess she decided she was just going to face it head-on, so that afternoon she had lunch down in the cafeteria rather than eat upstairs with the boys. So she walks out of the food area with Wallace Walker and her tray and acts like nothing's going on. Some clown decides to start clapping and then other people joined in, and it turned into a standing ovation. Mob mentality. Then the wolf whistles started. Must have gone on for a whole minute. But she just went to a table and sat down and dug into her salad."

"That must have been something."

"But the best part was after she was done," Stonetree went on. "It's maybe a half hour later, and nobody's left the cafeteria. I'd never seen it so crowded. A half hour later she stands up with Walker, and one guy starts to clap again. She looked over at him, and he stopped *real quick*. Then she slowly scans the whole cafeteria, and you can see these grown men cowering in their sandwiches, avoiding her eyes like she's Lady Godiva. For about ten seconds you could have heard a pin drop. Then she smiles and just strolls out like it's business as usual. I've got to hand it to her. It was really impressive. Nobody breathed for another minute. It was . . . it was like she'd wired the whole place to explode."

"The corporate princess has lunch with the commoners," McReynolds said. "When I first saw that picture, I thought *she* was SUE."

"So did a lot of people. They still call her that. Someone says 'SUE' and the reply is 'Mister or Miss.' 'This company has two great legs to stand on.' 'We're a leg up on the competition.' It goes on and on, corridor shots at their merciless best. I can see why she wouldn't have anything to do with you pricks from the Fourth Estate."

"Don't get uppity with me, Stonetree," McReynolds warned. "I can make you or break you."

They moved into the living room, sitting down in two chairs pushed close to a window. McReynolds set a tape recorder between them and picked up a legal pad lying next to it.

"Okay, Dave. Let me get adult for just one moment so we can establish some ground rules," he began. "What I want to do is record our whole conversation and then go back over it to take what I want. Everything you say will be considered on the record unless you tell me it isn't. But if you don't want it to be on the record, I want you to either say so before you give me the answer or indicate you'd like it off the record as soon as you respond."

"Hey, you're really serious."

McReynolds looked at him. "Of course I am. This is my job."

"This is fun."

"We'll see. Ordinarily I'd quote you as the source, but I agreed with Lane that all the comments about Pharmaceuticals or Entertainment from you would be attributed to 'a company spokesperson' or 'it was learned' or something along those lines. I've got most of the raw information I need for the article from research, you know, the trade press, other articles, so I just want to check some of my facts and pick up a little color to give the piece some dimension. Do you understand what I'm saying?" He paused. "I've essentially already completed it. This is just icing."

"Sure."

"I'll try to be as objective as possible with my questions, but I'd like you to be a little subjective, if you could, so I can present a better feel for the company. Seeing that we know each other, we'll probably get into some crap here and there and some irrelevant meanderings, but I want to impress upon you that what you say is fair game unless you say it isn't. Okay?"

"Come on, Robin." Stonetree frowned. "Does it have to be the third degree? I was looking forward to an enjoyable conversation, not this good cop, bad cop bullshit."

"No, we'll have fun," McReynolds assured him. "I'm just giving you this line for my own protection. I don't want you to get pissed off if I don't make you look like Walt Disney. Besides, like I said, I've got most of the info I need for the article, anyway. There are just a couple of areas I want to explore about Pharmaceuticals, a couple about Entertainment. We are not going to do a doctoral thesis here today."

"I don't know."

"Come on. We do this right and we both make out like bandits. Trisha told me you were really up on the whole picture."

"Maybe. You make it sound so ominous, though. And you're not known as Miss Congeniality."

"Look, man," McReynolds said with a frown, "we've known each other a long time and you know I'm not gonna make you look bad. The company, maybe, but not you. Besides, I wouldn't want to be on that bitch's shit list. Not me. I value my life."

"You're a wise man, McReynolds. There was this boy genius in Corporate PR, I don't know, he supplied the name of the photographer who just took the *Money* pictures, nothing else. She had his ass sacked after the article came out. He's probably still licking his wounds. So what do you do with the recording?"

"I have a court reporter I know put it in transcript form. You know—a 'Q' for me, an 'A' for you. A 'Q' for me. That's all."

"A court reporter?" Stonetree asked. "That must get pretty expensive. Why don't you just take notes?"

"I don't pay for it. Ashley wouldn't take any money to do it. I make her dinner, or we go to a movie or something. You think I'm made of money?"

"Ashley, the court reporter. Where did you get her?"

"Met her at the Walgreen's down the block. I was getting rubbers, she was getting birth control pills. Seemed like a decent point to build a conversation around."

"Figures," Stonetree replied. "Do I get to see this transcript when it's done?"

"Uh, if you want to. But you don't get to correct it, if that's what you mean."

"I don't know," Stonetree said, squinting at his interrogator. "I like being employed."

"Let me off, David. I'll be fair with you. And Trisha said you'd be great. She used that very word, I think. Come to think of it," he said, "I kind of got the feeling that she, uh, has plans for you, if you know what I mean."

"Really?"

"I don't think she'd be beyond taking advantage of you. In a friendly way."

"Now *you* let *me* off," Stonetree retorted.

"I'm serious, Dave. I know that tone of voice. Maybe SUE *is* heating up."

"Questions, please."

Q: For starters, why don't you give me the rundown, a little thumbnail history, of the Febrifuge Blue series, the way they indoctrinated you. That was Ruth's idea?

A: Well, he certainly was the one who pursued it. I don't think it was an original idea to pursue a treatment for CYD. A bunch of manufacturers went after it as soon as the envirus was partially, I don't know, isolated.

Q: Was it he who approached Dr. Camden or the other way around?

A: No, you had it right the first time. Ruth called Camden and essentially said he'd give him the world if Camden would just come to Southern Technology and work on a treatment for CYD. At the time Dr. Camden, I think, was— Can I go off the record?

Q: Sure.

Stonetree leaned forward and spoke in a low voice.

"The guy was just a college professor who happened to be the first person to partially isolate the envirus," he said. "He and Professor Young, I guess, did it at the same time. So Camden is probably making sixty grand a year, and Ruth calls him up and offers him an eight hundred thousand a year salary plus his own staff and state-of-the-art equipment. Probably got the guy laid along the way too. And, of course, the royalty agreement."

"And why shouldn't he get the guy laid," McReynolds chided Stonetree. "Camden only created the greatest of all the SUE money cows. He must have gotten offers from everywhere."

"Maybe," Stonetree replied. "All I know is that he got everything he wanted. Everything."

"So if he wanted to get laid, Pierre would have got him laid, right? Where do I apply for this job?"

"You apply for it in your dreams." Stonetree chuckled.

"Okay, let's get back on the record."

Q: So Ruth offered him the job?

A: And Camden came to work at Southern Technology. It took only a few months to come up with the first compound, Febrifuge Blue 100. The government was so crazy about us developing something that they approved it in about ten minutes. The FDA got the papers and said, "Okay, go sell it."

Q: Was he looking for a treatment or a cure?

A: Initially just a treatment. I mean, how do you cure something if you don't even know what it is? But Ruth really gave him a blank check to do whatever he wanted. He could work on treatments or he could work on a cure. Whatever he wanted.

Q: There was no pressure on him just to work on treatments rather than a cure?

A: No. He could do both or either. The initial focus may have been on treatment, as I said, but Camden was free to pursue his research on a cure too. The stories that Ruth forced him into a treatment-only posture are fiction. That was never done during Camden's entire tenure at SUE.

Q: Even though you're going to make a lot more money if everyone stays sick?

A: No, that's a red herring.

Q: What is a red herring? Have you ever seen one? What color are the other ones?

A: Beats me. Aren't they black and silver or blue and silver? You know, like sardines?

Q: They pickle them. Maybe they're usually green. So isn't it really in the best interests of SUE not to find a cure?

A: No, because someone is going to find it, and when they do, it's going to be Nobel Prize time.

Q: But the Nobel carries with it only about, what, six hundred thousand dollars? What were your gross sales of Febrifuge Blue last year?

A: We topped twenty-eight billion dollars worldwide during the last fiscal year. It's expensive to manufacture, though. You know that.

Q: And the profits on those sales?

A: The profits from Febrifuge are not singled out from the rest of our products, at least not that I am aware. We produce another sixty or so drugs. The Febrifuge Blue series is only part of it.

Q: Certainly the biggest moneymaker?

A: Maybe. Probably. What do you think?

Q: And if there were a cure, no one would need it.

A: Well, we don't know that at this juncture. First of all, it's not like we are the only company that makes treatments. There is Febrifine Green, Febrifal Purple, Febrium Yellow, and those are just our big competitors. There are a dozen smaller ones out there too. The Japanese have a hot one about to come out, and the Swiss are always snapping at our heels. If it was just us, I might agree with you, but right now there is a full, uh, I don't know. There is real stiff competition in the marketplace.

Q: But . . .

A: Let me finish this thought.

Q: Okay.

A: The search for a cure is going on all over the world. We know a lot more about CYD now than we did five years ago or even one year ago, a lot more about the whole envirus picture. Although we, I mean SUE, aren't currently as deeply involved in the cure research as other concerns are, we are looking at it and we may shift more in that direction as time goes on. No final decision has been made, yet, though. Yet, though? Though, yet? Which is right?

Q: We can fix that up.

A: Thanks. Are we doing all right? Am I doing this all right?

Q: Just fine. A little evasive, but otherwise good.

A: Isn't that what all great interviewees do? Get evasive?

Q: Get evasive or get cool.

A: You want to?

Q: Do you?

A: No, thanks. I need my job. I've got a Mustang I want to buy.

Q: Are you starting up on that Mustang crap again? Haven't you gotten that out of your system? Why don't you just buy one and get it over with? You know, here's the money—give me the keys. It's easy. You can do it.

A: It has to be the right one.

Q: Yeah. I said that about getting married, and look what happened.

A: Well, I finally tracked it down. I think. A 1967. With eighty-three hundred miles on it.

Q: How much?

A: Eighty-three hundred miles.

Q: That's unbelievable. Where did you find it?

A: Some guy. It's been in his family the whole time. He's got all the papers, everywhere it's been. This great story about his brother buying it. You could write a story about it. *Esquire* would buy it.

Q: Think so?

A: Sure. I was mesmerized by this guy. He's an original. Real quirky.

Q: Doesn't he ever drive it?

A: Hardly. It's like an heirloom.

Q: How much does he want for it?

A: Guess.

Q: In perfect condition?

A: Absolutely.

Q: I'd give him five, eight thousand for it.

A: Come on. It's worth a lot more than that.

Q: To you, maybe, but not to me. It's an old car. A Mustang. Big deal. The sixties were certainly an interesting period, but so were the twenties. Why not get an old Model T? Who cares?

A: I do. I want a Mustang, so shove it up your ass.

Q: So how much does the guy want?

A: More.

Q: Fifteen?

A: More.

Q: Twenty? A hundred thousand? How much does he want?

A: Fifty.

Q: Fifty? Jesus! Do me a favor and buy it. I *will* write a story about it. They'll put you in a home for the mentally infirm. Give me the money. I could use it.

A: Don't have it.

Q: So how are you going to buy the car?

A: I'm working on that. There must be a way to come up with a quick fifty thousand.

Q: How much do you have?

A: I've got about twenty thousand in the bank, but the guy told me the car is really too old for everyday use, so I've got to get the whole nut. No trade-ins.

Q: You're nuts. You really are. Let's get back to the subject. Let's see, where were we?

A: How much do you pay for maintenance here a month?

Q: Nineteen hundred. Really not bad for one bedroom. The bigger units probably cost, well, I know they cost a fortune.

A: It's a nice place.

Q: Back to work. Let's see, I think you said you weren't going to pursue a cure?

A: We haven't decided yet.

Q: That was what Camden's leaving was all about, wasn't it?

A: He and the company came to an amicable parting of the ways. It was not what it was made out to be.

Q: Well, then tell me what happened.

A: Dr. Camden had been given virtually everything he wanted at SUE by Pierre Ruth. And, in all fairness, Camden returned a great deal through his work. He reached a point where he decided that he wanted to devote most of his time to the research on cures. This decision did not fit in with the short- and mid-range plans of our company, so it was decided that Dr. Camden would not be retained as head of R and D.

Q: Who decided? Him?

A: It was mutual.

Q: I understand Trisha was behind it.

A: At that time Lane had taken over Pharmaceuticals, so I'm sure she had some input in the process.

Q: I've heard that she fired Camden so she could put her own guy in, that she didn't want to share the limelight with anyone, let alone the guy for whom they named the whole thing.

A: That's simply not true.

Q: I've also heard that a bunch of his books and notes and research were taken one night and locked away somewhere so he couldn't take them with him.

A: There is a bit of truth to that story. Under the terms of the contract entered into between Camden and SUE— Can we go off the record?

Q: Go ahead.

Stonetree stood up and stretched, then moved closer to the window. Six stories below he could see a group of what had to be cruisers leaning against a wall, motionless, like pieces of discarded furniture. Of the seven of them, not one could be older than twenty.

He thought about Sharon, he thought about research, he

thought about cures. For years the scientific community said a cure was just around the corner, and for years it remained a mirage. If only they could do it, now, today.

"So are you going off the record or are you going off the deep end?" McReynolds asked. "I've got other things to do today."

Stonetree sat down and leaned back in his chair, locking his fingers behind his head.

"Look, Robin," he began. "This guy was getting everything from us. In return we had the rights to all of his stuff. When the whole flap about what direction we were going to take regarding treatment or cure started, things evidently got pretty tense at the Home Office. Anyway, after one confrontation too many, they just sent Security down and locked up the whole lab until the dispute was resolved. That was it. Nobody stole anything from the guy. It was ours to do with what we wanted."

"Who ordered the lockup?"

"Are we still off the record?"

"If you like."

"Lane probably ordered the lockup," Stonetree continued. "But Ruth would have to agree with something as major as that. I mean, that's our bread and butter."

Q: Back on the record. And then Camden was free to go on to find the cure himself?

A: In his contract there was a no-competition clause in which he promised not to join up with one of our competitors for the period of two years after he left the company. That period, I believe, ended two months ago. He could conduct his own private research or hitch up with a school, which he didn't do, and we paid him a small fortune to fulfill our part of the deal. People like to make the guy out to be a big martyr, but he isn't. He lives a lot better than you or I do, that's for sure. He walked away with a package worth close to fifty-seven million dollars. That's not bad for two years of vacation. Wherever he went. Atlanta or somewhere.

Q: Yeah. He went to Atlanta. Wanted to be by all those CDC types, probably.

A: So you have to look at both sides of this, Robin. We're always made out to be the villains.

Q: Let's get back to profits. You really would prefer no cure, right?

A: No. Again, somebody is going to find it. We'd like to. But there will probably be years, decades of people with symptoms. Maybe the first step will be a vaccine rather than a cure. It's all up in the air. Anything could happen.

Q: Would you rehire Camden?

A: I doubt it. There's too much water over the bridge, or under it, or wherever it goes. He won't be back. I think he really did a number— Off the record?

Q: Sure.

"He really betrayed Ruth," Stonetree said. "Ruth gave him everything, and he turned on him. It's as simple as that. No love lost there."

"Yeah, but, Dave," McReynolds replied, setting his pad down, "SUE has made billions in profits based on Camden's research. And how do you figure he betrayed Ruth? Sounds to me like his only crime was to go one-on-one with Trisha. Sounds to me like his only crime was bad tactical judgment."

"Maybe. I don't know," Stonetree answered. "Having watched her up close, I don't think I'd want to be on the receiving end when she went off the reservation."

"Off the reservation?" McReynolds hooted. "Off the reservation? She practically *owns* the reservation. She can go wherever she wants."

"I'm not going to get in her way, that's for sure. You can take that to the bank."

"Can you imagine getting paid, what did you say, fifty-seven million to take a few years off? Man, that's for me. We gotta find another racket, you know?"

"After this article," Stonetree said with a bit of concern in his voice. "I may just be in the market." He paused. "So when do we go back . . ."

Q: On the record? Right now. So who's in charge now?

A: Hickey. Dr. Randolph Hickey. He runs R and D.

Q: Hickey was put in by whom?

A: Lane.

Q: And what's his claim to fame?

A: He's a good, hardworking scientist. He was on the staff before all this. He worked with Camden. He's been around a long time.

Q: And he follows the company line on treatment versus cure?

A: I'd say so. He's done some really brilliant work in the two years he's been in charge. He moved us into the one thousand series and beyond.

Q: Let's look at that evolution. Where is SUE and Febrifuge? What does the future hold for them?

A: As I'm sure you know, the first ones, the one hundred through five hundred product, are no longer in production. Check that. We sell some of the four hundred and five hundred in third world countries but not necessarily for CYD. Six hundred and seven hundred have been over-the-counter products for a few years. Very big market for those. Bigger than we thought. Eight hundred and nine hundred are both available through doctors and health services. One thousand is just coming out, and eleven hundred is in the early stages of development.

Q: I've seen some of the eleven hundred. Outside of SUE.

A: Where?

Q: Sorry. Can't tell you that. But it's there. In fact, Wallace Walker took me over to the lab when I was at SUE, and I saw some of yours. I asked an assistant if I could see some eleven hundreds, and he pulled out a vial of them. Light blue–dark blue capsule. SUE, then FF1100 in light green lettering.

A: That sounds right. I've just seen a picture of them.

Q: So they *do* exist?

A: Oh, shit! Come on, Robin. This is still off the record.

Q: No, it isn't. I'll give you a pass, though. But I did see them there, and they are out on the street already.

A: What was Wallace doing over in the lab? That's out of his jurisdiction.

Q: So, who's going to stop him?

A: No comment.

Q: They were testing some Bradshaw-4 Injectors. Some guys from Technology brought some over to settle a dispute with the Pharmaceutical guys about residue. I was just tagging along. Innocent as the freshly driven snow.

A: Sure.

Q: Let's talk about the Bradshaw-4. Not everything it was cracked up to be, huh? I gotta take a piss. Make it quick.

A: That's not our problem. That's a Technology beef. Talk to them.

Q: I did. You guys are getting destroyed in that market. The Japanese are about ready to take it all.

A: That's really outside my area.

Q: I'm about ready for a break. How about you?

A: Sounds like a good idea to me. This is interesting, though. You want the john first?

Q: If you don't mind. I'm gonna explode. I have to cut back on the coffee. Know what I mean?

A: Hurry up.

CHAPTER 7

BACK IN THE KITCHEN, MCREYNOLDS POURED FRESH COFFEE, and they sat at the kitchen table for a few minutes casually discussing the questioning. McReynolds seemed fixated with the subject of Camden's departure from SUE, and Stonetree figured he probably met with Camden and got a sob story from the scientist. Stonetree knew, though, that the entire Camden affair was a sore spot with a lot of people and decided the less he talked about it, the better off he would be.

He was amazed by the fact that McReynolds insisted he had seen Febrifuge Blue 1100 outside of the SUE lab. Febrifuge Blue 1100 was considered to be a breakthrough in the treatment of CYD. Rather than simply being a change in the chemical composition of an ancestor compound, 1100 went much further. It was augmented with a new substance synthesized by the research team. The animal test results were supposed to be tremendous.

The Febrifuge Blue 1100 research was being guarded, though, with an almost paranoid amount of security, so McReynolds's story of being shown a vial of capsules did not seem to ring true. Stonetree had never seen them and strongly doubted McReynolds had. He asked his interviewer who had shown him the capsules and was given a description that could fit half the employees at SUE. He asked if Wallace Walker had seen them too. He could not remember.

McReynolds talked about the women he was dating, and

Stonetree told him about London and Sharon and related the bowling-ball story. They agreed it had been too long since they'd gotten together for lunch.

After pouring a bit more coffee and moving back into the living room, the questioning continued.

Q: Okay, we're back on. Just a couple of more questions on the drugs issue, and then we can move on to the fun stuff. Ready?

A: Ready.

Q: How does the company feel about the abusive use of Febrifuge? What are you doing to stop it?

A: Uh, there are two types of abuse. Which one do you want?

Q: Either.

A: Well, first there is the abuse of the drug by people who have CYD and get it in their minds that if their doctor prescribes one capsule of eight hundred every two hours when symptoms are present, and if they take two or three or God knows how many capsules, then the symptoms will subside more quickly or they'll feel better or they'll be cured. It just doesn't work that way.

  The optimum dose of Febrifuge is just that—the optimum dose. If you have Class A-2 symptoms and the doctor says one eight hundred every two hours, you aren't going to feel better if you take two. In fact, you might even feel a little worse. We tell them in the advertising. We tell them in the labeling on the packages. We tell them until we are Febrifuge Blue in the face, but they will not listen. We had a report last week of a kid who got diagnosed and got a prescription and an injector and pumped sixteen capsules into himself. Of course, he was dead in a minute or so from heart failure. Just locked up and died. That can't be avoided. People are just stupid.

  We can't prove it yet, but our best estimate is that between the natural damage done by the symptoms and the contrary effects of Febrifuge or any similar product, people are probably dropping a couple thousand, maybe three thousand, brain cells per capsule per injection. And that adds up.

Q: You could get really stupid.

A: It's true. A shot of alcohol costs you twelve hundred brain cells. Look what happens when they are all added up. Look at you.

Q: Feels good getting there, though.

A: But people do a lot of unnecessary damage to themselves.

Q: And now let's talk about the totally unnecessary use of Febrifuge.

A: And its competitors. This is not just a SUE problem. All the manufacturers have it.

Q: Your qualification has been noted.

A: There has been an increase in the use of Febrifuge Blue . . .

Q: And its competitors . . .

A: And its competitors, by noncarriers, deezers, sixers, what have you, who take it for recreation. It's also taken by a growing population of carriers who think it will block symptoms before they activate.

Q: How about the carriers first?

A: Again, it's all a question of being misinformed. These people think if they take it when they are free of symptoms or in remission, then somehow they will stay that way. But it doesn't work. It has no effect. And they don't get the pleasurable sensations that Class D carriers get. Oh, they might be a little stunned by the right combination or a large amount of one series, and they might get an abnormally lower temperature for an hour, their heartbeats might slow down, but that's about it. Most of them learn fairly quickly, though. Some never do.

Q: And then there are the sixers.

A: And then there are the sixers.

Q: Our kind of people.

A: I suppose.

A: Who now account for how much use?

A: Our best estimates are that thirty-two percent of our products is used by the twenty-six percent of the population who don't need it—those who fall into Class D. Maybe higher, but we trust that figure.

Q: And it's on the rise?

A: We think so. It really seemed to jump when eight hundred hit the market. Big shipments suddenly disappearing. Employee pilferage in the plants and warehouses. It's definitely on the rise. We could see thirty-five percent before the end of the year. We can't stop it. It's not our fault. They haven't found a way to modify the formula to curb abuse by Class D carriers.

Q: Thank God.

A: No, Robin, this is serious. It should be stopped. It's just too popular. You walk into a doctor's office and ask for a prescription. He just gives it out. He's not going to test you. People go to two or three doctors to stock up on it. Or they buy it on the streets. What can you do? Remove it from the market?

Q: Never.

A: Of course not. But it has turned out to be an attractive drug to abuse by that segment of the population. No side effects. It clears the mind. It makes you feel— Off the record?

Q: Go!

"I have to tell you," Stonetree began. He stood and walked to the window. "I was down at Sirius, and this guy I know gave me a thousand and an eight hundred and it was bingo —I was there."

Stonetree looked down to the street and stared at the group of kids he had watched earlier. None of them appeared to have moved except one who was now lying motionless near the street. Passersby didn't hesitate or even bother to look. They had seen it all before, he thought.

"Yeah, I know what you mean," McReynolds replied. "I think you've taken a giant leap forward with the one thousand series. Maybe you pill pushers are really onto something for a change."

Stonetree grinned. "We do our best to keep the customer satisfied." He paused. "Have you done any eleven hundred?"

McReynolds stared back at Stonetree and slowly began to tap his pen on his knee. "Who wants to know?"

"I do."

"Well, Dave," he began, "we journalists have to protect our sources. You know, confidentiality and all that."

"I don't give a shit about confidentiality," Stonetree said, and laughed. "All I want to know is have you tried the eleven hundred?"

"Maybe I have and maybe I haven't."

"Well then, let's assume you have," Stonetree continued. "What's it like?"

"Sorry. Confidentiality. But if it helps you through the trauma of curiosity you're going through, I haven't tried it."

"Come on," Stonetree insisted. "I can tell by that smile on your face. What's it like?"

"No, really," McReynolds replied. "I've just seen it, that's all. Now let's get back to the matters at hand."

Q: Back on the record. Now, what's this about no side effects? Uh, I've seen some cases . . .

A: Well, sure. Too much of a good thing will do it to you. Get a little too cool and there goes the heart or the brain or the vision. But aside from the overdose cases, it's apparently no worse than taking a couple of aspirin or smoking a couple of weeds.

Q: Anything new on why it works that way on sixers? Why just them? Or, I should say, us.

A: No. It's still a mystery. They think once they unlock the way enviruses work, they'll be able to figure it out. It's probably all on the same answer sheet.

Q: I take it SUE does not subscribe to the theory that Class D carriers are simply—and I say this with a reasonable amount of humility—better than everyone else?

A: Oh, Robin, don't tell me you actually subscribe to that "better than them" bullshit. I'm really surprised at you, of all people.

Q: Hasn't there been some research supporting that conclusion?

A: Well, you can prove anything with a T test. Statistics can be interpreted lots of ways. It's all trash, though.

Q: Is that what SUE thinks?

A: You know what I mean. It's a sick thought. It went out with Hitler and that whole crowd. Tell me you don't believe it, Robin. It's really trash.

Q: I'm a journalist. I have to keep an open mind. What I believe is irrelevant.

A: Well, do you?

Q: No. But it would be nice, I guess. To be something novel, a better model. New and improved. Some people believe it. I'd say it's catching on. People talk about it. You know that as well as I do. We've got what you might call a genuine class struggle brewing out in the provinces. Maybe not next week or next month, but if you guys don't find a cure, something's going to snap.

A: Some people think Wexford is the Messiah too. Or a prophet.

Q: What a great transition! You ought to get into this business. I'll set you up.

A: The man is a pop singer. A great one, to be sure. Maybe one of the best, but he's a singer. That's it. Same as all of us. We're all the same.

Q: No, we're not all the same, Dave. That's a fact. That's all I was trying to get at. I wouldn't complain if I were you.

A: I'm not complaining. It's, just, I don't know. What else are we going to discuss? I'm getting tired.

Q: The man who brings salvation to wigs everywhere.

A: Like I said, the man is only a singer.

Q: And one of SUE's most valuable commodities. Have you ever met him?

A: No. Have you?

Q: No. Let's write him a fan letter. Maybe Trisha could set us up with him.

A: I was surprised to learn that she doesn't have much to do with him anymore. She got him into the company, and once he took off she went on to other things. She's not as concerned with the Entertainment Division anymore. She's much more involved with Pharmaceuticals. She made the transition look like she'd done it her whole life. She deals mostly with Wexford's manager, uh . . .

Q: Doug Smite?

A: Yeah, that's his name.

Q: Wexford has become a recluse?

A: Well, he started that about the time his second album came out. You start going onstage and people shoot at you or try to blow you up, I imagine the paranoia sets in. I don't blame him.

Q: Just for the record. What's his history as SUE's corporate pitchman?

A: Let me off.

Q: Give me the official party line.

A: Wexford was part of the first group of people signed to Southern Lights Records, brought in by Lane. That whole crowd—Tranq-Tranq, Peggy Quinlan.

Q: Go on.

A: So we put out his first album, "Seasons of Change," and Wexford was off and running. He charted seven songs off that album, five of them Top Ten. That debut album sold twenty million copies. It's still selling five thousand copies a week. Real popular.

Q: I bought a DAT and wore it out. Bought it on compact disc and that may be wearing out too.

A: Then a year later he puts out . . .

Q: "Tomorrow Comes the Dream."

A: Right. Didn't do as well as the first. Only twelve million. Can you imagine that? Twelve million copies, and they thought he was washed up.

Q: Quote you on that?

A: Not on your life. That's still my favorite album. I don't care what they say. That was around the time of the first attempt on his life, when his bass player got shot. I think that must have got him thinking about his life. Put everything into perspective for him. Gave him a new slant. He did that real strange piece for *Interview*. I think he must have turned the corner about then. He was imbued with a spirit. He invoked his muse.

Q: I've got a feeling you are building up to a climax.

A: By anyone's standards, I'd say it qualifies as a climax.

Q: A drum roll, please. And the winner is . . .

A: "The Shortened Life."

Q: Let us bow our heads as we praise the Lord. Tell our readers, David, about the scope we're looking at. Tell those fat, out-of-it toilet-bowl manufacturers what real sales are all about.

A: Well, back in the late seventies, there was this album called "Saturday Night Fever," which included songs by a number of artists, and it sold twenty-five million units or so. Everyone said that there would never be another one that came even close. And then, I don't know, eight or ten years later, Michael Jackson comes along just when videos are turning into art and dance clubs are coming back in, and he releases "Thriller" and it sells something like forty million copies and everyone shakes their heads and says that "Thriller" will never be touched, will never be equaled.

Q: And time passes . . .

A: And along comes this unemployed sandwich maker—I've got to tell you a story I heard about Wexford later concerning sandwiches—the man needs psychiatric help.

Q: For the record?

A: No. And he records this interesting little set of songs called "The Shortened Life."

Q: Which has sold how many units?

A: Total sales as of December thirty-first, all formats, sixty-nine million. Plus it still does thirty thousand extra units every week, like clockwork.

Q: For which young Wexford has been paid?

A: From us? For performance, or writing, or what?

Q: Total. For the fat guy out there reading this article.

A: About four dollars an album. Give or take twenty cents.

Q: Not bad for—how long did it take him to record it?

A: It was pretty quick. That was the last one he did in our facilities. I think he was there for two weeks. He doesn't like to screw around. He writes something, the band learns it, he does it, next song.

Q: That's over a quarter of a billion, yes, Mr. Toilet Bowl, a quarter of a billion dollars for two weeks work. And now, the big question, David.

A: I know what you're going to ask. We've had this question before. I will give you the party line and nothing more.

Q: Okay. Let's get the party line. Do you think the only reason the album sold so phenomenally well was the hysteria it helped generate in promoting the first Search for Survival blood drive, which in turn generated hysteria about the album?

A: No.

Q: So I suppose you won't tell me that Wexford was directed to write songs specifically designed to urge kids, albeit metaphorically, to give their precious pints of blood to a pharmaceutical company—a company that just happened to own his record company and also just happened to spend the largest amount of money that has ever been spent on the advertising and promoting of an album in the history of the recording industry—which in turn further fueled the sweet SUE money-printing presses.

A: No.

Q: And I suppose you won't tell me that the entire project, planned well in advance, did not go off precisely and successfully on schedule?

A: I can't tell you that because it's not true.

Q: That it was successful? Come on.

A: They were independent events. Did they become forever linked in the minds of the public? Yes. Did it make a ton of money for SUE? Yes. Were we happy with the results? Yes. Did we then try to plan it out the second time? Sort of. Were we as successful the second time? No.

Q: Let's take it from the top. The two were not planned together?

A: No, they were independently conceived and executed by two separate divisions of the company when the two heads of those divisions— Can we go off the record?

Q: Sure.

"From what I've heard," Stonetree said as he walked into the kitchen and poured more coffee, "Lane hated Mack Ennis, the guy who ran Pharmaceuticals back then, more than she hated Camden."

"Man," McReynolds called back. "That is a pretty serious case of hate. I wouldn't want any part of that love affair."

Stonetree returned to the living room and glanced out the window again. All the kids were gone, except for the one still lying silently on the sidewalk.

"There's a kid down on the pavement. Been there awhile."

"Oh, yeah?" McReynolds replied, getting up and standing next to him. "Doesn't look like any blood. His head—is that a guy or a girl?"

"Looks like a girl."

"Her head still seems to be attached. I didn't hear anything. I guess she didn't pipe herself."

Piping was the latest fad in suicides. It started in Florida and quickly spread throughout the country. It was quick, effective, dramatic, and affordable, all qualities of popular exits.

It didn't take much to complete a pipe job. All one needed was a twelve-gauge shotgun shell, about a foot of metal tubing, and a cheap firing mechanism that could be bought for ten dollars after an hour of asking around.

The piper then went through a simple procedure. The shell was inserted in one end of the pipe, held in place by its lip. The mechanism, the crackerjack box, was fitted over the end of the pipe holding the shell and clipped in place. The other end of the pipe was held against the forehead. Then, all the piper need do was fall forward.

A firm grip was a virtual guarantee of eternity, if the victim believed in it. The hospitals and homes were crowded with those who slipped or those who did not hold the pipe when it hit the pavement. Then there were the ones unfortunate enough to be standing nearby when a piper messed up.

"So what was the problem with Trisha and this Ennis character?" McReynolds asked, returning to his chair.

"Do you think we should go down there and see if we can help her?"

"Trisha? No, I doubt she needs our help."

"No, you asshole," Stonetree snapped. "The kid down on the street!"

McReynolds sighed. "So what are you going to do for her, Dave? Maybe she's dead. Maybe she just did a Bradshaw shuffle. Maybe she's taking a nap. Who the fuck cares? When did you become the great humanitarian?"

Stonetree tried to picture himself sprawled out on the sidewalk. He couldn't. Then he tried to picture Sharon. He couldn't.

"I don't know," he finally said, returning to his chair. "Sometimes I think our priorities get a little screwed up once in a while."

"Well, I know where my priorities are and I have to finish this article. Now sit down and answer these questions so we can get out of here."

Q: Lane and Ennis. For the record.

A: No one has ever taken credit for the first blood drive.

Q: But the Pharmaceutical and Entertainment divisions were under the same man, weren't they?

A: Yes. Jim Hare. Very popular guy. Lots of talent. He resigned a few years ago, and Lane took his job.

Q: Well, how could the group vice president not know that two of his divisions were putting together these huge projects and not make the connection?

A: You would have to talk to Mr. Hare about that.

Q: I did.

A: And?

Q: And he said he never made the connection. He also said he didn't listen to the records. How could he not know?

A: Everyone there says it was a fluke. No one associated the songs with a blood drive. Wexford even said he had nothing to do with it. The first one at least. Why would he agree to help with the second one and say he hadn't consciously been involved in the first?

Q: I don't know. I wish I could figure this one out. If I could, it would be a major scoop.

A: It never happened, Robin, I'm telling you. Wexford was even pissed off for a while when the craziness started. He wasn't in on it. That's what they tell me. I wasn't in on it, though.

Q: In on what?

A: The great conspiracy.

Q: How many pints of blood were donated?

A: Just about three million. And I trust you're using the word "donate" in a broad sense. We did pay out an average of about eighty dollars a pint. Plus we could use only a third of them.

Q: In cash and prizes. Records. Pins. Hats. Wexford Cryptos.

A: Those were toward the end but, yes, all of those things.

Q: So the blood could be used in research so SUE could produce better drugs than the competition and make billions more?

A: A better product was certainly a goal. That does not make it bad. Other companies and agencies have collected blood to use in treatment and cure research just as we have. No one has ever been as successful as SUE.

Q: But you have Wexford.

A: Yes, we do. That makes, say, the Centers for Disease Control better somehow?

Q: No. I just wish I could break the story. I can see Wexford and Pierre Ruth sitting in the mountains somewhere planning it out. What do you do with the blood, anyway?

A: I can give you a rough outline. The technical aspects are beyond me.

Q: Please, for Mr. Toilet Head.

A: Although we're still not sure what an envirus is, we've found that it leaves something in its tracks like, I don't know, coal falling off a coal train. This by-product is what has been used up until now as the medium against which a lot of the experiments are conducted. They use it to see how a given compound will respond under different sets of conditions, how a formula will act. They've also, I'm told, used it to try to develop a vaccine.

Q: Which is called what? The medium, I mean.

A: It's designated CY6A4. The trouble is, it is incredibly expensive to distill because of all the equipment and chemicals that go into the various reduction processes. Plus it is practical to do it only with batches of fifty thousand pints of raw blood—otherwise the expenses go off the charts. Plus the blood has to be tested to confirm that the donor was experiencing symptoms at the time of donation.

Q: You start out with a vat of fifty thousand pints of blood?

A: Essentially.

Q: Yuk! And what do you get from that? Can you imagine how that must smell? Hot blood?

A: After all is said and done, and done, and done again, fifty thousand pints of raw blood will yield approximately one pint of high-grade CY6A4. And even a lot of that one pint is just a medium to suspend it in. Once you've got it, though, it has a long shelf life.

Q: One pint? Pretty expensive stuff.

A: It is. But the really hard part is getting together a fifty-thousand-pint batch quickly enough to get it processed. Fifty thousand pints of blood, collected and processed in, say, forty-eight hours, is an incredible undertaking.

Q: Hence, Search for Survival number one. This is your last chance. 'Fess up now.

A: No conspiracy, Robin. It just worked out that way. We got lucky.

Q: Camden got fired around then, after the first big drive.

A: He quit. We went through this.

Q: And isn't it true that he was held responsible for the destruction of four pints of that CY6A4?

A: In an incredibly stupid move he decided he was going to do a spot check on the condition of the stored liquid. You are supposed to get three signatures to use a drop of it.

So he has four pints of the stuff and, because of the difficulty in getting fifty thousand pints of blood at the local drugstore, it's priceless. So he's screwing around with four pints, there's a fire in the lab, fire extinguishers, minor panic, and the stuff gets knocked into a drain. There is no excuse for that. I mean, I know it was an emergency, and it could happen . . .

Q: It could happen to anybody.

A: Perhaps. Insurance covered only part of it. That probably took care of Ennis too. Maybe eventually Hare. Mr. Ruth was not pleased. In fact, some people think it was that incident that split the two of them apart—Ruth and Camden, I mean. And they went way back. But that story has been told before.

Q: I've heard it from one other highly reliable source. Good. I can use it now. You'll not be quoted. Nor used as confirmation. This has been worth it.

A: Are we done?

Q: No, just a few more questions. You have nothing to do with his concerts or anything else?

A: No, just record distribution and publishing. Doug Smite handles everything else. Talk about marrying the boss's daughter. Except he married Wexford's sister. And, as I mentioned, he stopped recording at our studios. He now records at his own studio in that chateau he built up in Wyoming near Jackson Hole.

Q: And let's move on to his latest album.

A: "Marking Time."

Q: A major disappointment to the company?

A: Here we go again. It was like the comparison between the debut and second albums. How do you follow up on an album that sold more than any other in history, seventy percent more than its nearest competition? How do you do it? Simple. You don't.

Q: And he didn't?

A: "Marking Time" has done over twenty million units.

Q: And has been out for close to two years and is no longer in the top fifty, and it's a flop.

A: That's your characterization, not mine.

Q: Did you like it?

A: Personally? Not that much. It was a letdown. Rumor has it the next one will more than make up for it.

Q: Is he recording again?

A: Maybe.

Q: Come on, Dave. Give me a scoop here. I've got a little debt I need to pay back to one of my music-critic friends. If I could break this first, it would be great.

A: You didn't hear it from me. Promise?

Q: I'll turn off the recorder if you want.

A: Just remember you did not hear it from me, okay?

Q: Promise. I swear.

A: He's got a couple songs done already. The band got called up to Jackson Hole a few weeks ago. The stuff is supposed to be great. Maybe his best.

Q: Anything else you can tell me?

A: That's all we know right now. But he is recording. He owes us one more album under his contract. It might be out by July or August.

Q: Great. Thanks. Just a few more here. The second Search drive was a flop along with "Marking Time"?

A: Can't we quit? I'm beat.

Q: I'll tell on you. I'll call her up right now.

A: The second blood drive did not reach our expectations. Less than four hundred thousand pints. We could use only a fourth of them. It was a disappointment.

Q: And that time you had his cooperation.

A: Yes. He did those television and radio spots. It was a mistake. He should have just done his preaching with his music. He's not very convincing reading off a Tele-Prompter. I think everyone agrees it was a bad tactic.

Q: And Trisha takes responsibility?

A: Completely. She had projected between three and five million pints. I think she offered to quit when it bombed. Of course, Pierre probably thought it was cute of her to offer to quit and gave her a hundred-thousand-dollar bonus for her trouble. Don't put that on the record, please. I'm sorry. I'm exhausted.

Q: Wexford hasn't been seen in public for a while. Care to comment?

A: All right, let's go through the hot rumors. Is he dead? No. Did he come down with Class A-5 and become a vegetable? No. Did he have a sex-change operation so he could put out the greatest-selling album by a female too? No. Is he really a visitor from another planet? No. Do you want any more theories?

Q: No. I have heard a couple times that he has been sick, though. So what's the sandwich story?

A: I heard he had this little café built inside his house, maybe ten tables, and he has guests over occasionally and tells them they should go to this great little restaurant in town, and then one of his stooges takes them to this café. You know, in another wing of the house. They sit down and Wexford shows up and he's like the owner and chef and somebody is a waitress. So they look at menus, it's all sandwiches, and they order stuff and Wexford makes the sandwiches and comes over and asks if they like the place, will they tell their friends about it.

Q: Somehow I'm not surprised.

A: Me either. And so they sit there for an hour and then the waitress brings them a bill and they all laugh and then she says, no, it's not a joke, pay up. So they do and then the stooge escorts them out of the house to their cars and says good night. They think it's all part of the gag till they sit there all night and no one comes out, and they aren't let back in the house. And you probably are right—he has been sick, in his head. And I'm through. I'm beat.

Q: Interviews aren't that easy, are they?

A: That's for sure.

Q: I'm about ready to quit too. Anything you'd like to add?

A: Please go light on us in the article.

As he reached for the recorder, McReynolds pointed to a picture hanging on the wall behind Stonetree. "Remember her?" he asked.

"Good old Sasha," Stonetree replied, looking at the photograph. "Heard anything from her lately?"

"No." McReynolds sighed. "She called a few months back. Said the kids were fine and all that. Asked how I was, what I was up to. That's about it."

"That must be hard on you."

"Sometimes. You look a little run-down yourself."

"I am," Stonetree agreed. "This past week has been something. I've never worked so hard in my life. Lane is still out on the road. She gets back tonight, I think, but the pressure has already got me nuts."

"A little hard work will be good for you."

"Maybe for someone else," Stonetree said. "I don't think it's for me, though. I'm not used to it, and I doubt I will get used to it. It's too much. I'm already starting to regret it."

"Really. Just because of the hours?"

"Yeah. That, the pressure. The fear of doing something wrong. I made a mistake."

"It can't be that bad."

"Believe me. I was talking to a guy I know who knows the woman I replaced. Somehow I'd got it in my head that Julie, that's her name, decided she wanted to move on to something else. Well, it turns out she and Lane had been at a meeting with Ruth and a couple of other people and Julie started laughing about something. So Lane calls her up that weekend and says by Monday she wants an explanation of her behavior,

124 · JOHN PATRICK KAVANAGH ·

why she was mocking her in front of Ruth. So Julie sits out the weekend, goes in on Monday, and says it was a delayed reaction to an obtuse joke one of the other people made."

"You're kidding?"

"No. She just got the joke a minute after it was told. That's all. Dragon Lady didn't buy it. Told her to clean out her desk by noon."

"Jeez." McReynolds whistled. "That is terrible. And you wanted to go to work for this woman? What a bitch! You've got to figure Ruth is banging her. You know, wealthy chairman of conglomerate takes on hot ingenue. Look what she did to his old pal Dr. Camden."

"I was really floored. I couldn't sleep that night. Called up Tribe the next day to see if there was still a spot for me there."

"And?"

"They said maybe in a few months. They've had some cutbacks. And then I talked to Riley, and he wasn't too encouraging."

"Who's Riley?" McReynolds asked.

"My old boss. He's real sick and isn't coming back to SUE. Lane talked to him before hiring me. He told me he said I was a great guy and all that, but she never mentioned she was looking for someone. And he told me he would not have recommended to me that I take the job. Then he says there's another bed in his room, and he'll expect to see me soon. And then everyone at work, my old friends, they wish me well and all that but are avoiding me. I don't like it. I'm starting to believe she *is* the bitch everybody makes her out to be." He paused, then smiled. "In fact, were it not for an agreement you and I made just after Sasha split, about this vocabularic rut you had fallen into—"

"I know, I know," McReynolds interrupted, waving his hand.

"I would refer to Miss Lane by using the 'C' word." He paused. "But that would cost me one hundred dollars, American, and you ain't gonna get it, birdboy."

"Well, I wish you luck."

"Easy for you to say. If it wasn't—"

"Please, say no more," McReynolds interrupted again. "The interview is over."

Stonetree said his good-byes and went directly back to the Home Office to get back to work. He called Sharon to tell her she'd been right. She agreed. She asked if he wanted to get together that night. They had not seen each other since returning from England. Stonetree declined. Too much work, and not enough time. Strangely Sharon did not question his explanation or his motives. She said only "I miss you," and hung up.

He thought about changing his mind or calling her back but did neither. Too much work, and not enough time.

CHAPTER 8

The following weeks confirmed Stonetree's apprehension that things would get worse before they got better. Despite the fact that Lane was averaging only two days out of five in the office, her presence was always felt. Her eye for flaws always seemed to be hovering somewhere over his left shoulder. In the previous week he logged a total of fifty-seven hours at the Plaza. This did not take into account the time spent at home poring over reports or the few minutes he snatched here and there while on the Bullet.

The largest block of his time was devoted to discovering ways to cut expenses in Pharmaceuticals. His preliminary findings were not encouraging. During the previous year Lane had trimmed expenses to a minimum, and Stonetree was having a difficult time locating any areas where costs could be whittled down further.

Travel was virtually eliminated except for officers and the few managers who were required to transact much of their work out of town. Spoilage and waste were drastically curtailed, from multiple batches of capsules shipped free to doctors to the reuse of packing crates. The division payroll was decreased by an astonishing twenty percent, with some employees now handling the tasks that were previously the province of two or three. The free coffee was gone.

Receptionists or secretaries now conducted short tours of Pharmaceuticals rather than the blue-and-white-clad, saccharin Suezettes. Stonetree missed them, along with eating, sleeping, and watching television. He had difficulty remembering what it was like to have four or five hours to himself every night, not to mention Saturdays and Sundays. He never had time to run anymore or play an occasional game of handball or racquetball at the health club. This lack of exercise, along with his growing junk-food habit, made him feel sluggish and sometimes dizzy.

Maybe he had a brain tumor, he thought. But he didn't have the time or inclination to go to a doctor. He no longer read anything except SUE material. His eyes were so tired when he finally called it quits for the night that he couldn't bear to pick up anything from the growing stack of magazines in the family room. He couldn't work with the stereo on, so music virtually disappeared from his life.

He went to Sirius only once after "Lane days" began, he and Carl trying to figure out how to raise a quick $50,000 to buy the Mustang and be done with it.

Although they still talked on the phone each day, Stonetree had seen Sharon only three times since their return from England. The first was for lunch when business brought her into the city. They had a pleasant time, even a romantic one. Sharon looked good, sounded good, smelled good. They sat in an open café on a wonderful spring afternoon, holding hands and reminiscing about their trip. They walked through the streets for an hour with no destination in mind, just as they did in London. Meetings for both of them, however, curtailed any plans for an equally enjoyable night.

The second time, he spent the night at Sharon's apartment. She promised him a wonderful evening if he would just give her six straight hours of his undivided attention. The meal was excellent—raw oysters and some Chinese dish she'd dreamed up that Stonetree loved, and key lime pie.

They ripped through the bottle of Chardonnay he bought for the occasion before finishing the oysters and emptied another bottle before dessert made its appearance. They skipped the cleanup for a trip to the bedroom, where they made love melodramatically, falling asleep after being unable to decide who should get up to get the pie. Total elapsed time from greeting to unconsciousness: three hours and ten minutes.

Their final encounter was the previous Saturday when they

met for an argument at the deli near the bookstore. Sharon and one of her partners were thinking about buying out the third and opening a second shop eight miles away. Stonetree examined the plan they drew up and voiced a criticism regarding just about every point. Sharon was not pleased with his observations and told him so.

He was ticked about the amount of time and money the proposal would demand and suggested Sharon did not know the difference between staying afloat and getting in over her head. She responded that at least her head wouldn't float like that of Stonetree's last girlfriend. Stonetree retorted she at least had the sense to pay attention to people who had expertise in given areas. Sharon brought the conversation to an end by noting she could at least count to twenty without using her fingers and toes, had an IQ greater than her weight, and thought he should stop taking obnoxious pills. After she huffed out of the place, he sat there for another fifteen minutes alone, doodling on a napkin and wondering what the problem was.

The early publication of the *Fortune* article caught Stonetree by surprise. It was originally conceived as a cover story to be run in July, but the editors decided to narrow its focus and insert it in an earlier issue. As he walked toward his office, he was directed by Elaine to "report to the boss on the double."

Lane motioned him in while she railed at two of her other directors on a conference call and handed him a copy of the magazine. She indicated with a single gesture and facial expression that he should go back to his office, review McReynolds's work, and report back to her for a discussion. If her apparent mood was any indication of the content of the article, the morning was not going to be pleasant.

He returned to his desk after grabbing a cup of coffee and a sweet roll from the eighteenth-floor executive conference area. He sat on the window ledge and turned to the essay. "A Shift In Focus At Southern United Enterprises." So far, so good. Now, if Robin would just stay that neutral throughout the piece, Stonetree thought, he would still have a job at the end of the day. The good news was that the story did not begin with a cheesecake depiction of Lane. The bad news was that it began with a picture of Ruth and Walker standing in the chairman's office.

He was surprised to find that aside from a mention in the

fifth paragraph, the story did not deal with Pharmaceuticals or Entertainment until well into its second third. The entire first portion dwelled mostly on the recent achievements of Walker's Technology, Transportation, and Communications divisions, quoting him extensively and mentioning the rumor that he was being considered for the presidency of one of SUE's largest competitors.

The third part of the story was devoted to a scathing attack on Paneligan's Leasing, World Trade, and Retail operations, essentially stating what many at SUE believed—the only reason Paneligan was still around was that he was a college friend and former climbing partner of Pierre Ruth. Paneligan, by Ruth's own admission, had saved the chairman from certain death when he fell from a fractured ledge during a particularly dangerous ascent in the Andes.

The middle portion, which Stonetree read twice, was devoted to Entertainment and Pharmaceuticals. All in all, he reassured himself, it could have been much worse. Lane was portrayed as a competent and courageous administrator who was still in top form. McReynolds lingered on the failures, or perceived failures, of the second Search drive, Wexford's record sales, and the loss of prestige that accompanied Dr. Camden's departure. The phrase used to describe it was "under a cloud of accusations and half truths."

McReynolds fell for Camden's story, Stonetree believed, but certainly wasn't the first to take the side of the researcher. He thought too much space was devoted to the erosion of Febrifuge's market share and the continuing problem of abuse of the drug by Class D carriers. The flap over treatment versus cure was examined in detail, and Stonetree felt an impression would be left with the reader that SUE was concerned with profits first and human welfare second. Not that the inference wasn't true—after all, SUE was a business.

On the other hand, McReynolds waxed enthusiastic about the potential for the future. The new advanced Febrifuge Blue formula was portrayed as being closer to arriving at pharmacies than it actually was. The problems with the 800 and 900 series were glossed over, dismissed as almost irrelevant. Wexford's next album might rival "The Shortened Life." Lane was not beyond working more magic from her corner office. No reference was made to the famous *Money* magazine cover.

On the second to last page was a small insert of twelve postage-stamp-size head shots with accompanying names and titles captioned A FEW NEW FACES TO WATCH AT SUE. In the bottom row, third from right, smiled DAVID STONETREE—DIRECTOR, CORPORATE PROJECTS. And it wasn't a bad picture. In fact, he thought modestly, it might be the best he had ever taken. He was surely the youngest of his eleven costars, except for maybe the guy from World Trade and the woman from Communications, both of whom he'd seen before but did not know.

He returned to Lane's office, only to find her on the phone again. This time he seated himself on one of the couches and waited for her conversation to end—which it did, abruptly.

"I really do not know who these men think they are talking to," she said as she stood up from behind the desk. "Their secretaries? Their wives? Their sisters? They are going to have to wake up and open their eyes, or they might find there are no eyes left to open."

She tossed a tablet to one side of the desk and frowned. Then she flipped back her hair with a brush of her hand and a snap of her head. She joined Stonetree at the other end of the office. She perched herself on one of the arms of the couch and earnestly regarded him for a moment, a slight pout on her lips.

"So tell me what you think of Mr. McReynolds's efforts," she said in a measured tone. "Comments, criticisms, observations?"

Stonetree looked at her for an indication of what she wanted to hear. He could find none. "Well," he offered, taking a deep breath, "I think, overall, that it was, uh . . ." He hesitated, searching for an appropriately neutral adjective. "Balanced. It lacked some depth and could have done better in the clarity department. But it was balanced."

"David, we are discussing an article in *Fortune* magazine, not *Gourmet*. This is commerce we're talking about, not wine."

He swallowed hard and stared at her. *She is really sexy* was all he could pull from his thoughts.

"But you know, I think you're right." She smiled as she moved to the cushions. "I was a little aggravated by the harping he did about Camden, but aside from that I think he gave us a pretty fair shake. I didn't realize Wallace was in such big demand. Good for him."

Stonetree was relieved but couldn't decide if she was sincere in her praise of Walker.

"God knows we've had a lot worse done to us before," she continued thoughtfully. "McReynolds could have really screwed us if he put his mind to it. You must have done a good job on him. Thank you. I knew you would."

Stonetree smiled and shrugged the shrug of a superstar.

"And I liked that picture of you. Very flattering. The young women around here are going to be paying more attention to you. You'd better get used to it." She winked.

"I liked that one of you too," he replied.

"A little less controversial than some of my previous portrayals," she said. "This time *we* took the pictures and *we* developed the prints. No fuss, no muss, no negatives. I'll never let something like that get out of my control again."

They chatted for a few more minutes about the article and about the progress on the expense audit. Lane didn't appear excited about Stonetree's preliminary report, but she seemed too pleased with the outcome of the *Fortune* essay to care much, at least at that moment. She was returning to Seattle for the third time since Stonetree started working for her, and she was caught up in various details that needed attention before her departure.

She asked him how he felt about the job so far, and he lied. In fact, had it not been for the publication of the story, he probably would have ended their conversation by frankly admitting to her the job was a bit more than he felt he could manage much longer. He was tired of the pressure and the anxiety. He was prepared to step aside, even be dismissed, if that was what it would take to get his life back to some semblance of normalcy. Instead of a confession, though, he listened to her frank but concise praise of his efforts thus far.

"I know you've been spending a good deal of time here at the office," she said as he felt the end of the conversation approaching. "I know it can be a hassle to be here late or decide at nine o'clock in the evening you want to come in and tie down a few loose ends before a meeting the next morning."

A vacation, Stonetree hoped. An assistant. Maybe a day off.

"So I talked to Pierre the other day," she continued, "and he signed off on you getting a palm-print clearance."

A palm-print clearance was reserved for the officers and a

few selected directors only. It allowed entrance into the Plaza through two side exits and a rear exit at night and on weekends. It avoided the complications of the unusually tight security procedures that were in effect throughout the Plaza between six P.M. and six A.M. during the week and all day Saturday and Sunday.

"It's the least I can do to make your job a little easier," she said sincerely as she stood and returned to her desk.

Very generous of you, he mouthed silently as he left. *At least she'll be gone before noon, and at least I'll have a day and a half to stop the backward slide*, he thought. Maybe he would discuss his true feelings with her on the following Monday when she was back.

Returning from a quick lunch that afternoon, Stonetree picked up his messages and was delighted to learn McReynolds had called. He immediately went to his phone. He caught him just back from a long run, still panting a bit but sounding pleased with himself.

"Yeah, I did about six miles. Stopped at a pay phone for a minute and called you. I figured you'd be at lunch but wanted to try anyway. Ran all the way back. How did you like it?"

"I got a kick out of it," Stonetree responded excitedly. "It was really a relief. I've got to admit I was worried."

"I told you you were in good hands," Robin chided. "Just like at Allstate. You knew I'd come through for you. Now, was there really anything to worry about?"

"I guess not. But I'm still relieved. And thanks for the picture."

"Don't thank me, buddy. I picked up some nice cash for the three pictures of mine they used. It was my pleasure. How did the boss like the story?"

"She wasn't thrilled, but she thought it was reasonable."

"Shit," McReynolds said, and sighed. "What does she want? A testimonial? Tell her to take out an ad in the newspaper. She still working you hard?"

"Sure is."

"Still thinking about bailing out?"

"Sure am."

"Well, good," McReynolds continued, his voice taking on a more serious tone. "How would you like to get together this afternoon to discuss your future in the industry?"

"How do you mean?"

"I've got someone I want you to meet. He might be able to help you out, at least as far as SUE goes."

"Who? How would he help me?"

"He might be able to help all of us out. You gonna have an hour or so? Hurry up, I've got some stuff I have to do."

"Give me a little more information, huh?"

"Hey, I didn't steer you wrong about the article," McReynolds said sharply. "You can trust me on this too. What's the big deal?" he continued, now sounding conciliatory. "I've got to protect the identities of my sources."

"Okay, okay. I know, you told me. Just a little cranked up today, that's all. Where and when?"

"I'll meet you in the lobby of the Hyatt at, say, four o'clock?"

"Four?" Stonetree questioned. "Four? I was thinking about six."

"Let's compromise," McReynolds offered. "Make it five. In the lobby. See you there. I'll be the one with the trench coat and the stupid expression."

"All right. See you then."

Stonetree puzzled over the conversation for a moment, but then placed it in the back of his mind so he could devote his undivided attention to the picture of himself in *Fortune* magazine. Probably the first and last, he thought with a frown. He was simply not cut out to be a captain of industry, and trying to change that would be as hard, he mused, as changing the shape of the sun.

At 5:15 he walked into the lobby of the Hyatt and found McReynolds seated near the concierge desk, reading *The Wall Street Journal*.

"Sorry I'm late," Stonetree said as he tapped at the newspaper. "Did I miss anything?"

"I don't think so," McReynolds responded. "I thought maybe you'd changed your mind."

"Got stuck on a phone call. So where is the mystery person?"

"Upstairs."

"They work here? Or are they staying here?"

"*He* is staying here. Let's go."

As they rode to the eighth floor, Stonetree asked three times, in different ways, who it was he was about to meet. It wasn't one of Robin's girlfriends. It was no one Stonetree knew. It was somebody he knew of, and he should keep an open mind.

"I don't like this open-mind shit," Stonetree stated as they walked to Room 818. "That sounds a little weird to me. I mean, this isn't going to be kinky, is it? I don't want to have my picture taken with some transvestite midget you set yourself up with."

"Nothing like that at all." McReynolds laughed. "Much better. You'll see."

McReynolds knocked on the door with two sharp raps, waited a few seconds, and repeated the knock. Maybe it was a signal, maybe it wasn't. After a moment a slight man about fifty years old opened the door and said hello to them.

He was dressed in a gray tweed suit and brown tie, both colors which appeared in his hair and short beard. The aviator glasses he wore seemed somehow out of place on his weathered face. His eyes were deep brown and intelligent—eyes Stonetree recognized. The beard was new and the hair a bit thinner, and he was smaller than Stonetree recalled—but there was no mistaking who he was.

"David Stonetree," McReynolds said, gesturing toward the man, "this is Dr. Arthur Camden."

Stonetree hesitated for a second, then grasped the researcher's hand and shook it steadily. It was the most famous hand he had ever shaken in his life, and he felt a wave of admiration wash through him.

"Dr. Camden," he finally said. "It's a pleasure to meet you." He hesitated. "It's a little strange, though. I feel like I know you."

"Well, I'm sure you know of me, David," he replied with a reassuring smile. "I'm sure Miss Lane has briefed you on more than one occasion on what a deceitful, ungrateful, obnoxious son of a bitch I am. I expect it. It's like indigestion after too many hot dogs at a ball game."

He laughed heartily and led them to a group of chairs in the front of his suite. He then fetched three cans of beer from a small refrigerator, explaining he could call down for something else if they wanted. From the telephone in the bathroom, he said with a motion of his head.

After opening his can, McReynolds looked at both of them and then directed his comments to Stonetree.

"Dave," he began, "I know all of that stuff you gave me in the interview about the doctor didn't represent your personal feelings about him, did it?"

Stonetree was perplexed by the question. He looked at Camden and motioned for McReynolds to elaborate on his statement.

"What I mean is that you were essentially giving me the SUE side of the story, not your side of it. Right?"

Stonetree was still confused.

"Who's side of what? What are you trying to say?"

"What Robin's asking," Camden interrupted, "is, do you really think I'm the asshole I've been made out to be?"

"Oh. Well, uh . . ." Stonetree stumbled. "I guess I really don't have my own opinion. I mean, your accomplishments are known to almost everyone, and I'm sure that history will, uh, congratulate you, or whatever history does. . . ."

"And you think I'm an asshole," he said.

"If the truth be known," Stonetree said, relieved, "they have convinced me that you are indeed an asshole." He thought a moment. "And a pretty big one at that."

"Good for them," Camden responded, slapping the table. "I like working from an underdog position. Gives you an emotional advantage when you walk up to the plate. You know the crowd is with you."

"Dave," McReynolds said, "I know you probably think this is strange, but I want you to listen to Dr. Camden's story. That's all I ask. Just listen to the story. If you hear it and don't buy it, fine. You were never here. If you do buy it and want to get involved, fine. It's your decision. But listen with an open mind." He paused. "And promise me it won't leave this room."

"I don't understand. Buy what? Get involved in what?"

"Dr. Camden and I had two long talks when I was preparing the *Fortune* article."

"Well, I figured that," Stonetree said. "I wasn't born yesterday. I could tell by your expressions when we were talking that you had heard a different story." He turned to Camden. "Not that the different story might not be partially or completely true."

"Do you believe everything they've told you about the doctor?" McReynolds asked.

"I suppose it has to be taken with a grain of salt. There are obviously some personalities—strong ones—involved. But it's all secondhand to me. I only know what I've heard."

"So you'll give the doctor a fair hearing?"

"Sure. I don't know what that will prove, though. The article is out. I can't do anything."

"We'll see," McReynolds replied, patting Stonetree on the shoulder. "We'll see."

The first part of Camden's story did not surprise Stonetree. In fact, it tracked fairly closely what he believed to be the probable truth. Camden said it was pretty clear once Lane was given Entertainment that Pierre Ruth was grooming her for bigger things. It was also clear that no one should interfere with his plans for his protégée.

Ruth had no children, and his wife had been dead for years. In Lane he saw a reflection of himself as a younger man—the brashness, the arrogance, the drive. Lane was a woman Ruth could relate to. Ruth had nothing to consume him but his work, and she was a kindred spirit. If he was going to share his empire with someone, why not with this intelligent, appealing female rather than another middle-aged man? You didn't have to be a genius to figure that one out.

As her competitors, real or imagined, began to fall by the wayside, it became evident to Camden that his tenure was in jeopardy too. He presented the perfect test case for her, a chance to see if she could disrupt Ruth's personal as well as professional relationships.

The doctor approached Ruth at one time and voiced his concerns about the rumors he heard that Lane might be given the reins of Pharmaceuticals. Instead of keeping counsel with Camden as he always did in the past when the researcher advised him, Ruth launched into a tirade about how everyone resented Lane because she was a woman; everyone was afraid of progress and change, and no one knew her managerial skills as well as he. The decision as to who ran the divisions was his and his alone. If Camden didn't like it, he could submit his resignation.

Camden was shattered by what he felt was both a personal and professional betrayal. He contributed a great deal to SUE's success, and to be dismissed in such an offhand fashion was devastating. He did not resign at that moment, but he knew eventually he would have to leave, voluntarily or involuntarily. The anger and passion in the chairman's voice, and the ruthlessness of his suggestion, made it clear Lane could have anyone's head on a silver platter—she need only ask.

Instead of sloughing off, though, Camden decided to make the most of his remaining time at SUE. Still in possession of Ruth's mandate to pursue the path he wished, he shifted the focus of his work to a cure for CYD. He could never obtain another set of the tailor-made equipment and instruments he had assembled at the Plaza, and the opportunity to chase after the solutions to some of his theories became irresistible. Before his ouster he filled four fat notebooks with observations, sketches, and formulas on the question of cures. He felt he was onto something important, a breakthrough, when the rug of his career at SUE was pulled out from under him. The story he told of the end was not the same one Lane used to indoctrinate Stonetree.

Lane was promoted to group vice president much more quickly than even Camden anticipated. In fact, it happened the morning of the accident involving the fire and the destruction of the four pints of CY6A4. Camden, Hickey, and a few others were called to Lane's office to brief her on the incident. It was then that Camden first learned of her promotion.

After the briefing everyone but Hickey and Camden were dismissed. Hickey was with United Science when Ruth took control and was well regarded in the research community. Most people thought back then it was Camden who would work for him, not vice versa. Although there was friction between the two of them during the first months of Camden's control of Research and Development, a mutual, although purely professional, respect developed between them.

Lane asked for an outline of the major projects under way in R and D. She did not want money devoted to cure research and said she wanted it terminated as soon as practical. Both men protested. She said she had Ruth's complete support for any changes she wanted to make in R and D and she expected their complete cooperation. Camden continued to protest, urging her to reconsider. He felt close to a breakthrough. With another six months of work he might be able to save millions of persons inconceivable amounts of pain and anguish and save others from an early and painful death. He would never forget Lane's refusal: "This is a business. We are a corporation responsible to its shareholders. We are not a church. We are not a charity. If you disagree, I would suggest the seminary."

Hickey, before he could add his protests, was made the new head of Research and Development. Suddenly Hickey, too, saw the wisdom of concentrating on treatments rather than cures.

Camden was in an untenable position. He would have to give up both his autonomy and his search for a cure, not to mention his title and self-respect, if he remained at SUE. Rather than prolong the inevitable, he offered his resignation. Hickey then left so the two of them could discuss the terms.

Lane, it seemed, was prepared well in advance for Camden's resignation. She had a copy of his contract in a file on her desk and an opinion from Legal as to what consequences Camden's resignation would generate. It was all there. He would be awarded an extremely generous separation agreement, most of which, however, was conditioned on a few additional humiliations. He could not work for another private firm for two years, a condition to which he agreed when he was put in charge of R and D. He would continue to be paid two thirds of his sizable salary each month.

All of his current research, all notes, all projects, remained at SUE. This was from a clause in the standard release form he signed at the beginning of his employment. Additional royalties based on Febrifuge Blue sales would be paid to him toward the end of the two-year period if he continued to abide by the covenant-not-to-compete clause. The two years had expired nine weeks earlier. He'd been in the city forty-eight hours. There was a project he wanted to undertake.

From his bearing, his voice, and his facial expressions, Stonetree knew that every word he said was true. He was amazed. He could not believe Camden was so calm. Why hadn't he just strangled Lane and done the world a favor?

"Oh, don't doubt for a second that it didn't occur to me," Camden said as he bugged his eyes and pretended to choke the arm of the chair. "But I had to be rational about it. First of all, Pierre wasn't going to intercede. I called him later that afternoon, and all he wanted to know was if I resigned voluntarily. Period. He said we'd talk about it when things cooled off, but neither of us ever got around to making the call. It was really like a divorce. Have you ever been married, David?"

"No."

"It was like a divorce. So I couldn't go back to R and D as Hickey's stooge. It would have been too unworkable. Especially just doing Febrifuge again. They had a valid claim on all of my research. It was all spelled out in black and white. I had a wife, a couple of kids in college. I figured I could continue some independent work. Nobody else would be able to afford me or give me that kind of freedom. I know it might sound Machiavellian, but it came down to being comfortable and screwed or uncomfortable and screwed. I took comfortable."

"I understand. Completely." Stonetree nodded. "This story is quite different from what I was told, but I believe you."

"I found out later that Hickey probably knew about the whole thing in advance," Camden said. "When he got back to the lab after our little chat with Trisha, he personally packed up all of my things, with the help of some of my former associates, and turned them over to Security. Everything. Even the topcoat I had with me that day. My office was emptied in an hour. A week later I got most of it shipped down to me in Georgia, but a lot of it stayed behind—worthless junk they figured might be valuable to somebody else. Corporate paranoia at its best. It's frightening."

The three of them sat in silence for a few moments. Then McReynolds stood up and paced across the room, tossing his empty beer can up and down in his hand.

"So what do you think of Dr. Camden now?" he asked.

"Well," Stonetree began, looking at the researcher, "I certainly sympathize with you. I agree. You did get screwed." He turned to McReynolds. "But, Robin, I still don't get it. Why tell me?"

"Doctor, could you finish the story for Mr. Stonetree?"

"I've been working on the cure problem for the past two years. Actually both the cure problem and the symptom-reversal problem. Most of it has all been theoretical. I simply don't have the technology I had at SUE. I think I may have the answer now, but there is a big hole in the equation. I need some of my old notes to clear it up. I've got part of it, but I have to see the notes, my early impressions on a certain item. That, I think, will finish the puzzle."

"This is a big, big story," McReynolds said excitedly. "This is a major event. This is a Nobel Prize. We're talking about a cure for a major killer. You have to get involved in this, David. This is important."

"I realize it's important and all that," he replied with a question in his voice, "but I'm still baffled about what all of this has to do with me. I don't have access to these notes, if that's what you're getting at. I don't know where they are, and even if I did . . . I don't know. What do you want from me?"

"We need your help, David," McReynolds said. "We need it bad."

"This is crazy." Stonetree sighed. "Look, just tell me what you want, okay? If I can help, fine. If not, that's it."

"Are you willing to get involved?" Camden asked. "It could—I should say would—cost you your job if any of this got out. If we were caught. On the other hand, the rewards could be enormous, emotionally, financially, and otherwise."

"Why don't we clarify what you want," Stonetree said, growing tired of the mystery. "And then we can talk about rewards. I'm probably in too deep already."

"Let me put it all on the table," McReynolds said.

"Please," Stonetree replied. "What's this all about?"

"Dr. Camden needs to get at his four notebooks. We don't know where they are, but that really isn't important right now. What is important is that these notebooks still exist."

"How do you know?"

"I've known Trisha a while longer than you have," Camden answered. "She wouldn't destroy them. She figures they're worth too much. And in a roundabout way, she's right. To both of us."

"Anyway," McReynolds continued, "Dr. Camden left something behind in the laboratory. . . ."

"What?" Stonetree asked. McReynolds gestured to Camden.

"I'm the only one who knows this," the doctor said. "And I haven't told Robin and I won't tell you. You'll have to just assume for now that it's something Trisha would like to get her hands on. She'd be willing, I think, to trade my notebooks for what I have to offer her. Think of it as some pictures of her with her pants down. Something like that."

"So why don't you just call her up and tell her you want to make a deal?"

"I can't trust her unless I can deal with her at arm's length.

If I told her what I had, she'd be able to find it. She's no fool. She may be a lot of things, but not a fool."

"So you want to steal something from the Plaza to ransom your notes?"

"Something like that. Actually just borrow it until I can look at the notes."

"I understand. But what you're saying is that you want to take something and use it to shake SUE down. If I might be moral for a minute, what gives you the right to do that?"

"What gives him the right," McReynolds said, "is that he may have a cure for CYD, and SUE is not going to let him do anything about it. They don't *want* a vaccine. They don't *want* a cure. They want status quo. They want kids to keep dying so they can make more money. If you want to talk morals, why don't you go look in the mirror first? Kids dying. Our friends dying. You call that moral, Dave? I don't. It's bullshit. It's evil, sick bullshit."

Stonetree was stunned by McReynolds's angry outburst. Camden sat passively with a look of resignation on his face. Stonetree stood and stretched, then walked to the refrigerator, removing three more cans of beer. He returned slowly, seating himself next to Camden.

"Let's go over this once more," Stonetree began, addressing himself to the doctor. "You think you have a cure for CYD. You need a formula or something from your notes that are somewhere in the bowels of SUE, location unknown. You do, however, know the location of some"—he smiled—"compromising photos of Trisha Lane. . . ."

"That alone is worth the money!" McReynolds interjected. They all laughed, Camden the hardest.

"If you can get your hand on these photos, you'll let Lane have them back for letting you look at those notes of yours. A cure for CYD is discovered, and we all live happily ever after. Is that about it?"

Camden nodded. "That is precisely it."

"And there is no profit motive involved?" Stonetree asked cynically.

"Of course there is," Camden replied. "There is a profit motive in almost everything we do. I don't have to tell you what that formula would be worth, or what it would be worth to keep it off the market." He looked at McReynolds. "By the way," he continued, "I don't agree with our friend Robin that Miss Lane or anyone else wants to see people die. She has a business and she made a judgment call. I doubt she thinks there is a formula for a cure or something close to it in my notes. Valuable information? Yes. But not something that big."

"And profits."

"If I'm right, certainly the money would come in by the truckload." He paused and tugged at his beard, a look of serenity transforming his face into that of a weary but wise philosopher. "But I've got plenty of money now. More than I could ever give away. I like my house, but it's actually too big for us now that the kids are gone. You can see by the way I look that clothes have no meaning to me. I drive a five-year-old Mercedes that will outlast me. I'm wealthy as it is. Being a billionaire won't make me a better person."

"So what will?"

"The cure. The accomplishment. The satisfaction. You know, that feeling you've done more than just take up space on the planet. You understand that, don't you?"

Stonetree thought for a moment. "I guess so. I'm not sure . . . about any of this. All I see is getting fired, maybe getting thrown in jail. So you can be one up on my boss."

McReynolds hooted and jumped to his feet. "You know, Dave, you're really a piece of work! This man has a tremendous medical breakthrough, and you're worried about a shit job you don't want anyway. Damn it! I'm sorry I called you. I sure had you figured wrong. You're no better than Lane. You ought to get together. I'd love to see your children."

Stonetree could feel his face flush and his ears begin to ring. He felt dizzy, almost nauseated. He looked at Camden, who in turn looked away. McReynolds turned his back to him. He felt like running and hiding. He had never been more embarrassed in his life.

McReynolds hit him dead center, right between the eyes. Had he become that callous in such a short time? Had he really fallen for the lies? Was he becoming a clone of Lane, another heartless cog in the SUE machinery willing to sacrifice actual human lives so he could collect a paycheck twice a month a little while longer? Had he sunk that incredibly low? Was it *possible* to sink that low?

He started to stand up but was knocked back into his chair

by a sudden pain in his chest. *This is it*, he thought. *This is the end.* Sitting in a hotel room with a great scientist and an old friend, ignoring their pleas for help—pleas on behalf of humanity, just so he could pay his electric bills or subscribe to a few more magazines he didn't have time to read.

Was he really that loyal to SUE? Was he really that loyal to Lane? What would Steve Riley have done if he hadn't died? What would Sharon do if she were in his position and he was the one with CYD? What would a feeling, flesh-and-blood human do? Not a drone, but a real human being with real feelings, real emotions, real compassion.

He thought again about the blind man selling newspapers in London. He thought about Sharon the morning after they returned from there. He thought about two close friends lost to CYD, one by its hand, one by his own.

He never pictured himself as a savior. He wasn't a hero. Wexford was a hero. Hendricks's brother was a hero. Camden was a hero. Maybe McReynolds was a hero. But not Stonetree.

While he liked life, he didn't love it. So far he had managed to slide through. There were a couple of bad licks along the way, but none to write a tragedy around. Given the choice between a bang and a whimper, he would choose the latter with no hesitation. At least he was honest about it.

Something, however, was changing. He could not put his finger on it, or locate its point in space, but he knew it was there. What was it that Hendricks said—the view is always best from the edge of the cliff?

"Let's talk," Stonetree finally managed to say.

CHAPTER 9

AFTER AN HOUR OF DISCUSSION, STONETREE, CAMDEN, AND McReynolds agreed upon a plan of action. Stonetree said he would contact the others before five o'clock the next day to say if he would go through with it. He needed some time to consider the implications of such a decision. Kissing SUE good-bye was more complicated than kissing his cousin Tori in Colorado good-bye.

It was only three in the afternoon, but the commitment was there. He was ready to take a chance. He needed to make a break from everything, even if that break was spent in the unemployment line. This wasn't a kid swiping albums from K mart. This was insider corporate espionage, a crime punishable by the corporate death sentence.

Despite the fact that he had been up half the night agonizing over his options, he felt relaxed, even rested, for the first time in weeks. One way or another, his situation in life was about to change. Possibly for the worse, he thought. But if all went as planned, probably for the better.

If Camden was correct about the contents of the notebooks—if they held the missing link in his research—he believed he could have a rough model of the cure developed within eight weeks. Coupled with the rabid nature of the Food and Drug Administration's response to any CYD-related product, he could make it available within a few months.

Camden said he did not want to bind himself to another

conglomerate. He wanted to start a company from scratch, its sole raison d'être being the manufacture and sale of the new drug. If it was a success, billions of dollars in sales, year after year, would be assured. Camden would need people to run the operation, a task for which he held little interest. In that regard he would make no promises aside from stating he never forgot his friends. For the time being, all he needed was someone to open a door at SUE. He correctly guessed that Stonetree carried a palm-print clearance.

That was only the beginning. Who knew where the adventure might lead? Maybe this was the break he had always dreamed of, the once-in-a-lifetime opportunity to make it big without paying big. The worst SUE would do was ax him.

If he was willing to take a single chance, fame and glory and wealth would be tapping at his door. It was the bottom of the ninth, Camden said. No outs, nobody on base, SUE ahead one to nothing.

While McReynolds was intrigued with the cloak-and-dagger aspects of the adventure, his real motivation seemed to be the story. He could write an inside account about a cure for CYD and be a player in the epic to boot. He, too, could have it all at once without having to spend years waiting for a break. He had the biggest story he could ever hope for in his life and didn't want to lose it.

At first Stonetree felt he was being used by McReynolds, but the more he thought about it the more he realized it was Robin who was doing him a big favor, not the other way around. Even if it meant only the end of his few weeks on the eighteenth floor, Stonetree would be grateful.

Finally there was Sharon. Things were different since London, and Stonetree was worried. It was as if a stranger had come between them. Maybe it was the anxiety about her CYD, or maybe it was his betrayal of his former beliefs. It could be the bookstore, the weather, almost anything. McReynolds's scheme could save them. It could save Sharon's life.

The plan was simple. He would pick up Camden and McReynolds at 8:30 that evening. Hardly anyone would be at SUE at that time on a Friday night. His recent experience, wandering the halls late at night, guaranteed it.

Stonetree would admit the three of them through one of the Plaza's side doors. His guests would go to R & D opera-

146 · JOHN PATRICK KAVANAGH ·

tions, which occupied all of five and six, to retrieve whatever it was Camden had hidden there. Stonetree would go to his office long enough to count to one hundred and would then return to the first floor, where he would let all of them out through the same door.

His only real risk was being seen with them or being stopped by Security on the way in or out. Camden's appearance had changed enough since leaving SUE that it was doubtful he'd be recognized. If they were confronted, Stonetree would say they were friends of his from out of town and that he was merely showing them where he worked. Once out of the building, his role would be finished. Camden could approach Lane and make whatever deal he wanted. Stonetree would become a silent partner and wait to see what came of it. In the worst scenario, he kept telling himself, he'd be fired. And that, according to Dr. Fitzgerald's mind reader, was not such a bad result.

Stonetree took the disc over lunch to see if he was thinking as clearly as he believed he was. According to the results, he was right in the pocket. The idea of becoming a hero in return for helping to save Sharon and thousands of others registered so far into the purple that Fitzgerald thought the machine was broken. He was also almost as solid in his belief that the job was beginning to harm him both physically and mentally. He still showed some ambiguity about his relationship with Sharon but could not conclusively pin down its exact nature.

He did not feel that what he was prepared to do amounted to a crime, despite the Selfscan results. Dishonest perhaps. Seditious perhaps. But not a crime. He really did believe in the overall intrinsic good of the project. He also believed, only half to his surprise, that when all was said and done, he would be Lane's equal.

He called McReynolds first. He could picture the smile on his friend's face when he told him he was ready to lay it on the line. It would be a great adventure, they agreed. Serendipity at its best. McReynolds would be at the hotel at eight and wait in Camden's room.

He then called the scientist. Camden seemed pleased, but a little nervous. Aside from the possibility of being found out, of the ramifications among his colleagues in the scientific community for participating in what amounted to a major theft, he was apprehensive about returning to SUE. He had not been inside or even seen the building since he was fired two years before. He was prepared, though, he said firmly, and told Stonetree he should call from the lobby around 8:30.

A major theft. Stonetree thought about the words. A major theft. No, it wasn't theft. Camden didn't really want to *steal* anything, he just wanted to return it to its rightful owner and take a peek at some old research. That's not theft. A major *borrowing*, perhaps, but not a theft. Besides, who's going to be crazy enough to try prosecuting someone for saving millions of lives? Nobody. Simple as that.

The remainder of the afternoon passed quickly. Stonetree left the Plaza at 7:15 and drove to Sirius to have a snack, a single drink, and a cigarette. Carl rolled in about 7:45, and they chatted for a few minutes about the recent volatility in the precious-metals markets, about Kennard being arrested again (this time for possession of stolen property, of all things), and the latest gossip from SUE. At 8:05 Stonetree said he was leaving, a statement he guessed would merit another ten minutes of conversation and criticism from Carl. He arrived at the Hyatt at precisely 8:37. No apologies were necessary, Camden told him over the house phone. He and Robin had just finished getting dressed. They would be right down.

Stonetree puzzled over this statement as he seated himself near the elevators. Was he missing something? Was there more to the story than just— What did they call Watergate, a second-rate burglary? Was this going to be more complicated than he imagined?

All his questions were quickly compounded as the elevator doors opened and out stepped his two co-conspirators, smiling, arm in arm, in their black tuxedos. Stonetree's jaw dropped in exasperation, prompting laughter from Camden and a grin from McReynolds.

"You *are* kidding, aren't you?" he asked them. "This isn't a lark we're going on. This is serious stuff. What's with the tuxedos? We're not going to the prom."

"Wait till we get outside," McReynolds said as they made their way to the door and into the street. "It's okay. It's all right."

When they reached Stonetree's car, its flashers blinking as it sat in the no-parking zone, he inserted his key in the door but didn't turn it. "We're not getting in until you explain this," he threatened.

"Dave, this makes sense," McReynolds said, resting his arms on the roof of the Turbostar, and then his chin on top of them. "Did you ever read the Edgar Allan Poe story 'The Purloined Letter'?"

"You're going to give me a literature lesson? Jeez."

"Did you ever read it?"

"No."

"Well, it's a great story with a great moral. And the good doctor agrees with me, don't you, Doc?"

Camden nodded, straightening his bow tie.

"Keep talking," Stonetree said.

"So Poe wrote this story about a detective and his assistant who break into this other guy's apartment so they can find this letter that they want. Just like us. You with me so far?"

"Yeah."

"So they rip the entire place apart and can't find it. They take apart chairs, couches, tear up the carpeting, look in the john, everywhere. And they know it's there but they just can't locate it."

"So what?"

"So at the end of the story it turns out this letter is hanging in a frame right in front of these jerks, and they didn't see it. Right?"

"Get to the point, huh?"

"The point," he continued, "is that people always overlook the obvious! That's the point, you idiot. Come on, let's get on with it."

Stonetree stared at him for a moment. How could he have gotten involved in this, he wondered. Maybe it was not too late to make a quick exit. McReynolds and Camden had both lost their minds somewhere between three and eight P.M.

"So wearing tuxedos is supposed to help you find something over at SUE? What are you talking about, man?"

"Think about it, Dave," Camden said. "What would some-body in a tuxedo be doing at SUE on a Friday night? If you saw somebody, what would you think?"

"I'm not sure," Stonetree replied. "I guess I'd figure it was somebody who was called away from a banquet who had to take care of something at work."

"Somebody who worked, say, in the mailroom?"

"No. Somebody important. One of the executives."

"Exactly. And do you think your average security person is going to want to hassle an executive who has been called away from a big party to do something at work?"

"Of course not. No way."

"And that's why we got the penguin outfits. When we're away from you, we'll be on our own. We might have to bluff our way out of something. This way, we lessen our chances of being caught." He hesitated, waiting for a response. Stonetree slowly nodded his head. "And then, when we're done, we can crash a party somewhere. Nobody ever stops a man wearing a tuxedo."

"And we got one for you too," McReynolds added.

"Really?"

"No, but you can be our driver."

Stonetree could contain his laughter only for a few seconds. The tuxedos did make sense. He could use a party when this was over. He cleared a nervous frog out of his throat and opened the door.

As they drove to SUE Plaza, they reviewed the plan again. If they were stopped at the side door, Stonetree would say he wanted to show some out-of-town friends his office. If they met any resistance, they would leave. If they got through the door unmolested, he would take the executive elevator to eighteen, go to his office, kill a couple of minutes, and then return to the lobby.

Camden and McReynolds would take a different one to five. McReynolds would stay at the elevator, shutting it down for the two minutes Camden figured he would need to retrieve his prize. They would meet Stonetree downstairs and then exit through the same door. If all went well up to that point, they would be home free.

To add to their disguise, McReynolds wanted to carry a champagne bottle and Camden a briefcase.

"The briefcase is okay," Stonetree said, "but not the champagne bottle. That could only get us in trouble."

"You're probably right," McReynolds replied. "But I think we ought to slosh a little around in our mouths and smoke a cigarette. That'll give us a partylike smell. What do you think?"

"I guess for the two of you it makes sense, but not for me. I'm just there to pick something up. I just left."

Camden opened the champagne while McReynolds lit a cigarette. It was only half finished when they pulled onto the side street bordering the Plaza. Other cars were crowded along the curb, and Stonetree wedged his into a small space. They got out and looked around. There were only two people on the street, a couple kissing beneath an overhang down the block.

Stonetree led them to the side door. There was no guard at the security desk visible through the glass. Stonetree tried the door, but it was locked. It suddenly occurred to him he had never used the palm-print machine before, and his mind went blank as he stared at it.

"Dave," McReynolds said after a moment. "Are we going to do this sometime tonight or what?"

"Just wait a second," Stonetree replied. "I can't remember how to work it. She showed me how to use it, but I wasn't paying attention."

"Sheila?" Camden asked, a wide grin spreading across his face.

"Yeah! How did you know?"

"She showed me how to work it too. That must be a concentration test Pierre designed." He chuckled. "Flick the switch on the left, punch in your six-digit code, put your palm on the screen. That ought to do it."

Stonetree complied, and the lock on the door clicked. McReynolds pulled on the handle. It was open. They quickly walked to the elevators. A frail old man was pushing a huge broom down one hall, and Stonetree could see a couple of security people in the front lobby engaged in an animated conversation. They split at the elevators.

Stonetree's opened as soon as he pressed the button. He turned to look at his accomplices as the door began to close. Camden gave him the thumbs-up sign. The doors locked, and he pressed eighteen.

Nobody was there when he arrived. He got off the elevator and hurried to his office. He turned on the lights and walked to the window, peeking around the side of the blinds to look at the skyline. It seemed about right for a Friday, he sensed. From somewhere he could hear the up-and-down tones of a squad car or ambulance and felt his stomach twist a bit. Maybe the siren was on its way to SUE—to drag him away to a dungeon, to beatings, to spiders on the walls.

He turned off the lights and walked back to the elevator at a more leisurely pace. There was nothing to be afraid of, nothing to fear, he thought as he ambled along to his ride downstairs. What would Lane think if she ever found out about all this? How would she react? He wondered what it was that Camden had squirreled away in the massive complex.

If it was so important to Lane, how could it have been ignored for two years? Why didn't anyone stumble onto it? Was it really pictures? Or plans of some kind? Maybe, he mused, it was just a letter hanging in a frame. What had McReynolds called it? Purloined?

Again the elevator opened as soon as he pushed the button. He hopped in and pressed Lobby. He suddenly realized his heart was racing, beating furiously. His mouth was dry, and he was thirsty. He felt warm and a bit queasy. He was not worried, however. It would all be over in a few minutes.

He took a deep breath as the elevator stopped and the doors opened. He took three steps forward and looked around. No one was there. He took a few steps toward the door to look down the main hall that ran from the front to the back of the building. Standing in the front lobby was one of the security guards he had seen before. The guard was alone, staring back at him. Stonetree walked back to the elevators. In a moment one opened. It was them.

"We got it. Let's go," McReynolds whispered.

They slowly walked toward the side door. As they crossed the main hall, Stonetree saw the guard walking toward them. He sped up a bit and turned back to look when they reached the exit. Maybe the guard was going somewhere else. It was still clear. He stared at the palm-print device.

"Flick the switch, punch in the code," Camden reminded him. Stonetree pulled on the switch, then gazed at the telephone keyboard. Oh-three-one, he thought. Oh-three-one. What were the other three numbers? Five-oh-five? Oh-oh-five? Five-five-oh? That was it. Five-five-oh. He punched in the numbers and heard a voice behind him ask, "Gentlemen?"

Stonetree stopped and slowly turned, staring into the eyes of the security guard he had seen in the hall. He was young but big and nervous-looking. He was gently rocking his night-stick against his thigh. Stonetree smiled.

"Yes?" he replied, approaching the guard and looking at his nameplate. "Yes, Mr. Keeton. What can I do for you?"

"You're an employee?"

"Yes, I am."

"And you?" the man said, looking at McReynolds.

"These two gentlemen are my friends," Stonetree said. "They're from out of town. They are in town for, what was it?" He looked at McReynolds.

"A wedding," McReynolds offered.

"A wedding? On a Friday night?"

"Sure," he continued. "It's an old friend of ours. He's a musician. A sax player. This is his only night off."

"I see," the guard said. "And you are who?" he continued, turning his gaze back to Stonetree.

"Stonetree. David Stonetree. I'm the director of corporate projects for Miss Lane. Up on eighteen," he said, pointing toward the ceiling.

"Could I see your ID, please?"

He pulled out his wallet and removed the cards he kept stuffed on one side. He had his license, his Sirius card, two credit cards, a picture of Sharon, a folded twenty-dollar bill, a video club card, and a health club membership. As usual, there was no SUE ID card.

"I'm sorry. I must have left it at home. We came in through this door. I'm on the system."

"Show me," the guard replied.

Stonetree turned toward the machine. He pushed the switch off and then on. He punched in his identification number. He placed his hand on the screen. The lock clicked. He pushed on the door, opening it a few inches.

"See?" he asked. "No problem. Uh, we have to get going now. Good night."

"Mr. Stonetree?" the guard said as he took a step forward. "Yes?"

"There have been a few reported instances of employee de-falcation lately, and we have orders to stop anyone we might be suspicious of."

"And?"

"And I certainly wouldn't ask that you or your friends submit to a personal search or anything like that, but I would like to just take a quick look in that briefcase if you wouldn't mind."

"Mr. Keeton, this isn't necessary. Could we just leave, please?"

"I'm going to have to insist, Mr. Stonetree," the guard said, eyeing each of the three quickly, individually. "You know the rules. We can check bags anytime we want. That's the policy. I'm sure you've had a briefcase or two examined before."

Stonetree nodded.

"If you'd like, I can call up my sergeant," Keeton said, reaching to the small radio attached to his collar. "It won't take but a minute for him to get here."

Stonetree looked at Camden.

"I have nothing to hide from our young friend." Camden shrugged. "He may look in my briefcase if he feels it necessary."

"If you don't mind, sir."

Keeton pointed toward the security desk. Camden placed the case on its side and unlatched the two locks. He did not open it, but rather motioned to the guard to do so. The guard reached down and raised the top. Inside were eight small glass flasks.

"What's in those?" he asked.

"Apple juice," Camden replied.

"Apple juice?"

"Yes, Mr. Keeton. It's apple juice. Unsweetened, one-hundred-percent-natural apple juice."

Stonetree looked at McReynolds, who almost imperceptibly shook his head. He didn't know what to think or do. He smiled at the guard when he caught his eye.

"Can we leave now, Mr. Keeton? We are late for an engagement."

Just then two other guards stepped out of the main corridor and walked to where they were standing. One, named Cribbet, had sergeant stripes and looked mean. The other, O'Connell, was short and bore the same nervous look as his partner.

"Do we have a problem here, Keeton?" Cribbet asked. "What's going on?"

"These gentlemen were on their way out. Mr. Stonetree," he said, pointing him out, "is an employee and was showing his friends his office. I asked to see the contents of the brief-case," he continued, pointing to the bottles. "That's all."

"And the contents of the bottles?" Cribbet asked, looking Stonetree up and down.

"Apple juice." He sighed.

"Mr. Stonetree," the sergeant said, "I'm going to have to assume that there is not apple juice in these," he said, picking up one of the flasks and holding it up to the light. "I just don't believe someone would carry around eight bottles of apple juice and nothing else. I will have to assume that this is con-traband of some kind."

"I am," Camden said flatly, "what is known as a health nut. Part of my regime is a virtually constant ingestion of apple juice."

"That's about the dumbest excuse for a story I've ever heard," Cribbet replied.

"Now, just wait a second," Stonetree interrupted.

"Now, *you* just wait a second, mister," the sergeant shot back. "We have rules here, and everybody follows them. You are not leaving with those bottles. If it's nothing, you'll get them back on Monday. But they are going to spend the week-end with *us*," he added, nodding toward Keeton and O'Con-nell. "Nobody's fault if I'm wrong."

"It's not your property," McReynolds offered.

"Property?" Cribbet asked. "Property? I'll tell you about property. I know all about property." He paused. "Possession is ninety percent of the law."

"It's all right," Camden interceded. "No problem. If consti-pation sets in, it sets in. You can keep the juice and the brief-case over the weekend, Mr. Cribbet. I have no quarrel with that, but we do need to be on our way."

The sergeant squinted at Camden and closed the briefcase, pressing on the latches. He picked it up and nestled it under his arm, patting the end facing Stonetree.

"You just give us a call on Monday, Mr. Stonetree," he snarled. "We'll give you your apple juice back, if that's what it is."

Stonetree pushed the door open and grinned at the guard.

"Thank you, Sergeant Cribbet," he growled. "I'll see to it Miss Lane is advised of what an exemplary job you're doing."

"You just do that, sir," he retorted.

Stonetree could feel his stomach knot again and his face turn red. He motioned to McReynolds and Camden to follow him, and they exited together. As they stood on the sidewalk a moment, Stonetree looked back through the entrance at the three uniformed statues staring at him. "Let's get out of here," he hissed.

Nobody spoke until they were at least a mile from the Plaza. McReynolds finally asked where they were headed. Stonetree realized he thought "Hyatt" to himself but instead was driving in the direction of Sirius. "I'm gonna pull over," he replied. "Let's figure this out." After he parked he turned to Camden, who was wedged into the backseat.

"Well, Doctor," he began. "What happens now?"

"I'm not sure," Camden replied thoughtfully. "What do you think? Are you in trouble?"

"It depends on what's in the bottles." He sighed. "Could you please tell me what the bottles contained?"

"It's not contraband. It's harmless. Will you be in trouble if it's harmless?"

Stonetree thought for a moment.

"I'm not sure," he replied. "What was in the bottles? Do you know, Robin?" he asked, turning to McReynolds.

"Nope," he replied. "I'd like to know myself, though. How about it, Doc?"

"Take my word for it that it's harmless, it's nothing," Camden said with a bit of an edge in his voice. "Think of it as apple juice. Let's see what the security people do with it. We can wait till Monday, yes?"

"Well, maybe you can wait," Stonetree snapped, "but I'd like a little more information before I stroll into Miss Lane's office on Monday. I know how those Security nuts are. There'll probably be a report on her desk tomorrow morning. And I will be in trouble with a capital T if I don't have a good explanation for this. Now, what was in the damn bottles?"

McReynolds recoiled a bit. Camden sat up and smiled.

"It's apple juice, David. Unsweetened, one-hundred-percent-natural apple juice."

They all agreed it might be a good idea to split up and not talk for a couple days. They drove back to the Hyatt, where

Camden got out. He said he'd talk to them soon and wished them luck.

McReynolds just wanted to go home, so Stonetree drove him back to Wilson Towers. He invited him up for a drink, but Stonetree declined. Instead, they sat silently in the car for ten minutes, the radio playing softly in the background. Finally McReynolds let out a deep breath, mumbled good night, and got out of the car. He didn't look back when he reached the entrance to the high-rise. Stonetree thought of going to Sirius but decided he needed sleep more than anything. He drove home, exhausted and angry and scared.

He spent the entire weekend inside. Sharon was having more problems with the store and her partners, Tracey and Jim. She was in no mood to visit, which was just as well because Stonetree wasn't prepared to tell her what had happened. Instead, he stayed in his bedroom most of the time, reading, watching television, and napping. He felt like he should be drinking lots of liquids and eating bowls of soup. He did both. He called Hendricks, but there was no answer. He emptied out the refrigerator. He drank an entire bottle of Chablis with a bacon, lettuce, and tomato sandwich. Monday arrived quickly.

It was evident Lane was already in when Stonetree reached his office. He went directly to his desk, asking Elaine to join him and to shut the door behind her.

"Is Lane here?" he asked.

"I think so. Why?"

"I'm in trouble—at least I might be."

"Really?" she asked. "What happened?"

"I brought a couple of friends in here on Friday night to show them around. We got stopped by Security. One of them had some liquor on him or something. Anyway, here's what I want you to do—"

The phone rang. It was Lane. Could he please come to her office?

"Never mind," he said to Elaine as he hung up the phone. "I'm going to find out firsthand."

He walked down to Lane's office and looked in. She was reading a document at her desk. Rather than knocking to get her attention, he went directly to one of the chairs in front of her and sat down. She didn't look up immediately, but when she did she smiled.

"Nice weekend?" she asked.

"Restful," he replied.

"Good. Mine wasn't. I've been going over your last update on expenses. They're getting better—I think you might be onto something. I brought back some reports from your friend Taylor in Seattle," she continued, pointing to a document on the window ledge. "Go through them and tell me if you see anything strange. I think they blew a couple shipments of seven hundred but don't want to admit it. Some of the numbers look wrong, but I can't figure it out. Look at them, will you? I'm about ready to trim the payroll out there a few notches." She handed him the memo.

"Sure. Anything else?" he asked, rolling the paper into a tight tube.

"Umm, let's see. I talked to Columbia again, and now it looks like they are getting a little more anxious about The Bahamas. I stopped in Denver on the way back to talk with Doug Smite. He's being more difficult than usual. Wexford's new project has moved along considerably, but we are going to have some problems, I think."

"Anything else?"

She set aside her memo and picked up a pen. She pushed her horn-rimmed reading glasses up into her hair and leaned back in her chair, tapping the pen against the side of her head.

"You certainly are curious today, aren't you?" she chided him. "What brought on this 'anything else' attack?"

"Just curious to know what's going on. I like to keep on top of things."

"Oh, by the way," she continued, picking up a piece of paper next to the memo, "were you in here on Friday night with someone?"

Stonetree stared at her, trying to judge her mood. Once again he could not guess which way she was shifting. He stood up and looked out the window.

"Oh, did Security send you something?" he asked nonchalantly.

"Yes, they did. It says here," she replied, reading from the paper, "that you were showing a couple of friends your office, Security stopped you, they looked in one of your friends' briefcase, and it had eight glass bottles in it containing an amber liquid that your friend identified as apple juice, which Security didn't believe. Are they accurate up to that point?"

"Yes."

"So they seized the eight bottles which did turn out to be filled with your basic bottled apple juice, and you may reclaim the briefcase and its contents from them. Talk about paranoia." She laughed. "What did they think it was? Nitro?"

"It baffled me," Stonetree replied earnestly, trying to sound uninterested. "We told them. They had to take the stuff. I was really embarrassed. So were my friends."

"Well, as long as it wasn't alcohol, there's no problem. Did they really hassle you? I can check on this person Cribbet if you'd like."

"No, that's not necessary," Stonetree said, adding a magnanimous gesture of his hand. "He was just doing his job. No harm done."

She nodded. He turned and walked to the door. Just as he reached it, he heard her call him back.

"Oh, David? Can I have a few more minutes?"

He stopped and turned to her. "Sure, what's up?" he asked.

"Shut the door, would you?" she asked. He complied and moved back toward her end of the office, stopping about five feet in front of the desk. She rose from her chair slowly, carefully smoothing the sides of her snug, dark blue skirt. She stepped around to the front of the desk and rested against it, most of her weight supported by her downturned palms. She looked at him for a long moment, then smiled as she glanced toward the window.

"I'm not quite sure what you'll think of this," she began, continuing to stare out at the skyline. "It didn't occur to me until last night. It might sound a little awkward."

Stonetree leaned back a bit on his heels and put one hand into a back pocket. "What?" he asked, as confused as she seemed to be. He tapped the paper tube lightly against the side of his leg.

"Well," she began, finally looking back at him, "Wednesday is my birthday. I don't usually make a big production of it, and I don't plan to this year."

Her eyes seemed to search his for a sign of recognition. He gave none because he had none.

"Uh-huh. Go ahead."

"I've always thought people make way too much out of this thirty-third birthday thing. It's like New Year's Eve. People use it as an excuse to be ridiculous. I just don't subscribe to that."

"I agree. People do get out of hand."

"But I started thinking about it." She smiled as she brought her hands together and laced her fingers together. "And we all get only one thirty-third birthday. Someday I might regret staying here at the office till eight and picking up a sandwich on the way home."

"Did you want . . . to do something?" Stonetree offered.

"I don't have all that many friends, David—especially people close to my age. Everyone seems to be twenty years older. Now, don't think I'm a charity case."

"I won't. Did you want to do something?" he inquired again.

"How about this," she said as she looked back out the window. "Why don't you come over for dinner?" she asked, looking back at him.

"Dinner?" he replied. "At your place?" He could not believe his ears. What a great idea. Especially now that he still had a job.

"I'm not a bad cook. And we can just have a relaxing evening. Or, uh, would that cause any problems for you?"

"Problems?" he said with a laugh. "No, none at all. I'd enjoy that. I'd like to see your place too. Where do you live?"

"Wilson Towers. I moved in, oh, six months ago. It's pretty sharp if I do say so myself. Not that I get to *enjoy* it that much." She shook her head. "So, do we have a date?"

"Sure. Great. What time?"

"How about seven?" she asked. "I have to run some errands—I decided to give myself the whole day off."

"Fine. What can I bring?"

"A bottle of wine, maybe. A medium red?"

"No problem. What else?"

"Just you. Informal attire, of course." She grinned. "And although you still have a relapse once in a while, no 'Miss Lanes' or 'sirs,' okay? Just Trisha."

"I'll look forward to it," he said as he began to back away. "Seven, then?"

"So will I. Seven is fine."

He returned to his office for a moment, then decided to go down to the cafeteria. He found a few of his former colleagues from Technology and spent half an hour visiting with them. Then he got another cup of coffee and sat alone for a few minutes, wondering about Wednesday night. What to wear, what to bring, how to act.

She had, he realized, suddenly sparkled in front of him like the glint from the blade of a double-edged knife. Of all the suitors, all the men she could have chosen to mark the passage, he was the one who received the nod. Crazy world, he thought. He shook his head in wonder.

He thought about dropping by Fitzgerald's to find out if he genuinely wanted to have dinner prepared for him by Trisha. On second consideration, he knew that taking the disc to divine the answer would be a colossal waste of one hundred dollars.

CHAPTER 10

BY THE TIME THE LATE NEWS BEGAN ON TUESDAY NIGHT, STONE-tree had his plan for the next day. First of all, knowing that Trisha was going to take the day off, he decided to take a vacation day too. He'd sleep late and then maybe go for a workout at the health club. He called Sharon to ask if she'd like to have lunch with him, and she agreed. He was still baffled about the events of the previous Friday night, so he contacted McReynolds and they decided to meet for a drink at six. He wanted to do some shopping and, of course, there was a visit to the wine store.

He was awake at seven the following morning. He stayed in bed, however, until 9:00, getting up at 8:00 to turn on the television and catch the last hour of "Good Morning America." After two cups of coffee, a glass of orange juice, and a copy of *Insight*, he drove to the health club and put in a solid forty-five minutes of exercise. He followed with a half hour in the whirlpool and steam room and ten minutes in the swimming pool to cool down.

When he returned home, he agonized for a while over how to dress, and interrupted himself with another cup of coffee and half a *Rolling Stone*. He finally decided on a casual but chic look. This included his favorite sport coat and a shirt and tie that his younger sister sent him for his birthday. Finally, as a humorous touch, he dug through his junk drawer and found a Wexford Crypto, which he pinned to his lapel.

He was running behind schedule, so he called Sharon to tell her he would be late. Instead of the usual lecture about his chronic tardiness, she simply said she was looking forward to lunch, and he could pick her up at work whenever he wanted.

On his way there he stopped at the shop where he made most of his wine purchases and was greeted warmly by the manager. She was a woman in her twenties named Whitney who had large gray cat eyes and a penchant for using the word "grape" in as many inappropriate ways as she could. Her greeting to him was no exception.

"How *are* you today, Mr. Stonetree?" she asked him when he walked into the store. "It's really a grape day out there, isn't it?" She was one of those people who probably always paid with the correct change.

He agreed it was a grape day and began to describe what he was after, as far as wine went, anyway. A medium red. Fairly expensive. California would be fine. He wanted to impress someone.

"How expensive are we talking?" Whitney asked. "Is this a gift, or are you going to be enjoying it yourself? We do try to impress ourselves sometimes."

"Both, I guess."

"Do you know what it's going to be served with? Are we also cooking? Just cheesing?"

"No. She just said a medium red."

"Oh, a she," she said with a smile, her massive white teeth clicking a few times. "That lady you stop in here with sometimes, possibly? Is Sue her name?"

Stonetree chuckled. "No, Whitney. SUE is where I work. Sharon is the lady's name. Yeah, it's for her, or us, I should say."

"A romantic evening?" she continued.

"Yeah, you might say that," he agreed.

"So let's get the price range established. How high or low? You usually buy in the fifteen- to twenty-dollar range, right?"

"About there," he replied. "Why don't we think in terms of twenty-five to fifty. Maybe sixty."

"Oooo, that's *fun*," she cooed. "Now we're talking my kind of wine. My grape-grandmother always used to say that you have to treat yourself on a regular basis if you want to keep your sanity. Do I look sane to you?"

"No."

"That's because I don't treat myself enough. But let's do our *very* best for you."

They walked back to the domestic section and lingered fifteen minutes. Whitney extolled the virtues of each of six different California reds with phrases like "frisky but not aggressive," "quiet yet broad-shouldered," and "curious but not overbearing." He finally decided on a 1979 Stags Leap cabernet, described by his counselor as "graceful, sophisticated, and elegantly oaky," to which Stonetree responded, "Oaky, I'll take it." Whitney repeated the phrase four times. "I just *have* to remember that!"

At the cash register, it took a fifty-dollar bill and a twenty-dollar bill to cover the cost. Whitney agreed the price should also include a silver gift box and a large red bow.

"I hope you enjoy it," she called as he left the store. "If you can, decant it an hour before serving. And we're very grapeful for your patronage. Come back soon."

He arrived at the bookstore close to one o'clock and browsed through the magazine rack for ten minutes while Sharon finished a meeting with the other owners. She caught him off guard with a hug from behind and a suggestive hello. They walked to a nearby café, Sharon excitedly explaining that all the hatchets among the partners had been buried and that they were going to approach expansion at a slower pace. They would wait until they'd paid off more of their current debts before taking on new ones.

She stopped him at the door of the café and kissed him on the cheek, thanking him for the advice she earlier dismissed as condescending. After being seated and ordering a half carafe of house white, she apologized for her recent moodiness. The problems at the store, she said, had gotten to her.

She wanted to know everything that was going on in Stonetree's life. He listed recent events, except the previous Friday's escapade and his plans for the coming evening. He described Camden in detail, though, and said it was possible he might act as a go-between for the scientist and SUE. He wasn't at liberty to discuss it at the moment, however.

"Oh, David. That's allowed. You always get to tell those things, no matter how secret, to your doctor, your lawyer, and your wife."

He looked at her curiously. "My wife?"

"Or your lover, your girlfriend, whatever substitute you have."

"How many am I allowed?" he asked.

"Only one. Just me." She thought for a moment. "Which brings to mind an interesting point. Two, actually. When are we getting engaged, and when are we getting married?"

Stonetree's eyes widened a bit. He was stunned by the matter-of-fact tone in her voice. Six months earlier they had reached the point of booking a reservation at the best French restaurant in the city to make and accept the proposal. Three days before the appointed time, Sharon's sisters immolated themselves. Instead of spending the day looking at rings, they spent it at a double funeral.

Since then the topic had never come up. It seemed there was always an unspoken reason for delay. Sharon's grief, the store, the trip, now the CYD. Which, in an oblique way, was fine with him. Delay sometimes uncovers hidden problems, invisible difficulties.

The cards were on the table. He leaned back in his chair.

"Well," he volunteered, a slight hesitation in his voice, "that sort of frames the issue, as the guys down in Legal say. What would you like me to say?"

She rested her chin on her hand, a slight smile crossing her lips. She looked the best she had since they returned from London. Her eyes were clear and sparkling, and there was an air of steadiness and confidence in her movements.

She had regained the few pounds she had lost, and her cheeks were filled with color. *My God*, he thought, *I must be in love*.

Since the deaths of his mother and two close friends during one horrible summer a few years before, his emotions remained frozen. He had withdrawn from everyone, including himself, if that was possible. He refused to allow himself to get too close to anyone lest they be taken away in the middle of the night, never to be seen again. He would not allow himself the luxury of becoming lost in another heart. For a long time he sacrificed large amounts of pleasure to avoid small amounts of pain. He kept thinking he would shake it, thinking that the sense of loss and foreboding would dissipate. But his frozen heart held on like a badly sprained wrist, always there, not noticeable until used.

In England, for a few days, he thought he was turning the corner. For an instant, walking through the grounds of the Tower of London, it almost happened. He realized his heart was like a gem in the Jewel House, surrounded by thick stone walls, a vault impenetrable except by a master thief. He had squeezed Sharon's hand, hoping she would be the one to pull off the burglary. Somehow, though, the deed was never done, the crime not committed. So he continued on, locked in an emotional twilight, waiting for the lights to come up.

He was close again, that he knew, but as he stared across the table he could not make the commitment. Not today.

"I'd like you to say that you still want to marry me," she said.

"Why wouldn't I?" he responded, the hesitation still in his voice.

She sighed, and reached over to take both of his hands in hers.

"I know we wouldn't be the first couple it's happened to, and I'm sure we won't be the last."

"What are you talking about?"

She released his hands and placed hers palm down on the table.

"If you want me to say it, I will. I might be a little scared, David, but I'm not going to bury my head in the sand."

She looked around the restaurant. "None of this lasts forever. I learned that from my sisters."

And I learned it from my mother, he thought but did not say. *And Mary and Vince*. Everything she said was true. There *was* no guarantee. He was close, closer than he had ever been. If she just would have waited one more day.

He couldn't exist as a nomad the rest of his life, wandering the deserts of his soul, searching for the oasis that sometimes seemed to be just over the next sand dune. He couldn't continue waking in terror in the middle of the night to the sounds of a raid on his camp, only to find it was a nightmare he couldn't remember.

"I tell you what," he began. "I will make the reservations,

and we will have the dinner we were supposed to have last September. How does that sound?"

"It's a start." She smiled. "When?"

"Saturday?" He couldn't believe the word came out of his mouth, in his voice, so easily.

"It's a start," she repeated. "I figured you'd want more time to think about it."

"Why?"

"Because," she replied, taking his hands again and gripping them tighter, "sometimes you run your life like a business."

"But—"

"Let me finish," she said. "And I've been guilty of that too. I just decided last night that from now on I'm going to run my life like a life."

"And—"

"I started with Tracey and Jim," she concluded, "and you're next on the list."

"Lucky me," he said, half in truth, half in jest. More in truth than jest.

"In a lot of ways you are, David," she said softly, reaching across and placing her hand against his cheek. "But sometimes luck has a way of running out on us."

He grasped her hand. It was warm. He was close.

"Saturday is fine," she whispered.

"Then Saturday it is."

They ordered sandwiches and talked for another half hour—about the store, her health, London, the Mustang. After paying the bill, but before they got up to leave, she pulled a copy of the *Fortune* article out of her purse and asked him to autograph it next to his picture. He did, adding the greeting, "To one of my most loyal fans, love and kisses, Saturday or bust!" She took his pen and, having crossed out the last word, substituted "else!"

After dropping her off at the shop, he drove into the city. He spent an hour browsing through the stores in one of his favorite shopping areas, intent on finding a birthday gift for Trisha.

He was reaching a medium-to-high frustration level when he passed the window of a small knickknack store. He spied a curious little statuette, no more than two inches high, of a wizard leading a ten-inch dragon by a leash. It was perfect.

168   · JOHN PATRICK KAVANAGH ·

And reasonably priced—at least as compared to the Stags Leap. He had it wrapped, also in a silver box with a red bow. After a few more errands and a stop at the Plaza to finish a letter to Taylor, he left to meet McReynolds.

They met at a small bar near Wilson Towers. The place was filled with a typical Wednesday crowd when Stonetree arrived. He found his friend seated on a high stool near a window, a huge plant hanging directly over his head.

"I think you ought to get a hat like that," Stonetree said as he sat down across from him, pointing to it. "You look great."

"I've *got* a hat like this." He smiled. "I'd like to get into ivy next time. Something a little more informal. How's it going? Still got a job?"

"Yeah. Like I told you on the phone, Security did their report and that was it. And it really was apple juice. Did you get anything out of the doctor yet? I'm curious, real curious, to know what's going on in this little chess game."

McReynolds stopped a waitress and ordered another Bombay dry for himself and a Chivas on the rocks for his guest.

"Finally," he answered. "I finally got him to explain it to me. Had a long chat with him last night after I talked to you. He's back in Georgia. He'll be back here tomorrow."

"What's he doing down there? Did he have to go home?"

"Not to where he's been working. That's in Atlanta. He's got this other place down in Tiff County, where he goes to think."

"Tiff County? Where's that?"

"It's down in the southern part of the state. Maybe a couple of hours west of Savannah."

"Where's Savannah?"

"In the southern part of the state. Anyway, he takes a shuttle to an airport near his place, or sometimes he drives."

"How far?"

"A couple of hundred miles from Atlanta. It's worth it, though. I was down there with him once when I was doing research for the article."

"Oh, yeah? What's it like?"

"It's a rural area. His place is in between these two little towns, TyTy and Tifton."

"That sounds like a magic act or something," Stonetree said.

"It does," McReynolds agreed. "It's so quiet down there. Lots of those old mobile home trailers that look like small silver

· SIXERS ·   169 blimps. Like if you were in one for an hour in the sun you'd be dead."

"Oh, I remember those. Like a big hot-dog stand."

"Right. And there are lots of recreational places, lots of pecan stores, places that sell arrowheads, shit like that. Two kinds of women—real ugly or gorgeous enough to stop time in its tracks. I met this one, in a bar, her name was Donna Sue or Cindy Lou or something. I was in love instantly. She's about twenty-three and a cross between a country music singer, Miss Teenage America, the woman who taught me in third grade, and a hooker. I almost didn't come back."

"So what happened?" Stonetree asked.

"Nothing. Not after I bought her a couple of drinks and a guy in the bathroom told me she was married to a dude on the police force. No, thank you. Good-bye."

"You're not as stupid as people tell me you are," Stonetree said, shaking his head. "So, tell me about the place. The phone call."

"The place," McReynolds began, "is great. It's perfect. It's a two-bedroom one-story log cabin out on this pond in a wooded area. Farmish-looking except for this massive black dish antenna he's got up on the roof. It has to be twenty feet wide. He cannot be away from the Atlanta Braves during the baseball season or CNN Headline News anytime. He'll watch the same broadcast four, five times in a row. He's an information freak." He paused. "The inside is beautiful. A big, open living-dining room. Small kitchen. Nice den. Nice bedrooms. Two baths. The best of everything. He must have put a lot of money into it. So that's where he is. Thinking."

"So what did he say?"

"Well, first of all, he said he tried to get ahold of you at home a few times, but no answer. He won't call you at SUE. He's a little paranoid about that. He told me to tell you he'd tried. I told him I was going to see you today, so he gave me the story."

"Where did he get my phone number?"

"I gave it to him," McReynolds replied. "You're not listed, remember? Now, do you want to hear the story?"

"Shoot."

"Remember the CY6A4, the liquid gold he dumped down the drain, that stuff they made from the blood drives?"

"Sure. We talked about that."

"Right," McReynolds agreed. "The stuff is priceless."

"That's the impression I got from Trisha, from Lane. That really pissed Ruth off when the stuff got dumped."

"Well, it didn't."

"Didn't what?" Stonetree asked.

"It didn't get dumped. It's still there."

"The CY6A4? The four pints? It's still at SUE?"

"You got it. Still there, waiting for the dear doctor's triumphant return."

"But how?" Stonetree asked, amazed at what he was hearing. "Did he set the fire?"

"No. He said the fire really *was* an accident," McReynolds continued. "But he'd been thinking around then that he was about to get the boot and decided if he did, he wanted to make sure he got out with some of it so he could finish off his experiments. So he stashed some of it, but they threw his ass out before he could get to it."

"No shit."

"No shit, old stick. It's true."

"So why has he waited till now? Why couldn't he get somebody to smuggle it out before?"

"I'm not sure," McReynolds said, scratching his head. "I think it has something to do with his contract. If they knew what he'd done, I doubt if he would have continued getting his welfare checks."

"Well, that money they sent him is literally a drop in the bucket compared to what CY6A4 is worth. I don't like it. He could find himself in big trouble for this. Big trouble. That stuff would be priceless! You couldn't buy it for an armored car full of twenties!"

"I think he realizes that. I think he knows he might be facing some hard time in prison. He got religion after Friday."

Religion, Stonetree thought, the blood draining out of his face. Religion? He'd tried to steal. Oh, my God, that stuff's worth millions, maybe hundreds of millions. You could buy the "Mona Lisa" and then the Taj Mahal to hang it in. *Thank you, Lord, for not letting me get caught. I promise I will never, ever, the rest of my life do anything dishonest. I'll return those other Bradshaw-4's, and the albums I copped from K mart in eighth grade. I'll do anything. Thank you.*

"So what's with the apple juice?" he asked, hoping he wouldn't pass out.

"He told me he had a feeling they were going to be on the lookout for him over there, especially since he got everything due him per his contract. He figured, and I can see why he wouldn't even tell us about it, that maybe he should try a dress rehearsal of his CY6A4 recovery operation before the real thing. Also, if he was caught on the dry run, nobody would be in trouble, at least not with the law."

"That makes sense. I've got, well, I've got a small problem with it," Stonetree said hesitantly. "I would have liked to have known all this before. . . ." His heart was beginning to slow down, the light-headedness receding.

"Sure you would," McReynolds agreed. "So would I. But he probably—and I understand this too—wanted to check us out. It makes sense when you think about it."

"Yeah. I agree. He's no fool." *But I am, and a pretty big one at that.*

"So what he did was just put these eight flasks in the briefcase to see what would happen. He left the real thing where it was."

"Did you see it?" His heart hadn't exploded, the vessels in his brain hadn't burst. *Thank you, God. I promise, never again.*

"No. I was at the elevator. He wasn't gonna show me, not on the run-through. He's smart."

"And a good judge of your character." Stonetree laughed. *It's okay. I'm okay. No problem. You are* not *going to die.*

"Yours too," McReynolds retorted. "The doctor, I think, trusts you because he thinks you're not bright enough to lie very well."

"I can do it if I try," Stonetree replied softly. "So what now?"

"Well, he isn't going to do a repeat of Friday. He thinks it was just normal, getting stopped, but he won't do it again."

"So how does he get his notes?"

"I'm not sure," he replied. "I think maybe the dreams of the big story might have to be put on the shelf for a while, maybe for good. He won't do it again. He has too much to lose."

"Then why doesn't he just get somebody to go in there and bring it out for him?" Stonetree asked. *Not me, though. Never again. Never, ever again.*

"I really do not think," McReynolds said, leaning forward and lowering his voice, "that he will trust anybody to do it.

He took a stab at it, and that's it. He doesn't want to get into a serious game of hardball with Ruth or Trisha or anybody else over there. He's just not up for it."

"Well, then," Stonetree suggested, "why doesn't he just call up Lane or Ruth or the board and say, 'Hi! It's me. I've got four prints of CY6A4 and I'll trade it for my college notebooks'?"

"I asked him that. He said if he did, the first thing they would do would be to close off the whole Research and Development Department and dismantle it down to the steel girders until they found it. That makes sense too."

"You're right. Man, this is complicated. You ought to write a book about this." He paused. "But don't put my name in it, okay?"

"I'm trying to write, asshole. But as of last night, I've got only the first few chapters. And do not, I repeat, do not discuss this with anybody else. Even if we don't get to hit the jackpot on this, I do not want to screw this guy in any way. He took us into his confidence. We tried, we failed. I've got a feeling if sweet SUE found out about it, there would be big, big trouble. People would get hurt—maybe even us."

Discuss it with anybody, Stonetree thought. *Discuss it with anybody? If they suspended the first-degree murder laws for one minute, I'd ring your fucking—oops!—sorry, God. I'd ring your neck until you turned navy blue, Robin.*

"I won't tell anybody," Stonetree agreed. "This is a little too, uh, serious. You know what I mean? I thought losing a couple thousand in Las Vegas was serious. It isn't. This is."

"We might have to go down with the *Titanic* on this one. Big orchestra. 'Nearer My God to Thee.' The end. Good night."

"Are you sure he won't approach them? It's such a waste. I mean, if he's onto the cure." *Let* him *approach them. Not me. Never, ever, ever again. I promise.*

"That's what he wanted to do the serious thinking about. He wants to go over his notes and walk through all of his theories. He thinks maybe he can finish it off without his old research. It'll just take a lot longer. He's even thinking about signing on with someone else if he absolutely has to. But he doesn't want to go through it with SUE again."

"I guess." *Thank God.*

"It's funny," McReynolds continued. "When I was talking to

him, we got onto the Pierre Ruth issue. I didn't notice it so much before when I talked to the doctor, but last night I could really sense some pain, some hurt he still has over it. Like he was betrayed, sold out by his big brother, for your pal Trisha."

"Maybe he was." *I'm sure the guys who did the Great Train Robbery felt bad too.*

"I tried to keep an open mind about it and, to tell you the truth, I went into this thing taking the party line, believing that he essentially got what he bargained for. He's a big boy; he was on a level playing field. But it really is bigger than that. It's bigger than him or Ruth or SUE. It's bigger."

Stonetree looked at him quizzically. "What are you talking about? You're starting to ramble."

"Yeah, I'm sorry." McReynolds sighed, rubbing his eyes. "I'm exhausted. This whole thing has really got me down. It seemed so easy just a few days ago. I almost wish I hadn't gotten involved at all." He paused. "I suppose it's too late, though. I get maybe the biggest story in the history of science and I've got to keep it to myself. You cannot *imagine* how that feels. I know there are bigger issues here than my shot at a Pulitzer Prize. But, man, this hurts."

"It would have been a good story." *And maybe ten to twenty at a maximum security prison.*

"And the fame," McReynolds moaned, slapping his forehead. "The fame. When we were coming down the elevator, I could taste it. I could feel it in my pocket."

"Maybe we'll get a consolation prize." *Probation. I'd take probation. A hundred years of it.*

"Yeah. Sure. I'll give *you* a consolation prize."

"So what do we do now?" Stonetree asked. "Is there anything we should do?"

And then Sharon's face sparkled through his mind like the glint from the blade of a double-edged knife. In a few months she might be facing Class A roulette. She might get off with a warning, she might face the heavy fine. *Dear God, Mom, anyone who's up there listening. Please don't make me change my mind. Or if you do, make it work out for her. Somehow. Some way. Give me a signal. Somebody. Please.*

"I guess we just wait to see what Camden does. If he bags it, he bags it. That's it. You want to go have something to eat? I'm starving."

"No, thanks," Stonetree replied. "I've got some errands to run. Maybe after we hear from Camden."

"Okay, let's do it."

"But I'm glad we got together. This all makes a lot more sense now. I feel a lot better. I can relax a little, thank God. Both of us."

They finished their drinks, discussing the *Fortune* article. Then Stonetree got up to leave, shaking McReynolds's hand and apologizing for his friend's disappointment. And, in a way, apologizing for his own. If only it had all fallen into place like a train wreck run backward on a VCR. The dream of the big break, the easy way out, was gone. At least, he thought, if he'd lost out on one adventure, he had another waiting for him just a few blocks away. Just one more night, a few more hours, and he would straighten himself out, straighten his life out.

"So what are you doing tonight?" he asked McReynolds as they walked out of the bar. "A hot date, maybe?"

"No. I'll probably go back home and sleep. I'm really exhausted." He paused. "Maybe there *is* some rest for the wicked." He chuckled.

"Let me give you a ride," Stonetree replied. "I'm going that way."

He had to contain his laughter when McReynolds got out of the car and said good-bye. Stonetree wanted to get out, too, to protect the single parking space he'd found on the street. Protocol, however, required him to drive around the block a few times first and wait a little longer for the final scene of his nomad life.

CHAPTER 11

WHEN THE ELEVATOR DOORS OPENED ON TRISHA'S FLOOR, IT was obvious to Stonetree that all levels of Wilson Towers were not equal. The higher one went, the finer the appointments. Instead of the small love seat and coffee table on McReynolds's floor, the furniture in the second-from-the-top foyer was luxurious. There were Oriental rugs, couches, chairs, and tables. Two large lithographs accented the walls. Instead of numbers and arrows indicating which way to go, there was a brass plaque instructing him he would find "Lane" to his right. The guard in the lobby had told him he was expected.

He pushed the buzzer and heard her call out that she would be there in a minute. He heard the muffled sounds that always seem to accompany such a greeting. In a moment she opened the door. It was Trisha, but a different Trisha.

Her hair was fuller, even a bit disheveled. She was wearing more makeup than usual, especially on her eyes and cheeks. It conveyed a smoldering sensuality he imagined but had never seen. It was a perfect setting for her smile, decorated in deep red lipstick.

She was again wearing the necklace Smite had given her. Her black top was low cut, open, and blousy in marked contrast to the black skirt, which she must have poured herself into prior to his arrival. A thin red leather belt with two or three buckles, wrapped three or four times around, hung casually on her narrow waist and hips. Her black pumps complemented her perfect legs. She looked terrific for thirty-three, he told her, or, for that matter, any age. She leaned forward and kissed him lightly on the cheek, then methodically patted away the brand she'd left.

"That's sweet of you to say," she said as she closed the door behind him. "I've been preoccupied with this thirty-three thing most of the day. It's kind of exciting. I'm so glad you could come over." Her voice was softer than usual.

He handed her his two offerings.

"Oh, for me? How nice of you," she said, kissing his cheek again. "This one feels like wine," she said as she weighed the larger box. "I won't guess at the other. Let's save it for later, okay?"

Stonetree nodded and followed her into the kitchen, watching the shimmering fabric of her skirt cling tightly against her thighs.

"Can I get you a drink?" she asked as she set the packages on the large kitchen island. "I'm having scotch. This is number two for me already. But I figure," she said, flipping her hand into the air, "why not? We turn thirty-three only once, right?"

"Thank God."

"What did you do on your thirty-third?"

Stonetree thought for a moment. "It was a Saturday, a rainy Saturday. I stayed home, read, watched TV, ordered a pizza, cleaned out my closet, and went to bed." He shrugged.

"Now, I would have thought you would have gone out to celebrate, David," she replied, a touch of disappointment in her voice. "You just seem more earthy than that."

"Earthy?"

"Yes, earthy. You seem to like sensual things. You like wine, and I know you love music. Which reminds me. I've got a surprise for you later."

"For me? What?"

He pictured her reclining on the island. No, on a beach. In a black bikini. She'd have a half-drunk piña colada in one hand, with a small green umbrella poking out of it. It would be late afternoon, a sweet breeze drifting around them. The palms would rustle, the beginnings of a nap calling her away from her blanket. With her other hand she'd reach toward him, touching his elbow, distracting him from his book. She'd sigh, "Let's go back to the room."

"You'll see. Be patient. So let's get you a drink and I'll give you a tour of SUE *casa*."

"*Su casa?*" he asked. "Don't you mean *mi casa?*" The beach would be on the Pacific coast of Mexico. Hours from Guadalajara.

"No. SUE *casa*. Like 'the house of Southern United Enterprises.' They paid for the place."

He looked at her, perplexed. He blinked his eyes.

"I mean, they didn't buy it for me," she said with a laugh, "but they pay me enough so I could buy it. I'm a good girl, saved up my nickels and dimes. What would you like to drink?"

"Scotch would be fine. On the rocks, please."

"Let's see," she said, slowly tapping the side of her head with her finger. "We've got Chivas Regal, Johnnie Walker Black, Pinch, uh, some Cutty Sark if you have some nail polish that needs removing, and a bottle of some exotic limited-edition, only-five-hundred-bottles-made concoction. It's something special. Why not try some of that?"

"Fine. That sounds great."

He followed her out of the kitchen into another room that could be described only as magnificent. It was rectangular in shape, maybe thirty feet by fifty feet. The ceilings were higher than he was used to, and two entire walls were nothing but glass. These floor-to-ceiling windows afforded a panoramic view of the city to the west and south. The room was bathed in the glow of a lazy orange sun hovering above the skyline.

At the near end was a long, narrow Scandinavian-looking teak table with tiles in the center and seating for eight. The places at either end were set. Two candles were lit, flickering over a bowl of fresh flowers. A small bar sat in the corner. There was nothing along the longer glass wall save two back-to-back oversize love seats with matching tables. One faced the glow, and the other faced the large entertainment center on the inside wall. At the far end was a more traditional grouping of chairs, bookcases, and shelves. Rugs of different sizes covered about half the oak floor, and soothing nondescript abstract paintings were spaced perfectly on the walls.

"This is beautiful," Stonetree gasped. "What a view!"

"It is, isn't it?" she agreed. "Sunset is my favorite, but at night it's pretty too. There was supposed to be a formal dining room and a living room, but I decided to have just one large open space. I think it works."

She reached to the shelf behind the bar and grasped a small mahogany case. She opened the top and removed a thick crystal bottle.

"Doug Smite sent this to me the day the fourth or fifth single went Top Ten off the first album. I notice you have your Crypto on tonight, a very nice touch." She smiled. "Is this to be an all-SUE night?"

"No," Stonetree replied, starting to unpin the Crypto. "No Wexford."

"I didn't mean you had to take it off," she said. "Just no SUE. And I didn't say no Wexford. There's always room for Wexford." She laughed, a sound the symphony could never duplicate.

She dropped some cracked ice into a glass that looked to match the bottle, and handed it to him.

"Anyway," she continued, "he sent me this. He knew I liked scotch. It comes with a handwritten letter from the distillery that made it. Let's see," she said, pulling a document from the box. "Um, it was aged for twenty-four years in Scotland. There were only five hundred fifty-four bottles produced. Each of the bottles was handblown in Waterford, Ireland. Each of the boxes was crafted in Austria. The pedigree of the scotch is blah, blah, blah. Each of the bottles is numbered. The royal family got numbers one through forty-eight. This particular bottle is number one sixty-nine." She looked back at him. "Try it." He did.

"This is definitely good scotch." He nodded approvingly.

"It should be. I was at a restaurant one night, and they happened to have purchased two bottles of it. And for only sixty dollars a shot, you could have all you wanted."

Stonetree's free hand involuntarily rose to cup his other. "Sixty dollars?" he wheezed. He looked into the kitchen at the two silver boxes on the table. Maybe, he thought, he should have gone an extra few yards.

"Oh, that reminds me," he said, taking another sip of the potion. "The woman at the wine store told me she thought the wine should be decanted about an hour before serving. . . ."

"And you would like a funnel and something to decant it into," she stated.

"You read my mind. Have anything?"

"I'm getting better as a mind reader," she said, pulling open the doors of the cabinet behind the bar. "Will this do?" she asked as she handed him a cut-glass carafe and a matching funnel.

"Great. And a corkscrew, please."

He walked to the kitchen and retrieved the wine. He returned to find her leaning against the dining table in the same posture she used at the office.

"You know," he said, handing her the box, "you lean against the front of your desk just like that. You did that on Monday."

"Someone else told me that once," she said, opening the gift. "Oh, how nice. Stags Leap. And seventy-nine. Very good. This is perfect. Thank you very much." Kiss three.

"And that's three kisses now," he said, summoning all the objectivity he could. "Which is three more than I had before I walked in. I must be doing something right."

"You are," she purred. "This will be a very special evening." She placed her hand on the upper part of his arm and squeezed lightly. "I'm really glad you came over. I've been looking forward to tonight all day." She looked at the bottle again. "This is so thoughtful." She gazed back at him. "Why don't you decant it, and we can relax for a while."

He pulled the cork and poured the wine gently, practically tipping the funnel to the level of the bottle. He doubted if there was any sediment in it, but it sure did look professional. She watched him, leaning against the side of the love seat, facing the city, in what Stonetree christened "Trisha pose one."

After finishing the transfer, he fussed over whether to replace the large silver top of the carafe. After twice on and twice off, he left it off and set the vessel on the table. He picked up his scotch, and with the addition of a bit more ice, joined her.

"I'm delighted with the wine," she said with a touch of whimsy in her voice. "You saved me from a monumental decision. If you didn't bring it, I was going to invade another treasure Doug sent me. It was just after *Life* eclipsed the competition. Chateau Margaux 1903, if I recall." She paused, taking a sip of her drink. "Plundered from the *Titanic*." She paused again. "Maybe another night."

Stonetree went blank. He could buy his Mustang with what that one bottle was worth, he finally concluded.

She asked if he wanted to listen to anything in particular. He replied, "Anything you'd like, except Peggy Quinlan's new album."

"What a disappointment, that record," she said. "Oops! No business talk. How about some Mozart? That's good sunset music."

He nodded and watched as she bent over to pull a few discs from the lower shelf of the electronics hutch, her knees not bending an inch. "How about the sound track from the movie they did about him? It has one of my favorites. I believe it's called 'Piano Concerto Number Twenty in D Minor.' They played it over the credits. I love it."

"Fine."

She placed the disc in one of the two players, pushed, flicked, or turned about twelve switches and knobs, and sat down next to him just as the music began. It was soothing, gentle, and even though his classical knowledge was light, recognizable Mozart.

They watched the sun begin to set and the city lights wake to the approaching dusk, one by one. They talked about music and about whether a movie about Wexford would be made in two hundred years and would use his middle name as a title. They decided that Edward, as in Donald Edward Redal, could lead to some confusion among theatergoers, and that Donald or Redal would not be of much use either. They talked about the *Fortune* article, agreeing they both received calls from well-wishers, Stonetree mentioning that someone even asked for an autograph. He told her an abridged version of the Mustang story.

"It's getting a little dark in here," she said, standing up. "Come with me. I'll light the place up and give you the tour."

The rest of the condominium contained two and a half baths, a spacious guest bedroom, and a smaller room with nothing in it. There was a den, which was not as immaculate as her office. Some gold and platinum records and various awards lay unhung in a corner, books, magazines, and reports

182　　· JOHN PATRICK KAVANAGH ·

cluttering the desk and furniture. There was a large utility room and an equally large storage area that could actually be considered yet another room.

And then there was the master bedroom suite. It contained a sitting room, a third full bathroom, and a commodious main room. Everything in it—the bedspread, the rugs, the wallpaper, the furniture, the lights—was either black, white, or gray. Her bed was no exception—a sleek black lacquered affair sitting against the far wall.

"Colorful, cheery place," Stonetree said deadpan.

"It is on the stark side," she replied, "but I like it. Everything else in the place is an earth tone. I wanted something a little different in here."

On the side wall was a painting, perhaps three feet by five feet. Deep gray lines slashed over a light gray background. He didn't need to see a signature this time. He'd seen a similar one at the National Gallery in Washington. It was Jasper Johns, probably from the early eighties.

He walked to the far wall to examine another painting. It was also rectangular, perhaps four feet high, maybe thirty inches wide. A light pink flame rose from its base and spread across the gray wash, reminiscent of O'Keeffe's metaphors. The upper half was dominated by a penciled circle and arrow, forming the universal sign for man. The three points of the arrow were accented by three ragged holes in the canvas. There were an equal number of long brass shell casings following in their wake, a trio of vindicators off on a search-and-destroy mission.

The lower half was dominated by another penciled circle and cross, forming the universal sign for woman. The three lower points of the cross were accented by three smaller holes in the canvas. There were an equal number of shorter silver shell casings nuzzled into the tip of the flame, awaiting the arrival of the vindicators.

At the top of the painting, in three-inch block letters, was stenciled the phrase COMBAT ART. At the bottom of the painting, also in three-inch block letters, was stenciled the phrase COMBAT SEX.

If these pictures were what he thought they were, he figured he was standing in between thirty to forty million dollars' worth of art.

He turned back toward the first painting and pointed at it. "This is Jasper Johns?" he asked.

"Yes." She smiled.

"I saw one similar to it once, at—"

"The National Gallery in D.C.?" she interrupted.

He nodded.

"I've seen it too. They were executed the same year, probably the same time, or, at least, around the same time. I would expect Mr. Johns, like our boy, works on a number of pieces simultaneously. Great artists have that capacity." She paused. "They don't view the world in the linear way most of us are confined to."

"Where—where did you get it?" Before she could answer, he added, "Did you buy it?"

"A little out of my price range," Trisha replied. "At least when I received it."

"Received it?"

"It was a gift," she continued. "A rather extravagant gift, but a gift nonetheless."

Stonetree took a sip of his scotch, stared at the painting a moment, then took another sip.

"May I ask from whom?"

"A secret admirer," she whispered, and motioned with her hand that he shouldn't pursue the issue further.

He returned his gaze to the smaller piece.

"This is a Lionne-Demilunes?" he asked.

"Pre-trademark." She walked to the painting and, touching its frame, adjusted it a bit.

"How long have you had it?"

"It's been five or six years now. I was flying back from Minneapolis, and I was sitting next to this guy. He owned an art gallery."

"Here? Go on."

"So we got to talking," she said, "and he gives me this line about how he thought I should drop in sometime to see some paintings."

"Go on."

"So a few weeks later I've got a couple hours to kill and I remember his offer, so I stop by the gallery. As it turns out, he just received sixteen paintings by this new artist. . . ."

"You've got to be kidding," Stonetree marveled, recalling her first meeting with Wexford.

"True story," she replied, adjusting the painting again. "So I'm waiting for a cab, and he starts hanging them and I see this one and I say 'Wrap it up, it's going with me.'"

"You're kidding, aren't you?"

"Nope." She turned and began to walk toward the door. "He even tossed in this little packet of photographs, a dimestore album of the photographs of the paintings that Jean sent him when he was trying to find a gallery to carry his work."

"I don't even want to know what it cost," he said, following her out of the room.

"Then I won't tell you," she replied, not breaking stride.

Stonetree stopped. She continued her leisurely pace toward the windows. "But you'd tell me if I *did* want to know?"

She hesitated, then slowly turned to face him. She took two steps forward, then paused again.

"Back then," she said, "it cost about what I made every couple of weeks. It could have been what I made in three months, but I would have bought it anyway. I just had the feeling. I knew it was right."

"And now?"

"And now?" she replied, raising her hand to the opposite shoulder. "When I was negotiating the purchase of SUE *casa*, I went out for lunch with Rae Wilson, the woman who built the Towers. Somewhere during the conversation, about lighting I think, it came up." She raised her other hand to the other shoulder. "She offered me the east penthouse in exchange for it."

"You didn't take it?" Stonetree asked.

"You're not in the east penthouse, David."

He looked around the room, then back at the painting. *Yes, she was right. We are not in the east penthouse. And*, he mused, *we're not in Kansas anymore, Toto.*

"And then," Trisha said, "the guy with the gallery calls me up a year later. He calls me up and says Jean has put together his first portfolio of photographs, fifty sets of ten impressions, eleven-by-fourteen black and whites, and he wants his first patrons to have first crack at them."

"Really?"

"So I drop down the next day, you know, at lunch. He takes me into his office in back, and there's Lionne-Demilunes munching away on a submarine sandwich, trying to figure out if he should stamp the photographs with his new fuh."

"His what?" Stonetree asked, taking another sip.

"His fuh." She placed her hands behind her neck and raised her head a bit. "It's a . . . like a rubber stamp. They use them in the Orient, like a signature. It's divided into four quadrants. Each one means something. He started to explain it to me, but I had to get back to the Plaza for a meeting."

"So what happened?"

"Well, he'd already signed and numbered all the portfolios, so I said, 'I'll take set twenty-six. Why don't you just stamp every *other* one of the photographs for me, and I'll be on my way.' "

"And?"

"Jean thought that was hilarious, so he put *two* stamps of the old fuh on five of mine and left the other five of them blank." She paused, raising her head a bit more. "Only set like it in the world." She paused. "I'd show them to you, but they're in a vault."

Stonetree turned back to look at the Lionne-Demilunes, then the Johns, then back at the Lionne-Demilunes.

"That second c-o-m-b-a-t." Stonetree smiled, nodding his head. "Do you accent that on the first syllable or the second?"

"Depends on my mood," she said, and smiled back.

They sat on the love seats and talked another half hour about the insignificant and the informational. He was surprised to learn she had been engaged briefly, about a year, when she was in college. Both her parents were dead. She saw her older brother one holiday a year. She talked to a younger sister every weekend. The only sports she enjoyed were tennis and horseback riding but had not done either in years. He asked if she danced, and she replied she hadn't since high school.

She did not like pets, never had one, never wanted one, and would never change her mind. She thought learning how to pilot a helicopter would be interesting, but she doubted she'd ever have the time. Her favorite thing to do when she was frustrated was work.

If she ever left SUE or, more accurately, *when* she left SUE, she wanted to travel and consult on a part-time basis. She was losing interest in the popular music business and had asked Wallace Walker twice if he wanted to swap Technology for Entertainment. He'd declined on both occasions. Finally, she said she was getting hungry.

Most of dinner was already prepared: salads, a side dish of fettuccine primavera with snow peas and shrimp, and the main course, veal parmigiana. "With a tomato sauce handed down for generations in our family," she said as she pulled it from the oven.

After holding her chair, he poured her a glass of the wine. He set it in front of her, draping a napkin over his wrist and mumbling a nonsensical phrase in French. She sipped.

"No," she said, motioning him away. "Don't speak to me in French. Speak to me in Californian. It's all I'll listen to when I drink domestic wine."

They both laughed. He poured a glass for himself and sat down at the opposite end of the table.

"This is exceptional, David," she said, setting her glass down and applauding lightly. "Great choice. I think it will go very well with the food."

"Happy birthday, Trisha," he said, lifting his glass to her. She lifted hers in response. "Wait. Before you drink, I have a toast. Let me remember it." She lifted her glass higher. "Okay, I remember," he continued. "May the sky of your life be filled with just enough clouds to form a beautiful sunset." He paused. "Pretty good, huh?"

She sipped the wine and let the rim linger at her lips. She placed it to one side and cocked her head slightly. "And?" she replied in a soft voice, "don't I even get a birthday kiss?"

He felt a sheet of flame spread through his body. *It has already reached this point*, he thought, *and most of the evening is still ahead*. He looked down the long table at her. The candlelight seemed to soften her angular features and made her look younger, more innocent than beautiful.

For a brief moment he felt the tug of his rational self. He knew involving himself in any way with Trisha would bring him nothing but trouble. He was simply not in her league, was not the type who would fit into the circles she seemed to enter and exit so easily. She might have use for him as an administrative assistant, and she might have use for him as in-home entertainment on a birthday she decided at the last minute to celebrate. But that was as far as it went. He was nothing more than another part of her collection of accoutrements, another cog in the machinery that made her life a little easier, a little less unrehearsed.

She could have pop stars, she could have chairmen of the board, she could probably, even without her position and her power, have any man she wanted if she put half a mind to it. By some quirk, by some odd set of circumstances, by some incredibly unpredictable combination of events, he now found himself no more than a nod away from the lips of a woman he lusted after since the day they met. Why had she picked *him* for the passage?

Stonetree had, like so many others, spent maybe thirty seconds, a few days a month, mesmerized as she walked through the cafeteria or passed in the hall. His was one of countless heads that slowly tracked her when she was within eyesight, her effect on them like that of a massive oscillating fan blowing through a forest of tall, thin pines.

Maybe it was only a kiss she wanted and nothing more. If he gave it to her, there would be no harm done, there would be no cause for alarm. If there was something more she wanted, it could certainly cause problems. He was always true to Sharon. He never cheated. He never wanted to, never had the desire. Well, maybe the desire but not the urge. She was the one who said "all bets are off" after her sisters died, not him. Saturday loomed in the distance but was still part of the future, not the present.

Following Trisha's lead would bring him nothing but trouble, he repeated to himself. In the end it could cost him Sharon, his job, and maybe even some dignity. To allow himself to take her cue would make him not much more than a starstruck groupie, ready to trade on himself so that for just one night he could live a fantasy about which others could only dream.

He thought all this, but very briefly.

They pushed away from their chairs, as if on a signal, and moved slowly toward each other, their eyes locked like radar. She calmly raised her arms when they met and placed her hands gently on the back of his neck. His hands rested on her waist and then, without hesitation, moved effortlessly to her hips.

She drew in a shallow breath and partially closed her eyes as their lips touched, closing them completely as her tongue began to play with his teeth, pushing at them curiously. He first felt the pressure of her chest on his, and then the rest of her body as it pressed against him, grinding closer. He could feel her smiling, a low purr of satisfaction vibrating in her throat.

"See, that wasn't so bad, was it?" she asked, taking a deep breath and licking her upper lip.

"No," he said, shaking his head slightly and releasing his grip. "And I do hope you are having a happy birthday."

"I am." She returned to her chair. "And it's not even nine yet. You don't turn into a pumpkin at midnight, do you?"

He shook his head again.

CHAPTER 12

DURING DINNER TRISHA AGAIN TOLD STONETREE SHE HAD A SURprise for him that he would genuinely enjoy. While clearing the dishes, she returned to the subject, turning it into a guessing game.

"All right," she said as she flicked off the kitchen light and walked to the bar. "You've got enough clues. You must be able to guess what it is. I think I'll have a Bailey's. Would you care for one?"

"Please," he responded. "Give me another clue."

"Tell me what you know already."

"Uh, let's see," he began. "It's very special. It's something that, knowing me, you know I'd kill for. There is only one place in the city I can get it, and that's right here." He tugged absently at the waist of his pants, shifting position, his heart trotting ahead a bit. "It's something a lot of people would die for," he continued, gazing at her as she poured the liqueur, "and you can't think of anyone who deserves it more than me. So far, so good?"

"Absolutely," she said enthusiastically, passing him a glass and taking him by the hand. "And if you will just follow me to one of the love seats, which is the best place in the room to enjoy this little treat, I'm sure it will all become clear as the proverbial bell."

She led him to the couch facing the inside wall of the room, walked to the entertainment center, and leaned against it, facing him.

"You really haven't guessed?" she asked, giving him what could be described only as a seductive smile.

"No. I need a few more clues."

"I'll give you three."

"What color is it?"

"Black, black with red trim," she replied as she latched her thumb around one of the lengths of her belt. "That's one."

"You said I could get it only here," he began. "Will that always be the case? Is this the only place I'll ever be able to get it?"

"Well," she said thoughtfully, "the first time is always special. But in, oh, I'd say less than six months you'll probably be able to get it anywhere you want. Not like tonight, but a reasonable facsimile. It won't be exactly the same as it is tonight, but it could get even better."

The drinks are starting to get to me, he thought. He could not believe it was real, that she was standing there and telling him in a roundabout way he was about to be taken to paradise. His eyes shifted slightly, away from hers.

"Isn't that the necklace Doug Smite gave you?" he asked, not looking back at her.

"Yes, it is." She smiled. "Is that your third and final question?"

"No," he replied, wanting to up the stakes a bit. "Can I hold it in my hand?" he asked, setting his drink down and positioning himself to stand up.

"Only if you promise to put it back in the tape deck when you're done with it." She laughed.

The words seemed to dart over his head and bounce off the window behind him. *Put it back in the tape deck*, he thought. *Is that really what she said? Did I only imagine it? Am I drunk? I know I'm kind of high—I feel good, but I'm not drunk. I don't feel* drunk. He wished he had a cigarette.

"Uh, could you repeat that?" he asked, squinting a little and retrieving his Bailey's.

"I said," she replied, holding up her hands as if to balance her words, "you can hold it if you promise to put it back in the tape deck. Now, if that isn't the best clue in the world, I don't know what is."

He was baffled. He was disappointed. He wanted to leave. Was he that dense? Did he really think, and this was before starting on the wine at dinner, that for one moment she was interested in anything more from him than a pleasant evening's companionship? More than two colleagues celebrating one's birthday? Was he so fatigued he was seeing things that weren't really there? Did he actually believe the primary purpose for going to her apartment was for her to celebrate the passage by taunting him till his eyes popped out?

"I'm lost, Trisha," he said, sinking into the cushions. "I have no idea what you're talking about. I give up."

She reached up to one of the components and gingerly picked out a tape with a red label.

"Do you know what this is?" she asked, holding it toward him.

"A cassette," he responded.

"Any cassette?"

He looked at it closer. He was relaxing again. There was no reason to be disappointed because he never really expected anything anyway. Well, maybe for a while he did, but that was just the liquor thinking.

"I'm not sure. I can't read the label from here. I can't read the writing."

"Enough suspense," she said, walking to join him. "Take a look, and then take a guess." She handed him the tape.

He studied one side. In black block letters he read the titles—"No Reply," "I Know There's Something Going On," and "Heaven." On the reverse side were three more titles— "She Couldn't Take Her Eyes Off Me," "Take Me Away," and "True Blood Brothers." "No Reply" seemed to ring a bell. The other five titles drew only blanks.

"What do you think?" she asked restlessly. "Tell me what you think."

"I think cassettes are a little on the primitive side for a system like yours."

"Not this one," she said. "But my friend Doug was thoughtful enough to add an anticopy squeal that almost blew out the right channel. Paranoid hillbilly. But what do you think?"

"I don't know." He heard her words but could not make a connection.

"Do any of the titles sound familiar? A couple should."

"Well," he began, returning the tape to her. " 'No Reply' sounds familiar. Wasn't that a John Lennon song, a Beatles song?"

She nodded excitedly.

"And the 'Something Going On' song," he continued. "That was done by some Swedish group, I think. Wasn't it . . ." He hesitated. "Wasn't it the song that Wexford . . ." He searched his memory, trying to make the connection. "The song has something to do with Wexford. Something about his divorce?" He paused. "The English guy, the little one who plays drums, uh, Collins. He wrote it. He recorded it a few years ago."

She nodded again.

"I just can't place it, though."

"Sure you can."

He thought for another moment. Then it hit him.

"Now I've got it," he said enthusiastically. " 'I Know There's Something Going On.' Wexford played that for the encore at the Pittsburgh concert. Everyone said he was trying to get at his wife, to let her know in public that he knew—"

"She was having fourteen or fifteen affairs," Trisha finished for him.

"Yeah. He was just finishing up the song when the kid threw the hand grenades. How could I forget that? Is this a recording from the concert? With the explosions?"

"Better."

"That's all I can think of. He did it only that one night. He's never recorded it."

"Not until now."

His eyes widened. "Do you mean," Stonetree began, thinking that maybe he really *was* about to receive a special surprise, "that you have a recording of him covering a song written by someone else?"

"Uh-huh."

"That he recorded in a studio?"

"Uh-huh."

"I *don't* believe it," he said, hoping he was wrong. "You have a tape of Wexford doing somebody else's music in a studio? He *never* covers other people's songs. Never."

"Not until now, David," she said in a teasing tone. "But you are about to experience firsthand that sometimes even our boy is capable of breaking his own rules. And not only has he recorded *one* song written by someone else," she continued, carefully handing the cassette back to him, "but he has recorded *three*."

194   · JOHN PATRICK KAVANAGH ·

He couldn't believe it. He was holding history in his hands. He felt them tremble a bit.

"And in addition," she purred, looking at him and then at the tape, "he has recorded three new songs." She looked up at the ceiling as if to offer a silent prayer. "If they are any indication of what's to follow, they will not only satisfy the critics and the public that 'Marking Time' was just a minor lapse, but will also launch a third Search for Survival drive with a vengeance."

"These are the new songs, the ones you mentioned to me before the interview?"

"In your very hands. And only one person outside of Jackson Hole, Wyoming, has heard them, and you are sitting next to her."

"Where did the tape come from?"

"Our friend, Mr. Smite, had it expressed to me this morning. I've already listened to it a dozen times today. I could have listened to it a hundred," she added. "Interested in hearing what our favorite star has been up to, tucked away in his castle . . ."

"Of course I am!" He laughed, his mood beginning to brighten.

". . . avoiding his adoring fans?"

She walked to the tape deck and dropped the cassette into the machine but did not switch it on.

"Evidently," she said, turning to Stonetree, "our boy has taken this whole divorce thing much harder than anyone thought. Doug told me he tried for months to put it down on paper but couldn't do it. So finally he decided he would just fire off some songs by other people. The emotion he put into them is really striking." She thought for a second and lowered her voice. "He must still be wild about that woman, despite what she did to him. Ready?"

He nodded, and she activated the machine, raising the volume of the system considerably. She sat next to him as the first two songs played. They were about lies, about betrayal, about longing for someone despite her crimes. The sense of loss in his voice was so exquisitely painful, so powerfully angry, Stonetree felt embarrassed. It was as if he were eavesdropping on another man's most private thoughts and fears.

· Sixers ·

195

As the chorus on the second song faded away, Trisha stopped the concert with a remote control.

"What do you think?" she asked.

"It's great," he replied. "It's beautiful. It's so sad, he's so angry. And he sings those lyrics as if they're his own. If I didn't know better, I'd say he composed them."

"A little sparser than he writes. Not the wordy images he likes to paint."

"True, true," Stonetree agreed. "A few less syllables than one might expect. He played the lead guitar on the second cut?"

"That's an easy one."

"Sure. I guess that was a rhetorical question. Anything else?"

"He doubled on a synthesizer on 'Something Going On.' Plays one of the acoustic guitars on 'No Reply.' Ready for more?"

They listened to the third track.

"That's a strange little song," he offered when it finished. "Where did it come from?"

"It was originally done by a group called Eurogliders," she responded. "They were from Australia, I think. Quite good. I'm not certain what became of them. With songs like that, they must be somewhere now. Maybe they changed their name."

"It's so haunting. But I don't think that one was directed at his wife, do you?"

"I'm not sure. Maybe not. But he's trying to get at something."

"When he talks about not wanting to live somewhere, do you think he's talking about Jackson Hole?"

"He lives alone there now. Must get lonely."

"Maybe it's more than that," he replied. "Maybe, I don't know, it's got almost a religious feel to it. Like he really *is* talking about heaven, like he's tired of being alive." He hesitated. "I heard he was sick. Is he?"

Trisha sighed. "Uh, from what I know, he hasn't been well."

"You wouldn't know it from the music."

"He's just not been well, David," she said, turning and looking out to the black sky. "In fact, Doug and I are going to have a face-to-face about it. Soon. Very soon." Her voice trailed off.

"When?"

"Probably Friday morning. Doug's coming into town. We've got to get a few things straightened out. He's being difficult about the new album, the next contract, if there is one."

"Is Wexford going to leave?"

"Maybe. I'm not sure. We have a lot of problems. But," she said, her voice mellowing as she walked to the hutch and turned the tape over, "we can save that for later. You *have* to hear his new songs. How about getting us a little more Bailey's?"

He did, and they met back at the love seat. She directed the system to play, and they listened to the first track.

"No question he can still rock with the best of them," Stonetree said as the song ended. "He hasn't kicked like that for a while. Great guitar work. I wonder who *that* song was about."

"Sure wasn't his *wife*," she replied. "Who do you think it is?"

"I have no idea. Somebody he wanted or wants, though."

"Didn't you catch the symbolism? About how the woman had everything she wanted? And the six rings on her fingers?"

Stonetree looked down at her hands. She wasn't wearing any rings.

"No, not *me*. It's symbolic, though. The six rings. It's obvious—she's a sixer. That's what he wants."

"Him?" Stonetree questioned. "Not Wexford. Anybody but him. He'd never write that in a lyric. He's on the other side of the coin." He thought about his statement. "Is that it? Has he got it? Is he dying from CYD?"

"No," she replied reassuringly. "No, he's not . . . dying from CYD. But that's not the point." She let out a deep breath. "But I think he is saying that some people might be more desirable than others."

"Huh? No, you don't believe that, do you? Did he tell you that?"

"No."

"Smite?"

"No," she said impatiently. "You don't have to be told that. It's there, in the song."

"I don't buy it."

"You might not buy it," she replied, an edge in her voice. "But a lot of other people will. They'll want to hear it. They'll want to think that it would be good to get this whole CYD thing out of the way, to have everything normal. Don't you agree?"

"I agree that people would like to see CYD disappear," he responded, still not understanding her insistence. "Who wouldn't? But I really think the song is, uh, not going that far. He just doesn't say it."

Her eyes searched his, showing a combination of disappointment and frustration. She bit at her lower lip.

"David," she said, a false calmness in her voice. "We may soon launch a third blood drive. The last time we did it, it was a colossal failure. We cannot let that happen again. The only thing that will make it succeed is if Wexford gets it across to those thousands of walking test tubes." Her voice began to constrict. "The time has come to help the cause again."

She stopped, obviously reconsidering her remark.

"I'm sorry," she apologized. "That was thoughtless."

"I understand. I didn't think you meant it," he replied, his old doubts raising their heads.

"They just *have* to take it seriously this time around."

She stood up and paced to the window and back, clasping her hands nervously, biting at her lip again. She sat down next to him, dropping her head onto his shoulder for a moment. He thought about putting his arm around her but didn't. She sat up and looked at him intently.

"This third blood drive is *so* important, you just cannot imagine," she said. "This will be our last chance. We'll never get to do it again. We'll never have an opportunity like this. And there are only two people who are going to make it happen or not happen, and that's me," she said as she pointed to the stereo, "and Mr. Redal. Period."

She seemed to be genuinely concerned, but he wasn't sure. He *was* sure that the evening was beginning to lose its charm, and he did not want to add to the already dissolving spell.

"Trisha, I'm sure it will be a success, believe me," he said. "I know it means a lot to you, to everyone. We'll do it."

She let out a satisfied sigh. "I know, I know. I'm just so nervous about it."

"Have a little more Bailey's."

"How about something a little better?" she replied.

"Like what?"

"Oh," she said, snapping her head and brushing back her hair, "seeing as I run Pharmaceuticals, I'm sure I might be able to find something around the house." She paused. "Samples, maybe."

He looked at her, methodically rubbing the back of his neck. There was no mistaking the reference, but he wasn't sure how he should play it. He knew she was well acquainted with the use of Febrifuge Blue for nonmedical purposes. She wasn't born yesterday. She was Class D. She'd read the reports. She was the keeper, the mistress of the elixir.

She knew that even if CYD disappeared from the face of the earth, twenty-six percent of the population would buy the drug, legally or otherwise. Did she use it herself? If he asked and she didn't, the insult might not be forgiven. If he asked and she did, he might sound presumptuous. But the chance to ice over with her was too good to pass up.

"Like what?" he replied as flatly as possible.

"Come on, David. This isn't a test. Security isn't hiding under the sofa. This won't be, what did they call it in *1984*?"

"The year?"

"No, the book," she said, touching his arm as if she wanted to see if he understood a punch line. "Thoughtcrime, that's it!" She crunched her fingers into claws and affected a snarl. "And I am the Thought Police."

He laughed. She could actually be playful.

"Like what?" he repeated, smiling and raising an eyebrow.

"Do I have to spell it for you?" she teased. "F-E-B-R-I . . ."

"F-U-G-E."

"Yes. One one zero zero."

"Eleven hundred?" he replied, a small shock rifling through his chest. "I didn't think—"

"It was available?" she asked. "It's not. Well, it's not unless you know the right people." She winked.

Stonetree didn't reply but only stared at her, looking for recognition. Was it a taunt? Maybe there really *were* Thought Police.

"I'd understand if you declined," she said earnestly. "If I were in your position, and I know what it feels like to receive"—she hesitated, searching for a word—"an unexpected suggestion from your superior. Believe me, I've had my share, both unexpected and otherwise."

He relaxed, but just a bit. She sounded sincere, one former assistant talking to a present assistant.

"But that's not what we're doing here tonight." She thought for a second. "Yeah, I've been given that line a couple times too."

"I can imagine."

"This is funny." She sighed, touching his arm again. "Talk about role reversal. All right, let's start over. We're here tonight only to . . ."

He laughed.

"Okay, I know, I know," she urged. "You're right. There's no way to say it. I give."

"I believe you," he replied. "I was even surprised you asked me over for dinner. I'd think twice before, say, inviting Elaine over for dinner. People take it wrong, no matter what your intentions."

"Did you take it wrong? I'm sorry if you did."

"Oh, no, no," he replied, shaking his head. "I knew you just wanted to share your birthday with someone. Nothing else." He hoped he was wrong.

"Good, I'm glad you understand. It's as simple as that."

His shoulders drooped a bit. At least he was getting to hear the new Wexford material.

"And maybe it's best we pass on the eleven hundred too. I'm not a serious customer, anyway," she said. "Maybe some other time."

He had blown his chance. He frowned. He'd had it but lost it.

"I'd like that," he said in a doleful tone, hoping she'd reconsider.

"You know, I am just like everyone else. People get a picture of me in their mind of the premier bitch executive. But I like to relax and enjoy myself."

She stood up and smoothed her skirt gently on the sides.

"There're a couple of good years in me before I turn into the monster they imagine me to be."

She turned and walked leisurely into her den, returning in a moment with a Bradshaw-4, setting it down on the coffee table. "Maybe later if we change our minds," she said. "Are you ready for the next song? I promise I won't go into one of my corporate spiels this time."

He nodded, and she cued the next selection.

Stonetree could not recall ever hearing a Wexford song like this. First of all, it was a ballad, a style that never seemed to suit Wexford's delivery. Secondly, there wasn't the swirl of his usual six- or eight-piece accompaniment. Instead, there was only a piano supplementing his lone voice on the first two verses. Then the addition of a bass guitar and some percussion, sounding like an afterthought when it entered at the vocal bridge. The synthesizer during the second vocal bridge initially seemed to promise a powerful ending, but all the instruments, save the piano, disappeared before the final lines. Stonetree was impressed.

"That is a number-one hit for sure," he said. "He hasn't lost the touch."

"It was beautiful, wasn't it?"

"And that's not something I associate with him. He can be romantic, but it's usually a harder type of romantic. That was a real love song. A ballad."

"It floored me," she replied.

They talked for a few moments about the song, comparing it to his earlier works and those of other artists. Stonetree still believed too much could be read into anything Wexford did, and he thought to himself that this might be just another lyric having nothing more to say than that the singer wanted someone in his life to keep him on an even keel. His former wife supposedly did just that when he was dealing with the immense personal and professional pressures generated by the unexpected, unbelievable success of "The Shortened Life."

Trisha saw more in it, however, and right now it wouldn't hurt to give her some encouragement. He sensed that the third Search for Survival drive meant much more to her than just a tactic to help Wexford's sagging career or a way to generate enough CY6A4 to propel Febrifuge research and production to new levels.

"So what's the last song?" he finally asked. " 'True Blood Brothers'? Sounds almost Indian. American Indian?"

"And wait till you hear it," she said, moving to the stereo. "The first sixteen bars or so will give you that very feel immediately. It lasts through the whole song. It's almost as if you expect to hear a kind of chanting in the background, as if the big battle is about to begin. He told me once that one of his great uncles or somebody was Cherokee." She paused. "I never believed it. Maybe it's true."

"So let's hear it."

"The best for last," she cooed. "I've saved the best for last."

CHAPTER 13

I was thinking just this morning
Of the friends I've had, I've had a few.
Some have lasted through my journeys,
But I lost some ones I thought were true.
We have all had friends and lovers
I reach in the night to hold them sometimes.
They are gone, these true blood brothers,
They'd give me their blood, and I'd give them mine.

Seems we hit the streets too early—
They worked in the factories,
I worked in the bars.
They would come to hear me singing,
We'd laugh afterward and chase after stars.
But they're gone, these true blood brothers,
I'd give everything to see them again.
Can't replace life lost so early,
Make no mistake, I'll help out my friends.

We forget that life is chances,
Some chances we might not see the dawn.
But the sunlight's now upon us
Let's give it a chance, we won't be wrong.
We must love our true blood brothers
Forget about sorrow, forget about pain.
Take our chance before tomorrow,

They loved us before, let's love them again.
They loved us before, let's love them again.
They loved us before, let's love them again.
They needed us then, let's love them today.
They needed us then, let's love them today.
They loved us before, let's love them again.
They loved us before, their time's at an end.
They loved us before, let's love them again.
They loved us before, let's love them again.
Our sisters, our brothers, let's love them today.
Our sisters, our brothers, let's love them today.
They loved us before, let's love them again.
They loved us before, their time is at hand.
They loved us before, let's love them again.
They loved us before, let's love them again.

Stonetree noticed Trisha relax as the song began, a song that did indeed sound like a chant, a tribal invocation, a call to arms, an anthem. She rocked gently to the incessant rhythm, the smile on her face growing with each line. Color filled her cheeks as the track drove relentlessly to its climactic ending.

He was stunned by the simplicity of the lyric, the seductiveness of the tune, the tremendous ease with which Wexford moved from a small tale about his early days into an apocalyptic vision of the future. A future based in large part on the generosity of the listener. Stonetree was struck with his own gullibility, with the fact he believed for more than a minute that Trisha was not in control of the situation, in control of her own fate. She didn't need any of the other songs. This one provided more than she would ever need. She had struck the mother lode.

Neither of them spoke after the final chorus faded. The apartment fell into a comfortable, almost churchlike silence, broken only by the faint, repetitive notching of the cassette winding to its end.

"So what do you think?" she finally asked. "Did you like it?"

"I was mesmerized," he replied, somehow exhausted by the onslaught of images. "I still am. It's a lot like that song they did for the food drive for, uh, Africa."

"Better."

"Much better," he agreed. "And only one person. I mean the lead vocal. No cast of celebrities. Just Wexford and his dreams."

"His dreams about stars. Isn't it wonderful?" she said, shifting toward him and propping an arm lazily on the top of the love seat. "I don't think he'll ever be able to top it. This is his masterpiece."

Stonetree thought about the concept for a moment. A masterpiece. Few people could ever claim a masterpiece. He certainly could not, and probably never would. Only a small, select circle of geniuses would ever, could ever, create something so right, so perfect.

"I really am at a loss for words," he volunteered. "It's as if I don't even want to begin to take it apart, break it down into its components."

"The music, the lyric, the arrangement," she offered quietly. "I know what you mean. You want to enjoy it but not touch it. It captures you, surrounds you."

He thought again about the difference between creating a masterpiece and only experiencing one.

"Would you like to hear it again?" she asked.

"No. I think once is enough. At least for tonight. I imagine I'll hear it a thousand times in the future. We won't be able to turn on the radio and not hear it." He paused. "I'd like to be able to remember it just the way I heard it, here, with you, before the rest of the world got hold of it."

"I know how you feel," she replied. "It's something. We are the only civilians outside his chateau, the only people outside of Jackson Hole, who have ever heard this song. Maybe we can tell our grandchildren about it someday."

"Our grape-grandchildren."

"What's that?"

"Oh, nothing. Just something a friend of mine would say."

They sat silently for another few minutes.

"But I don't get it," he finally said, turning to her. "What was your concern about the other songs? You never thought they mattered one way or another, did you?"

"Oh, I did, and I still do," she assured him. "One song, even this one, might be written off. A series of them could never be."

"You're kidding me now," he replied. "That song isn't open

to interpretation. It's as though Marketing got inside of him. It's perfect. The other ones are just icing on the cake, let alone anything else he comes up with. Did we commission this song or something?"

As soon as he said it, he regretted it.

"David," she said in her schoolteacher tone, "I could never do that—and wouldn't do that. As if he'd listen to me. No, of course not."

"I didn't—"

"It was like pulling teeth to get him to do the video last time, and that was a flop, let alone getting him to write an advertising jingle for SUE. No way on earth could I do that. I've made a lot of sales in my time, but I wouldn't even think of trying that."

"I didn't—"

"We've got enough problems with him already, let alone trying to turn him into our corporate songwriter, our poet laureate. He's crazy enough as it is. That's all I need, him thinking we are trying to control his artistic output. That would be suicide."

She seemed to realize she was getting carried away, and fanned herself with her hand to let him know she was finished.

"I was just curious to know if you had talked to him about it, that's all."

"No, I didn't," she said calmly. "I've talked to Doug about it, a possible drive, I mean. I'm sure he passed along my comments. I'm sure they discussed it somewhere along the way. Smite knows how important this is. Believe me, he knows."

"So what happens next?"

"I'm not sure," she replied thoughtfully. "It's really up in the air at this point. Smite and I have to have, as I said, a very long talk. We've got a lot of problems that have to be resolved. I think he sent me the tape as a way of getting my blood pressure up to a ridiculously high level so he can work from a position of strength. He can be a real bastard when he wants to be. I think we are about to see him raise it to an art form. He can be tough."

"But we have at least one more album coming under the contract, don't we? They have to give us that."

"Well, of course they have to give us an album," she said,

standing and stretching, her hands plowing through her hair. "But we could get ten songs from our boy singing in his bathtub, serenading the shower curtain. We have no artistic control over what he gives us. None at all. I gave that away, what we had, when we renegotiated after 'Life.' We could get," she continued, stretching again, "forty-four minutes of him snoring along with a music box, and that would satisfy his commitment. Morally it wouldn't, but try to tell that to his lawyers."

"But you made him," Stonetree protested.

"I got him started," she said, sounding genuinely humble but proud of her accomplishment. "But if it wasn't me, it would have been somebody else. You should have heard him the first night I did. I wish I had *that* on tape. He was *so* good. He just didn't know it at the time. Things have changed a lot since Philadelphia."

He nodded.

"But that's the way it has to go," she continued. "How about some background music? A little more Mozart? You look tired. Do you want to call it a night?"

He perked up immediately, widening his eyes. "No, I'm not tired. That song just took a little wind out of my sails. One more Bailey's maybe?"

"Or how about if we finish His Majesty's scotch? You go get it. I'll pull out another album."

He went to the bar and turned to watch her reach for a new disc just as she had done before. While getting some ice from the bucket, he noticed his gift still sitting in its box on the island.

He returned to the love seats, winding down along with the evening. Trisha now sat on one facing the windows. He wondered about the real reason for the invitation. He puzzled over the mixed signals, the contradictions. She was right; he was tired. There were, however, fifteen more good minutes left in him.

"You didn't tell me of your concern about the first two songs," he said as he sat next to her. "Why did you get me so worked up when you knew you had the Hope diamond?"

She looked at him mischievously.

"I was just setting you up for the kill," she replied.

"I should have figured as much," he said, taking a sip of his drink. "You're like the guy I want to buy the Mustang from. He did the same thing. Got me eating out of his hand."

"It worked, didn't it? You have to have that car now."

"I guess so."

"And maybe you can do something for me, now that I have your attention."

"Me? Like what? You had my attention as soon as I walked in tonight." Ideas, concepts, scenarios. An island.

"I know," she replied. "And you being here with me has been very, very enjoyable." She leaned toward him and gently touched her lips to his cheek. "Thank you. Again."

"So what do you need my attention for?"

"Oh, it's a work-related thing. We don't have to discuss it now. It can wait till later."

"No. Go ahead if you want. I don't mind if you don't mind."

"Could we?" she asked sincerely. "I was the one who said we wouldn't."

"Really. If you want."

"It's a little involved. You're sure you wouldn't mind?"

"No, be my guest."

Trisha pulled her legs up onto the couch and shifted toward him, her necklace dangling slightly in front of her. She ran a finger slowly around the rim of her glass, her head tilting a bit, her eyes locking onto his.

"It involves an imposition on one of your friendships," she began, her voice low and serious. "And that's not something I would ask for casually. I like to keep business and friendship separate and not get them depending or existing on or for each other. To do so is to ask for the loss of one or the other. Or both."

"I agree."

"Sometimes, though, there can be an advantage for everyone. If it's not something you'd want to do, I'd understand completely."

He nodded.

"Believe me, I would," she added.

"I'll certainly listen," he replied.

They both took a sip of their drinks.

"Your friend, McReynolds, the one who wrote the *Fortune* article?"

208   · JOHN PATRICK KAVANAGH ·

"Yes."

"Do you think maybe you could approach him regarding one of his sources, maybe, without offending him, ask him to get in touch with that person?"

"I could certainly ask. Robin would listen, anyway. I don't know if he'd agree. He's funny about things like that."

"I can imagine," she replied. "And I understand journalists and protection. I respect it."

"So what do you want me to ask him?"

"I'm certain that during the course of his research he had occasion to contact Dr. Camden."

Stonetree felt a pain in his chest, and his face began to tingle.

"Would he have said anything to you to indicate that? Do you think he talked to him?"

He took another sip of his drink and a shallow breath. "He did say that he talked to Camden along with a number of other people." •

"Do you think he has a good relationship with him? Do you think Camden would trust him?"

"Why? I'm not sure."

"The reason I would like to know is that I would like to be able to communicate with the doctor through a neutral third party, someone who is not connected to SUE, someone who would be credible to Camden. Someone the doctor would trust."

"Why?"

"If a communication went to him from SUE, or from any of us, especially me," she continued, "it would be immediately suspect. We all have our own paranoias, real and imagined, and I'm sure he would be skeptical about anything we proposed to him directly."

"Have you tried?"

"No. The matter I want to talk to him about has to be kept off the record, as they say. And I just can't, for various reasons, contact him myself."

"I could try."

"No, that would be the same as me doing it. That's why we need a third party, someone not involved with us. Not directly, anyway."

She ran her fingertip around the rim of the glass again, her eyes not shifting from his.

"I could ask Robin," Stonetree said. "I'm sure he'd listen. What did you want to talk to Camden about? I'd have to tell him that."

"It's a very sensitive matter, a very important one," she said, setting her drink between them. "Before going any further, you'd have to promise me, and I don't think I need to even ask, that this will all be held in the strictest confidence. It cannot be discussed with anyone else at any time for any reason. You agree?"

"Sure. Whatever you say. What is it?"

She picked up her drink and walked to the hutch, flicking off the Mozart and turning to an FM station. Airy jazz filled the room where a harpsichord had been. Stonetree stared out at the skyline as she began to speak from behind him.

"I have reason to believe," she said, "that the CY6A4 that supposedly was destroyed the day of the fire in Research, the day that Dr. Camden decided to leave SUE, was not, in fact, destroyed. At least not all of it."

She seated herself next to him, a troubled look on her face. "Oh?"

"I'm not certain how, or why, or when, but I believe Dr. Camden took some of the reduction with him."

"How?"

"I don't know. But I believe he did. Hickey thinks so, too, although it's only just recently that we began to take it seriously. The doctor's contractual obligations to us have terminated, and I think the time has come to find out if it's true."

"What would happen to him if it were true?"

"As far as retaliatory measures?" she asked.

"Along those lines, yes."

"Nothing," she replied. "Absolutely nothing. I have no desire to pick a fight with Dr. Camden. We have seen our way through the past two years with no problems, and I do not want any now. It goes without saying that we have caused enough distress for each other, intentional and otherwise, to last a lifetime. He is now free to go where he wants, do what he wants, and pursue his own ends. He abided by our agreement, better than I thought he would, and I'll be the first to wish him luck in his future endeavors."

"Even if he stole it?"

"That's old news. I'm interested in the future, not the past.

210   · JOHN PATRICK KAVANAGH ·

We all make mistakes. You have, I have, we all have. I just want to move on."

"Why do you want it if he's got it?"

"It's ours. We need it."

"But assuming he doesn't have it, those new songs and a third Search drive would get us all we wanted, wouldn't it?"

She thought for a minute, then passed her glass to him.

"David, why don't you get us just a little more? Do you have a few minutes?"

"Sure." He went to the bar and poured the scotch, and then just a bit more into each glass, methodically adding two ice cubes to each. This was perfect, he thought, just like "True Blood Brothers." Here Trisha was asking for the impossible, and he could provide it effortlessly, establishing himself in her eyes as a trusted, talented colleague. He could get Robin an inside track on anything that came of the union, and possibly, just possibly, get Camden the papers he so desperately needed.

No prison, no probation, just the accolades of Trisha, his new confidante. There would be other dinners, other soirees, him sitting to her right hand, sharing her secrets, her asides.

Despite the lateness of the hour and a familiar fogginess descending on his mind, he returned to his hostess with a slight swagger, an air of confidence. He wasn't so tired. The big chance had arrived. Not the one he entertained at the beginning of the evening, but one he was nonetheless happy to take.

"I think I could set something up," he stated, handing the glass to her.

"You could?" she asked, sounding relieved and pleased. "Do you think you really could? You don't know how much it would mean."

"But I'd have to know a little more."

"For instance?"

"Well, if Dr. Camden has the CY6A4, why would he suddenly want to give it to us?" He emphasized "us."

"Oh, that's easy," she replied. "Ever since he quit, SUE has been in possession of a body of research he left behind. We own it, under his contract, but it's really of no use to us. Hickey has been through it a couple of times. These notebooks he left behind, they're all indecipherable meanderings. It's like

Greek to everyone. Dr. Camden has a peculiar style of writing. It looks like Arabic. No one can make head or tail of it. But I'm sure he can, and I'm certain he'd like to have them back. He's welcome to them—if we get something in return."

"The CY6A4?"

"Precisely."

"But what about the next blood drive? That won't do it?"

"It should if it works," she replied. "But that's a long way off. Maybe six months to a year. We need it now."

"That long?"

"That long. We need it now. Tomorrow. Yesterday."

"More research?"

"In a way. We need the raw product."

"I don't understand," he said, puzzled at the course of the conversation. He wondered if he was missing something or getting confused. Maybe the scotch was finding its mark.

"It cannot leave this room, David," she cautioned. "No one—not McReynolds, not Camden—finds out why we want it. We agree?"

He stared at her. It was a question of honor. A matter of confidence.

"Yes. We agree."

"During the past six months or so, a number of tests have been conducted by Dr. Hickey on variations of the Febrifuge formula, some of them involving the actual use of CY6A4 in the compounds."

She stood and perched herself on the arm of the love seat, her eyes scanning the entire room, finally coming to rest on the coffee table behind the two of them.

"During the course of this research," she continued, "our entire supply of CY6A4 was exhausted, including some we were able to obtain from another source. And we need more. There are presently no other ways to get it."

"For research?"

"For production."

"Of what?"

"Of a compound. Something new we have."

"Eleven hundred?"

"No. The eleven hundred we've got. We can produce as soon as they work out all of the kinks. It needs more testing, but it will be worth it. The one thousand is coming along. We're clear on one thousand, and we can make what we need for the masses."

"You said you had some eleven hundred."

"I do. It's there, not in quantity, but that is not our concern right now."

"Is there another generation?"

She nodded. "Twelve hundred is on the drawing boards, but that's about as far as it's gone to this point. Conceptually Hickey feels he has it. Of course, with all the structuring and all of the cross-checks, we have a long road ahead. But at least there *is* a start."

He wondered why he was not informed of this for the interview but realized secrets such as these made SUE the power it was in the marketplace.

"I'm getting lost," he said, genuinely confused. "What is it you're leading up to?" he asked.

She looked at him intently.

"Nobody," she said. "Not McReynolds, not Camden."

"Agreed."

"Dr. Hickey was working on a few theories and quite accidentally stumbled onto a very intriguing compound. He mistakenly transferred about a hundred times more CY6A4 into a batch than he meant to. After reducing it, he realized what he had done and then tinkered with ways to extract it. During the course of this procedure, he ingested some. He liked the result."

"Which was?"

She moved from the arm back to the cushions and continued in an intense, soft tone.

"As you know . . ." she said, then stopped. "Well, you probably don't know, but Dr. Hickey, like you and I, is a Class D carrier. It's funny—I think the scientist who first synthesized Teflon, and the scientist who discovered lysergic acid diethylamide, both did it accidentally too. Maybe it's all luck."

"What makes you think I'm Class D?"

"You are, aren't you?" she asked with surprise in her voice.

"Yes," he said. "I am."

"The compound he created may prove to be of extraordinary benefit to us."

"To us?"

"To Class D carriers. Sixers. What have you."

Stonetree was baffled. She was starting to sound like Mc-Reynolds.

"So what is it?" he asked, a touch of playful sarcasm in his voice.

"This isn't funny, David. This is not a sophomore prank in the high-school chemistry lab."

"I'm sorry. Go ahead."

She shifted herself away from him slightly but continued to stare into his eyes.

"Dr. Hickey may have run across something that could be, as I said, of extraordinary benefit to us. At least some of us."

He thought for a moment. "I really don't subscribe to that," he finally said.

"I'm not asking you to subscribe to it, David. I don't *care* if you subscribe to it. We want to produce some more of it to see what it does, where it will take us." She turned back toward him, smiling slightly. "You cannot subscribe to it because there is not enough to go around."

"That's why you want the CY6A4?"

"That is why I want it."

"How much do you have left?"

"Of the CY6A4? None."

"No, I'm sorry," he said, shaking his head. "Of the, what is it? Do you have a name for it?"

"Officially, no."

"Is it, will it be the next Febrifuge? Thirteen hundred?"

"No. I highly doubt it will ever be in the marketplace. The costs would be astronomical. We just want to see where it will take us."

"So what's it called?"

"For right now, Dr. Hickey calls it Sapien II."

"That's an odd name. Was there a Sapien I?"

"It's just a name, David. Talk to Dr. Hickey. It's not important. I'm not concerned about what he calls it. I'm concerned about what it does." The edge in her voice was as sharp as a brand-new razor.

"Can you tell me more about it?" he asked.

"I can do better." She smiled. "Do you recall the report I gave you on my impressions regarding reorganization of the three divisions? The one I sent to Pierre?"

He remembered it. It was a massive document, highly detailed, exploring different possibilities for restructuring SUE's eight units into a more rational and more easily managed scheme. Pharmaceuticals and Technology would end up under the supervision of one Trisha Lane.

"Of course. It was brilliant. Has Mr. Ruth responded yet?"

"Not yet." She sighed. "But I expect his positive reply soon. That's not the point I was trying to make."

"I'm confused, then."

"How long do you think it would take you to put a report like that together, from conception to final draft?"

"Oh, man," he said, considering the mass and scope of paper. "I have no idea."

"How long would it take?"

"With all the projections and everything? And writing it? Two or three weeks, maybe more."

"I thought of it, played with it one morning while being driven to work. After a few other things, I sat down at ten and started dictating. It was done at three-thirty. You read the first draft, essentially."

"I don't believe it."

"You should," she said, "because it's true. And," she added, "that was twelve hours after I'd tried Dr. Hickey's mistake." She laughed and brushed back her hair. "Maybe we should call it DHM—Dr. Hickey's Mistake!"

If what she said was true, and now he was beginning to believe her, maybe the idle gossip of cocktail parties did have some merit. And if it did, he would be a beneficiary. Perhaps one of the biggest.

"If you did that report in one sitting, and you think it has something to do with Hickey's mistake, I'd sure like to try it! That's incredible!"

"So would the rest of the world," she agreed. "At least twenty-six percent of it. Quantities are limited. Is it getting warm in here?"

"Not really."

"You look a little warm. I am. Don't you think it's late enough for you to loosen your tie?"

He reached for it.

"Here, let me," she said, taking the knot in one hand and pulling a loop with the other. "Now, isn't that a little better?"

"I can't complain." He paused. "So there's none of this left?"

"With the stabilizing agents he added and a medium to hold it, he put together all of thirty-four capsules."

"That's it?" he asked, thinking there were probably a few thousand. "That's all?"

"That's all. And there remains a total of twenty-two. Twenty of them are locked in a vault at the Plaza. The rest were used in testing."

"You said twenty in the vault. Someone has the other two?"

"I do," she whispered. "In the den. Perhaps tonight would be an appropriate time to, uh, test them."

He stared out the window.

"Of course," she continued, "when the two I have are gone, that will be it. For now. With the CY6A4 Dr. Camden has, we could produce more. Find out where it takes us."

He looked back to her, feeling anticipation rise from the floor.

"Do you really want to?" he asked.

"Only if I know that we can produce more. Do you still think you might be able to impose on McReynolds to talk to the doctor?"

"I'll ask him," he said, pausing to collect his thoughts. "But you knew I would, didn't you?"

"Of course I did, or at least I hoped you would," she replied, lowering her hand to his thigh and gently brushing it with her fingernails. "Maybe some firsthand experience will turn you into a believer."

She went to the den. When she returned, she picked up the Bradshaw-4 and sat down next to him, placing the injector and two capsules the color of 1100's on the coffee table in front of them.

"Maybe you'd like to hear Mr. Redal's three new songs again?" she asked. "Maybe that would get your attention back?"

"No, once was enough."

"This music that's on is fine, then?"

"Yes, fine. I like it," he replied, listening to a saxophone playing a dreamy break. "It's nice. It's . . . sexy."

"When Dr. Hickey first told me about this," she said in a casual tone of voice, "I was, of course, interested. When I didn't believe what he told me, I decided the best way to judge was to try it myself. Then I understood what he was talking about."

"How many times have you . . . tried it?"

"Twice. But after the first time, I knew it was special. I told Doug Smite about it—he's willing to do or try anything if he feels there's an advantage for him. He, in turn," she continued, beginning to look quite satisfied with herself, "told his meal ticket about it. Wexford was searching for something to unstick his mind, and I think he found it."

Stonetree felt his jaw drop a bit. Now it was beginning to make sense.

"And he—"

"And he wrote and recorded the songs you heard tonight."

"You mean—"

"Yes, David. You heard them. Amazing what the introduction of a friendly substance into a body can do, isn't it?"

"I never would have guessed," he replied. "He's not the type. He doesn't drink, doesn't smoke. Bad-mouths drugs whenever he gets a chance. What's the story on him? What's happening to him?"

"What's happening," she replied in a measured tone, "is that our little friend has decided to wake up and smell the espresso. Welcome to the real world."

"He doesn't need anything to write great material," he protested. "He's been doing it for years."

"Oh, I agree with you, David," she responded, not trying to mask the patronizing tone in her voice. "I agree with you one hundred and twenty-six percent. The material is there. The material is there in a lot of us. It just has to be coaxed out sometimes. Do you understand what I mean by coax?"

"I think so."

"Sometimes," she said, "it is difficult to do whatever it is we do best. Civilization has been tampering with ways to unlock potential since civilization began."

Her voice had once again taken on its schoolteacher tone.

"Everybody wants to have an edge. You do, I do, Wexford does, the man in the moon does."

"So?"

"So maybe we've got the edge. Maybe we can control the edge. Maybe we found what it takes to connect what we wish we could do to what we *can* do." She paused. "Maybe we found the bridge."

"The drug?" he asked.

"Of course the drug, David." She sighed. "Why do you think I'm going through all of this?"

"All of what?"

Now it all made sense, he thought. She invited him over for one reason and one reason only—to get to McReynolds. To get to Camden. To get to anyone she wanted. Anyone but him. What was worse, he signed up for the entire program without the slightest hesitation. It wasn't the scotch. It was him.

She moved closer, raising her hand slowly and placing it on the back of his neck. Her eyes twinkled, just like the lights of the distant suburbs.

"You really don't understand, do you?" she asked.

"I'm—I'm not sure."

"David," she said, "I could do this alone if I had to." She paused. "But I don't want to."

He looked at her, this woman who had bounced him around like a basketball the entire night. What did she have in store now? What manipulation was hiding behind those eyes?

"Only five people know of the existence of Sapien II. Dr. Hickey, Smite, Wexford, you, and me. I'd like to keep this our own little secret for a while. You'd agree with that, wouldn't you?"

He wanted to ask her if Ruth knew about it, or Walker, but he didn't have to. He had entered the inner circle. He didn't need to ask. He knew. They were not in control of the agenda anymore. She was. And she wanted to share the control with him. She was tired of everyone being twenty years older. She wanted to bring in a new guard. She wanted to choose her confidants. And he was one.

"Of course."

She turned to the table and picked up one of the capsules. The cover of the Bradshaw-4 popped open with two beeps. She rolled the capsule from her palm into one of the chambers, shaking the unit to get it to drop into place. She then stood and walked the few feet to the windows, her form a shimmering silhouette against the background glow of the city. She turned to him, washed in the dim spray from the track lighting overhead.

"This is not a miracle drug that will save all of humanity, David," she began, her voice low and sultry, blending in with the music he heard behind him. "This is not cocaine or LSD, opium or hashish, an upper, a downer, or a stopper. It is not Febrifuge. Maybe a distant cousin, but it has its own identity."

He felt as if he were in church, the church Wexford had gone to, and she was the goddess he had sung about. There could be no mistake about it. Six rings or not, she was the goddess.

"While the temporary effects of this compound are certainly interesting, it's the long-range effects that might prove to be the breakthrough."

"Breakthrough to what?" Stonetree asked.

"To knowledge, to potential. What do you think makes Mozart and Einstein different from you and me?"

He pondered the question for a brief moment and could not resist the first thought that popped into his mind.

"Their hair!" He laughed, leaning back on the cushions and motioning toward the stereo with his hand. "It has to be the hair."

She stared at him with an intensity he could almost touch. It was warm, like sitting on the hood of his car on an autumn afternoon. But it was not a friendly warm. It was a dark warm. Until she could no longer hold back her own laughter.

"What am I going to do with you?" she asked. "Where did I go wrong?"

He had misjudged her. He wasn't being used. If anything, he was going to use her.

"What does it do?" he asked.

"We're not completely sure yet," she replied. "We know it builds a bridge between possibility and reality. For me it's been like, I don't know, like having layers of clothing removed. Each time I've taken it, I get closer to the essence, to the core, to whatever it is in me that feeds my mind. I've tapped it."

"You really have or you think you have?" he asked, actually beginning to believe her.

"You saw my paper," she said flatly. "That wasn't drugs talking. That was me talking. After it seems to wear off, it leaves something. That's the only way to explain it." She paused. "I want you to see for yourself."

She leaned against the brace between two of the windows and placed the injector against her wrist. She stared at him as she activated it, the crackle coming precisely in beat with the music. Her eyes closed, and she raised her head slightly.

She turned it a bit, as if to listen to a far-off sound she couldn't pinpoint. She stood there for a minute or so, not moving or even seeming to breathe.

As her eyes slowly opened, all he could see were two immense black pupils rimmed in light blue. She stared at him much the way a cat would consider a ball of yarn. Her free hand, beginning at the other wrist, moved gradually up her arm to the top of her shoulder. It rested there a moment and then, by degrees, returned to where it started. She blinked a few times and breathed deeply.

"How do you feel?" he asked, thinking it was a stupid question. Her entire demeanor told him she was just fine.

"I feel," she said, moving toward him and edging herself into the cushions, "a little playful. I think we've had enough serious conversation for tonight, don't you? Or," she added, "did you have to get home?"

"What do you think?"

"I think you ought to stay a while longer. We're both adults. We can stay up as long as we want. You don't have to be anywhere, meet anyone, do you?"

He shook his head. "No."

Suddenly her eyes widened a bit, and she again took on a statuelike appearance. It was at least thirty seconds until she returned from wherever she had been.

"You still look a trifle warm." She took a deep breath. "I think I have something that might cool you down a bit."

She pressed the button on the unit, and the lid sprang open. She turned it over and the light, dusty residue floated to the floor. Leaning to the table, she picked up the remaining capsule, placed it in the device, and closed the lid against her chin.

"Allow me," she whispered.

He held out his left wrist, shaking it a couple times to dislodge his watches. He rested the back of his hand on her thigh. She lowered the injector and it crackled, surprising him enough that he recoiled slightly. She began to lift the unit from his wrist, and he felt an old, forgotten memory begin to rise from his subconscious. Then he was suddenly *inside* the memory.

It was an overcast, heavy late-summer day, when he was a young boy living a child's life in a small town. School, he knew, would begin in just a few weeks, but those few weeks, like the summer, would last forever.

He was in the little grocery store a few blocks from his house, alone except for his bicycle parked against the streetlight out front. The store was old and not very bright inside. Mrs. Dattore, an old, chubby, kind woman who sometimes spoke with words none of his friends knew, stood behind the flat, low counter, smiling as she always did.

His grandmother gave him a dollar bill the night before, to spend as he wished. It was not for his education, which was like school but older. The morning was spent in the backyard, in the cherry tree, thinking about what he could buy with his fortune. There were many possibilities. It was after lunch, when his sister was being put back into her crib in the living room, that he decided to go to the little store to spend part of his money.

He walked in knowing exactly what he wanted. And now his face, his torso, was being washed with the icy blast from the freezer he leaned into. The milky white air blurred his vision and curled around his ears; the loud hum of the freezer blocked out all other sound. He tried to reach down farther, to grasp an orange Popsicle from a light brown, folded-over, half-empty cardboard box at the very bottom.

If he could just be bigger, he thought. If his fingers were just an inch longer, the prize would be his. If he fell into the freezer, which he knew he wouldn't, Mrs. Dattore, or the firemen, or his mother would come to pull him out. You can't keep your head in the freezer too long, he knew, or your eyes might never be warm again.

The humming subsided, and the icy air was gradually replaced by a warmer, lighter sensation. Stonetree felt a wave of tranquility, almost a dead, silent calm wash over him. He opened his eyes and saw Trisha's face smiling at him. She was closer than before. The scent of her perfume, of her body, filled his nostrils like a million fresh blossoms flooding a greenhouse. It was almost as if he just awoke from a nap he didn't need. He felt incredibly lucid. A moment before, he recalled, he was fatigued and drowsy and drunk. Now everything was vivid and sharp, the music from the stereo sounding like a sound track from a movie.

"You see," she said, smiling and motioning with her hand to the injector, "this is more than a small laboratory mistake. You are now part of the future, David."

His first thought was to ask her what future she was referring to. Then the second wave hit him. It seemed to have emanated from the base of his spine. He sensed it just before it rocketed into his brain, exploding quietly like a distant fireworks display.

For a moment it was as if his entire body, his entire being, turned to ice. Solid, frozen, eternal. As quickly as it began, it was gone, replaced by the warm, damp weight of the air, and the cool, tart taste of his treat.

From his vantage point atop the stack of boxes in the parking lot, he could see the world. He could smell the world, he could taste the world. The roar to his right reminded him he could hear the world too.

The machine lurched to a stop just a few feet in front of him. It was different from other cars, certainly different from the ones that carried him and his sister on errands. This one smoked and blared music and seemed to sweat. It was as red as blood.

A man in a white T-shirt and jeans got out on one side. From the other a girl, but not one like his friends from school. She was sweeter, and shaped differently from them.

She was taller than the man and also wore a T-shirt. Something was pressing against the fabric, and he thought for a moment about what might be hiding behind it. Her lips were very red, her shorts were very short, her legs seemed awfully long, and why would anyone want to wear shoes like that?

The man walked around the back of the car and took the girl by the hand. Stonetree stared at her, and she laughed. The man stopped in front of him, a wide grin on his face.

"You'll understand someday, kid," he told him. "It'll make sense. I know how you feel."

And now it made sense.

He blinked, and the vision was gone. How long had he been back there, he wondered. His eyes shifted to Trisha's lips. Her smile was the same, the same as it was before the wave, the same as the girl in his memory.

"I was back in my old neighborhood when I was a little kid," he said as if he were talking about the day before yesterday. "I was there. It was so clear."

"Were you cold?" she asked. "Was it a cold day?"

He sensed a third wave approaching, but it broke before it

reached him. Or maybe it passed over him so quickly it only seemed as if it broke.

"Part of it," he replied. "I've never . . . I can't believe how clear it was."

"And now?"

"Now? Now I feel . . . I'm not sure how to describe it. I feel fine, wonderful, in fact. It's like we never had anything to drink tonight."

"Squeeze your hand. Make a fist like this." She held out her hand and slowly drew her fingers together into a tight ball. He imitated her.

"God! I can feel every little muscle, every little nerve, like following the impulse from my brain, down my neck, through my shoulder, down my arm. This is amazing!"

"It'll get better. Especially tomorrow. Wait till you see how you'll feel then. It's like having the gift wrap taken off your brain. You'll never think so clearly. It's something." She hesitated. "And then there's the second time. It's cumulative. It remains."

He nodded and lifted his other hand, squeezing it and relaxing it. The sensation was indescribable.

"We still don't know exactly what it will do or where it might take us," she said, standing up and stretching her arms to the ceiling, small pops blasting from her joints. "It somehow unlocks the memory, expands the thought process." She paused and leaned against the brace. "And it's capable of doing some other interesting things to the senses."

"Like what?" he asked, shifting toward her and relaxing against the cushions.

"Well, color for one," she said. She reached down to her belt and toyed with one of the buckles, finally unfastening it. "I like the way the color of this belt contrasts with the rest of my outfit. I think red and black is a very intriguing combination, don't you?"

The belt unwound and dropped to the floor.

"Yes, I do," he replied. He could feel his heart begin to beat faster. A warm familiar pressure began to build in the center of his body. He'd been there before, a long time ago. Or maybe it was just a moment ago.

Trisha tugged at her blouse, pulling the tails out of her skirt, first from the back, and then from the front.

"Do you like this blouse?" she asked, her red fingernails lazily opening each of the buttons. "I love silk. And black makes it even better. Wouldn't you agree?" Her hands dropped to her sides.

He nodded again but said nothing. The pressure was building. It seemed to be everywhere.

She turned and walked a few steps across his field of vision. His eyes riveted on her hand as it slowly disappeared into a sleeve. The blouse slid off her back, then the other arm, in one fluid motion. He didn't think she was wearing a brassiere. Now he knew he was right.

"I've noticed you've been paying some attention to these," she purred, cupping her breasts in her hands and lifting them slightly. "I thought you might like to see them."

Stonetree started to get up, but her head motioned him to stop. He froze for a moment, supported by his palms. Then he lowered himself back onto the cushions.

"Just watch now." She licked her upper lip. "Anticipation is what great sex is all about."

He nodded again, unable to speak. She took the few steps back to her original position. She unfastened her skirt and let it drop to the floor. She absently kicked it away to one side and faced him, revealing a deep red satin garter belt holding up her black stockings. And nothing more. She raised her hands to the sides of her head and began to run her fingers languidly through her hair, brushing it back more and more with each motion.

"I must have been fixated on this red and black combination," she cooed, her hands continuing their movement. "I bought this whole outfit today, just for tonight. I do hope you like it. I've never seduced anyone before. I wanted to make sure everything was right." She again cupped her breasts in her hands, looking at each of them for a moment. Then she gazed back at him. "What do you think, David?" she asked in a taunting voice. "Do you think I might be able to seduce you tonight?"

He stood up and took a step toward her, stopping to absorb the vision standing before him. She held out her hand, and he took it.

"Come with me," she said, leading him toward the bedroom. "I don't want anything to distract us for the rest of the evening."

He followed her. There was really no other alternative. It really was too good to be true. Dream or not, he wanted it to last.

CHAPTER 14

THE NEXT MORNING STONETREE MADE THE TRANSITION FROM sleep to full consciousness in one motion, bypassing the in-between zone. His eyes opened, and he stared at the thin sheets of light entering the room through the cracks in the black blinds. He sensed he was alone and that it must be close to eight. Rolling over, he looked at the clock radio next to the bed. It was 8:15.

His clothes were draped over a chair in one corner, and a large white terry-cloth robe was lying sideways at the bottom of the bed. There was no sound save a dull hum from a location he couldn't place. He sat up and reached for the robe, noticing an envelope on top of it. Opening it, he found a note in Lane's handwriting.

David—
Thank you for last night and the early morning. Take the day off and see if you can contact McReynolds. I'll see you tomorrow at 9.

Trisha

On the way home he replayed the events of the previous evening over and over in his mind. They were all very clear, as if captured on videotape. He kept forwarding and reversing to his favorite parts. He spent a lot of time watching the end of the epic.

After showering and making a pot of coffee, he called McReynolds. His friend answered on the third ring and sounded as if he'd been asleep. His drowsiness disappeared, however, when Stonetree began to tell him about the "phone conversation" he had with Lane the previous evening.

McReynolds said he would try to reach Camden as soon as possible and would call back when he could arrange a meeting. Stonetree told him he might be busy as the morning progressed, but he would call him back if they didn't connect.

He then called Carl, who apparently was also asleep.

"God, how late do you stay in bed every morning?" Stonetree chided him. "It must be nice to be on welfare."

"Hey, I had a rough night last night. I was at the club till it closed. Had a real good crowd. I think I fell in love, but I'm not sure."

"Did she fall in love with you?"

"I'm not sure about that, either," Carl responded. "There's nobody in bed with me. I was real drunk. I think I still am."

"Well, go take a shower and meet me over at Willie's. You know, that joint down the block from Sirius. I want to talk to you."

"About what? What's the rush? Can't we talk about it some other time?"

"Look," Stonetree said. "This is going to be your chance to pick up some easy money and might also get me a little more interested in your next project with Smitty. You gonna meet me?"

"I'll be there, chief." He laughed. "Give me forty-five minutes or an hour, okay?"

"I'll see you at eleven."

"Right."

Stonetree was on his way out the door when the phone chirped. It was McReynolds.

"Dave, I got hold of the doctor. He came in late last night. I guess he was real antsy to get back here to try to get something going. He looked at his own stuff and decided he still needs the notebooks. I told him about your conversation with Trisha, and he was excited about the possibilities. But I got the distinct impression he thinks maybe he's being set up."

"Set up?" Stonetree asked, half in amazement, half in frus-

226   · JOHN PATRICK KAVANAGH ·

tration. "Why does he think he's being set up? What the hell does the guy want?"

"He wants his research, Dave. But look at it from his point of view. You work for the woman, you're her right-hand man. You break into SUE with us, and we get stopped by the guards. I mean, he's got to be a little careful, you know."

"So why would I change from last Friday? What's different now?"

"I don't know, but he sounded skeptical. He said we could get together tonight and talk about it, though, if that's okay with you. Over at the hotel."

"Let's see," Stonetree replied, going through a mental timetable. "Yeah, I can do it. But it might have to be later in the evening. I've got a shitload of stuff I have to take care of."

"Okay, when?"

"Would eight be all right?"

"Sure. I'll call Camden. Call from the lobby again. If we're not there, we'll leave a message at the desk."

"Good. I'll be there. Bye."

As he drove to meet Carl, Stonetree's mind began to flood with distinct lucid images from his past. He could remember with incredible clarity how the guard who led the tour of the Tower of London looked and sounded, down to the lint on the insignia of his long red coat. He recalled the first time he ever kissed a girl, *really* kissed one. It was on a dark outdoor stairway, on an autumn night, when he was in his freshman year of high school. He remembered the first time he walked into the Bally casino in Las Vegas, how he was struck with its size and its high ceiling, and how he sat down at a blackjack table and lost his four days of gambling funds in less than an hour. He recalled his entire first day of kindergarten.

The decision to go with his instincts hit him in a rush of pros and cons as he left Wilson Towers that morning. In between Lane's floor and the lobby he decided he had to eliminate the nagging question of the Mustang once and for all. He no longer had any spare room in his life to worry each day about buying it, not buying it, affording it, not affording it. The time had come to remove the issue from his agenda, if for no other reasons than it would give his friends some relief and it would give him something to drive while the Turbostar was in for some warranty maintenance work.

The time had come, he decided, to take a chance. He could see his old college friend, Pete Radek, sitting across from him at a poker table in the recreation room of Pete's fraternity house, a cigarette dangling from his lips. He would taunt Stonetree with phrases like "If you want to win like a champ, you have to bet like a champ" and "No guts, no glory" and "If you want to play like the big boys, you have to pay like the big boys." Stonetree chuckled as he swung the Toyota off the expressway. "If you want to play like the big boys, you have to pay like the big boys," he whispered.

As he drove the last mile of his trip, he recalled everything Carl told him about what affected the price of gold on the futures market. Oil prices, military spending, military cutbacks, military unrest, political unrest, political assassinations, religious assassinations, religious beliefs, unemployment, industrial need, depression, inflation, stock prices, food prices, clothing prices, booze prices, the time of year, the time of day, the money supply, the domestic economy, foreign economies, who won the World Series, the whims of traders, the whims of hedgers, the whims of speculators, the weather, and the price of tea in China.

Virtually everything and anything could cause the small ticks that sometimes made fortunes but more often destroyed them. If someone had divined the secret of the ebb and flow of the precious metals commodities market, he was not about to tell. Carl stood up halfway and saluted as Stonetree sat down.

"You look awful, Carl."

"And boy do I feel it. I gotta knock off this running-around business. It's a young man's game."

"Young man, shit," Stonetree replied, motioning to the waitress to bring coffee. "You're only twenty-five years old."

"Twenty-six as of last week." Carl frowned. "It ain't gonna get any easier." He paused and looked at Stonetree. "So what's up, my man? How are we gonna get rich today? You ready to cough up some coin for the cause?"

"Better than that. I've got twenty thousand I want to put in play."

"Hey, that's nice. That's all right. I knew you'd wise up."

"Today."

"Sure. You can give it to me today. We won't be doin' anything for a few weeks, but I'll keep it safe for you."

"No, Carl. I want to do it today."

"Today? Twenty thou? You're nuts."

"Well, why not?" Stonetree asked. "I've got a hunch."

"And I've got a hunch you need a break." Carl laughed. "You just don't stroll in and buy some contracts on a hunch. You've got to do your research. It takes time."

"Look, Zigs," he continued in an even voice, "I'm going to do it and I'm going to do it today. I can go open a commodities account if I want, but I figured I'd cut you in."

"Okay. Tell me more."

"Here's what we do. I suppose you get a discount on large trades and you can cut the commissions down?"

"Sure. But not with Smitty. He still doesn't have his license back. I've got an account through Hutton, though. I've had it for a few months. Made some money too. Not a ton, but I've done all right. The broker there, Tommy, he's good. He'll take care of you. How much we gonna trade?" he asked, lifting his cup.

Stonetree quickly reviewed his calculations. "I want to go three hundred contracts of gold."

Carl began to cough and turned his head, spitting his coffee onto a busboy passing by.

"You want to trade what?" he asked, his eyes wide.

"You heard it right."

"Don't you mean you want to control three hundred ounces of gold? That's three contracts, my man. Not three hundred. You had me crazy there for a minute." He pulled out a five-dollar bill and handed it to the young man as he wiped off his apron.

"No, Carl. I want three hundred contracts."

"Stoney, do you know what you're saying?"

"You tell me."

"Okay," Carl began, leaning back in his seat and staring out the window at two women walking by. "You and me go over to Hutton and sit near the tickers, right? You decide you want to buy, to go long three hundred contracts of gold at, say, six hundred eighty-five dollars an ounce. What you now have on your hands is the responsibility for thirty thousand ounces of gold. You understand me, Davey? Thirty thousand ounces. That's a three followed by not two, not three, but four very large zeros. Thirty thousand with a capital three."

"I know, Carl. I'm an accountant. I can add. I can even multiply three hundred times one hundred in my head."

"So you now have," he continued, "these thirty thousand ounces of gold which you bought to play with at six eighty-five. That's what? Twenty million dollars? Then you look up and find that those contracts are now selling for six eighty-four ninety an ounce. You just lost yourself three grand in the blink of an eye. And if it ticks down another ten cents, you just lost yourself another three grand. You got the picture?"

"Yeah," Stonetree responded, cracking his knuckles. "I know all that. Can we go now?"

"And what happens when it hits the wire that OPEC is lowering oil prices by five bucks a barrel or something? You is finished, with a capital F. No house, no car, no nothing."

"We'll put in a stop a dollar below where we get in. The maximum we lose is thirty thousand."

"No, no." Carl laughed. "The maximum *you* lose is thirty thousand. I'm only there to help." He paused. "For which I get what?"

"My love and affection," Stonetree shot back. "Along with two thousand if we hit it right. If I crap out, I'll give you a couple Bradshaw-4's and I'll buy you a couple cocktails at the club."

"You're on, Davey," he said. "You're dumber than shit, but you're on. Let's do it."

"I've got to stop at the bank and pick up the cash. I've got twenty-three. Am I good for the rest?"

"You're good for all of it, pal," Carl replied, extending his hand, which Stonetree shook. "E. F. Hutton, here we come!"

On the walk to the brokerage house they agreed on the basic strategy. When Stonetree thought he was ready to take the plunge, Carl would call his broker on the house phone and have him place the order for three hundred contracts of June gold with a one-dollar stop, limiting the potential loss to thirty thousand dollars. He would not get the broker back on the line until the price had shifted to within twenty cents of the price they would sell the three hundred contracts to make a thirty-thousand-dollar profit. Carl would watch the board and handle the phone, and Stonetree would watch the news tickers. Long or short was the only remaining issue.

When they arrived, they positioned themselves as planned. To warm up, Carl called the broker to tell him what to expect and to haggle over a reasonable commission.

"He'll do it for twenty-nine hundred dollars, both ends," Carl said. "And that is dirt, dirt cheap. He's giving it away. But we have to finish the trade today. Okay?"

Stonetree nodded.

"Right, Tommy. You've got a deal. Wait for the call." He turned to Stonetree and gave him a thumbs-up signal. "You're on your own, but I'll be here to stop you before you get the cyanide in your mouth."

Stonetree returned the signal and began to follow the computer screen that carried financial news. After a moment he shifted his attention to the screen carrying world and national news and finally to the one carrying sports, regional, and local news.

He returned to the financial news and noted that a sharply smaller crop of oranges was expected the coming season in Florida. A bad sign for Popsicle lovers everywhere, he thought. In times of crisis the price of gold rises. He looked up at the board. June gold contracts were trading at $681.20. He nodded to Carl, mouthed "long," and pointed at him with both index fingers, bending his knees a bit and smiling. Carl placed the call and in less than a minute hung up the phone.

"You're filled," he said, walking back and placing his hands on Stonetree's shoulders. "Welcome to the land of supernatural greed." They sat down on a ledge and stared at the board, watching for the numbers to change. In a moment they did, the June gold contract losing twenty cents.

"That little flicker of the lights cost us six thousand, Dave," Carl said. "This isn't pretend anymore. This is for real money. You sure you want to do this?"

"Yes."

"You can walk away right now. With commissions it's less than a nine-thousand-dollar loss."

"Do you like Popsicles?"

"What? Now? You're facing financial disaster, and it's snack time?"

"Just asking," Stonetree replied.

"When I was a kid, I loved them. My favorite was blueberry, then grape. Banana if I could get it."

"How about orange?"

"Nah. Orange Popsicles were for the commoners, the people with no imagination, no class. *Everybody* liked orange ones."

"You saying I've got no imagination?"

"Nope." He coughed, looking at the board. "But you just dropped another three grand. We're in five figures now. Want me to call Tommy?"

"No." Stonetree grinned. "It's an adjustment, that's all. It'll come back up. There was some bad news on the ticker. The world is going to hell."

"Oh, yeah?" Carl said as he got up to read the screens. "What was it?"

"Keep reading. Let me know when you see something."

Carl pulled a chair up to the consoles and sat down. Stonetree gazed at the board and began to run through his album collection, alphabetically, artist by artist. By the time he reached Presley's "Greatest Hits," the price of the June contract had ticked down another twenty cents. Including commissions, he would be out about eighteen thousand dollars if he quit now. He began to think about what he could buy for eighteen grand. For starters, about two thousand albums if he bought them on sale.

He thought about driving through the countryside on a cool autumn afternoon with a Bahamas tape blasting away, Lane sitting next to him holding his hand with a blissful smile on her face. They'd be driving to the middle of nowhere to spend a long weekend alone—no SUE, no Camden, no nothing. Just the two of them, and the birds and the bees.

Then he replayed the same scene, except this time it was Sharon with a blissful smile. They were also driving to nowhere but going there fast. Then it was Lane, and then Sharon again. He wondered what the gas mileage on the Mustang was, and if Lane would ever take him horseback riding.

"Hey, we got something hot here," Carl called.

"What's that?"

"It says here a woman out in Honolulu got sick of pineapples and she started an organization to have their sale banned on the islands on Sundays. Her husband is a vice president at Dole. He's filing for divorce. Great story!"

232   · JOHN PATRICK KAVANAGH ·

"Come on, Carl. This is supposed to be serious, remember?"

"It is serious. If I was married to her, it would be real serious. Like first-degree murder."

They both looked up at the board. June gold had ticked down another ten cents.

"We're more than halfway into the big hole," Carl moaned. "We don't have much more room, Stoney. Want me to get Tommy on the line?"

"No, let's play it out. It's only money."

And, Stonetree thought, *it* was *only money*. Would the loss of thirty thousand change the world? No. Neither would the gain of thirty thousand. It was all a game, not being played there, but at some other place where Radek's big boys played. He was just a passive observer, another small pinion in a large profit machine.

It was no different from SUE. You had a job, you lost a job. The corporation functioned with you, without you, in spite of you, regardless of you. Ruth could go, Walker could go, Lane could go, Wexford could go. It didn't matter—the game continued, only the players changed. Some were bigger than others, but when it came right down to it, in fifty years it wouldn't mean shit. But it mattered to Camden. Maybe he was right about making a contribution. Maybe it did change something. He could afford to be a philosopher. With a massive nut in the bank he could afford to do just about anything he wanted.

And Wexford. He put together the biggest, fattest album in history in a couple weeks and took in more money from that one project than a lot of countries—*countries*—used up each year to run the whole operation. Where was he? Locked away in some ersatz medieval castle with a bunch of bodyguards, a sandwich shop, and a broken heart. He was afraid to set foot outside of his stronghold lest somebody put a bullet through his skull or drop a bomb on him. Was that living? Was that what it was about to be rich and famous? His goddess and his public and the one love he ever had so far out of reach he couldn't buy a pole long enough to reach them?

No, it was just money. Like his grandmother told him, and he thought she invented the phrase, it can't buy happiness. Or peace. Or contentment.

"Holy shit!" Carl yelled. "Oh, baby, get yourself to the trading floor!"

"What's up?" Stonetree asked.

"Libya just announced—the defense minister announced— that they've got nukes and some missiles and they ain't afraid to use them! Oh, baby, get to the floor!"

Carl scampered over to Stonetree and put his hands on his shoulders again, both of them looking up to the board.

"That's good news, for us, anyway?" Stonetree asked.

"You bet your ass, just as long as it gets there on time. Those stories usually hit the floor fast—this could change everything. Just pray it gets there before we get stopped out."

The lights of June gold flickered, but when they rested, they spelled out $680.50.

"Oh, shit." Carl sighed. "Come on, sweetheart, you can do it. You can do it."

"Is it time to bail out?" Stonetree asked, watching an old man a few seats away folding a cigarette in his hands, half of the tobacco falling from the pouch directly into his lap.

"Of course not! This could really turn it around."

He walked to the phone and called the broker, returning in a moment with a calm expression on his face.

"Tommy is ready. I mean, the stop order is already in if it dips to six eighty twenty. We're in pretty deep. You want to go all the way?"

Stonetree sunk into his chair. "A friend of mine used to tell me not to go 'the lick.' You heard of that?"

"No. What is it?"

"We used to play poker for a half dollar, a dollar. Those were the wagers. But if you wanted to go halfway, seventy-five cents, it was called 'going the lick.' "

"Yeah, and?"

"And we ain't going the lick. Not this time. I'm not going it anymore."

The board flickered again. June gold was up thirty cents to $680.80.

"Okay, they must have heard about it," Carl said reassuringly. "Those bastards on the floor got the news. Now we're in business."

The board ticked up another twenty cents, and then another thirty, and then another twenty. In fifteen minutes it was up another ten, to $681.60.

"They got the word. World War Three, here we come," Carl whispered.

The board sat at that figure for another fifteen minutes, each minute repeating the same plateau.

"We're up twelve grand before the commission, Dave. It might be stuck there. It could correct anytime. You want to call it a day?"

"Not yet," Stonetree said, watching the old man roll another cigarette. "We've got our whole lives."

"Oh, don't start on the Philosophy 101 with me, man. This is cash money we're talking about. Come on, let it go. Get out."

The board flickered and the new June gold price was $681.90.

"More than halfway there." Stonetree smiled.

It flickered again—$682.10.

"Call him," he ordered Carl. "We're out."

"I thought you wanted six eighty-two twenty?"

"Call him. Now! We're out!"

The board flickered again. The price had jumped ten cents.

"Carl, you got him yet?" he yelled.

"It's ringing. It's ringing."

"Carl, get us out!"

"Okay, okay. I'm trying . . . Tommy? Zigs. Sell the gold. Now!"

Carl returned and sat down, a film of sweat covering his forehead.

"He put in the sell order. We got out with a big profit."

"How much?"

"Have to wait and see."

They waited. And waited. The broker would call back when he had a confirmation of the sale. The lights of the board continued to flicker. In the fifteen minutes they sat there, the price of the June gold contract had risen to $682.70. Carl said he wanted to drink.

"For what? To celebrate?"

"No, to keep *me* from committing suicide. Look at that contract. If we got out now, we'd be up forty-five grand. Forty-five grand! I feel sick."

"If you want to play like the big boys," Stonetree said, "you've got to pay like the big boys."

Carl answered the page for Mr. Zigeras. The contract was

sold at $682.30. After commissions, the credit to his account was $30,100.

"Can we get the money now?" Stonetree asked. "Do we have to wait?"

"We don't wait for anyone." He chuckled, shaking his hand. "We just walk over to the cashier's cage and have a check made out."

"Am I good for your two thousand till tomorrow?" Stonetree replied. "I've got an errand to run."

"You're good for all of it," Carl replied, shaking his hand again. "Shall we say Sirius at seven on Friday? I'll pop for a bottle of Dom Pérignon. What say?"

"What say? I say fine."

Hendricks agreed to meet Stonetree at the train station at three, and he was there as promised. On the way back to his house they talked about the weather, about the upcoming elections, about riding on trains, and about the Libyans having the bomb.

"Who cares if they have a delivery system," Hendricks said as he unlocked the front door of his house. "Nuclear war? Sure. That's gonna keep me awake tonight. I had a toothache last week, an abscess. The dentist gave me some penicillin and the pain was gone in three days. And you want me to worry about a fifty-megaton bomb dropping into my backyard? I've got other things on my mind."

They walked into the living room, and he motioned for Stonetree to sit down on one of the couches. He put on some music. It was the same song about living away from the city, safe from crime. Stonetree asked who performed it.

"Ganymede."

"Never heard of them."

"Probably never will, either. Not your mainstream group. Good album, though."

Stonetree thought for a moment. Maybe now was the time to start trading.

"I'm a record company executive. You didn't know that, did you?"

"No," Hendricks responded. "You want a beer?"

"Sure," Stonetree replied. "To celebrate."

He returned with two cans and set them in front of his guest. Stonetree looked at him and then at the beers. Hendricks looked at him and then at a painting of a court jester hanging on the wall. Stonetree looked at the painting and then at Hendricks.

"Nice painting," he said. "Where did you get it?"

"It was a gift from an old friend of mine. Probably reminded her of me. I thought you were an accountant?"

"I am. Or I was," he replied as he picked up his drink.

"So what are we celebrating?"

"I'm here to buy the car."

"I figured that. You go to school for twenty years and you pick up something here and there."

Stonetree handed him the other can. Hendricks lit a cigarette and tossed his guest the pack.

"I wish I would have had one of these last night."

"A beer?"

"No, a cigarette," Stonetree replied, lighting one and inhaling deeply. "I had some scotch last night. This stuff that they made only five hundred bottles of. Really expensive."

"Did it give you a buzz?"

"Yeah, I guess."

"So will this. Save your money."

Stonetree reached into his shirt pocket and pulled out a check, examining it and handing it to Hendricks.

"That is a certified check from E. F. Hutton made out to me in the amount of thirty thousand one hundred dollars," he stated. "I'm sure you can see that."

"If you think I can see it, why did you tell me?" Hendricks smiled, blowing a long stream of smoke toward the ceiling. "You came up here to give me a vision test?"

"No, no," Stonetree protested. "It's just a figure of speech."

"And what do you propose I do with this figure of speech?"

"I'd like you to accept it, after I endorse it over to you, as partial payment for the car. I'll give you my personal check for the rest."

"Oh?"

"If that's acceptable to you."

"The old certified-check gambit."

"What do you mean?"

Hendricks leaned back in his chair and looked at the court jester, first blowing a smoke ring toward it, then one toward Stonetree.

"One of the favorite games of defense attorneys, when they feel themselves getting backed into a corner, is to have a certified check cut in an amount for which they think they should be able to get out of a bad case. Usually they do it just before opening arguments or after the jury has been chosen. They take the certified check and dangle it in front of the nose of the plaintiff's attorney. Trial lawyers love the smell of money, but they go absolutely wild over a certified check. It's like catnip to them. It usually works, too."

"I wasn't aware of that," Stonetree replied, taking a sip of his beer. "I suppose that could be pretty convincing."

"It worked for me every time."

"Think it'll work today?"

"It already has." Hendricks extended his hand to him. "You just bought yourself a Mustang. And a damn good one, too."

After filling out the title transfer and exchanging it for the two checks, Hendricks said he wanted to take the car for a short spin before he turned it over. They went into the garage and removed the tarp, which Hendricks folded neatly and placed in the trunk on top of the briefcase.

He told Stonetree to wait in the house and to make himself at home. He backed the car out of the garage and onto the street, but then pulled it back onto the driveway and shut off the engine. Stonetree asked him if anything was wrong as he slid off the driver's seat.

"No, nothing's wrong," Hendricks said. "I just decided that I don't need to take it for another ride. I've still got the memories. Besides, it's not his birthday and it's not Thanksgiving, and there aren't any provisions in the rules for farewell rides."

"But you're certainly welcome to take one," Stonetree responded. "I don't mind waiting."

"No," Hendricks replied, grasping Stonetree's hand and placing the keys in it. "The car's yours. Enjoy it and take care of it. You might not find another one like it."

"I know, and I will. Thanks."

They shook hands and Stonetree got into the car, closed the door, and rolled down the window.

"Say, Jay," he said. "I know before you told me that it wasn't any of my business what you were going to do with the money, but that your brother wanted you to do something creative with it."

"That's right."

"I'm still curious. Would you mind?"

Hendricks leaned over and placed both his hands on the top of the door.

"Well, I suppose it's part of the history of the car." He paused a moment. "I met this woman, a young woman, who's a nurse here in town. She works with these teenagers who've gone through the worst CYD symptoms, the ones that are supposed to kill you. But these kids didn't die. Most of them have brain damage and eyesight and hearing loss. Some are just zombies. They sit all day and stare at a chair or a picture on the wall, or at nothing."

"It must be horrible."

"It is. It's heartbreaking. So anyway, I was with her one day over there and I got to thinking how good we have it, people who are healthy, live in nice homes, drive nice cars. We take it for granted. I do, anyway. So, I decided maybe it was time that *I* set aside a little time to be thankful for what I've got."

"So what are you going to do?"

"I'm going to work there for a year, as a volunteer. The money from the car should just cover my expenses for twelve months. I won't be living like a king, but those kids don't either. Enjoy yourself."

"I will. And thanks for telling me. I appreciate it."

"Take care. Take care of the car," Hendricks said, patting the hood once before it rolled down the driveway and onto the street.

Stonetree made it home in less time than he expected. The trip was shortened by a few stretches down two-lane highways on the outskirts of the city, where he tried to bury the needle of the speedometer. And on one stretch he finally did.

CHAPTER | 15

STONETREE WAS OUT OF HIS HOUSE AT SEVEN AFTER A CALL TO McReynolds. He walked into the lobby of the Hyatt at precisely eight o'clock. He picked up a house phone and was directed by Camden to report to Room 823. He knocked twice as Robin had the first time he'd visited Camden, and was ushered in by the doctor. He sat down on the couch in the living room of the suite. Camden looked calm, McReynolds tired and nervous.

"So, David," the doctor began in a comically formal tone. "Robin tells me you are the bearer of an interesting offer from your superiors. Perhaps you'd like to tell me about it."

"I'd be happy to, Doctor," he replied. "In just a minute. I have a bit of news I'd like to share with Mr. McReynolds, if you wouldn't mind." He turned to Robin and grinned. "I bought the Mustang today. It's downstairs."

"Hey, that's great, Dave," he said, shaking his head and turning to the doctor. "Dave has been eyeing an old Ford Mustang for a long time. I guess he finally cracked open his piggy bank and broke down. Is that right, Dave?"

"Yeah, something like that," he replied. "It is really something. You've got to see it to believe it. Maybe we can all go for a ride later." He looked at the doctor, who seemed perplexed. "Or," he added, "maybe not. Back to business."

"Tell him what Trisha said," McReynolds ordered, pointing to Camden.

"Well, Doctor," Stonetree began. "I'm not sure how it came about, what caused it, but I had a conversation with Miss Lane last night, and she expressed an interest in exchanging your notebooks for the CY6A4 you have." He looked at both of them. "It's as simple as that."

"As simple as that," McReynolds repeated.

"As simple as that?" Camden asked, arching one of his eyebrows. "She just conveniently decided that, one, I had some CY6A4 and, two, she'd like to exchange my research for it? Doesn't that sound a little strange to you, Mr. Stonetree?"

"It sounds coincidental to me," he replied. "But not strange. In fact, it sounds pretty fortunate. It seems to solve a lot of problems for you." He folded his arms, relaxed and satisfied.

"And apparently for her," the doctor added. "What exactly did she say she wanted it for?"

"Research."

"On what?"

"She didn't say."

"Why else would she want it?"

"I don't know."

"They must be onto something, something important."

"I don't know."

"She gave no indication as to why she wanted it?"

"No. For research."

"Did she say research?"

"I don't recall."

"And she wants to trade the notebooks for it?"

"She indicated that. She said Hickey looked at them and couldn't figure anything out. She said they were written in Arabic or something."

"They would be difficult for anyone else to read. I knew that. Was Hickey there?"

"No."

"Who else?"

"No one. We were on the phone."

"Then how do you know no one else was there?"

"I don't. I just assumed it. Did you go to law school, too, Dr. Camden? I feel like I'm on the witness stand."

"Hey, lighten up a little," McReynolds interrupted.

"*You* lighten up a little, Robin," Stonetree barked. "I'm just carrying some water here. That's it. I'm not on trial."

"You are, in a way, David," Camden said in a softer, less confrontational tone. "It just sounds a little suspicious to me. You can appreciate that, can't you?"

"Sure I can," he replied, picking up his keys and pacing back and forth in front of them. "I know it sounds crazy, but that's how it happened. Believe me. It's true."

"So why did Lane approach you, and why now?" he asked.

"Doctor, she knows that I know Robin. She figured he had talked to you for the *Fortune* article. She said you'd be skeptical about anyone from SUE contacting you directly, so she asked me if I would contact Robin and ask him if he would get in touch with you to see if, I don't know, a meeting of some kind could be arranged. And that's it."

"How does she know I've got the CY6A4?"

"I don't know."

"How do you *think* she knows?"

"I'm not sure. She said something about your contract being up with the corporation, that Hickey said something to her. He's the one who thinks you have it. But they're not sure."

"Why does Hickey think I have it?"

"I don't know."

"Why do they think I suddenly want to trade for it?"

"I don't *know*, damn it!" He went to the refrigerator and got a beer, half of which he drank before returning to the conversation.

"Look," he said, squeezing the can in his hand. "You got the message, okay? You've got it. If you want me to get out of the way now," he continued, his voice rising, "so you can go cut your deal with her, it's fine with me. I don't need this shit."

"Dave . . ." McReynolds began.

"And don't give me that 'Dave' shit, either, Robin," he yelled. "I went out on a real limb for the two of you last Friday. I could have gotten both of my nuts cut off in that little escapade, and now all I get from the two of you is 'why this?' and 'why that?' If they would have found out who you were that night, the two of you wouldn't be out of a job. *I* would. So let's keep this in perspective, okay? I just don't need the hassle."

"Your point is well taken, David," Camden said apologetically. "I guess I did get out of line. Why don't you sit down, and we'll talk about this with a little less passion."

Stonetree sat down.

"Last Friday I had a good deal to lose too," the doctor continued. "Maybe the world had something to lose. And our friend Robin . . ."

"Robin didn't have shit to lose but a story."

"And a real *big* story, too, Dave," McReynolds snapped. "Don't forget *that*. Things are tough all over."

"I know. I'm sorry. Let's get on with this. Yelling at each other won't accomplish anything. Let's go."

McReynolds went to get two more beers and turned off the television which was flickering in the background.

"All right, let's all put our heads together and see if we can make some sense out of this," Camden began in a measured voice, tapping his foot and seeming to try to put together a large mental jigsaw puzzle without touching the pieces. "It really doesn't surprise me, when I think about it, that they think I've got the CY6A4. I like the fact they think it's off the premises. If Hickey thought it was there, he might have figured out where I put it."

"That's probably true," McReynolds said.

"But I wonder why they think I'd *still* have it, that I haven't used it all up. Any insight into that question, David?"

"No, Doctor," he replied. "I don't think she ever mentioned an amount. She just said that you had some *or* all of it. I don't think they have any definite idea about it. They might just be guessing or assuming that you do."

"Yes, that's possible. But it doesn't seem to be the way Lane and Hickey would operate. Lane is the type to conduct a scorched-earth policy."

Stonetree thought about the previous evening. Yes, she could get things pretty hot when she wanted to, he recalled, and then grinned.

"So you agree with me, David?" the doctor asked.

"Yes, sir," he replied, continuing to smile. "I agree with you completely. Not the type to try to seduce you, use the velvet gloves."

"Oh, I wouldn't agree with *that*," Camden objected. "First she tries to get things done with honey. If that doesn't work, then the whip comes down. And hard."

Stonetree finished his beer and nodded his head.

"You have a rough day with that Mustang?" Robin asked. "You're really knocking the suds back."

"Just thirsty, that's all."

"I think if we're going to do something, we ought to do it quick," McReynolds said, turning to Camden.

"Why?" the doctor asked.

"Because if they just decided you might have the CY6A4, it's only a small jump for them to consider that it might still be at the Plaza. If they think that, it's only a small step to dismantling the place."

"You're right."

"And if, for whatever reason," he continued, eyeing Stonetree, "they want to make a deal, it would probably make sense to talk to them while their interest is up rather than giving them time to start changing their minds."

"I guess I'd rather take my chances in front of them instead of trying it behind them again," Camden replied. He turned to Stonetree. "Then it's settled. When do they want to talk?"

"I imagine we could get hold of Lane right now if you want," Stonetree offered.

"We don't want to seem *too* eager," the doctor replied. "Why don't you just tell her tomorrow morning? Tell her you got Robin, and he got me and I'm ready to talk."

"When?"

"Right then. We can do it then. You call Robin, he'll call me. Get it over with."

"But do you trust them to make an honest deal?" McReynolds asked. "They screwed you once before."

"She'll keep her word," Stonetree said.

"That does raise an interesting logistical point." The doctor sighed, smoothing his beard a few times. "I'm a bit reluctant just to walk into the lab and point to the CY6A4 and say, 'Here it is, where are my notebooks?' Any ideas, David?"

"I'm not sure," he replied. "There must be a way to keep it all aboveboard."

"One possibility," Camden continued, "would be for me to tell them that I was going to do an unknown number of dry runs through the lab, walking down to the street level and out the door. They would never know when I had it or when I didn't. Then we could work the trade on more neutral ground."

"That's a good idea," McReynolds said. "Keep those bastards honest."

"I could actually take it out on my third run."

"Why three?" Stonetree asked.

"Because people always think you're going to do things the third time around, and they'd figure I knew that so I'd probably do it on the second run-through. This way," he continued, a bemused expression crossing his face, "we fake out everyone including ourselves."

They all laughed.

"Maybe the guards too," McReynolds added, and they all laughed again.

"Well, that does it, then," the doctor said, standing up. "We'll do it tomorrow. Robin," he continued, turning to McReynolds, "you said you had an engagement later on?"

"Yes, I do. Are we done here?"

"I think so. Perhaps David could give you a ride to wherever you're going. I'd like to take a little spin in his new treasure too, if he wouldn't mind." He turned to Stonetree, his eyes widening comically.

"I'll pass on the ride," McReynolds said. "My appointment is just a few minutes from here."

"Come on, Robin. Come down and see it," Stonetree pleaded.

"I'd still like a test drive," the doctor stated. "I used to have one of those babies myself, a long time ago."

Stonetree nodded. "Let's go."

In the parking lot the men "oohed" and "aahed" over the car for a few minutes before parting. McReynolds again declined the offer of a ride, accepting a raincheck instead. Camden hopped into the passenger seat, and Stonetree piloted it to the entrance of the garage. "Which way?" he asked.

"I don't care," Camden replied. "Wherever you'd like to go." Stonetree swung the car to the left and gunned the engine just enough to attract attention.

"How long have you known Robin?" the doctor asked.

"Oh, I don't know," Stonetree replied as he switched on the radio. "Five, six, eight years. He was married to a friend of mine from college."

"And you trust him?"

246   · JOHN PATRICK KAVANAGH ·

"Sure," he replied, turning to him with a curious look. "Why?"

"I just wanted to make sure. I asked him the same question earlier in the evening about you. He said you could be trusted to a fault. He really likes you, respects you."

"Well," Stonetree said with a smile, "we've seen each other through some ups and downs. I guess that can build up trust between two people. He went through a very rough period after Sasha left him. We had some crazy times back then."

"I think he's a good man too," the doctor agreed. "A little ambitious, I'd say, but he'll outgrow that. On the other hand, even though you don't want to hear this, I still have a few reservations about you."

Stonetree pulled the car over to the curb, into an empty taxi zone, and shut off the engine. He turned to the doctor with a frown.

"Okay. I can understand some hesitation on your part," he said flatly. "Doctor, you have much more to lose than I do. I *do* want to help you because it might help me and, besides that, it's the right thing to do." He paused. "But I don't know what to change to eliminate your fears. What do you want from me?"

"Do you remember our first conversation, back at the Hyatt?"

"Yes."

"Robin was in the bathroom or something, and you asked what I thought of Selfscan."

"Right. You told me you thought it was interesting, but it would take a few years to perfect."

"But that the inventors had done a reasonably good job with it."

"Right."

The doctor looked out the window. Stonetree did, too, and he sensed he was about to receive quite an insult.

"I'd like to get you on the disc and see how you respond to a couple of items," Camden said.

"Oh, come *on*," Stonetree blurted out, rubbing his eyes. "You *have* to be kidding. What is that going to prove?"

"It'll prove to me that I'm not being set up."

Stonetree looked at the man, a man he had grown to like

after just a few meetings, but one he had almost despised just a few weeks before. Camden was calling him a liar, simple as that. He might be a lot of things, have his own set of neuroses and weaknesses, but he wasn't a liar. At least not to Camden. At least not on important issues.

"Shit, great," he replied, a tone of resignation in his voice. "Sure, why not? Maybe we can find someone with a rubber hose, too. They could beat it out of me."

"Dave," the doctor protested softly, "you have to understand. I don't think you're lying to me. I believe you."

"Then why the disc?"

"I've made some bad judgments about trusting people in the past." Camden groaned. "And I knew them a lot better than I know you."

Stonetree told Camden to wait a minute and got out of the car, walking to a pay phone to call Fitzgerald. He recalled that his therapist kept hours till nine P.M. on Thursdays. After he was put on hold for two minutes by the receptionist, Fitzgerald finally took the call. He was fully booked, he said. Could it wait until the next day? Stonetree told him it was critical to get in that night, and finally Fitzgerald relented, agreeing to see him at 9:30.

Halfway back to the Mustang a wave of realization washed over Stonetree just as a wave following the crackle of a Bradshaw-4 would. He didn't understand truth. He understood only shades of it. He couldn't remember the last time he'd ever leveled with anyone, ever really laid it out for all to see. It wasn't maliciousness that guided him, though. It was misunderstanding. It was pain.

He didn't want to disappoint. He didn't want to harm. So his version of reality was filtered through buffers, synthesized into a product with which no one would take offense.

Instead of looking in a mirror and asking questions, he paid Fitzgerald rent money, so to speak, of a hundred bucks a crack—two hundred and eighty-eight thousand dollars a month to borrow *his* mirror. But even in Fitzgerald's six-foot reflector, he saw only what he *thought* was the truth, which wasn't necessarily the truth at all.

What was the point? Whom was he kidding? Worst of all, when would he get caught?

Stonetree and Camden drove to the therapist's office and waited in the car until 9:25. Stonetree gave Camden a detailed account of his purchase of the car that day, including his luck on the commodities exchange. Camden said he was relieved to hear of the way he obtained the money. The doctor related some stories about his former sports car, a 1966 white convertible, and how he used to love driving through the Georgia countryside at breakneck speeds.

When they reached the doctor's office, it was empty. They waited a few minutes and then Stonetree called Fitzgerald's name. He called back, saying he would be there in a moment. As he entered the office from behind the receptionist's desk, he came to a startled halt when he looked at the two visitors.

"You didn't say you were bringing anyone with you," he began, staring at Camden. "And a famous someone at that." He extended his hand. "Dr. Camden?"

The doctor shook Fitzgerald's hand enthusiastically. "Yes, that's correct. And it's nice to meet you, Dr. Fitzgerald."

"The pleasure is all mine, believe me."

"Dr. Fitzgerald," Stonetree said, "isn't there a doctor-patient privilege, you know, like with a priest?"

"Why?"

"Because I would appreciate it if you forgot you met Dr. Camden, or at least forgot that you met him with me. Is that okay?"

"Why? I don't—"

"It's a long story, and I won't bore you with it. I realize you're doing us a favor by sticking around."

"No problem at all. I—"

"So if you could just plug me into the scanner and let me show the doctor how it works, I'd appreciate it."

"Well, I'd be more than happy to participate in any demon—"

"Dr. Fitzgerald," Stonetree said, trying not to sound ungracious. "I know you love to show it off and I know that you'd like to pitch Dr. Camden, but, uh, I have a little issue I have to resolve with him. It's of a confidential nature, so we're just going to go into the room, turn down the lights, and be out of your hair before you know it. Maybe some other night, huh?"

"That's fine, David," he replied, turning to Camden. "I trust you won't think I was trying to sell anything, sir."

"No, not at all, Doctor." Camden laughed. "I've been known to get pretty enthusiastic about new technology too. Perhaps I could come back another time." He placed his hand on Fitzgerald's shoulder. "I would like to try it out myself. With your guidance, of course."

"Of course! That would be fine. So let's get David set up, and I'll leave you to the project you're engaged in."

They walked into Room Two, and Fitzgerald began to adjust the machine to fit Stonetree's profile. The alcohol he could account for, and a cigarette earlier in the day, and even the obviously excited state his patient was in, but the readings were still not to his liking, and the test responses were giving unusual results. Fitzgerald thought for a moment.

"I'm not sure why," he finally said, "but we are getting an awful lot of high end out of you tonight. Have you taken any amphetamines today, anything that would boost your brain activity?"

"No."

"There's enough punch coming out of you—well, look at the screen."

They all did. Random spokes, in no particular order or pattern, were appearing. Even after the screen was cleared and no one said anything, the spokes returned.

"It sure beats me." The therapist groaned. "It usually is much easier, Dr. Camden. Any Febrifuge," he said, and looked at Camden, "or anything like that today, David?"

"No." Stonetree thought for a minute, slumping into the chair. "I did have some last night, though."

"How much?"

"I'm not sure. I don't remember. I was distracted."

"What series?"

Stonetree looked at Camden and felt a rush of embarrassment.

"I don't know. I can't remember. It was, uh, a lot, though."

A massive purple spoke appeared on the screen, but only Stonetree noticed it. "Yeah, uh," he said, speaking louder and faster. "And I'm worried about the commodities thing, about the Mustang, about war and famine." He hit the clear button.

"Well, let me keep trying," the therapist said. After a few

moments the screen had calmed down, and the test responses were flat enough to satisfy Fitzgerald. He went through a quick explanation of what he should do, and then walked to the door.

"Don't I get the usual send-off, Doctor?" Stonetree asked.

"Oh, of course." Fitzgerald cleared his throat. "And remember, David," he said in a solemn tone although there was a smile on his face, "always seek the pain, no matter how truthful it might be."

Stonetree roared. Camden held back his laughter.

"Or something like that," Fitzgerald blurted out quickly before he left the room and closed the door behind him.

"All right, Doc," he said, clearing the screen. "Here we are. What do you want to know? I'm not afraid to talk."

Camden looked at the screen and then at his patient.

"Bear with me, David," he replied in an apologetic voice. "I don't like doing this. I can imagine how you must feel. Just a few things, okay?"

"Shoot."

"Make a statement that you're not setting me up."

Stonetree hit the clear button and turned to the shimmering disc. "I am not setting Dr. Camden up."

Three blue spokes and one purple spoke, followed by a green one, appeared on the screen.

"Clear it," Camden ordered. "Next—that Robin is not setting me up."

"I don't know if that's true," he protested. "Only what I believe."

"Do it, please."

"Robin is not setting up the doctor."

Again, three blue spokes, one purple, one green.

"Good. That's comforting." The doctor sighed. "That makes me feel a whole lot better. Could you just try a few more for me?"

"Shoot."

"Tell it you're not happy you bought the Mustang."

"Why? What's that got to do with anything? I *am* happy I bought it," he said, clearing the screen.

"Humor me, David," Camden said enthusiastically. "I just want to see a comparison. I want to see a negative now that I've seen a few positives."

"Sure." Stonetree hit the clear button again, staring into the small black circle. "I'm not happy I bought the Mustang."

An orange spoke, followed by two yellows, another orange, and a green appeared on the screen and began to swirl.

"That's funny," Stonetree said as two pairs of spokes, one yellow and one green, entered the field. "I know I wanted it more than that." Another two pairs of yellow and green spokes appeared.

"I guess the mind really *can* play tricks on us, Dave." Camden patted him on the shoulder. "The things we think we want, I guess, aren't always what we really want."

"Reminds me of a song," he replied, hoping his ordeal was over. "There's this woman talking to this guy, and she says something like 'Your wife only knows what you need, but I know what you want.' Wish I could remember who recorded that."

"Sounds wise to me," Camden said, gazing at the screen. "And so, it seems, is this machine Dr. Fitzgerald has here. I've just got one more thing I'd like to ask you."

"Go ahead."

"But again, I really don't need to. I'm satisfied. Let's get going."

Stonetree charged the visit to a credit card and after an extended good-bye, Camden declining twice to set up an appointment, the three of them left the building together. Fitzgerald stopped to see the car and then went on his way. As the two of them returned to the hotel, Stonetree couldn't contain his curiosity about Camden's final but unasked question.

"So, what was the last question you wanted to ask me?" he inquired with an air of confidence. "I could have handled it. Shit, I was involved in corporate espionage last week, and now I'm about to help retrieve the Rosetta Stone of medical science. I'm pretty tough."

"It's really pretty personal. I was just playing a hunch. It's nothing."

"Come on. Tell me."

"I was going to ask you if you wanted to get involved with her."

"Who?" he asked, a lump rising in his throat, his hands gripping the steering wheel tighter.

"Lane. I was going to ask if you wanted to crank her, that's all."

"But why?" Stonetree challenged. "Why ask a question like that?"

"Just a thought, my young friend." He laughed. "Nothing more."

"Would you have an affair with her if you had the chance?" Stonetree blurted out.

Camden smiled. "I'd be telling you a lie if I said the thought had never crossed my mind," the scientist mused. "A thought I suppose a lot of people at SUE have had. But although I'm a country boy, I do have a few smarts. And one of those smarts is that you don't stick something into quicksand if you don't want to lose it."

Stonetree nodded his head, but why he wasn't sure.

CHAPTER | 16

STONETREE WAS PROUD HE ACTUALLY MADE THE BULLET RUN HE counted on, only to have a fifteen-minute delay spoil his plans to arrive at SUE Plaza before nine. As it turned out, he walked into the lobby at 9:10. He skipped a trip to the executive lounge area and went immediately to Lane's office. He found her immersed in a quarterly and had to knock on the doorjamb twice to get her attention. She looked up and motioned him in.

"Good morning," he began, walking up to her desk.

"Hello, David," she said flatly.

"I wanted to thank you again for having me over last, uh, the other night."

She looked around him toward the door, then gazed at him curiously.

"What goes on outside this office should not be discussed in it," she stated, then leaned back in her chair and frowned ever so slightly. "That is the way it has to be. Period."

Stonetree turned his head toward the windows, then back to her, wondering where she put her other self when it wasn't in use.

"I got hold of McReynolds, and he contacted Camden."

Her eyes brightened and she leaned forward, smiling. "Go on," she ordered.

"Camden is in town. He'll talk to you. He said this morning."

"Excellent," she murmured, rising to her feet. "I knew I

could count on you, David." She extended her hand, and he shook it without enthusiasm. "So how do we arrange it?" she continued excitedly. "How do we set it up? Where do we do it?"

"I'm supposed to call McReynolds. He'll call Camden. After that I don't know."

"Well, call him, call him," she directed, pointing to the phone. "I'll be right back. Just get him on the phone."

As she walked out of the office, Stonetree pulled his notebook out of his pocket and looked at the inside cover, where he had written down the number of the Hyatt. Lane walked back into the office just as the operator told him she would connect him to Camden's room.

"Let me talk to him," Lane said, requesting the phone with her outstretched hand. Stonetree pressed down on the receiver.

"Now, do *you* want to talk to him or do you want *me* to talk to him?" he asked, trying hard not to sound presumptuous.

"Oh," she said, biting her lower lip. "You do it. I just got carried away."

He looked through the list of phone numbers in the back of his book and found McReynolds. He dialed the number and got an answer in three rings.

"Hello?"

"Robin? Robin, this is Dave. How are you this morning?"

"Fine. What's up? Where are you?"

"I'm in Trisha Lane's office, over here at the Plaza."

"Is she there?"

"Yes."

"Oh. What now?"

"Miss Lane would be happy to meet with Dr. Camden this morning. . . ." He looked at Lane. She nodded. "At about . . ." He looked at her again and she whispered, "Anytime. Anytime the doctor would like."

"Only the doctor," Lane said.

"And only the doctor," he said into the receiver.

"What about me?" McReynolds asked.

"Only the doctor," he replied. "Could you call us back here at the Plaza when you contact Dr. Camden and let us know when to expect him?"

"Okay, you got it. He's up and ready to go. Is an hour soon enough?"

"An hour from now?" he asked Lane. She nodded.

"An hour would be fine, Robin. We'll look forward to your call."

McReynolds called back ten minutes later, saying that Camden would be at the reception desk on the main floor at 10:30, and would they have someone there to meet him. Stonetree repeated the message, and Lane nodded her assent. As he hung up the phone, he noticed that something had caught her eye at the far end of the office. From behind him he heard a voice with a midwestern twang say, "Well, hello, gorgeous. How's my lady?"

Stonetree turned and saw a face it took him a moment to associate with a name. The man was about his age and height but huskier, more muscular. He was dressed in what looked to be expensive clothes, especially his soft, rust-colored leather blazer with its sleeves pushed up to his elbows. His hair was medium length, brown, and curly; a darker mustache covered his upper lip. His beagle-brown eyes seemed to blend well with his deep tan and decidedly rugged demeanor.

At the juncture of the thumb and index finger of his right hand, Stonetree noticed what at first he thought were a series of cuts. Then he realized it was a design, a tattoo. The spider web stretched to the man's wrist, the innkeeper of the maze sitting on the raised bone.

"Hello, Doug, how are you?" she said, walking toward him. "I wasn't expecting you till later in the day."

"Gotta keep on the move." He laughed. "Hey, nice necklace," he said, flicking his finger at his gift. "Nice tits too. Any more like you left down on the farm?" He looked at Stonetree. "Oh, sorry, babe. Didn't realize you had company. Us poor old farm boys from Terra Haute just come up short in the manners department sometimes." He laughed again.

"Doug," she said, "this is David Stonetree, my assistant. David, this is Doug Smite."

They shook hands, Stonetree saying he was pleased to meet him. Smite said nothing but instead returned his attention to Lane. Stonetree looked at his own hand to see if the spider had jumped onto him.

"You look a little happier than you did last time I saw you," he said in a surprised voice. "Have you been eating right and exercising like I told you?" He looked at Stonetree. "Is it all right for us to talk in front of your ass-sistant?"

Lane leaned against the edge of a chair and looked at each of them individually, Smite first, then Stonetree.

"David can stay if it doesn't offend you," she finally said. "He's bound to get involved in this sooner or later."

"In what?" Stonetree asked.

"Oh, we got big, *big* problems this week, Davey," the man said. "Serious, *serious* problems. Which I hope our dear Trish-abelle is going to solve for me before I go off in a huff."

"I got Wexford's songs," she said in an energetic tone. "I like them a lot. Did you bring the rest with you?"

"I've got a total of eight more songs, six of which are marginal, two of which are pure crap. I figure you can get one short album out of the fourteen."

"That's it?" Lane asked. "That's all? I thought you said he was living in that studio?"

"He was. But a lot of it was reworks of the same songs, over and over and over. There's one song on there called 'American Love Story.' He must have done twenty different versions of it. Still came out like pig shit."

"So you've got the masters?"

"For all fourteen. On three reels. All locked safely away somewhere in this fine city where precious little claws can't reach them."

"I want to hear the other eight."

"I brought a cassette with me," he said, reaching into his jacket pocket, pulling it out and tossing it to her. "You can listen to it till hell freezes over, but it won't make those songs any better. The six you heard are the ones he did before he decided he needed a little help from his friends at SUE. After that it all fell apart. Pure crap."

She looked at the cassette and dropped it onto the cushion. "You mean he recorded the six *before*? Not the reverse?"

"No, it done done him in. He's stupid. He couldn't control it."

"And the masters for 'Blood Brothers,' for, uh, 'Take Me Away'?"

"I told you, precious. I brought all fourteen. Your baby Doug brought you all fourteen. It works out real easy. You give me twelve of something," he said in a low snarl, "and I give you fourteen of something." He looked at Stonetree. "Don't mind us, Dave. Me and Trishabelle here *always* talk to each other in numbers." He turned to her. "Don't we, babe?"

"Always in numbers." She looked toward the door. "Mary," she shouted, "would you close my door, please. No calls, either."

"Yes, Miss Lane," she responded.

After the door was closed, she motioned for him to sit on one of the couches at the other end of the office.

"How is he?" she asked, nervously fingering her necklace.

"He'll be okay as long as they don't pull the tubes out of him," he said blankly. "Actually that's probably a little too optimistic. I doubt that we'll ever see our boy ride a bicycle again, let alone perform. The doctors say he might never snap out of it." He coughed. "They say he might just stay in that little frozen twilight zone of his mind forever, till some kind soul like me takes pity on him and puts him out." He coughed again. "We'd better find us a new headliner quick, Trish."

"What a sad, foolish man."

"Not foolish, Trisha. He's a fucking asshole dumbshit motherfucker!" He stood up, rage flowing into his words. "And look at my sister! They get divorced and what does *she* get? Four million a month for a couple years? That's it? Why didn't he o.d., freeze his fucking brains into oblivion while they were married?" He began to shout at the top of his lungs. "Huh? Answer that one! Now, who's gonna get his six hundred million? His fans? The fucking government? Jesus Fucking Christ! And you call him *foolish!*"

Stonetree's jaw dropped a bit.

"Doug, be sensible," Lane interjected. "Yelling won't change anything. The party's over. Forget it."

"*You* forget it!" he screamed. "You're set for life. I've got things to worry about."

"Don't give me that 'poor boy from Indiana' shit!" she screamed back. "Your farm with the cedar deck the size of an average Broadway stage plus the first fifty rows! Your gold-plated Harleys! Your . . . what? Your four vacation retreats, each with its own little stable of chippies to keep you happy! That's what I like about you, Doug. You've got expensive tastes, except when it comes to women! Spare us all the bullshit this morning, okay?"

Stonetree's jaw continued to drop.

"Bullshit?" Smite roared. "Bullshit? Don't start telling me about bullshit, Trishabelle. If I deal bullshit, I do it with a small 'b.' I do friendly bullshit. I don't do big-time corporate bullshit. I don't do it with a capital 'B.' "

"And the reason you don't," she spat, raising her right hand and pointing at him, "is that you never learned your alphabet, you pitiful hillbilly!"

"Watch your mouth, honey."

"Watch your ass, Doug," she growled, "or somebody might bore you a new set of specifications. You understand? You might manage him Doug, but I own him."

"Bullshit."

"And next time you go to the beauty parlor," she said, "tell them you want a refund on your hair. Tell them somebody told you you looked like a department store mannequin."

"I have a certain style of living to which I have become accustomed," he said in a measured voice. "I do not plan to make the type of adjustments my sister made. I plan to stay on top, and what I do with my hair is my own fucking business."

"All right," she said, motioning him to sit down. "Now that we have had our respective hysterical outbursts, let's look ahead of us. David," she said, shifting her eyes to him, "what Mr. Smite was trying to articulate is the fact that Wexford injected too much of a certain drug and is now convalescing at his home in Jackson Hole."

"Don't patronize me, Trisha. I'm not putting up with that!" Smite half yelled, half growled. "Just remember who's got those tapes."

"And you remember who has the ten capsules?" she shot back.

"Twelve," he said.

"Ten, Doug. That's all there is. That's the truth. Ten."

"And not one less," he demanded. "I'm getting bored with this game of yours. Let's do it now."

"Where are the tapes?"

"Don't worry where the tapes are, Trisha. You give me those capsules."

"Not just yet," she said.

Smite started to get up, but she pointed at him in such a threatening way and glared at him with such an icy stare that he stayed on the couch.

"We all have our deals to cut, Doug," she hissed. "You have a deal, I have a deal—"

"Even old Davey here has a deal," he interrupted, laughing nervously and pointing to Stonetree. "Don't you, Davey?"

He didn't respond.

"And I have to get all of my ducks in line before we get all of your ducks in line," she continued venomously. "Is that too hard for you to understand?"

"Go ahead, babe."

"I hope that by the close of business today we will all have what we want." She turned to Stonetree. "David, would you please go down to the lobby and wait for Dr. Camden to arrive? When he does, bring him up here."

"Anything else?" he asked, looking at Smite.

"Not from me," Smite said. "Camden? *The* Camden, as in boy-are-my-eyes-bloodshot?"

"The same." Lane sighed.

"Hey, I'd like to meet him if you don't mind."

"You can say hello, but then you're on your way. We agree?"

"I just want to shake the man's hand, that's all. If it wasn't for him, I would have thought all along I was just drinking too much. Now at least I know I'm afflicted." This time he roared.

Stonetree went to the main-floor desk, but Camden was not there. He passed the time chatting with the guard and getting a visitor's tag for his guest. In a few minutes he saw him enter the building. He walked toward the scientist quickly, extending his hand.

"Hello, Dr. Camden. My name is David Stonetree, and I work for Trisha Lane. If you will just follow me, I'll take you up to the office, pronto. Just follow me, please."

As they rode up to eighteen, Camden whispered, "I guess we just met, is that right?"

Stonetree nodded.

When they reached Lane's office, the closed door and loud voices from inside told Stonetree that Smite was still there. He knocked on the door, and Lane asked who it was. He slowly opened the door and said, "I have Dr. Camden with me." She motioned him in. Looking past Stonetree with a look of anticipation on her face, she said, "Hello, Arthur."

The scientist took a few steps into the office, then stopped, as if hesitant about entering a cold lake. "Hello, Trisha," he replied. "You look well."

"So do you," she replied. "The beard is new, isn't it?"

"Since last time, yes."

She took a step toward him. "Your wife?"

"She's fine, thank you." He turned to Smite. "I don't believe I know your guest."

"Arthur Camden, Doug Smite. Mr. Smite is Wexford's manager. Doug, you know who the doctor is."

"Yes, Doctor." He shook his hand. "I'm pleased to meet you. I don't meet many intellectuals in my line of work."

"Nor I in mine," the doctor replied. "Nor any of those young women who follow you around."

"Not me, Doctor. They follow *him*, not me."

"Mr. Smite has his fair share of fans, too, don't you, Dougie?" Lane grinned. "Please, have a seat, Doctor," she continued, motioning to one of the couches. "Mr. Smite was just leaving." Camden sat on one of the couches.

"Maybe I'll stick around a few minutes, Trishabelle," Smite responded. "I have a stake in this conversation too."

"That won't be necessary." She scowled. "The doctor and I will be able to dispatch this much easier the less interference we have."

"Oh, you never know," he shot back, seating himself next to the scientist. "I can be real *helpful* during a tough negotiating session."

"Doug, please."

"And I'm familiar with the terms being discussed, too. You don't mind, do you, Doctor?" he asked.

"If Miss Lane has no objections, I have none," Camden said.

"I do, a number of them." She sighed, sitting down across from them. "But I'm not in the mood to argue about it. David, close the door, please."

"Do you want me to leave?" he asked.

"No," she said, motioning to the door. "You might as well stay. Just close the door."

262   · JOHN PATRICK KAVANAGH ·

She looked at the two men as Stonetree closed it. "No calls, Mary," she shouted. She then took a deep breath and addressed Camden.

"Doctor, I'll make this short so we don't take up too much of Mr. Smite's incredibly valuable time."

"I always appreciated your directness, Trisha," Camden said. "You always manage to get to the point quickly. I like that in a woman."

"I'm sure you do, Doctor," she said, motioning for Stonetree to sit on the ledge. "As I said, let's make it short."

She crossed her legs and flipped her hair back.

"Doctor," she began, "is it your understanding that all of our contractual obligations have been satisfied?"

"It is."

"There remains the matter of four pints of CY6A4 that were supposedly lost during an accident in Research. I have reason to believe they are in your possession."

"Is that so?"

"Yes, it is, Doctor," she snarled. "Would I be correct in that assumption?"

"You might be."

"So?"

"Let's assume you are. Let's also assume you have some notebooks of mine."

"Let's assume that too," she agreed.

"Well, am *I* correct?"

"I have some notebooks of *ours*, Doctor," she stated. "They contain your thoughts, but they belong to us."

"Continue."

"I would like to exchange those notebooks for the CY6A4. That is the offer, pure and simple." She stood up and walked to the window, leaning with her hands on the ledge next to Stonetree and gazing out at the city.

"Don't let her get too close to you, kid," Smite chortled. "You might get hurt."

"Shut up, Doug!" she snapped, continuing with her back to them. "If such a proposition is of interest to you, Arthur, we can talk. If you aren't interested, we can terminate the discussion."

"I love it when you talk that way, Trishabelle," Smite said sarcastically.

"Doug," she said softly, turning to him, "would you please stick it up your hillbilly ass."

"I'm sorry, babe," he said, grabbing one of the pillows on the couch. "I'll be good. You have to excuse me, Doctor. She just gets me excited when she talks that way."

"Does Pierre know about this?" Camden asked, ignoring Smite's comments.

"I'm the group vice president over Pharmaceuticals, Doctor. You should have realized that a long time ago. Would you like to see one of my business cards?"

"That won't be necessary, Trisha," he said, shaking his head. "The two of you speak as one. I'll deal with you."

"Good," she replied. "Right now would be fine. I don't suppose you brought the stuff with you, though."

"Hardly. Not something I'd want to carry into enemy territory. You'd agree with that, wouldn't you, Mr. Smite? You seem like a reasonable man."

"Absolutely! I like you, Camden. You're all right. Now we're making some progress." He turned to Lane. "See, Trisha. I told you I could help things along."

Lane sighed and returned to the couch. "So what would you propose, Arthur?"

"Well, first of all, I'd like to see those notebooks of mine— I'm sorry, of *yours*, if it wouldn't be too big a problem."

"That's reasonable," she replied. "David, go over to the cabinet behind my desk. Open it, and on the left side on the bottom you'll find them. Bring them back here, please."

Stonetree went to the bureau and retrieved them. There were three blue ones and a green one, maybe two hundred pages each, bloated to twice their original size from folds, wrinkles, and the countless spills they must have taken from years in the laboratory. Together they seemed to weigh about what a thick Sunday newspaper would.

For the second time that week he was holding history in his hands. If he counted the Mustang's briefcase, three. If he counted Trisha, four. He carried them to the coffee table and set them down.

"My old friends," Camden murmured, gliding his hand across the covers. "There's a lot of me in these old books." He paused and looked at Lane. "May I look through them for a moment?"

"Be my guest," she replied with a tinge of impatience in her voice. "It's all there, don't worry."

He picked up the first and rifled through the pages, many of them sticking together. Then he picked up the second and repeated his examination. The third blue one drew more of his attention. He paged through it slowly, the smile on his face growing larger with each turn.

"This was the low spot," he said, looking at a page and then at Smite. "Did you ever think you were onto something, Mr. Smite, only to find it was nothing more than a dead-end street?"

"All the time, Doctor. It comes with the business."

"Look at this trash," Camden said, tearing a few pages out of the book and dropping them on the table. "Trash. Junk. Wasted years."

"What are you doing, Doctor?" Lane asked. "That's our property."

"Oh, I know it's yours, and you can keep it!" He chuckled, ripping out a page, and then another, letting them drop to the floor. "All those years of thought, and I wasn't thinking a goddamn thing."

"I don't . . . understand, Arthur," she said, her voice constricting. "This *is* what you wanted, isn't it? These are the notebooks, aren't they?"

Stonetree could sense panic in her voice, as he did when she talked about Wexford's songs.

"Well, there might be something of use in the blue books," he said, placing the three of them in the neatest pile he could. "There might be something I'd be able to resurrect someday. But the green one is the charm."

He picked up the final notebook the way a father would caress a sleeping infant. He opened it and looked at the first few pages, almost lovingly, Stonetree thought. Then he set it on top of the others.

"Yes, Trisha, these are the books. I'll trade."

"Thank God," she said.

"Thank God," Smite repeated.

"And what is *your* concern in all of this?" the doctor asked Smite.

"I'm just here protecting my interests, like you," he replied. "You have something Miss Trishabelle wants, and I also have something she wants. Trisha, on the other hand, has something you want, and there is also something I would like to obtain from her sweet little treasure chest. We take care of each other, and we can all go on our merry way, just like in the movies."

"I saw a movie once," Camden said in a familiar voice. "There was a man who had something, and when he decided to give it back, he got himself in a lot of trouble. Ended up in jail."

"Oh, you don't have to worry about that," Smite replied. "I doubt anyone wants to tell the newspapers about this little transaction. Nobody wants to look bad. That's why we have the door closed. This is a backroom deal. Isn't that right, Trish?"

"What's your point, Doctor?" she asked absently.

"I would like some assurance that this matter will remain closed after its completion. I would like to know that there will be no retaliation, legal or otherwise, if we effect this exchange."

"Fine with me," Smite said.

"Doug, would you please keep out of this," she ordered. "Doctor, what do you want? Five lawyers from Legal to come in here and draft a twenty-three-page release form? Is that it?"

"Nothing so elaborate, Trisha. I understand the need to keep this among ourselves. Your word, as the head of Pharmaceuticals, will suffice."

"You've got it. Are we agreed, then?"

"Well," Camden continued, "maybe we could immortalize it for future reference. Do you have a pen, Mr. Smite?"

"Here you go," he said, handing him an elaborate gold and burgundy affair. Camden picked up the loose papers and found one that was blank on one side.

"Let's see," he said. "This is what, the twenty-ninth?" he asked as he wrote the date at the top of the page. "Now, the wording. How about," he continued, writing on the page, " 'Southern United Enterprises will, let's see, forever hold harmless Dr. Arthur Camden' . . ."

"Hey, I like that," Smite said. "You've been a lawyer too?"

"No." He looked at Stonetree. "I've been accused of that

before, though. Maybe it could be a second profession for me. One doesn't have to be too smart to handle it, I guess."

"They're all bloody fucking leeches—pardon my French, Doctor."

"Arthur, get on with it, would you?" Lane ordered.

"Right. Where were we? 'Will hold harmless Dr. Arthur Camden for his act of returning some CY6A4 to SUE against any criminal or civil charges or prosecutions, and will not inform anyone of his returning them.'"

"Wait," Smite blurted out. "You need that consideration stuff. Write down 'for ten dollars received in hand.'"

"Why?"

"Just do it. They do it all the time."

"I can't believe this," Lane moaned, crossing her legs and holding her face in her hands.

"All right," Camden said. "Let's see—who gets the ten dollars?"

"I'll give you the ten dollars. I'll give you a million," Lane screeched. "Just do it!"

"All right," Camden said. "For ten dollars received in hand." He then signed it and passed the paper to Lane.

"You want *me* to initial it?" she asked.

"Please, Trisha. And I'll hide it away in a safe-deposit box, so when the FBI comes for me, I'll be able to tell them it's all a misunderstanding."

She reached for the pen and signed the paper, then tossed both of them onto the table. Camden picked up the paper, folded it carefully, and placed it in his shirt pocket.

"So, now that you have your memorandum, Doctor, can we get on with this? I've got an important meeting a little later in the day with Mr. Ruth about my reorganization plan. Can we move on?"

"Who are you eliminating now?" Camden asked. "Walker? Paneligan?"

"Let's stay on the subject. Do you have the CY6A4 with you?"

"No. Let me make a proposition."

"Please do."

"Some of it or all of it might be here on the premises. Some of it might not. I would like to be able to check on it first. Then we could meet later and we can all make our exchanges."

"Now we're getting somewhere," Smite hooted.

"What's your idea, Arthur?"

"I would like to go down to R and D for a few minutes, unmolested."

"Alone, never. You just can't do that."

"All right. You can send your assistant, Mr. Stonetree, with me. Would that help?"

"Maybe. What happens then?"

"I'd like everyone cleared out of the main lab. I'll then turn out the lights so the cameras won't be able to monitor me. I'd like to check something, that's all. I've got a flashlight, a small one, in my briefcase. Then I would like to leave the Plaza, again, if you wish, with Mr. Stonetree, to see if my progress will be interrupted along the way."

"This is insane," Lane said in exasperation.

"And then maybe I'll walk back in and do it again, maybe a third time, and soon I'll be satisfied that I can go on my way. Then we can meet later and exchange our goods. Would that be acceptable?"

"If it's got to be that way. I suppose we don't have a choice, do we?" she asked.

"No choice, Trisha."

"So where do we all meet?" Smite asked. "I've got to get my stuff too. How about at my hotel?"

"Forget it, Doug," Lane said. "Try again."

"Then how about the doctor's place," Smite retorted. "Or how about your little love nest, Trishapoo?"

"What I would suggest, if I may," Camden said, "would be a place that's public in the sense that other people would be around us, but private enough where we would have some control over our conversation. Any ideas?"

"I know," Smite volunteered. "I hang out with the guys who run a nice club here in town called Sirius."

"That whorehouse," Lane spat out. "I'd prefer the Hyatt."

"It was no whorehouse when I was there, Trisha," Smite said. "Don't worry. You won't be propositioned. The boys can set us up a table away from everyone, where we can talk. Maybe even have a bottle of champagne to celebrate."

"It sounds acceptable to me," Camden said.

"All right, anything you want," Lane conceded. "This is getting more tedious by the minute. What time? I can be free at five. Is that acceptable to everyone?"

They nodded.

"Arthur, you'll bring the CY6A4. Doug, you're responsible for the master tapes. I'll bring the notebooks."

"And my little Care package, Trisha. And nothing cute— except you."

"Nothing cute. Let's just get this concluded. That's all I want."

She made a phone call and returned.

"Arthur, the lab will be empty and the lights out when you get there. There will be one security guard at the door with instructions to allow you and Mr. Stonetree in."

"No guards."

"We have to have at least one."

"No guards."

"All right, no guards. I'll call. Are we done? Are we agreed?"

The men nodded.

"Then we'll meet at the whorehouse at five. See you there, gentlemen."

Stonetree and Camden left, taking the elevator down to the fifth floor. Aside from a few people walking in the halls, it was the usual lunchtime lag period. None of them that he could tell were from Security. They walked to the main door and opened it. The lab was dark except for the soft glow of LED lights on various instruments.

Camden switched on all the overhead lights and looked around. Apparently satisfied, he flicked them off again and told Stonetree to stand at the door. He disappeared into the lab for a few minutes, then returned, motioning to leave. They caught the elevator down to the first floor and walked through it out to the street.

"Now we go back in?" Stonetree asked,

"Is your car here?" Camden replied.

"No. Took the Bullet in today."

"All right. Then here's the rest of the plan. I'd like you to go home and get your car and meet me back at the hotel before five. I'll get in one of those cabs over there," he continued, pointing to a line of three, "and drive around awhile, make a few stops, and go in and out of a few suspicious-looking places. Eventually I won't get back in the cab and I'll be gone."

"Where?"

"Back to the hotel. Robin is going to meet me there. We want to discuss a few things, make sure we've covered all the possibilities. Then you meet us and we can chat and then go to this—what's it called?"

"Sirius."

"Sirius, yes. We'll go there and make the exchange. What's this place like anyway? What types of people go there?"

"If Smite knows the Brown brothers, it's not the best of signs. Some pretty sleazy stuff can go on there. But it meets your requirements."

"Good. I'll see you later, then. Keep the faith. We're almost there."

They shook hands and Camden left in the cab, his briefcase held tight under his arm. Stonetree went back into the building and back up to eighteen to report. Everyone was gone. He called Sharon at the store but was told she'd gone home sick. He called McReynolds and Carl but received no answers. He stood in his office a few moments, wondering if he'd ever see it again. He was nervous and scared. But he knew in a few hours it would all be over, for better or worse.

CHAPTER | 17

STONETREE WASN'T CERTAIN WHY CAMDEN WANTED A CAR FOR later in the day, but he was grateful for the chance to return home to choose one. He needed to unwind from the events of the morning. On the way there he thought about reading or possibly taking a nap, but neither seemed appropriate once he was inside the house. It looked a bit strange to him. It looked like a place he visited rather than lived in. He decided to take another shower.

He shaved again, he washed his hair again, he brushed his teeth again. He stood for an extended period with a warm spray beating on his face, then, for an even longer period, with the temperature up, he let the water pound on his back. It felt so good to be able to stand there, in no hurry to stop, breathing in the steam and allowing his muscles to unknot beneath the heat.

After fifteen minutes he'd had enough. Drying off and throwing on his robe, he made his way down to the family room simply to sit in the silence and drink a glass of orange juice. He was just placing the bottle back into the refrigerator when the doorbell rang. He went to the front, pulling the shade aside a fraction of an inch to see who was there. It was Sharon, her arms holding two brown bags.

"Hi!" she greeted him as he opened the door. "Surprise! It's only me!"

"This *is* a surprise," he replied, trying to figure out why she was there. "I called you at work. They said you went home sick."

"I *am* sick." She nodded, kissing him. "Lovesick, that is. I just had to get out of there. I've been working too hard."

"I know."

"Soooo," she said with a smile, "I decided, seeing you said we'd be able to get together tonight, that I would sneak over here, lower the lights, chill some wine, put on some music, create some delightful snacks, and then, after all that, make mad, passionate love to you five or six times. How does *that* sound?"

"It sounds great. That last part has a ring of science fiction to it, though."

"Science fiction?" she asked, raising a single eyebrow. "Science fiction? Not at my bookstore. Over there we call it desire. Sometimes lust, but usually desire."

"Is it quality or quantity you're after?"

"Both. Like I told you the other day, I'm going to run my life like a life." She paused, then laughed. "But I'll meet you halfway. Four times," she said, holding up the same number of fingers on her free hand.

"Two," he replied. "Maybe."

"We'll see. You'll regret your doubts."

"I do appreciate your confidence in me. I'm always excited to have somebody drop by to tempt me."

"And what are *you* doing here?" she asked, looking around the living room. "You're okay, aren't you?"

"Yeah, I'm fine. Remember I told you about a possible exchange of something between Lane and Camden?"

"Yes, but you wouldn't say what was being exchanged."

"Well, they had a meeting this morning and later on they're going to make the switch. It's pretty bizarre."

"Why bizarre?"

"Now Wexford's manager is in on it too. It's really weird. Tapes, drugs, secret plans, everything."

"So when does this all happen? Today?"

"Yeah. Later on," he replied. "I'll really be happy to get this over with. It's getting too confusing."

Sharon placed the two bags on the coffee table and flopped onto one of the loveseats. Stonetree flopped next to her.

"So is this still a top-secret mission," she asked, "or are you going to cut me in on it?"

He regarded her for a moment, weighing whether the time had finally arrived in his life to step over the border. Trisha Lane, and everything that came with her, was just an illusion. In fact, if he didn't know better, Wednesday night was nothing but a dream.

Sharon was real. Her affection was real, her problems were real. Maybe he could do better, he mused, but he could also do much worse. Lane had told him he was now part of the future. Perhaps she was correct. But he realized, maybe for the first time in his life, that there was also a present. And it was right now.

Sharon was who he wanted. Sharon was always who he wanted. Since that first time he saw her at the bookstore. Since their first kiss. Since the Tower of London. She was the one. There would never be another one like her. Never, ever.

"Yeah, I guess you can be trusted." He smiled. "I'll cut you in on it."

He related everything he knew up to that point. Everything except the attempt to retrieve the CY6A4 the previous Friday and his visit to Lane's for dinner. Sharon was enthralled.

"A bit more exciting than unpacking cookbooks," she said.

She kissed him once lightly, and then he kissed her back with more passion. He felt good. In a few hours he'd be a hero to everyone. Maybe Lane would give him his own unit. Maybe Camden would want him to return to Atlanta. Maybe Doug Smite would turn him into the next Wexford. The weekend was supposed to be partly cloudy, with highs in the sixties. A perfect time to take a ride in the country.

"And I have a little surprise to show you in the garage," he finally said.

Her eyes widened. "Oh, David, you didn't, did you? Did you? You did!"

And she loved it. She'd never cared one way or another about cars, but this one, she said, was an exception. She fawned over it like a mother over a bride, and Stonetree finally had to tug on her arm a few times to get her out of it.

Back in the living room she kept switching back and forth between her interest in SUE and her enthusiasm about the

Mustang. Stonetree thought that for the first time he could remember he would really enjoy having her around all the time. All the time. Forever.

He went to his bedroom to get dressed, and she followed, sitting down on a low chest of drawers and watching him through the bathroom door.

"Can I go with you to meet Dr. Camden?" she asked.

"With me?" he replied. Ordinarily he would have dismissed her suggestion out of hand, but now he thought otherwise. "I don't know. He's already a little leery about the whole situation."

"I just want to meet him, that's all. The way you tell it, he might be the man who finds the cure for CYD. And if he does and he wrote his autobiography, I could say I was with him that day." She went to him and put her arms around his chest, watching both of their reflections in the mirror. "And then maybe he'd remember me when I'd write and ask him to autograph his book at the store." She paused. "What do you say?"

"I don't know." He sighed. "I don't know how long it will take. It could be hours."

"Okay," she said. "I'll tell you what. Let me go down to meet the doctor, then I'll take the Bullet back here and get started on dinner. You can call me when you're getting close to finished. If worse comes to worst, you'll get home late and have me greet you at the door with a glass of wine and little else. Not a bad deal to start the weekend, if I do say so."

He thought about it. He liked the idea. He could even meet Carl at Sirius, give him a check, and be back before eight. He was ready for the break. Finally.

"Okay, you're on," he agreed. "But just to say hello. Then you've got to let us finish the business part."

She nodded, deciding that maybe a book-signing party might be a little too much to expect.

As they drove into the city, Stonetree related the story about the gold trade and about the purchase of the car. Sharon was amazed he would take such a chance with his money. Then he detailed the story about the Mustang, his conversation with Hendricks, and the man's plan for the money.

"I think that's just wonderful," she said after he finished. "What a touching, wonderful thing to do. Certainly a tribute to the memory of his brother." She thought for a moment.

274 · John Patrick Kavanagh ·

"Do you ever think you could do something like that, David? Take off a year to care for others?"

"Couldn't afford it," he replied.

"What if you could?"

"Afford it? No, still wouldn't do it."

"Why not?"

"It would be depressing, being around sick kids all day. Who needs it? Why, would you?"

She thought for a minute. "Maybe not a year, but I could see doing it part-time if business at the shop ever calms down. Pure satisfaction. Just knowing that I was doing something for someone else. Just giving instead of taking."

"You give a lot to me."

"Well, I try," she replied. "But there has to be something more to it. I've got the store, I've got you . . . sort of."

He glanced over at her and then stared ahead at the road. And he had her, sort of.

"Which reminds me," she continued. "What's the story on tomorrow night? Are we going to take the little step toward the big step, or am I going to have to come up with a new set of excuses?"

"I told you I'd make the reservations," he replied, feeling a little pushed into his corner of the car. He told her he'd make the reservations, but he'd forgotten.

"And I'm sure you did. It's just that I've gotten anxious about everything." She paused. "I just want us to be happy. I want there to be more of a reason for the things I do."

"Is that you talking?" he asked, reaching over to take her hand, "or is it the CYD talking?"

She turned with a glare in her eye, but he continued before she could reply.

"Now, don't take that the wrong way," he admonished her. "This hasn't been a picnic for me, either. But that's not the point."

"What *is* the point?" she asked in surprise.

"The point," he replied, squeezing her hand, "is that I love you, and everything is going to work out fine."

She turned away from him and stared out the window. In a moment she released his hand to reach into her purse for a tissue. He waited until she dabbed her eyes before taking her hand again, and the damp tissue, back in his.

"So now what's wrong?" he asked.

She turned to him, her entire body sliding sideways in the seat.

"Nothing is wrong," she replied, half sobbing and half chuckling. "I've just realized in the past few days that a lot of things are right." She took a deep breath. "And I want them to stay right."

"Stick with me, sweetheart," he growled in a Bogart voice he had yet to master.

When they entered the lobby of the hotel, Stonetree saw Camden walking away from the registration desk. He approached the doctor, Sharon trailing behind.

"Well, David, you brought a friend, and a pretty one at that."

"Dr. Camden, this is Sharon Neville. Sharon, this is Arthur Camden."

"Oh, please don't be mad at David," she said. "I made him bring me along so I could meet you. I've never met anyone famous. I'll leave now if you want."

Camden smiled and shook her hand. "It's very nice to meet you, Sharon. You must be the young lady I've heard David talk about. I'm charmed."

"Oh, so am I. I even use your competitor's drugs."

"Ahem. Well, it's always nice to meet a satisfied customer." He looked at Stonetree. "Perhaps we could go up to the room for a few minutes and talk. But then, I'm afraid, David and I will have to be on our way to our engagement."

"Oh, I can leave now," she repeated.

"No, that won't be necessary. Come. We have time to chat for a few minutes, don't we, David?"

"If you'd like, Doctor. We're only ten minutes away from where we're going."

They went up to the suite, and Sharon asked if she could use the bathroom. Stonetree and Camden sat on the couches, the doctor pulling a receipt from his shirt pocket.

"Are you nervous?" he asked.

"A little," Stonetree replied. "Maybe a little more than a little. I don't even know if I'm supposed to be here. I went back to the office after you left, but everyone was gone. Did you get back here all right?"

"Yes, everything was fine. No problems. Maybe I'll go into the spy business."

"I still think law school is what you should do next," Stonetree said, shaking his head. "You really had Lane on the ropes with your contract demands."

"All part of the plan, David," he replied. "You'll see. It was just a precaution."

"Did Robin meet you back here?"

"Yes, as a matter of fact," Camden replied, a look of concern crossing his face. "I'm a little bewildered about a couple of things. Something doesn't fit with him."

"Really?" Stonetree replied, more out of curiosity than interest. "What makes you say that?"

"When you talked to Lane about me, did you ever tell her where I was staying?"

He thought for a moment. "No."

"Are you sure?"

"Yes, I'm sure. All I said was that you were in town. I never even said you were in a hotel. Just that Robin would call you."

"You're absolutely sure?"

"Positive. Why?"

Camden stood up and slowly began to pace back and forth. He seemed about to ask another question when Sharon walked back into the room.

"This is certainly a lovely place," she gushed. "Now, this is living. Why do you look so serious?"

"We have to talk about something, Sharon," Stonetree said. "I think you'd better excuse us now."

"Oh, okay. I'm on my way. Could I have the keys for the car? I left my purse on the seat."

"Your purse? Oh, jeez. Sure," he said, pulling the keys out of his pocket. "Better yet, why don't you get a newspaper downstairs and wait for us in the lobby? We'll be down in, oh, ten minutes. Would that be too long?"

"Oh, no. That's fine. It was certainly a pleasure to meet you, Doctor," she said, walking toward the door. "Good luck in whatever you do." She waved, closing the door behind her.

"So what's the problem, Dr. Camden?" Stonetree asked, resuming his seat.

"I don't know if it's a problem. There are just a few things that concern me."

"What about the hotel?"

"Oh, yes," he began, tugging at his beard. "When we were

in Lane's office, discussing a place to meet, she said she'd rather go to the Hyatt than to the club. Just before that Smite had suggested we go where I was staying. It might be a coincidence. Does she come here for meetings?"

"I don't know."

"Does Lane come here a lot?"

"I'm not sure. Not that I am aware."

"And then there's this," he said, handing him the receipt. "At one-thirty Robin was leaving and I turned on the TV to watch 'Headline News.' I know it was one-thirty because I looked at my watch. Robin asked to use the bathroom and then left. I went in to use it and, for some reason, I noticed the phone was wet. I figured if he wanted to use the phone, he just would have asked, right?"

"Right."

"So I called down to the desk and asked if my phone had been used. They said it wasn't on my bill yet, but they had a printout of all the calls made from the room which I could look at. So I went down to check. That's when you saw me." He pointed to the receipt. "Do you recognize this phone number? It was called from here at one thirty-one P.M."

"Five five five, two nine seven nine," Stonetree said out loud. "No, I don't."

"They looked at the log, and he was on the phone for less than a minute."

"That's his exchange. That's around where he lives. Maybe it's his cleaners or something."

"I don't know," Camden said.

"Let's call information. They'll tell us. I've got a number you can call, and they give you the owner's name and the address."

Stonetree made the inquiry, only to discover the number was both unlisted and unpublished.

"Beats me," he said, hanging up the phone and looking at the doctor. "Are you really concerned?"

"And then there's the interview he did with you."

"What about it?"

"He played part of the tapes for me."

"Oh?" Stonetree asked, a bit surprised. "Why did he do that?"

"To introduce you to me, I guess."

"Well, then, what's the problem?"

"Do you remember the last thing you said to him, at the end?"

"No. Should I?"

"Was it something about your wanting him to have mercy on you?"

"Oh, yeah, that's right. I did say that. You're right. So?"

"That's the impression I got too. But there's more on the tape, and it didn't sound like you were being interviewed, that you knew you were being recorded."

"Like what?"

"First you talked about a picture of his wife, I think."

"And then?"

"And then you said some things about Lane you probably wouldn't have said to *anyone* if it was being recorded. Something about a 'c' word."

"I did?" he asked, his legs wobbling slightly as he stood up. "And he played it for you?"

"Twice. To show me how sincere and courageous you were. And simple."

"He said that?"

"The implication was there."

Stonetree searched his mind for other anomalies he had noticed but could think of none. "I don't know," he finally said. "I'm surprised."

"I'll tell you what I'd like you to do," Camden began. "Robin said he would wait at his apartment to hear from us. Why don't you go over there and satisfy yourself that everything is right."

"Do we have time?"

"You go there yourself. I'll take a cab to this Sirius place. Would a driver know where it is?"

"Sure."

"I'll go there and wait for you outside. We don't have to go in and meet them till five."

"If you want me to, I'll go. Are you sure?"

"Yes. Do it. I'll see you later."

They shook hands and Stonetree left.

Sharon intercepted him in the lobby, a concerned look on her face.

"What's wrong, David? You don't look too happy."

"I've got to go check with my friend McReynolds about something, that's all."

"Let me go with you."

"No," he said as they walked toward the car.

"Why not?"

"Because it might get a little ugly."

"Why?"

"I'm not sure," he said. "Something came up. Something might be wrong. I can't tell."

"Let me go with you," she insisted.

"No. It might be dangerous."

"David!" she yelled, grabbing his arm and turning him around just in front of the Mustang. "David, listen to me. Ugly I can handle," she insisted, looking into his eyes. "As long as it's with you. Can't you understand that? When are you going to get that through your head?"

"What?" he demanded.

"I love you. I just want to be with you. To share with you. To protect you . . . from yourself."

They held each other for a moment. Stonetree thought of holding her hand at the Tower of London. And the walls around him.

"Get in," he said. "We don't have much time."

His thoughts raced as they made the short drive to Wilson Towers and raced more as they approached the elevator. *Five five five, two nine seven nine*, he said to himself. *Five five five, two nine seven nine*, he thought as the doors closed. *Five five five, two nine seven nine*. Where had he heard that number before? As they walked to the apartment, he reached into his pocket and removed his notebook, flipping to a section where he listed names and phone numbers for quick reference. About two thirds of the way down the second page he found it.

He rapped on the door twice. McReynolds opened it almost immediately.

"David?" he said, taking a step backward and looking at Sharon. "What brings you here? I didn't expect to see you till later."

"Oh, really?" he replied, stepping into the condo with Sharon close behind. "Where were you expecting to see me? I don't recall making any plans along those lines."

280 · JOHN PATRICK KAVANAGH ·

McReynolds closed the door and stepped back. "Oh, I don't know. I just figured. Who's this?"

"This is Sharon. Sharon, this is Robin."

"Oh, *you're* Sharon." McReynolds smiled. "Nice to meet you. Dave talks about you all the time." He turned to Stonetree. "Come in. Could I interest you in a cocktail?"

"I'll have a scotch," Stonetree replied. "Sharon?"

"Uh, do you have any white wine?"

"White wine and a scotch, coming up."

McReynolds returned with the drinks quickly.

"So, what brings the two of you into the neighborhood?" he asked, smiling at both of them now. "A little dinner maybe?"

"No, just thought we'd drop by to say hello," Stonetree said. "What are your plans for the evening?"

"Oh, I don't know." McReynolds shrugged, reaching for a cigarette from the table. "Want one?"

Stonetree took it.

"Nope, no big plans," their host continued. "But you know what I always say, Stoney."

"No rest for the wicked."

"You got it." He turned to Sharon. "Did you like the way our friend here came out in the *Fortune* article? I took the picture."

"With his new camera," Stonetree added, walking to the desk and picking it up. "Old Robin here loves his new toys. Don't you, Robin?"

"I sure do. It's a nice camera. Sharon, do you take pictures?"

"No, I don't," she answered.

"And he buys *dangerous* toys too," he continued, opening up the blue box and removing the Beretta. "Dangerous toys." He disengaged the barrel and nudged the shell out halfway, then nudged it back and closed it. He walked back to the couch and showed it to Sharon. "Robin thinks somebody's after him. Don't you, Robin?"

"Hey, Dave," he began. "Put that back. It's *not* a toy. It's real."

"I know," he replied, rolling it from one hand to the other. "Has it been fired yet?"

"No," McReynolds said, starting to stand up.

"Stay there, Robin," Stonetree ordered.

He hesitated, then sat down.

"Got any Febrifuge around here?"

"Sure, Dave. Always keep some around. Want to get cool?"

"Got any thousand?"

"I might."

"Any eleven hundred?"

"Hey, Stoney," McReynolds said, putting out his cigarette. "Lighten up, okay? I don't need this attitude of yours, whatever it is."

"Got any Sapien II lying around?"

"Listen, man," he shot back. "I don't need you coming in here and giving me shit. Maybe you ought to get to your dinner engagement."

"We're not going to dinner, Robin," he replied, continuing to roll the gun. "Not until we clear a couple things up."

"Like what?"

"Like a tape you played for Camden."

"What about it?"

"There was more on the tape than I thought. What's the story?"

"Maybe there was. So what? We were there to get your thoughts, remember? You knew it was on."

"Not at the end."

"So what? What else you want to know?"

"How do you fit into this, Robin?"

"It's a story, man. A big, big story. Come on, I've got things to do. What else?"

"How long have you known her?"

"Who?"

"You tell me."

"No, you tell *me*! What the hell are you talking about, man? Let me off, okay?"

"How long have you known her?"

"Look, Dave," McReynolds said, relaxing into the couch and smiling, his hands resting on his knees. "I know you've got a few questions you want answered, and I'm sure I can clear it all up for you." He looked at Sharon. "But this is a rather confidential matter, you know. Maybe we can talk about it later, huh?"

"How long, Robin?"

McReynolds jumped to his feet. Stonetree raised the Beretta

and pointed it at his head, both of them staring fiercely at each other. Then he cocked it.

"David!" Sharon cautioned. "What are you doing?"

"Yeah, listen to her, Stoney. What are you doing?" McReynolds asked in a flat tone. "Don't get carried away. We don't have to have problems. I can explain this." He looked at Sharon. "Tell him to put it down."

"David," she said, "what is the problem? Why are you doing this?"

"Stay here," he told her, pointing toward the bedroom with the gun. "Let's go in there and talk, Robin. We ought to be able to clear this up quick, don't you think?"

"Fine, man," he agreed. "Just fine. Let's go in there and talk it out."

Stonetree stood up and motioned with his head for McReynolds to walk to the other room. He followed him and closed the door behind them.

"Okay, what do you want?" he asked Stonetree as he sat down on the bed. "What's the problem?"

"How long have you known her, Robin?"

"Oh, I don't know." He sighed. "Three months, maybe four. I met her on the elevator one day. I recognized her from the *Money* article. Told her I was doing a piece on SUE. We had a couple of drinks."

"And?"

"And I did the piece on SUE."

"What else?"

"And I did the piece on SUE. So far."

"What next?"

"A book."

"On what?"

"I'm not sure yet, Dave." He smiled nervously. "Lots of possibilities. Lots of possibilities."

"You're setting him up, aren't you?"

"Who? Camden? Nope, just bringing some consenting adults together to resolve some of their differences. That's all."

Stonetree rubbed the butt of the pistol against the side of his head. He still didn't know how deep McReynolds was into the arrangement, or the precise role he played, or what he was doing in his friend's apartment holding a gun while Sharon sat in the living room.

"So what happens now, Robin?" he finally asked.

"Beats me. No idea. I'm out of it for now. So are you. Put away the gun, huh?"

"What happens now, Robin?"

"Uh, let's see. Camden goes to Sirius. Camden turns the stuff over to Trisha. Trisha gives the capsules to Smite. Smite gives the masters to Trisha. Trisha puts out the album. SUE runs the blood drive. Trisha makes more Sapien II, or three or four or a million. The possibilities are endless." He settled back on the bed. "Lots of possibilities, huh?"

"What's Camden get?"

"A kick in the balls if he's lucky."

"What about his notes? The cure."

"He's holding stolen property. Trisha isn't. The stuff belongs to her. The notebooks do too. Camden's lucky if he keeps his ass out of the penitentiary."

"So what about the cure, Robin?"

"Not my problem, pal. I'm out of it for right now. Sapien II could be a big story, Dave. The biggest yet. We might be at the dawn of a new age. And I'm gonna be right there, recording it for prosperity. I don't need a cure. I'm part of the future."

"You make me sick," Stonetree snarled, moving toward the closet. "How did you get sucked into this?"

"Hey." McReynolds said with a laugh. "Interesting choice of words. You ought to ask yourself a few questions like that. We're not all lily white, are we?"

"Turn over," Stonetree ordered as he pulled a handful of ties out of the closet.

"Cut the melodrama, man."

He lowered the gun, a foot in front of McReynolds's face, and thumbed the hammer. "I'm not kidding, Robin. Better yet, here," he continued, tossing him the bunch of ties. "Around the ankles. And tight."

"Okay, Dave," he said as he began to wrap one of the ties around his legs. "You're a big boy. You make your own choices."

"That's right."

"But I've got news for you," he said, knotting the tie twice. "This deal goes bad and Smite finds out you wrecked it, you can kiss your ass good-bye."

"I'll take my chances," he replied. "Roll over, on your stomach. Put your hands together."

"And he's not the type to let people off," McReynolds hissed as Stonetree tied his wrists together. "He's crazy. He'll kill you. He's been in a bad, bad mood lately."

"Haven't we all," Stonetree added. He dropped the gun and looped a tie between his captive's ankles and wrists, securing it with three knots. He rolled McReynolds over on his side, breathed deeply, and picked up the gun.

"And Trisha won't be very happy with you either—what's left of you." McReynolds smiled. "No more of those romantic, secluded nights."

"So she got you too, huh?"

"More than once, pal," McReynolds said. "But again, I live right here in the neighborhood." He paused. "But don't take it personally, okay? I don't. Neither does Trisha."

"I guess," Stonetree replied.

"See?"

"I guess I'm really not much better than you." He thought for a moment about whether it would be a good idea to put some tape or something over McReynolds's mouth to keep him quiet but decided against it, figuring it would take a would-be rescuer more than five minutes to get someone into the apartment after he and Sharon left. And a five-minute jump was all he wanted.

"Listen, Robin, I'll come back or I'll send someone back. I'm gonna rip the phones out. Do me a favor and don't be a hero." Stonetree tore a cord out of the wall and crushed the plug with his heel.

"I think *you* want that distinction." McReynolds smiled crookedly as he laid his head down and closed his eyes. "It was nice knowing you."

Stonetree began to leave but hesitated and turned back toward his captive.

"Why did you do it to me, Robin?" he asked, a lump rising in his throat. "After all this time, after all these years."

"Opportunity knocks only once," McReynolds replied. "So you have to take your chance when you see it. You just happened to be the doorman. Like I said, nothing personal."

"I'll send someone," Stonetree said, patting his friend on the leg. "See you later."

As they rode down in the elevator, Sharon didn't ask any questions, and Stonetree didn't offer an explanation. He looked at his watch. It was 4:50. He looked at his list of phone numbers. He couldn't believe he could be conned that thoroughly.

CHAPTER 18

THE MUSTANG SCREECHED TO A HALT IN FRONT OF SIRIUS. IT WAS a few minutes after five, and Camden was nowhere to be seen. Stonetree jumped out of the car, telling Sharon to stay put, and walked hastily to the first gate. He recognized the guard and walked past the line of twenty people waiting to get in.

"Hi," the bouncer said. "You don't have to show me your card." But he did not open the remaining barrier.

"Was there a guy with a beard, about fifty, standing here?"

"Yes, sir. There was. He's inside now. Are you Stonetree?"

"Yeah. Why?"

"He asked me if I knew you. Said he'd be inside. His name is Camden."

"How do you know?"

"The boss told me to let him in."

"Thanks," he replied, handing the boy a twenty-dollar bill and turning toward the second gate.

"Oh, Mr. Stonetree?"

He turned back. "What?"

"Is she with you?" he asked, pointing to Sharon as she ran up.

"Huh? Oh, Sharon!" He paused for two seconds. "Yes, she is."

There were no customers on the upper landing, and the dance floor and its surrounding area were empty as they walked in. Stonetree squinted around the upper level as his eyes adjusted to the low light. He didn't recognize any of the three waitresses standing at the bar.

"Do you see him?" he asked Sharon.

"There he is, I think," she replied, pointing to a high table beyond the dance floor and ledge. The table and its four high stools stood alone and empty in the middle of the safety zone, about ten feet in front of the furnace. Empty, that is, except for the slight figure of Dr. Camden. They raced down the right side stairs and across the deserted dance floor, reaching the table at the same time as the owner, Kennard Brown.

"This is a private table, boy. You'll have to leave," he ordered.

"Oh, hi, Kennard," Stonetree said. "How are you? It's okay, I'm expected."

"That's correct, Mr. Brown," Camden said. "He's with me."

"I was told three people," the man growled. "And these two ain't them."

"Mr. Smite will approve. Could you send a waitress over to take our order?"

Brown snorted and glared at Sharon, then walked slowly away, turning his head a few times to glare again.

"Robin set you up," Stonetree whispered. "They know all about us. He's been talking to her."

"I was beginning to suspect." The doctor sighed, looking at Sharon. "Trust is hard to come by these days."

"Let's get out of here, Doctor," Stonetree urged. The scientist began to get up when they heard Kennard's voice behind them.

"Stay," he ordered. "The waitress is on her way. You don't need to go nowhere."

"Just going outside for a little fresh air, Kennard." Stonetree motioned to the upper landing. "Unless we could use the back door?"

"You ain't going nowhere, cousin. Now, sit there and wait for your guests. Take care of them, Kristin," he ordered the waitress. She walked over and greeted Stonetree with a lascivious smile.

"Well, hello, David," she cooed, squeezing his forearm. "I've never seen you without a tie. This is a beautiful shirt."

Sharon frowned and looked into the furnace as the jets of flame turned from blue to red.

"Hi, Kristin. You look nice today too."

"Only nice?" She pouted. "Last time you were here, a few

weeks ago with Carl, you said I looked, what was the word, smashing."

"Yeah, well, you do today too. Could I have a Chivas?"

"On the rocks," she added.

"And, Doctor, you'll have . . . ?"

"A beer would be fine. Any kind."

"And Sharon . . . Sharon?"

"Oh, me? Me? I'll have a glass of white wine. I love white wine. It's so smashing," she replied, eyeing the waitress.

"Isn't this a cute outfit?" Kristin asked, calling the bluff.

Stonetree smiled. "Very," he said. "That's it for now."

The waitress turned and stepped away, bumping into an agitated Doug Smite. He had changed clothes since the morning. He now sported a black leather sport coat with a diamond lapel pin in the shape of a shooting star with a flowing tail. He wore a dress shirt and tie, and faded jeans. Stonetree also noticed a small gold stud in his left earlobe but couldn't remember if he'd seen it that morning. Smite carried three boxes marked 3M Mastering Tape, tightly bound together with twine and a plastic handle that strained under the weight of the foot-long cube.

"Hello, Doctor," he said, setting the tapes on the floor. "Who's she?" he continued, glancing at Sharon.

"A friend," Stonetree replied.

"This is no place for friends, friend," he said roughly. "Would you excuse yourself, lady?"

Stonetree placed his hand on her shoulder. "Sharon, go sit over in one of the lounge chairs, huh? We won't be long."

She began to walk away, but her progress was halted by Brown, who was leaning at the ledge surrounding the dance floor.

"It's okay, Kennard," Smite shouted. "Let her go. And what the fuck are *you* doing here?" he demanded, turning to Stonetree.

"He drove me here. He can stay," Camden said.

"Fine. Trishabelle ought to be here anytime. How do you like this place, Doctor?"

"I was looking at that newspaper headline over this, this . . ." Camden answered, motioning to the inferno behind him.

"The furnace," Smite said.

"Yes, this furnace. Two people jumped into it?"

"Fried like a Sunday morning breakfast." Smite laughed. "The first people ever to *be* barbecue instead of eating it!"

Kristin walked up to the table. She handed Stonetree his scotch, Camden his beer, and looked around for a customer for the wine.

"I'll take that one," Smite said, pulling it from her hand. "Thank you, Kennard," he called to the owner, toasting him. "Honey, you are about the most beautiful creature I have ever seen. Kristin, is that your name?"

"Yes, it is, thank you."

Smite took a sip of the wine and spit it back into the glass.

"This tastes like piss." He grimaced, looking at Camden and then at the waitress. "Why don't you bring us a bottle of Dom Ruinart, Kristin," he continued, wiping his mouth on his sleeve, "and four or five glasses."

She looked at Stonetree, then back at Smite. "I'll be happy to, sir."

" 'Sir'!" Smite roared. "You don't have to call me sir, honey." He paused. "You can just call me honey, honey."

"Anything you say, Mr. Honey."

"You are incredibly gorgeous. Do you know who I am?"

"No," she replied. "Are you a friend of David's?"

Smite looked at Stonetree and frowned. "Yes, I am, darling. My name is Doug Smite. And I also am a friend of Wexford's. I'm his manager. In fact," he continued, polishing his lapel pin, "you're just the type of girl we want to put on his next album cover." He leaned toward her. "How would you like to fly to Indiana with me later on tonight, and we can discuss this in more detail?"

"Really?" she asked.

"Yes, really."

"Well, David is *my* manager." She laughed, turning to leave. "You'd better discuss it with him."

"Really?" he replied, perplexed.

Stonetree saw Lane approach from behind Camden. She was wearing a black trench coat, one arm holding the notebooks, a neutral expression on her face.

"Well, we all seem to be here," she said as she set the books on the table. A hiss rose from the furnace as the streams of fire grew brighter and changed from red to hot white. Stonetree felt a blast brush against his right side. The music increased in volume and switched from a slow dance tune into the first number-one song of Wexford's, "The Pine Ridge Clipper." Lane turned toward the dance floor. "Our boy."

"Our boy, our dumbshit boy," Smite added. "Do you want a drink, Trish?" he asked.

"No, thank you," she said, looking at Stonetree. "Let's just get this over with. Are we agreed?"

Camden looked at her and bent forward a bit, staring at her intently.

"What is the purpose of this whole charade, Trisha?" he asked. "Why all of the pretense? If you wanted the CY6A4," he continued, pulling a small glass flask from his coat pocket, "why didn't you just call me up and ask for it?"

"I wasn't sure you had it," she replied.

"Till when?"

"Till I was told you did."

"By whom?" the doctor asked.

She looked at Stonetree again. "A friend of yours."

Camden looked at him and smiled at her. "He never told me, Trisha. And he doesn't know *now* if I've got it. McReynolds?"

"McReynolds."

"So what was the point? Why now?"

"We need it, Arthur. We're onto something. Bigger than Febrifuge. Bigger than you."

"What is it?" he demanded in a measured voice. "I want to know what it is."

"That's not your concern, Arthur. It's my discovery, not yours. Sorry, this one stays off the record."

Camden looked over his shoulder at Brown, who had been joined by two of the club's enforcers, one of them tapping the large brass handle of a walking stick in his hand. Then he looked at the three at the table. He stood up from his stool and took a step backward toward the furnace.

The waitress returned and set a champagne bucket and four glasses on the table. Smite shot the cork into the furnace and then filled each of the glasses. He lifted one to Lane, but she refused. He emptied a glass in a few gulps and then refilled it, setting the bottle down on the table.

"How about you, Doctor?" he asked, raising a glass toward the scientist. "Why don't you join in the celebration?"

"Yes, that's a good idea," Lane added. "I'll explain it all to you after we make our exchange."

"That answer is not good enough, Trisha," he warned her. "I want to know what it's for, or the deal is off."

"Now, Doctor," Smite interrupted, relaxing his arm on the table and staring at Camden. "The rules of this game are no longer in your control. I do not want any trouble from you. Trisha does not want any trouble from you. Those three gentlemen standing over at that railing do not want any trouble from you."

"You manage Wexford's career, Mr. Smite, not mine." Camden paused a moment and looked at the flask, then took another step back. "And was that a threat?"

"No, Doctor," Smite snarled. "That was a promise. Don't fuck with me and you won't get hurt. Kennard's dogs there look real hungry."

"They do look something, but I'm not certain what," he agreed. "And you look a little thirsty, Mr. Smite. Perhaps you'd like something more to drink?" he asked, holding the flask toward him. "Or maybe not."

With a quick flick of his wrist the doctor tossed the bottle into the furnace, a flash and a loud pop announcing its disintegration. Kennard moved toward him, and Smite stood up. Camden crouched a bit and held his open palms toward both of them.

"One more step and I swear to you I'll dive in with the rest of it!" he shouted. "And that is a promise, Mr. Smite. Don't tempt me!" He pulled out another flask.

Brown looked to the table, and Smite motioned slowly for him to return to the ledge.

"Tell him to get lost," Stonetree said to Camden.

"You keep out of this, David," Lane warned. "I can't protect you here."

"Tell them to get lost," the doctor directed.

"We're okay here, Kennard," Smite announced. "We just need a little more privacy. The doctor here is a little nervous. Why don't you and the boys leave us alone."

"I don't want no one throwing shit into the furnace, Doug. I don't want it."

"Kennard, don't worry," Smite said. "You have any damage,

I'll take care of it. No sweat. Just leave us alone for a few minutes. There's hardly anyone here, anyway."

Brown looked around, then back at Smite. "We got them in line out there, Doug. Get this over with. I want to open."

"Don't worry, don't worry. And don't worry about your little campfire. I've got all the damages, understand? Go have one on the house."

"I *am* the fucking house. I got people in line. Get it over with."

"Dave," Smite said, reaching into a pocket and pulling out three Kruegerrands. "Go give these to Mr. Brown, would you?"

Stonetree walked the ten steps and handed them to the owner. Brown looked at them suspiciously.

"That's to cover your delayed business, Kennard. Plus I get all the damages. Leave us alone for ten minutes, okay?"

Brown tossed the coins a few inches in the air and caught two of them in his other hand. The third was retrieved by one of the bouncers.

"The place is yours." He motioned to the flames. "You've got fifteen minutes. Throw the fucking stools into it if you want!" he roared, turning and pushing the guards away with him.

Camden relaxed a bit but held his position near the furnace, passing the second flask back and forth in his hands and staring at Lane.

"That was an incredibly stupid and costly thing to do, Arthur," she said. "Do you know how much that little temper tantrum was worth?"

"Eight ounces?" he replied, raising his eyebrows. "Priceless. You can't buy it many places these days, can you, Trisha? In fact, I know you can't get it anywhere."

"Perhaps," she said. "Which is why I came to you. Now, can we conclude our agreement?"

"As soon as you tell me what you plan to do with my part of it," he stated.

"I told you once, Arthur. It is none of your business. Now, let's get on with it."

Camden flicked the second bottle into the furnace, recoiling slightly from the flash of light. "I asked you, Trisha. What's it for?"

"You know something, Doctor," she said as she removed her trench coat, revealing the outfit she'd worn two nights earlier. "I went home after a discussion I had with Mr. Ruth this afternoon, and I thought about a portion of that conversation in which your name came up."

"I'm listening."

She reached into one of the notebooks and removed the pages Camden had torn out that morning. She took a step toward him, then a few toward the furnace. Stonetree watched her hands as she leisurely folded the papers. "And he asked me, as we talked about my reorganization plan, to describe the problem I had with you two years ago."

"And?"

"And I told him," she said, tossing the papers into the furnace and watching them disappear in a puff, "that my biggest problem with you was that you could never tell the difference between what was intrinsically valuable and what you personally *thought* was valuable. I told him I felt the gap was incredible. And it's true." She returned to her seat. "What do you think?"

"I think you should refrain from incinerating those notes," he warned her. "They are much more valuable than you could imagine."

"Maybe to you," she said as he took a third flask from his pocket, "but not to me. Now, why don't we start with one of these blue ones that evidently contain your unbridled genius." She picked up the top notebook and held it toward him. "Now I'll give this to David, and he can give it to you. You give him a couple of those flasks, Arthur, and we can finish this up before you know it."

"You can be back in Atlanta tonight, Camden," Smite added. "Don't be an asshole, all right?"

"I told you, Trisha," the doctor said in an even, almost sleepy voice, large drops of sweat forming on his forehead, "I want to know what you plan to do with the CY6A4. Tell me, and we'll be done."

"Sorry, Arthur—the notebooks for the reduction. That is what we agreed on. Nothing more."

"The deal has changed. What do you want it for?"

"None of your *business*," she spat out.

Camden looked at her and twice pretended to toss the flask

294   · JOHN PATRICK KAVANAGH ·

into the flames, each time prompting her to scream "No!" On the third toss he let it go, and it exploded in a bright orange flash.

"You bastard!" she howled. "You stupid bastard! I can play your game too!" She arched the notebook from her hand, and it tumbled end over end into the furnace, disappearing in a brief fizzing sound. "There! Are you happy, you stupid old man?"

Camden wiped the sweat off his forehead. He had an odd, almost mad look on his face, Stonetree thought.

"Are you okay, Doctor?" he asked. "It's boiling over here. You'd better sit down."

"I'm all right. I can sit later. First we finish this." He reached into his inside pocket and withdrew a fourth flask. "What are you going to do with it, Trisha?"

"You're sick, Arthur," she replied. "You're not well. Let's get you out of here."

"Come on, Camden," Smite added. "You'll fry over there. You look like you're dying."

"I'm fine, just fine," he replied, wiping more sweat off his cheeks, then rubbing one of his eyes. "What do you want it for, Trisha?"

"I'll tell you, I'll tell you!" she yelled, slapping her palm on the table. "Just get away from the fire. You'll pass out. You'll fall in."

Camden staggered a few feet from the flames, motioning to Stonetree to give him room. Then he looked at the furnace and took a step back.

"Tell me, Trisha. Now." Stonetree pulled one of the stools from the table and set it behind him. Camden placed a heel onto one of the support rungs and leaned on the cushion with his free hand.

"We came up with a formula, a very important discovery," she began. "A chemical to unlock our minds, our potential."

"Who?"

"Hickey."

"What is it? The next generation? A new series?"

"No," Lane said, propping her chin on one hand, her elbow resting on the notebooks. "Something different, exciting, important. Words you don't understand, Arthur."

"Tell me more."

She stood up and stretched across the table, bending low and grasping the opposite edge of the table with both hands, her necklace hanging flush with her face.

"It is beyond Febrifuge, beyond everything," she said softly. "It is a compound, an elixir for a new age. A new age that doesn't belong to you, Arthur. It belongs to me, and me alone."

The doctor wiped his cheeks again and blinked through his watering eyes, a confused look distorting his face.

"Wait," he said. "Is this a compound that actually uses the CY6A4? You actually add it to the compound?" he asked.

"Yes, that's right. Now you're starting to understand."

"In what multiples?"

"What do you mean, in what multiples?"

"In multiples to the synthetics you put in Febrifuge Blue? In multiples to those? How much?"

"I'm not certain I follow you. I don't know what you mean."

"The multiple, Trisha. You've been around," he said in a stern voice, dragging his sleeve across his forehead. "Let's say there is one fiftieth of a unit of synthetic in the formula for the eight hundred series. How much more would you put into this compound of yours? Ten? Twenty?"

"A hundred," she said, a suspicious look in her eyes. "Why? Why do you care?"

"A hundred," he said, looking into the flames. "A hundred sounds about right." He opened a button on his soaked shirt and looked at Stonetree. "She did say a hundred, didn't she?" he asked.

"Yes, sir, she did."

Camden convulsed a couple of times, and Stonetree stepped toward him. But he realized it was not coughing, instead a low chuckle that rose from the scientist's chest, soon replaced by laughter. He looked at Smite and Lane, their faces blank, changing from white to blue as the furnace did the same. It felt cooler, even though he knew it wasn't. The doctor removed another flask from his coat.

"Tell me you're pulling my leg," he said in a mocking tone. "Tell me you're kidding, Trisha."

"I'm not," she said. "It's the truth. Believe me."

"And Hickey told you about this, Trisha? Is that right? This discovery?"

She nodded.

"And did he tell you the name of it, Trisha? Did he tell you the name of it?"

"He has a name for it."

"Did he call it Sapien II?"

She straightened up, a bewildered expression quickly replaced by rage. "Who told you that?"

"Nobody had to, Trisha," he answered, finally sitting down on the stool, the hand holding the flask dropping behind the backrest. "I invented it. And you tossed the whole formula into that fire."

She stepped toward Camden but was grabbed from behind by Smite, her blouse tearing at the shoulder as she was pulled back. A long, heavy, gold-bladed knife appeared in his other hand, its point directed at the doctor.

"I don't know what the problem is between you two," he growled, looking at Lane, then Camden. "But you're going to have to work it out between yourselves later. Give me the capsules, Trishabelle."

"Give me those bottles," she said to the scientist.

"Back where I come from, Doctor," Smite snarled as he picked up the remaining notebooks with his free hand and wedged them under his arm, "little boys like me grow up with knives like these and learn how to use them." He glanced back at Trisha, then at his surroundings. "I can slit a grown hog from end to end in just one motion. I can cut a piece of rope thicker than your cock in one motion. I can do a whole lot of things you wouldn't imagine in one motion. But, most of all, I can throw."

Camden stared back, motionless, the sweat dripping off his face.

"I learned how to throw," Smite repeated, letting the weapon drop to his side. "Throw as pretty as can be. I used to stand out in the backyard with my brothers. We'd stand there for hours, tossing our blades at a big oak tree no farther away from us than you. Had a little circle on it 'bout the size of a man's heart. And I learned to cut dead center every time."

The flask dropped from Camden's hand and shattered on the floor.

"Now we're gonna play a little game of backyard tossing, Doctor," he said. "We're gonna play us a game for money, and here's how it goes. I'm gonna ask you just once to walk over here and give me the bottles you got left, and I'm gonna hand you these books. Then I'm gonna give Trishabelle those bottles and Wexford's swan songs, and she's gonna give me those Sapien capsules. And then the game's over."

Camden stared back at his inquisitor with half-closed eyes, his hands shaking at the ends of his limp arms.

"But if you don't do what I ask, you're going to find old Doug's knife somewhere between your shoulder and your stomach. And I'm gonna walk over and take those bottles from you. But you won't care because you'll be dead. Do we have an understanding?"

Camden's mouth opened slightly, but he did not speak.

"Come over here, Doctor," Smite ordered. "Come over here or you're history." He raised his arm, the handle of the knife resting on his shoulder. "I said, come over here or you're history."

Camden remained still. A look of animal rage jumped onto Smite's face as his arm cocked. Stonetree pulled the Beretta from his pocket and leveled it at the attacker, the hammer clicking open. "Stop!" he shouted.

Smite froze. Stonetree heard Sharon yell, "No, David, no!" from behind and to his left. Camden lurched to his feet and shook his head. Sharon ran up to Stonetree's side.

"Down on the table, Doug," Stonetree ordered. "The knife and the books. On the table." The man followed his instructions.

"It's all right, David," Camden said. "It's all right. Don't do anything. It's all right."

He held the gun steady. "So what's the story, Doctor? What is it?"

"Yes, what is the story, Arthur?" Lane asked, stepping back to the table. "Now that we've all calmed down." She sneered at Stonetree. "Put the gun down, David."

"The knife, Trisha," he replied, motioning with the gun. "Into the furnace, please."

She picked it up and tossed it into the blue wall of flame, a burst of yellow and a thunderous crack greeting it. Stonetree lowered the weapon to his side.

Camden straightened his clothes and pushed his wet hair back on his head. "I can't believe you'd be so foolish, so ignorant, Trisha." He walked to the table, staring fiercely into her eyes. Picking up a glass of champagne, he then returned to slump into the stool. "You never were that circumspect to begin with."

"What do you mean?" she asked, running her finger across the cover of one of the remaining notebooks. "I've tried it. I know."

"And I'll tell you what you know, and what you don't," he began. "I came up with that concoction you've fallen in love with three years ago. It was an accident, wasted a lot of CY6A4. But I decided to see what it would do."

She stared blankly at him and bit hard on her lower lip.

"The rush of euphoria, the freeze, the tranquilization, the awareness, the brilliant memories—yes, I know all that. Once, and once only. It will unlock your memory, Trisha, and make you think you control the past and therefore, maybe, the future. And it explodes millions of brain cells in the process. Probably tens of millions. I'm surprised I can still talk after that experience."

She continued to stare, the grip of her teeth on her lip becoming stronger.

"Fed some to a couple of innocent rats and a monkey down in the lab," he continued, the confidence of knowledge flowing through his words. "Sort of a last meal for them. Cracked open their little skulls afterward. Cracked them open and found little balls of mush, almost liquid." He rose from the stool and shook his head. "Maybe you can take it once, Trisha. Maybe twice. Maybe you got off lucky like I did. Do it more than that and you might be in trouble. You could go into a coma or lose your eyesight. It just depends on which cells decide to blow."

Lane dropped onto her chair, her makeup barely concealing the ashen tone of her face.

"And that could happen to you, Mr. Smite, as sure as you're standing there. From one farm boy to another, you'd better take my word on that."

"Hickey," Trisha said in a weak voice. "Hickey."

"Yeah, I told him about it a few months before I left," Camden said, shaking his head again. "I told him and he was all eyes and ears. I figured he wouldn't leave it alone, that he'd have to see it for himself. He's a fool too. I even told him the name I gave it. Named it after that poor monkey I killed. Poor old Sapien II. I wonder where his monkey soul is today?"

"You're serious, ain't you, Doctor?" Smite asked.

"Serious as a heart attack, Mr. Smite," he replied. "Old Pierre smiles only about once a month, but this might get a little laugh out of him." He paused, staring intently at Lane, his sleeve again wiping his forehead. "I gave him a call today, Trisha. Thought the time had arrived to come to terms with him. And, you know, in some respects he was still on your side, still in your corner."

"That shouldn't surprise you," Lane replied, standing and slowly moving around the table. "Pierre doesn't make mistakes when it comes to judging relative strength."

She took another step toward the scientist. Stonetree moved in between the two, facing her. The brilliant light from the furnace made her eyes glow and her face glisten. Her disheveled hair and clothes only added to this vision of pure contempt.

"Leave the doctor alone," he warned her. "He'll give you what he said he would. Just leave him alone."

"And who are you to tell me what to do?" she asked. "Get out of my way, David."

"I said leave him alone," he replied, raising the gun slightly. "I am not going to allow you or anyone else to harm him."

The flames of the furnace turned from blue to red. Stonetree could hear music in the background but could not place the song. Sweat was dripping into his eyes, making them sting. The Beretta felt like a feather. He knew he was in trouble, more trouble than he could imagine. "I'm right," he said almost in a whisper.

"You're right?" Lane repeated, an air of innocence in her voice. "No, you're not, David. You're confused. Your loyalties are confused. You don't work for Camden, you work for me." She paused. "And I want those other flasks the doctor has. Don't make this difficult for yourself, David. Don't make this difficult for me."

"Leave him alone."

Lane looked at the tear in the shoulder of her blouse, tugging on the material to straighten it a bit. She returned her gaze to Stonetree.

"You have to make a choice, David," she continued as she absently toyed with a button of her blouse, already half ripped away. "It's like I told you the other night, you're now part of the future."

Sharon grabbed the champagne bottle by the neck and smashed the side of it against the table. She then took a few steps and held the jagged weapon an inch from Lane's throat.

"And I'm telling you," she growled at Lane, "that if you take one more step, you're part of the past."

Smite yelped and started to clap. Lane stepped backward and leaned against the table. Sharon dropped the bottle to the floor and looked at Stonetree, a slight smile appearing on her lips. "I think you four can finish up now," she said as she picked up a glass from the table and stepped away from them.

Lane smoothed her skirt. She looked at each of them in turn, settling on Camden. "Arthur, this has been a trying day," she said. "Take your notebooks and go back to Atlanta, please." She turned to Smite. "The capsules are in my coat, Doug. Leave me the tapes, and we'll talk later."

She then returned her gaze to Camden, a gaze so rife with contempt it could slice through the wall of fire behind them, Stonetree thought. "Legal tells me the witnessing was enough," she growled. "You fuck with me for one more second, you go to prison. Grand theft. And I'll make it stick."

Smite reached down to the floor behind him and picked up her trench coat, setting it on his stool.

"I'm not sure those capsules are yours to give away, Trisha," Camden said. "Or those notebooks. Pierre might have something to say about that." He turned his head toward the second-floor landing. The rest of them looked up, following his lead. The silhouette leaning at the railing, black against the glare from the doorway behind it, was recognizable to anyone who had worked at SUE very long. The silhouette waved its hand and turned and left, walking out into the late-afternoon sunlight.

"You might have won this battle, Arthur," Lane yelled, grabbing the notebooks, "but I'm sending the rest of your dreams to hell!"

She turned toward the furnace, positioning her arm to send the scientist's research into oblivion. A figure from behind a pillar appeared in a flurry and snatched away the notebooks. "Control yourself, Trisha," the man said. "That's SUE property, not yours."

She snapped her head around to look at her molester. "Wallace!" she cried in surprise. Smite reached down, grabbed the boxes holding the tapes, and took a step away from Lane and Walker, clutching the cases to his chest.

"No need to panic, Mr. Smite," the man cautioned in an even voice. "We have avoided serious problems thus far. Let's keep it that way."

"Who the fuck are you?" Smite demanded.

"I'm Wallace Walker, one of Miss Lane's colleagues," he replied, raising his palm in a conciliatory gesture. "I have been given temporary authority by our chairman, Mr. Ruth, over Miss Lane's divisions. Am I to understand that those are the masters for Wexford's next album?"

"Maybe."

"Well, maybe you'd be interested to know that a good friend of mine is a high-placed law enforcement officer here in the city. In fact, he is the regional director of a certain government agency, a federal agency, best known by three initials. Are you familiar with that agency, Mr. Smite?" A slight grin crossed Walker's face. "He tells me he has a file on you. His name is Fine. Nick Fine."

"I might know of him."

"Well, I called this friend of mine and told him you might be involved in something of interest to him. And he has a few of his employees waiting outside, perhaps wanting to talk to you. He arranged for Mr. Ruth, myself, and a few of his employees to circumvent that long line of people Mr. Brown is holding at the door of this establishment. If you'll please set those tapes down and leave, you might be able to walk away unmolested. If not, you take your chances."

Smite hesitated a moment and then placed the tapes on the table. "Can I leave now?" he asked. "I think I've got another appointment waiting for me. I'm done here with your 'colleague,' Miss Lane."

Walker waved to someone at the other end of the first floor. "Yes, you can leave. Someone will contact you soon so we can have the papers signed. Good day." He extended his hand, but Smite only glared at each of them and left.

"This is colossal stupidity." Lane sighed. "There's been no damage done here, Wallace. Can we sit down and talk this through so we don't end up with a big misunderstanding?"

"I think there has been some damage done, Trisha. You've

destroyed, oh, what would you say, Dr. Camden? A pint of CY6A4?"

"About that," he agreed, placing four flasks on the table.

"I didn't destroy anything," Lane protested. "Not a thing except a moldy notebook."

"A quite valuable notebook, Trisha," Camden said. "A very valuable one."

"Did that one have your precious vaccine formulas in it?" she asked, running her hands through her hair, an arrogant tone in her voice. "Well, gentlemen, don't worry. I have a beautiful set of copies of these notebooks back in my office." She turned to Walker. "You see, Wallace," she protested, "no harm done. You really didn't think I'd ever torch those, did you?" She hesitated. "Pierre knows that."

"I got all I wanted this morning, Trisha," Camden put in, pulling a paper from his shirt pocket and unfolding it carefully. "It's all on the back of our contract." He held it up to the light. "Just one formula. A very long one, I'll admit. One I couldn't chance upon again for years, but it's all here." He tapped his head. "And now it's all up here too."

Stonetree felt Sharon's hand close around his.

Lane shook her head as if recovering from a punch. "So, all's well that ends well." She smiled, reaching into the pocket of her trench coat and placing a small box on the table. "No harm done, except Dr. Camden's insane threats and his destruction of the CY6A4."

"It's only apple juice," the scientist said, picking up one of the flasks and opening it. He took a large gulp, burped, and then smiled. "Apple juice."

"Then I am truly at a loss. What was destroyed, then, Doctor? Wallace," Lane said, turning to him again, "can you enlighten me?"

He looked at Camden.

"It's all in the notebooks, Trisha," the doctor said, patting them. "Or three fourths of it, now, at least."

She looked at him, then at the notebooks, lifting one of the covers and running her hand over the discolored, bloated pages. She then looked at Stonetree, just as the realization appeared on his face.

"I had to leave it somewhere, somewhere I knew it would

be safe," the scientist said, his voice filled with irony. "I knew these books would never be destroyed, that you'd guard them forever. Very absorbent," he continued, placing his hand over hers. "Like a sponge. Like a greedy sponge."

They all stared at the notebooks for a long minute. Then the crowd began to filter in, and the music grew louder. And, again, Wexford's voice could be heard over the hiss of the furnace.

"Mr. Ruth would like to see you in his office at seven, Trisha," Walker said. "I'd suggest you go home and change first. Dr. Camden, if you would be kind enough to meet with me tomorrow at nine, we can talk about all of this. I think you've had enough for one day. On behalf of myself, Mr. Ruth, and Southern United Enterprises, I would like to express our apologies."

Camden nodded.

"David," Walker continued, "I'm not sure about you. We'll have to consider this escapade you've involved yourself in. We can talk Monday."

"Yes, sir. I'll be there."

Stonetree looked at the scientist and smiled weakly.

"Thank you, David," the doctor said, holding out his hand. "I mean that."

Stonetree shook it. He turned to Lane, a faint smile appearing on her face. "I'll see you around campus, Trisha. Take care of yourself."

She made no reply.

"Can we leave now, David?" Sharon asked. "I'm making dinner for you, remember?"

"Dinner?" He laughed, putting his arm around her. "After all of this you want to go home and make us dinner?"

"Well," she replied as she beamed at him, "maybe you should do something about Robin first, but I'm really hungry. This cops-and-robbers stuff really builds up an appetite."

Stonetree thought about the Tower of London.

"Better yet," he said, "you know that place we're supposed to go tomorrow?"

He hesitated. She nodded. He hesitated one last time.

"Why don't we just go tonight? I'm getting a little hungry myself."

EPILOGUE

STONETREE HEARD THE PHONE CHIRP AS HE OPENED THE DOOR of the Turbostar. His first thought was to ignore it and continue with his plans for the steamy summer Saturday. Instead he walked back into the house and picked up the cordless in the family room.

"Hello?" he said as he wedged the phone between his head and shoulder.

"David?" the voice replied. "David? This is Trisha."

He smiled and sat on the couch, hesitating a moment before answering.

"Hello, Trisha."

"How *are* you?" she asked with an enthusiasm he recognized. "I was just sitting here having a cup of coffee and thinking about you and thought I'd give you a call. What's new? What have you been up to?"

"Just living out here in the suburbs."

"I heard you're not at SUE anymore."

"No." He chuckled. "No more SUE."

"They didn't ax you too, did they?"

"Well," he began, picking up a half-eaten doughnut and taking a bite, "not really ax." He paused, looking to the clock in the kitchen and then at his watch. "I had a long talk with Wallace after our get-together, and we both decided it would be best if I considered my options."

"Must be nice," she responded. "I was simply fired."

"Yeah? Well, my options came down to going back to Technology and counting beans for the rest of my life or two years' pay plus my benefits and taking a hike."

"And?"

"And I took a hike. A long one."

"I'm surprised. I figured they'd make you an officer and give you the distinguished service medal."

Stonetree pulled a pillow behind his back and stretched out a bit, resting his feet on top of the coffee table.

"Well, I sort of hoped for that too, but it just couldn't work out that way. They were happy with the outcome and everything, but when it came right down to it, I was stealing company property. So I really can't complain. I could be in jail with your friend Smite."

"Now, David," she said in her schoolteacher tone, "if there is one thing I want you to get out of this conversation, it is the fact that I knew absolutely nothing about the bombing of that police station. Absolutely nothing. You do believe me, don't you?"

"Sure. Why?"

"Oh, I don't know. They've been here twice to question me about it. And I simply don't know anything. Nothing. You do believe me, don't you?"

"Look, if you don't know anything, you don't. No point in getting worked up about it." He hesitated and then continued. "Besides, what's the worst that could happen if you did? You got a lawyer?"

"Of course I do. But I don't *know* anything, all right?"

Stonetree looked back at the kitchen and saw Sharon drag herself in, wrapped in the huge yellow robe he bought for her a few days before. She yawned and rubbed her eyes, then opened the refrigerator door. She slowly removed a carton of milk, then just as slowly replaced it.

"So what have you been doing with all your time?" Lane continued. "Taking it easy?"

"No, not really," he replied, taking another bite of the doughnut and motioning to Sharon to join him. "I'm doing volunteer work at this place called Parkwood House. I do a lot of work with A-5 survivors. Keeps me pretty busy."

"I'm sure it's very rewarding."

"As a matter of fact, it is," he agreed. "How about you?"

"Me?" she asked brightly. "I just got back from two weeks in Paris with my sister. Did the whole tourist thing. Nonstop. But it's good to be home. I feel like I need a vacation from my vacation."

"Your sister?" Stonetree chuckled. "I think old Robin would have been a lot more fun. He even speaks French, if I recall."

"Don't even mention his name to me," his caller shot back. "That little friend of yours really turned out to be a waste of time. He's a real lightweight."

Sharon yawned again as she crawled onto the couch and snuggled closely against Stonetree. In a few moments she would be asleep again, if she wasn't already.

While treatment was still in its early stages, the seven-day Camvac regimen was proving to be even more effective at curing humans than it had been in the ninety-seven percent of the lab animals that showed positive responses in the first trials.

Sharon was on her fifth day of the program and had thus far demonstrated a textbook response. She had already lost eight pounds and could count on dropping another five by the time Tuesday arrived. Despite the fact that she was sleeping close to twenty hours a day, the extreme fatigue and listlessness was a small price to pay.

The weight would return as quickly as it was lost, the fatigue replaced by what was best described by patients as "cold, fresh energy." The brilliant dreams most patients experienced, focused on peace and tranquility, would subside, but the memory of those dreams would endure.

Stonetree squeezed Sharon's shoulder and shook her gently, but the most she could give in response was another yawn. "Are you awake?" he asked softly.

"What did you say?" his caller asked.

"Oh, nothing," Stonetree replied.

"Would you be interested in coming over for dinner sometime?" Lane continued. "There are a couple things I'd like to talk over with you," she said. After a brief pause she went on. "In all honesty, I really did enjoy the first time. What do you say?"

"Why me?"

"Why not? I've given up holding grudges. What do you say? For old times' sake."

"You're not really serious, are you?" Stonetree asked, genuinely curious about her response but not the invitation.

"Like I said," she responded in a level tone, "I've given up holding grudges."

"But I don't think my wife has given up holding broken champagne bottles to people's throats—have you, Sharon?"

He squeezed her again but got only a sigh this time.

"Oh, I see," Lane said.

"See you around campus, Trisha," he said with a smile as he clicked off the phone.

After setting the phone to the side, he put his other arm around Sharon and kissed her nose. He was a bit alarmed at how cold she felt, but then remembered that a temperature in the ninety-four- to ninety-five-degree range was not an uncommon side effect of Camvac.

"Are you going to use me for a pillow all day?" he whispered, brushing her hair off her forehead. "This is a busy weekend. If I'm going to take care of you, I've got to get the errands out of the way. What do you say? Let's get you back to your kip."

She opened an eye halfway, curled still closer, and seemed to smile, but then she was out again.

Stonetree nodded, then reached as far as he could to grasp the weekend edition of *Newsglance* he had picked up the night before.

The bold headline shouted: CAMDEN IS EVERYONE'S MAN OF THE YEAR!

Time magazine had broken its long-standing policy and would feature the scientist on its cover in two weeks, no other person being a possible contender for its Man of the Year award. This despite the fact the year had another five months to go. Next week the scientist would receive the Medal of Freedom from the President.

The Nobel Prize for Medicine was a cinch for next year, his second, as was probably the Peace Prize, which would be his first. One of Camden's biggest concerns was what to do with all the statues and medals and plaques, and Stonetree, on his visit the previous week to Georgia, suggested that they all be housed in the lobby of the soon-to-be-constructed headquarters of the Camden Foundation.

The doctor had invited Stonetree down to brainstorm the

idea a month before and then asked him to return to consider the details. One of those details was who would run the operation, and, as Camden reminded him, "I don't forget my friends." The pay was more than Stonetree could imagine, and the work would be fascinating.

Pierre Ruth had offered the world to the doctor if he would just enter into a licensing and distribution agreement for Camvac with SUE, and Camden had accepted it—including a three-hundred-and-forty-one-million-dollar initial endowment for the charity that now bore his name.

While flattered with the offer, Stonetree had asked Camden for some time to consider it. He wanted to make sure Sharon came through Camvac without a hitch, there was still a month left on the commitment he gave to Parkwood House, and there was—what was that third item?—oh yeah, he thought with a smile. The honeymoon.

Camden told him he understood, would not take no for an answer, would give him until the middle of September to see the light and, if he didn't, would personally come to get him and drag him back to Atlanta.

As a final incentive the scientist offered Stonetree a 1967 Mustang to replace the one his protégée had traded back to its original owner for a nearly flawless two-carat diamond. That, Stonetree agreed, might just do the trick.

He couldn't get the newspaper open without disturbing Sharon, so he merely flipped it over to see what was going on in Entertainment.

Wexford had finally come out of a three-month coma and was said to be optimistic about his future. Although he could no longer play the guitar or piano, he did tell the interviewer he hoped to perform again, somewhere, somehow. No date had been set for the release of his next album, if there was one.

Artist Jean Lionne-Demilunes was in the process of filing a lawsuit against an imitator in Australia who was making a small fortune selling paintings similar in appearance to the artist's COMBAT ART, the major difference being that the pretender was labeling her work WOMBAT ART.

The new Chin-Chin Davis movie was the box office leader for the sixth week in a row, author Sven Moyer's *Four Corners* was on top of the best-seller list for the seventh week in a row, and yet another re-release from The B-52's was at the pinnacle of the music charts, for the third straight week, "The Summer of Love."

From somewhere else in the house, or possibly from down the block, or maybe only in his own thoughts, Stonetree could hear the refrain of the chorus and its bouncing, hopeful message.

He tapped his finger on Sharon's shoulder along with the beat. She looked up at him with a mixture of curiosity and confusion.

"What is it?" she asked.

"The summer of love," he whispered.